THE HOPE THAT
KILLS

JOHNATHAN
WEBBER

Published by Webber's Nook Publishing Limited 2023
Copyright © Johnathan Webber 2023

ISBN: 978-1-7392857-0-8

Cover design and typeset by riverdesignbooks.com

To Laura,
for your unwavering encouragement and support.

CHAPTER 1

THE SOFTLY BACKLIT ANALOGUE CLOCK turned 1:00 a.m. as Councillor Irving Hargreaves brought the sleek four-door Mercedes to a stop in front of the metal railing that separated the car park from the nature reserve beyond. By the time the thin, arrow-like second hand had completed two sweeping revolutions of the clock's elegant, square face, Councillor Hargreaves was dead.

Not that this fact would have been obvious to anyone walking past. There was no blood to draw attention and no visible injuries to indicate anything amiss. The councillor's body was slumped slightly forward with his chin resting lightly on top of his chest, but he remained surprisingly upright, held in place by the seatbelt which still tightly crossed his torso. He could easily have been mistaken for simply being asleep.

Faded words, now barely legible, on a rusting metal sign that clung stubbornly to a weather-beaten wooden post rising out of the windswept ground just in front of the Mercedes warned that overnight stays were prohibited, but the car park was public property and secluded and it wouldn't have been the first time a visitor had sought to grab forty winks here. There was little chance of being disturbed. Regular evening patrols of remote car parks like this one, that served the numerous beauty spots dotted around the headland overlooking Torbay's large horseshoe-shaped bay, had been one of the first casualties of recent local council cutbacks. In the summer, you might have expected to share the space with any number of people – teenagers looking for a place to drink, couples after some privacy or (for the more adventurous) those seeking an audience – but not tonight. Not this early on a cold, cheerless Tuesday morning in the middle of November.

At three minutes past the hour the passenger door behind the driver's seat opened and a shadowy figure emerged silently into the night. The door closed soundlessly behind them and the light that had momentarily illuminated the inside of the Mercedes, briefly spilling out across the vehicle's immediate surrounds, was extinguished as suddenly as it had appeared. Perhaps reminded of something, the figure turned and stared in the direction of the sea. Though hidden from the car park by the rolling contours of the headland, Berry Head's short, stubby lighthouse was no more than four hundred feet in front of them, beyond the railing, sited close to the edge of the giant limestone cliffs that rose powerfully out of the dark, uninviting waters of Tor Bay. Tonight, like every night, it would be radiating its concentrated shafts of light out across the water. A beacon of hope in the dark.

The figure stood perfectly still for several seconds. The long, floor-length coat that concealed their entire body stirred faintly as a gust of wind blew across the desolate landscape. They wrapped their arms tightly around themselves against the cold before proceeding to look all around. Slowly. Methodically taking in every part of their surroundings. They moved in a clockwise direction, their whole body rather than just the head, although beneath the peak of a floppy hat pulled down low over their forehead, sharp eyes flicked left and right with the beat of a metronome. Gravel crunched loudly beneath weighty leather boots as they turned.

Apparently satisfied they were alone, the stranger opened the driver's door and leaned into the vehicle.

Councillor Hargreaves' eyes were open, but they didn't see the figure bent over him. They stared ahead blankly, devoid of even the dullest spark of life. The councillor's limp hands rested submissively in his lap, just above a dark stain that was spreading steadily across the front of his recently pressed beige trousers.

By the time the clock displayed eight minutes past the hour, Councillor Hargreaves was alone once more, the ticking of the clock his only companion and the only sign of life. The dark clouds that had covered much of the sky since just before his arrival suddenly cleared, revealing a bright three-quarters full moon. It bathed the councillor in a rich, warm glow the unsuspecting might innocently have termed healthy. A shadow passed across his surprisingly serene-looking face as the reflection of a smaller, less flashy car driving towards the narrow country lane that bordered the entrance to the car park was caught in the rear-view mirror of the Mercedes. The car moved slowly, the light from the recently unveiled moon guiding its path. Only once it had pulled onto the road beyond, did its headlights come on.

The call arranging the meeting had been received only about three hours earlier. Councillor Irving Hargreaves had not been expecting it. He'd just poured himself a second whisky and was about to settle down in front of the television when the phone rang. Frustrated by the intrusion, he answered somewhat gruffly. The person on the other end did not speak at first, perhaps startled by Irving's tone. When they did, the voice was muffled. It sounded distant, as though they weren't talking directly into the phone's mouthpiece or, as Irving soon realised, were trying to disguise their voice.

Irving strained to hear what they were saying. He didn't recognise the voice and the caller hadn't offered their name. In normal circumstances he'd have just hung up, assuming it to be a wrong number or some cold call or other. He'd been receiving them frequently of late, much to his irritation. He often wondered why he maintained his landline. No one of importance ever called him on it anymore. Everyone used his mobile now.

But this evening something gave him pause, made him continue listening. He didn't know what. Maybe it was the lateness of the hour – he always had a sinking feeling when the landline rang after 9:00 p.m., less so with his mobile, fearing bad news. Perhaps that was why he kept the home phone – some self-destructive appetite for pain and misery. Although, he was glad for the uncharacteristic display of patience on this occasion. The words may have been indistinct, but the content could not have been clearer. They had the information he was after, and they were willing to share it. But it had to be tonight. And it had to be somewhere quiet. Somewhere they wouldn't be seen together.

At first, the clandestine nature of the demand had seemed completely unnecessary to the no-nonsense businessman turned local councillor. Why couldn't it wait until the morning and be at a sensible time and in a civilised place? Then he heard the urgency in the caller's voice. They sounded scared and emphasised how much they had to lose. Irving was hooked. The information must be dynamite to warrant such extraordinary precautions, he reasoned. When the caller made it clear they would only meet if Irving promised not to divulge how he'd come by the material, he reeled himself in. Besides, the whole thing felt like a scene from a James Bond novel. What man could refuse?

As Irving put down the phone, adrenaline coursed through his body. He poured his whisky away – he needed a clear head and was thankful he'd only had a nip before-hand – and spent the next couple of hours pacing around the spacious living room of his detached two-storey prop-erty situated in generous gardens a half mile or so back from the seafront in Paignton. He kept replaying the con-versation in his mind – analysing each word, desperately trying to find a clue to the nature of the information, or the identity of the mystery caller. At half past midnight he went upstairs to change into a pair of casual chinos. It might be late, and he might not know who he was meeting, but he had standards to maintain.

The roads were deserted and the drive along the coast from his house in Paignton to the old military fortifications on Berry Head would only take around fifteen minutes. Paignton, a traditional British seaside resort with a certain faded Victorian charm, was positioned in the centre of Torbay in South Devon, England, flanked on its northern side by slightly larger and glitzier Torquay, with the smaller but arguably more famous fishing town of Brixham to its south. Berry Head was the name of the coastal headland that formed the bay's southern boundary. It lay to the east of Brixham and was now a local nature reserve, although for several hundred years its vantage point over the deep, sheltered waters of Tor Bay had seen it maintain a con-tinuous military presence. Today, however, the old and crumbling fortifications were guarded by nothing more than a small herd of North Devon cattle, and you were more likely to see bats or guillemots patrolling the area than military personnel.

Irving was anxious as he drove, the adrenaline still not completely out of his system. He sat slightly forward in the driver's seat and concentrated hard on the road in front of him. He'd always disliked driving to Brixham, though not because the drive itself was difficult. In truth, it wasn't hard to drive anywhere in the bay, except perhaps during the peak summer months when the roads were clogged with tourists and caravans dominated the area's narrow streets. Besides, the opulence of the Mercedes meant there was no hardship in any journey. No, it was more of a psychological issue. Given its location, nestled at the southernmost tip of the bay, the sole road into the town led only to the harbour and the watery expanse of Tor Bay beyond. That road in was also the only road out. Irving felt hemmed in whenever he visited, which he only ever did when he absolutely had to, typically nowadays on official council business. But tonight felt different. He almost welcomed the journey.

The vast panoramic sunroof flooded the inside of the Mercedes with the rich, warming moonlight from a cloudless sky that didn't appear to have any end. Irving looked at his reflection in the rear-view mirror. The sagging skin under his eyes had become the prominent feature of his face over the past few months, seemingly without him even noticing. He almost didn't recognise the face staring back at him. When had he grown so old? But of course, he *was* old. Comparatively speaking at any rate, although he looked much older than he felt. He needed to ease back a bit, start looking after himself better. Maybe a holiday was in order. An opportunity to relax and recharge. A reward for a job well done perhaps. After all, this would be over soon. Who knew, he might even convince his daughter to go with him. She hadn't spoken to him for almost six years but, after tonight, everything would be different.

The road followed an inland, largely elevated path from the coast, but loosely shadowed the contours of the bay which lay to Irving's left as he drove towards his destination. Houses were built on both sides of the road, those on Irving's right typically constructed taller to afford them a glimpse of the sea over the roofs of those they faced. As he passed Broadsands, a residential area named after the long, sandy beach that hugged the coast at this part of the bay, there was a brief pause in the monotonous urban scene, providing Irving a momentary glimpse of the sea. In the distance, intermittent shafts of light emanated from the lighthouse at Berry Head. From his position, the narrow pulse of light looked faint and appeared far off. He checked the clock on the dashboard. 12:47 a.m. Irving pressed down more heavily on the accelerator pedal beneath his right foot and the powerful petrol engine responded instantly, effortlessly taking the vehicle over the speed limit. He hated being late for anything and had no intention of starting now.

On the outskirts of Brixham, Irving slowed and took a gentle right turn at a fork in the road before immediately starting to climb the narrow streets lined with identikit terraced housing that covered the hillside surrounding the town's picturesque harbour below. The houses were built densely, and the roads were steep, seemingly even narrower than throughout the rest of the bay. Irving eased further off the accelerator, down to only 10 mph, and concentrated hard as he steered the Mercedes between the rows of tightly parked cars that lined both sides of the road. Their owners had parked them with two wheels mounted on the pavement, but even then, the wing mirrors of the Mercedes passed with only inches to spare. Irving could feel the tension spreading across his shoulders. He thought about turning on the seat's massage function to help him relax, but there was no time. He was close now.

Berry Head was situated at the end of a narrow country lane only wide enough for a single car to travel along. The lane dissected open fields on either side that completely disconnected the tourist spot from the nearest homes, themselves hidden behind a dense canopy of tall evergreens. The hedgerows that lined the lane had not been cut for some considerable time (another victim of recent cutbacks) and they crowded the Mercedes as it passed, even slower now, no more than 5 mph. At the end of the lane, Irving made the 90-degree turn into the car park, the powerful headlights illuminating the vast open space in a big slow arc. Outside, ominous dark clouds had appeared suddenly in the sky, as if from nowhere, cloaking everything in darkness. Shadows emerged at the edges of the high-powered beams, forming sinister shapes that played tricks at the periphery of Irving's vision.

The car park was empty save for a lone, featureless car parked at the far end, its bonnet pulled up tightly against the rusting metal railings that designated the end of the gravelled parking area. Irving steered the Mercedes towards it, coming to a graceful halt with his passenger window adjacent to its driver's side door. There didn't appear to be anyone inside.

Irving looked at the clock and smiled. He was right on time.

Outside, the wind swept silently over the open, uninhabited landscape. The ground beyond the car park was covered in a low-level brush of thick, heavily gnarled branches that intertwined intimately to create a convoluted maze. Covered in sharp thorns, they looked impenetrable to anything but the smallest and bravest of animals. Irving could see a couple of narrow paths criss-crossing the site, but they quickly disappeared into the dark. None of the vegetation appeared taller than a metre although he noticed a clump of four defiant oak trees growing in the distance, their trunks leaning at a 45-degree angle in deference to the prevailing wind. Irving looked on as their bare branches appeared to wave at him, wildly, like the arms of the characters in the Punch and Judy puppet shows he used to watch on the seafront as a child.

Darkness descended all around as he switched off the engine. It was an absolute darkness, the sort only found in such an isolated spot. The rhythmical ticking of the clock was the only noise inside the heavily soundproofed car. Irving found it strangely reassuring. He was about to undo his seatbelt when the Mercedes was unexpectedly filled with light. Momentarily disoriented, he realised it was only the powerful, oversized vanity light in the vehicle's ceiling panel positioned in front of the rear-view mirror, directly above his head. He instinctively looked towards it.

Temporarily blinded, he was suddenly aware of the distant sound of waves, and he could taste the damp, salty air on his tongue. He would forever associate the sea with his childhood. At once, he was transported back, to a time when he'd been walking along Paignton beach with his grandparents, pulled by the promise of a cone of chips from the small wooden kiosk at the end of the promenade. His grandparents were struggling to keep up with him. He kept stopping to make sure they were still there. They were. And they were happy. They were laughing and joking as they walked hand in hand, ignoring all his pleas to speed up.

A gentle thud somewhere over his right shoulder shattered the memory and brought Irving crashing back to the present. The inside of the Mercedes was dark once again and black spots had invaded his vision. They danced around in front of his eyes in a sea of spinning white light.

And then he sensed it. He was no longer alone. Someone had joined him inside the car and were now sat directly behind him.

Irving attempted to turn his body to see who it was. The sudden movement caused the belt to catch, restricting his movement and pressing him with surprising force into the enveloping grip of the leather seat.

Instinctively his head dropped forward as he tried to adjust the belt, gripping it firmly in his fist, but his attempts only seamed to tighten it further. He could feel the breath being squeezed out of his lungs.

He started to panic.

At that moment something was forced over his head. He took a sharp intake of breath as his head was pulled backwards against the headrest. He could feel his heart beating much faster than usual. He tried to take another breath but there was no air to breathe.

He finally released his grip on the seatbelt and raised his hands in front of his face in a bid to ward off the attack. But it was too late. His arms ached and he suddenly felt tired. Really tired. His head rocked forward slightly and was then pulled back sharply as he felt the ends of whatever was covering his head tighten around his neck.

As he gasped his last few airless breaths, Irving felt warm shivers course through his body. Had someone turned on his massage seat, he wondered, as a surprising calmness flooded over him. He was aware of his arms dropping heavily into his lap before his mind drifted into total blackness.

CHAPTER 2

THE CURSOR FLASHED IN THE top left-hand corner of the screen. Peter Norton shifted awkwardly on his chair. He'd been sitting in front of his laptop for the last two hours, waiting for inspiration to hit. So far, nothing. It was eight thirty in the morning, his deadline was at five that afternoon, and he still had no idea what he was going to write for the *Torbay Times*, the weekly printed newspaper covering Torquay, Paignton, Brixham and their immediate surrounds, today. A heavily chewed lid from a ballpoint pen stuck out of the corner of his mouth. White streaks had formed at the pointed end, like lava flowing down the sides of an active volcano. Peter was always troubled when the words wouldn't come easily. As a journalist, words defined him. They were his superpower. He felt strangely exposed when they dried up.

He threw the piece of mangled blue plastic onto the notepad that lay next to the laptop and stood. The lid bounced off a page covered with elaborate doodles before dropping off the table and getting lost among the dense patterns of the brown carpet that covered the floor. Peter stretched and made his way into the small galley kitchen just off the dining room-cum-lounge where he'd set up his makeshift office on the circular, wooden dining table that had come with the rented flat. Maybe more coffee would help.

As he filled the kettle, Peter looked out of the small, wooden-framed window above the kitchen sink. Condensation covered the inside of the single-glazed windowpane, obscuring the view. He ran his hand across the glass, from left to right, forcing individual water droplets to merge into parallel streams that collected in puddles on the windowsill.

The slow rising winter sun sat just above the horizon, like a brightly coloured beachball floating aimlessly on a deserted swimming pool. Peter breathed in the view and was momentarily transfixed by the gentle, hypnotic motion of the colourful little fishing boats that bobbed up and down on the water in the harbour below. He could see the end of Paignton's Victorian-era pier over the roofs of the houses to his left and the outline of Torquay's headland beyond that. In the distance to his right, the imposing cliffs that held the historic military fortifications of Berry Head rose like sentries out of the sea. Facing this twenty-plus miles of beautiful Devon coastland, and dwarfing it all in terms of size and scale, were the calm, sheltered waters of Tor Bay. The dreamy blue waters filled Peter's vision and he immediately felt himself begin to calm. The water always had that effect on him. If words were his superpower, then the sea was his elixir. It centred him and helped put his problems into perspective. In comparison to the vastness of the ocean, everything else seemed trivial.

That view had been the primary reason for renting the dingy one-bedroomed flat overlooking Paignton's small, idyllic harbour. It was as far removed from the flat he'd shared in London with Frieda, his former fiancée, as he could imagine. And that was the point. Peter had wanted, needed even, a complete change of scene as he attempted to rebuild his life and career. The fact it was cheap was a bonus. The sudden and unexpected move south had hit him hard in the pocket, and it wasn't as though the 1970s décor bothered him. He'd been renting the flat back in the town where he'd been born and spent the first eighteen years of his life for almost twelve months and hadn't made a single attempt at homemaking in all that time. If challenged, he'd probably have pointed to it being a temporary arrangement, but the reality of his situation was beginning to make that a difficult argument to run.

Just then, Peter heard the familiar ping of his email chiming in the other room. He plugged in the kettle and went to investigate, hoping for inspiration. It was from his friend Steve Earl. Not inspiration then, but a distraction. Good enough.

Peter had met Steve on his first day of university. After being assigned adjacent rooms in the halls of residence, they bonded over a mutual love of football and quickly became close friends. Following graduation, they both moved to London for work and lived together for several years in a flat share. When Peter moved in with Frieda, Steve took the opportunity to return home to Manchester, keen to make a name for himself in his own, smaller back yard. Peter hadn't understood that decision at the time. He couldn't fathom why anyone would want to give up a promising life in the capital to move home, dismissing it as a backward step. Recent events in his own life had forced him to revisit that rather crude conclusion and he now conceded that decisions are often more nuanced and rarely black and white. Since moving back to the bay, Peter had found himself thinking a lot about the choices he'd made, speculating what his life might have been like had he done just one or two things differently. But every time he came to the same rather depressing conclusion: he wouldn't do anything differently if he ever had the chance to go back. When pushed into a corner, he would always come out fighting. And he would always do what he thought was right. It was just the way he was.

Peter opened the email. There were no words, just an attachment. Typical Steve. In person he was the friendliest person you could hope to meet, but electronically his chat was abrupt at best and often, like today, non-existent. Steve argued it was more efficient. Peter just thought it odd. Rude even. He still wrote emails like formal letters though, so realised he probably wasn't the best person to judge. Despite political correctness, Peter clicked on the link fully expecting some wholly inappropriate joke or image to appear, and was surprised when an entirely normal black and white photo filled the screen. It was of four people, three men and one woman. The woman was smiling but each of the men stared moodily at the camera. The clothes and hairstyles harked back to a different era, suggesting it had been taken many years earlier. It was a social setting. Not one that was familiar to Peter, although he did recognise one of the men.

Peter was staring at the picture when his phone started to ring. Steve.

"Hey mate, what's up?"

"Morning Peter." Steve sounded full of energy. Peter knew he was an early riser. He'd probably already been to the gym or run a half-marathon. Not for the first time, Peter wondered how they were such good friends. "What do you think of the photo, then?"

"Photo?" Peter joked, sensing an opportunity for some fun.

"Nice try. I know you've already looked at it."

"How so?"

"It's Tuesday!" Steve paused as though no further explanation were needed. When Peter didn't respond, he continued. "You have a deadline tonight and you leave everything to the last minute. Not your fault I know, you're just terrible at time management. Something about not wanting to stifle your creative genius. Anyway, I'm willing to bet you've already been up for hours tapping away on that computer of yours."

Peter laughed. "No one likes a smart alec! Besides, you're wrong. I may have been sat here for the past two hours – I'll concede that – but I haven't managed to write anything yet."

"Oh dear. That bad, eh?"

"Just a temporary creative block. Something will come to me soon." Peter hoped he sounded more confident than he felt.

"So, what's got the great Peter Norton stumped? Still the big development story that's been keeping you busy ever since you retreated to Devon, or is that finished now? You mentioned something about it coming to a head the last time we spoke."

"Yeah, still Oldway Mansion. Although the final council vote is next month, so the finish line is in sight." He paused but, sensing the sarcasm in his friend's voice, quickly continued. "It's getting interesting as a matter of fact. We're coming under pressure from both sides to make our coverage favourable. That raises a host of questions around journalistic independence and integrity. You know, all those things I take so seriously."

"Sounds wild" replied Steve flatly. After a brief pause, he continued. "You're wasting your talents down there, you know that don't you, Peter? You used to work for the *Times* for God's sake. You were their top investigative reporter. Now look at you. Reporting on lost cats and who made the best jam at the local village fête."

"Thanks for the vote of confidence!" Peter tried to sound insulted but in truth he appreciated the honesty.

Besides, he knew his friend was probably right. Even so, he felt like he needed to defend himself. "And that's not fair. The intern beat me to the big village fête gig this year!" He laughed at his attempt at humour, but it came over as a bit hollow.

"Seriously though, it's not *that* bad. This development story for one is fascinating *and* it's important to the local community. I feel like I'm doing something worthwhile. Oldway Mansion has been here for the past hundred and fifty years. It's a beautiful building, mate. Architecturally stunning. You're a property developer, I know that's something you can appreciate. The council have let it fall into disrepair in recent years. They say it's through a lack of money; the conservationists argue it's nothing more than a cynical ploy to push through a sale and line the council's pockets in the process. Now I don't know who's right, not my place to judge, but I do know the stakes are high and, whatever the final decision, it will have far-reaching implications. Our readers have a right to understand the arguments on both sides so they can make an informed decision based on *all* the facts." Peter wasn't sure who he was trying to convince more, Steve or himself, but wondered whether there might be something here he could turn into an article for the newspaper today. He decided to see where his thoughts took him.

"The whole question of whether the council should sell an historically important building to the private sector, to become a hotel and private members club accessible only to the wealthy, or transfer stewardship to the local preservation society who plan to restore it to its former glory and maintain it as a public resource, feels quite relevant right now. Following the pandemic, people are beginning to cherish their public spaces more than ever. Should the privileged be able to buy access to these places to the exclusion of others? It's the David versus Goliath story for the modern age. And then you've got climate change. People are looking locally now, thinking about ways to be more sustainable." He paused, realising he was starting to ramble. "And besides, it's not like I had a choice, is it?"

"You always have a choice, Peter. There are other newspapers, and other cities. Places where newsworthy things happen. Manchester, for example. You know us Northerners don't care about anything that happens in London. The way you left the *Times* would probably be enough on its own for one of the papers up here to offer you a job."

"Maybe. I'll think about it. Anyway, this picture?"

"Oh yeah, I thought you'd like it."

"Is that who I think it is?"

"The one and only."

"So, what's it all about?"

"Remember I told you about that pub we're developing? Into a boutique hotel."

"The one that used to be the headquarters for a group of old-school gangsters back in the sixties and seventies. The Buford Boys, wasn't it?"

"Burford Boys, yeah, that's right. The hotel's themed around them and their story. Rooms named after the members. Lots of photos from back then on the walls. You know the sort of thing. Celebrating an important piece of Manchester's history and keeping it alive for future generations. Not too dissimilar to what the conservationists are trying to achieve with Oldway Mansion, I suppose."

"Except they don't see a hotel as part of their plans! But, yeah, I can see the parallels. So, what's George Best got to do with it?"

George Best, arguably one of the most recognisable footballers of his generation who most famously played for Manchester United, stared back at Peter from one edge of the photograph. His right arm was draped around the very broad shoulders of the man standing next to him. The woman was next in line. She stood close to the second man, on his other side, her body turned slightly towards him, although Peter noted she wasn't touching him. The third man, on the far side of the image, completed the quartet. He stood next to the woman, but with a noticeable gap between them, as though he wasn't really part of the group. To Peter's surprise, it was the man next to the footballer who appeared to be the focus of the picture.

"It turns out that gangsters were local celebrities back then," continued Steve. "This photo proves it. The guy in between George and the woman is Harry '*The Torch*' Bannister, infamous leader of the Burford Boys and a nasty piece of work. Had a penchant for setting things on fire, apparently, hence the moniker. People as well as places if the legends are to be believed."

"Blimey. Are you sure that's going to attract people to your hotel?"

"Absolutely. It all adds to the experience we're trying to sell. People love that sort of stuff, always have done. George Best is a case in point. Arguably one of most famous footballers of his generation and even he wanted a photo with Harry."

"Is this Harry character still around then? If so, I hope he's happy with what you're doing. He doesn't sound like the sort of fella you'd want to get on the wrong side of."

"I don't think I've anything to worry about on that score!" Steve chuckled. "He went to prison in the early eighties for some white-collar fraud or other. By the time he got out, Manchester was a completely different place. I don't think he exactly went straight, but he effectively disappeared."

"Well, let's hope he stays that way." Peter studied the photo again, focusing this time on the woman and the third man. She was attractive, no doubt about that, with a mischievous glint in her eyes. Peter wondered what her story was. She looked much younger than George and Harry. Perhaps no more than eighteen years old. But it was the third man who looked most out of place. While the other three were focused on the camera, he just looked startled by it. He certainly didn't look happy to be in the photo. "So, who are the other two? Anyone I should recognise? The guy on the end doesn't appear particularly impressed to be in the company of greatness. Obviously not a football fan!"

"Ha, obviously not. No idea who they are. Just hangers-on, I guess. Anyway, you'll have to come up for a weekend soon, let me show you round the place properly. You've not been up since that whole thing in London. It would be great to see you. And it'll do you some good to get out of Devon for a bit." He paused. "You could arrange to meet an editor or two while you're here. Dip your toe in the water, see how the land lies."

"Sounds good." Peter hoped he sounded more enthusiastic than he felt. "It might have to be in the new year now though. Once this Oldway Mansion story is finished."

"No problems, just let me know. And promise you'll think about your career situation."

Peter had only just disconnected the call and put the phone down on the table when it started ringing again. He picked it up without checking the screen.

"I promise I'll think about it, okay?"

The silence which greeted him gave Peter pause and he brought the phone away from his ear to look at the screen. Marcus, not Steve.

Marcus Payne was his editor at the *Torbay Times*. Peter cursed under his breath. Had he realised who was calling, he might not have been so quick to answer. Marcus had a habit of lecturing Peter, on all manner of subjects, and he often phoned before a deadline to provide 'helpful' tips and advice. Last week his sermon had been on efficiency, but that had just been the latest in a long list of subjects. Peter found it annoying and often let the calls go to voicemail. Not that Marcus seemed to take the hint. In truth, his only crime was trying to streamline the journalistic process, something Peter took as a personal insult. For him the story was everything. You followed it no matter where it took you and regardless of what it uncovered. In the same way, he didn't believe the creative process of recording and presenting the story could ever be defined by a set of rules. After all, that freedom to pursue the truth, and the independence to present it as he saw fit, was the reason he'd become a journalist in the first place.

"Sorry, Marcus," Peter finally managed. "I didn't realise it was you."

"Peter?" Marcus was almost shouting, his voice an octave or two higher than normal.

"Yes, hi Marcus, I'm here. Sorry, I thought you were someone else."

"There's been an unexplained death." The words came quickly. "You need to get yourself out there. Now. My sources tell me it could be Councillor Irving Hargreaves."

"What?" It was all Peter could manage, his own voice louder than he intended.

"This is front page news, Peter. It could push our numbers through the roof."

"Back up a minute, Marcus. You're not making a lot of sense."

"If it *is* Councillor Hargreaves, I want you to combine the report of his death with the update piece you're currently writing."

"Yeah, about that…"

"I can push your deadline to around seven p.m. Now get yourself up to Berry Head and keep me posted."

"Wait, Berry Head…" But the line was already dead.

Peter put the phone down on the table and smiled. He almost skipped back into the kitchen to make the coffee, pouring it into a to-go cup he pulled from the cupboard rather than the empty mug that stood next to the kettle. He'd just found his angle.

CHAPTER 3

"Any idea about cause of death?"

Detective Chief Inspector Bobby Redhill walked towards the crime scene while speaking to the back of the forensic pathologist who was leaning over the still-seated body of Councillor Irving Hargreaves. The bulky driver's-side door of the imposing black Mercedes stood open, creating a formidable barrier between them, and blocking the inspector's view inside the vehicle. Only occasional flashes of the pathologist's vivid blue coveralls above the blacked-out window told him the victim was not alone.

Since arriving on site five minutes earlier, Bobby Redhill had already been brought up to speed by the crime scene manager. There wasn't much to tell: the officers who'd responded to the 999 call had retreated to a safe distance upon determining the occupant of the Mercedes was dead and, having secured the witnesses who'd reported the incident, had proceeded to establish an outer cordon adjacent to the entrance of the car park in a bid to preserve vital evidence. With the site and the investigation now under his direct control, Bobby approached the primary crime scene anxious to find out more. He knew they could simply be looking at death by natural causes or possible suicide, but instinct told him there was more to it. He wasn't sure why – perhaps it was the remote location or the expensive car (more likely both) – but he had a bad feeling and had long since learnt to trust his instincts. The young male officer patrolling the inner cordon lifted the police incident tape as Bobby approached, at the same time risking a furtive glance at the detective's feet. *Presumably checking I'm wearing the regulation protective overshoes,* Bobby noted approvingly as he ducked under.

As he reached the car and stepped around the door, Bobby spoke again. "What about cause of death then, Jake? Or do you expect me to guess? I need to know if we're looking at anything suspicious." He stood still, waiting for a response, hands stuffed firmly into the deep pockets of his trench coat. None came. As the bright early morning light glinted off the pathologist's crinkled paper suit, Bobby was reminded of one of the kingfishers he'd seen on television last night – some nature programme foretelling the end of the world at the hands of climate change that lamented how animals were disproportionately bearing the brunt. He recalled the presenter saying the birds were native to tropical regions of Africa and Asia. *As out of place in this part of the world as a suspicious death*, he thought.

Bobby spoke again, more forcibly this time. "Talk to me, Jake. I haven't got all day!"

"Are you speaking to me?"

The question took Bobby by surprise. As did the voice. It wasn't the one he'd been expecting, although it did appear to be coming from the Mercedes. He refocused his attention on the kingfisher as it retreated from the vehicle. As it turned to face him, a look of confusion spread across the detective's face.

The ill-fitting coveralls could hide many things, but they couldn't disguise an extra foot in height or two stone of missing padding around the stomach. Even with the hood drawn tightly, the pale skin and warm, friendly face looking back at him was unmistakably female.

"You're not Jake."

The words were a statement but came out more like a question.

"No, quite right." The pathologist smiled warmly. "Good observation. And not easy in this get-up. There's nothing remotely flattering about them, is there?" She puffed out her cheeks and squatted down slightly on her haunches, much like a sumo wrestler might before a fight, as though to exaggerate her point. "Were you expecting Jake Twyford?"

"That's right. The forensic pathologist. Is he on holiday or something?"

"Oh, Jake retired. Must be two months ago now. I'm his replacement." She removed a plastic glove and held out her hand. Bobby immediately noticed her long, slender fingers. The nails, cut short, were perfectly rounded and covered with a translucent clear lacquer. "I'm Faith. Faith Andrews."

"Right, yes. Of course. I should have remembered about Jake. Two months you say? I don't know where the time goes." Bobby reached out to meet Faith's hand with his own. "DCI Redhill. Pleased to meet you." He paused but felt the urge to continue speaking. "Everyone calls me Bobby."

Faith's bright blue eyes shone with the same warmth as her smile. "Pleased to meet you, Bobby."

They stood there looking at one another for a few seconds before Faith broke the silence.

"You were asking about cause of death?"

"Yes, yes, absolutely." Bobby broke eye contact and looked down at his feet. "What's your best guess at this stage? Suicide or murder?"

"Well, actually, I can already be quite certain that this was murder." Faith's words were accompanied by another broad, infectious smile. Bobby wondered whether she was always this happy. Not that he was complaining. It made a welcome change from Jake's permanent scowl. "Or perhaps I should say this man did not die from natural causes. That much is clear." As she corrected herself, her face took on a more serious expression, as though trying to convey the gravity of her words.

"Are you *sure* the death wasn't from natural causes?" Bobby was surprised by the frankness of the response. Jake had been a fantastic pathologist, but he was cautious. He would never give a definitive opinion until everything had been checked and rechecked and he was certain his findings could be fully supported.

"I'll be able to tell you more after the autopsy, but he was suffocated, no doubt about it. There's evidence of petechial haemorrhaging in his eyes and he's clearly voided his bowels. There's also bruising on his neck. Not horizontal like you might expect to see with strangulation. These bruises appear more vertical, starting off low at the front, just above the Adam's apple, and rising as they move round the back of the head, behind the ears." She demonstrated, with her hands positioned around her own neck as she spoke. "He might have been attacked from behind. Perhaps with a plastic bag. Something like that at any rate." She stepped back and pointed at the victim's neck. "See, the bruising is quite narrow and faint." Bobby stepped forward and bent down to look at the area of the man's neck that Faith was pointing to. He could make out some light marks, rising slightly from front to back as she'd demonstrated. When he stood up again, the pathologist continued. "Either way, it doesn't look like suicide. Besides, we haven't found whatever was used to asphyxiate him and dead men don't usually tidy up after themselves." She paused. "That's usually the woman's job." The laugh which accompanied these words made Bobby chuckle even though he hadn't thought the comment funny.

"Do you think he was killed inside the vehicle?"

"I think that's likely, yes. You can see he's still wearing his seatbelt. When I get him back to the lab, I'll be able to tell for certain."

"Anything else at this stage?"

"Nothing obvious, but we'll process the area and let you know what we turn up."

"Okay, great. Thanks, Faith. That gives us plenty to be getting on with. I'll let the CSIs know we're looking for a plastic bag or something similar as the murder weapon. It could have been disposed of somewhere nearby since it's not in the vehicle." Bobby looked around the floor, as though the missing item might simply be lying there beneath his feet. "Any thoughts on time of death?"

Faith considered the question for a moment. The smile was gone now, and her forehead furrowed slightly with concentration. "Not more than ten hours ago. But he's been dead for at least six."

"So, somewhere between eleven last night and three this morning. A strange time to be up here," Bobby muttered, almost to himself.

"I suppose it depends on what he was doing here, doesn't it?" Faith raised a knowing eyebrow. "I can imagine this sort of isolated spot being quite appealing in the right circumstances."

Bobby could think of several activities that might fit the description, but thought Faith had something specific in mind. His cheeks reddened slightly as he considered the most likely, and he quickly decided to move the conversation on. "You're right, of course. Hopefully we can find some other evidence that helps explain the why. What time will you be conducting the autopsy?"

"I assume it's urgent?" She gave him a playful smirk. "Shall we say three o'clock? I don't like working on an empty stomach so will want to grab lunch first." Faith gave Bobby another, final smile before returning her focus to the body in the Mercedes.

As he walked away, Bobby was surprised to find himself thinking not about murder or the events that had taken place on this remote outpost last night, but rather Faith Andrews and whether she was single and might consider going for a drink with him.

CHAPTER 4

PETER NORTON CHANGED INTO HIS usual work uniform of navy-blue jeans, black wool polo shirt and dark brown leather Chelsea boots. He grabbed his car keys from the cabinet beside his bed and stopped at the dining table to pick up his laptop and mobile phone. At the stand in the hall, he selected his favourite coat. He'd bought the army-green bomber-style jacket with mahogany-brown shearling collar the Christmas before last from a boutique in London's Covent Garden. He'd been shopping for a gift for Frieda, last-minute like always, but had returned home only with the present for himself. He shuddered as he recalled her reaction to only having some bath salts and a box of garage bought chocolates to open on Christmas morning.

He wondered now whether that was the first indication things weren't going to work out between them, his sub-conscious telling him he wasn't as invested in the relationship as he should have been. He hadn't seen it at the time. He'd been too caught up in his own success, in his perfect life, with his dream job and his beautiful fiancée.

Now he didn't think *perfect* existed.

The door slammed shut behind him, jolting him back from the unexpected memory, and he bounded down the stairs, taking them two at a time. In his head he repeated Marcus's words – '*an unexplained death…it could be Councillor Hargreaves*' – and for the first time since he'd left the *Times* last year, he felt the familiar buzz of excitement that had always accompanied the scent of a big story.

He smiled. Maybe he could make a go of things here after all.

The single, bare lightbulb that hung from the ceiling at the foot of the stairs hadn't worked since the day he'd moved in and, as he emerged from the dim stairwell into the bright November morning, his eyes took a moment or two to adjust.

Despite it being the middle of the prime commuter hour, there were only a few people milling around. To his left, an elderly couple, clad in matching beige ensembles, shuffled along the pavement towards the convenience store below his flat. On the other side of the road, a young mother supported her infant son as he stood on the harbour wall and looked down on the boats below, pointing excitedly and making indecipherable yet unmistakably happy sounds. Overhead a group of seagulls squawked loudly as they swooped down upon the remnants of someone's fish and chip supper that had been discarded in the gutter overnight.

Many of the local businesses situated around the harbour were seasonal. They were shut up for the year, tables and chairs piled high inside empty cafés and restaurants, now barely visible through dirty windows and graffitied shutters pulled down tight.

It struck Peter how the area around the harbour had two distinct characters: one full of colour and noise and infused with an unmistakable energy, the other quieter and less hopeful. It was almost as though winter threw a veil over the bay, shrouding it in shadow and encouraging it to hibernate. But bright, sunny days like today served as a timely reminder that the seasons were cyclical. Happier, more prosperous times might be behind you, but others were always just around the corner.

Peter pressed the button on the black fob that hung from his jangling bunch of keys and the amber indicator lights of a bright red two-door Audi coupé parked in front of the convenience store flashed twice. The Audi was the only thing Peter had to show for his ten-year stay in London. Apart from more debts than he cared to think about, and an ex-fiancée who remained angrier with him than he thought the previous twelve months of separation fairly warranted. The car was a luxury Peter could no longer afford, but he hadn't been able to part with it. It served as an extravagant comfort blanket. A reminder of what he'd achieved in the past, and the success he wanted to taste again.

He got into the sporty, leather driver's seat and closed the solid door with a reassuring thud. Peter put on his aviator sunglasses and sat quietly for a moment, his finger hovering over the starter button which pulsed red in anticipation of his impending command to start the engine. The wholly unnecessary but delightful theatrics of this luxury vehicle never failed to make him smile. He felt like a fighter pilot sitting at the controls of his multi-million-pound machine, going through his final pre-flight checks before embarking on his latest daring mission. The aviator sunglasses and pseudo–American Airforce flight jacket he was wearing also helped, of course.

The engine fired with a satisfying growl and Peter could immediately feel the vibrations from the engine as they passed through the low-slung seat up into his body. As he pulled the Audi away from the kerb he ran through the essentials of his mission.

His destination: Berry Head.

His objective: the truth behind the death that had been reported there. Oh, and a five-hundred-word article with a new and exciting angle on the Oldway Mansion development story, to be delivered in time for the next edition.

Traffic was light as he made his way along Dartmouth Road, heading out of Paignton towards Brixham. Peter had a smile on his face as he drove. *Nothing interesting ever happens in Devon, eh Steve? Shows what you know!*

He passed the leisure centre where he'd learnt to swim. As a child he'd favoured the pool at Torquay's newer conference centre. All his friends had. It had a flume, part of which travelled outside the building, and a wave pool. But his dad had insisted on the pool in Paignton. A proper pool he'd called it. Peter could hear his voice now: '*How are you going to swim with all those people just bobbing up and down, getting in your way?*' Since he'd moved back to the bay, Peter had been swimming at the leisure centre every week. Never the pool in Torquay. He'd been surprised at how quickly he'd reverted to old routines. After university he assumed he'd outgrown his hometown, it was too small and provincial, but it was the first place he'd thought about when things had got difficult in London. And this morning it seemed more appealing than ever.

The Audi's front windows were down, and Peter rested his arm on the doorframe as he cruised along at the speed limit. He decided to put some music on. He'd got into the habit of listening to one of the local radio stations whenever he was in the car, keen to hear about anything that might classify as an interesting story. But today he already had his story, so he thought about putting on a CD. He couldn't remember the last time he'd listened to one. The Audi had a six-disc player and when he turned it on, CD4 started playing automatically, presumably from where it had left off however many months before. Peter recognised it immediately as a playlist Frieda had put together for him when they'd first got together. The song playing had been one of her favourites. She'd always made them get up to dance whenever it came on, no matter where they happened to be at the time. Peter smiled at the memory and started to sing along. Progress, he thought.

Peter was still singing as he entered Brixham, but quickly turned the music off as he climbed the narrow residential streets. He needed to concentrate. Marcus had told him to get to Berry Head but hadn't been more specific. Without more detailed instructions, Peter's plan was to head towards the old military fortifications. He thought that's what most people meant when they referred to Berry Head. He hadn't been up there for years, not since a school project in secondary school, he guessed, but he knew there was a car park just inland from the headland and he figured he could park there and have a look around if it wasn't obvious where the incident had taken place. Besides, he knew there'd be any number of locals hanging around who'd be only too happy to point him in the right direction.

He needn't have worried.

As he approached the lane that led to the car park, he was forced to stop. Three police cars had been deliberately parked across the road, preventing any vehicular access. Peter pulled into the kerb, reverse parking between an ancient Ford Fiesta and a battered-looking Toyota pickup truck that might once have been blue. The Audi stood out in this company and Peter hoped it wouldn't draw any unwelcome attention from the locals. It was only then, as he took in the scene through the windscreen, that he realised there weren't any locals around. In fact, he couldn't see a single other person.

The red and blue flashing light bars on the roofs of the abandoned emergency vehicles threw long, threatening shadows over everything in their path, tricking Peter's brain into seeing movement and activity where none existed. As he got out of the Audi, Peter was confronted by an eerie silence. He walked towards the mouth of the lane cautiously, half expecting someone to jump out and stop him, but no one did. There was no sign of anyone in the lane either, although his view was disrupted by hedges that grew out wildly, as though intent on meeting in the middle. Peter stood still for a moment and listened. He sensed the direction of the wind was probably blowing any sounds away from him, out towards the sea, but nevertheless he thought he could hear something in the distance.

He took a deep breath and started to walk purposefully down the lane, eager to discover the story that awaited him at the other end.

CHAPTER 5

"Is everything okay, sir?" Detective Sergeant Matthew Grainger walked towards DCI Bobby Redhill who was staring off into the distance, apparently deep in thought.

"Sir?" DS Grainger repeated his question, more forcibly this time, although he made sure not to raise his voice or sound aggressive. Grainger had only worked with DCI Redhill for around twelve months. Not enough time to become friends, but he thought they'd developed a good working relationship during that time. Even so, he'd learnt enough to know his boss expected a degree of deference from subordinates. Grainger was working on that though. Slowly. Training him.

"What's that? Ah, Grainger. What do you want?" Bobby spoke without looking at his sergeant. In fact, his demeanour hadn't changed at all. Grainger thought his attention was still elsewhere.

"You were miles away, sir. Penny for your thoughts."

"I was just thinking about the situation we have here." Bobby paused. His face didn't give much away, although that wasn't unusual. He was known around the station for being hard to read. When he'd first been assigned to Bobby's team, Grainger had noticed several more seasoned colleagues sombrely shaking their heads while others had offered him an encouraging slap on the back. It still happened from time to time, not that Grainger had ever understood it. He enjoyed working with Bobby. Besides, he knew his boss had been through a lot over the past couple of years and thought he deserved to be cut some slack.

"It's not good," continued Bobby, looking his sergeant straight in the eyes with an intensity that made the younger man blink and look away. "There's going to be a lot of interest in this case. We need to get on top of things, and quickly. Has the scene been fully secured?"

"Yes, sir." Grainger took the opportunity to consult his pocketbook. He could feel Bobby's emerald-green eyes on him as he flicked the pages. He didn't know why, but whenever Bobby stared at him like that, he felt strangely guilty. It was like those eyes transported him straight back to his childhood, to one of the all-too-frequent occasions he'd been forced to stand in front of his father after doing something wrong. He took a deep breath to clear the thought from his mind. "The immediate scene was locked down by the officers who responded to the initial emergency call. That was Harris and Armstrong, sir. The 999 call was logged at six thirty-three a.m. and our guys were on scene just after six forty-five." Grainger flicked to the next page. "Erm, six forty-seven to be precise. This area gets busy during the day, with locals and tourists, and is popular with dog walkers and runners. Fortunately, given the hour, we don't think anyone has trampled over the crime scene. Not this morning at any rate."

"Any CCTV?" Bobby asked.

"Nothing like that, no. There might be some private cameras on the houses further down the road, back towards the town, but this is an isolated spot up here."

"What about the entrance?" Bobby looked over Grainger's shoulder. "I can see it's open now, but is it locked at night?"

"There are the remnants of what appears to be a barrier at the entrance. Nothing to suggest it was in operation last night though. It's been partially reclaimed by the hedgerow and is completely rusted so it looks as though it's been out of commission for some time. Harris told me he was able to drive straight in when he arrived this morning. The car park is owned by the council, so I'll check with them."

"Okay, do that."

"Do you think the perpetrators also came in a vehicle then, sir?"

"I don't want to rule anything out," responded Bobby thoughtfully, "but this is a car park, our dead body is in a car, and you've already pointed out we're in an isolated spot, so it feels possible at this stage. We should canvass the neighbourhood for sightings of anything unusual last night. Make that any time over the past week or so. Our perpetrators could have been here beforehand to carry out reconnaissance. And make sure the team going door-to-door ask about home security cameras and camera doorbells. Anything with a view of the road heading down here. It's the only way in so any vehicles would have had to use it. Anything else?"

"There's a café just over there." Grainger pointed vaguely in the direction of the cliff edge. "You can just about see its roof from here." Bobby followed his sergeant's arm, but his blank expression suggested he couldn't make anything out, so Grainger continued. "It doesn't open until ten during the winter, according to the notice on the door anyway. And it closes at four at this time of year, so probably outside our window, but I've asked the guys working the cordon to notify me as soon as the owners arrive. I'll check whether they've seen anything suspicious. Oh, and the forensic pathologist is here looking at the body."

"Yes, I've spoken with Faith already."

"Oh, Faith is it, sir?" Grainger regretted the comment instantly.

"Yes, Ms Andrews. Faith. The forensic pathologist. I spoke with her just now." Bobby didn't look impressed. He was staring again. Grainger managed to ride through it this time without looking away. He thought his boss suddenly looked embarrassed. "Did you know Jake Twyford had retired?"

"Yeah, great send-off. A few sore heads the next day!" Grainger chuckled before noticing the blank expression on the older man's face. He suddenly remembered that his boss hadn't been there. He couldn't recall whether he'd been invited. He assumed so, everyone from the station had. But then his boss wasn't much for social occasions. "I think you were busy that night, sir. You signed his card though and put something in the kitty."

Bobby didn't respond. He looked thoughtfully at the small but growing crowd that had started to congregate at the end of the lane, on the other side of the police tape. Grainger followed his gaze. It was a diverse group. There were several people with dogs, presumably out for their morning walk, and a whole family unit comprising father, mother and brace of young children. They were standing together in a semicircle, the two adults book-ending their offspring, each of them sipping a steaming mug of something and nibbling on a triangle of toast, as though they were watching the local bonfire display. To their right, a young woman bounced a screaming baby on her hip and a couple of teenagers clutched mobile phones at the end of fully extended arms. Grainger thought they looked like Daleks.

"And can we stop the videos please?" Bobby admonished his sergeant. "We'll be moving the body soon and could do without it being all over the internet. Let's show a bit of respect for the deceased and his family, shall we?"

And with that he walked off leaving Grainger alone in the middle of the busy car park.

Bobby examined the familiar face staring down at him. It looked peaceful but unmistakably sad at the same time. The open eyes were strangely red. Bloodshot. Like his brother had been crying. But there were no tears. He looked down the wiry, athletic body, a longer version of his own, and stared at his brother's legs as they dangled unmoving in the air, like he was floating.

"Is everything okay, sir?"

The urgent-sounding voice brought him back to the present and the memory faded. He felt the warm sun on his face.

"Sir."

Bobby saw DS Matthew Grainger standing next to him. His sergeant was tall and thin. Not the sort of presence that could be easily missed. He wore a suit, like always, but this morning he'd teamed it with a short, waxed jacket. Bobby wondered whether that was intentional, because they were on site out in the sticks. His sergeant probably thought it counted as the countryside. Bobby had to concede that Grainger was always smartly dressed, but somehow he managed to look permanently scruffy. It was a constant source of frustration to Bobby who took pride in his own appearance. He couldn't help but think it somehow reflected badly on the way Grainger did his job, although he realised how unreasonable that was.

Bobby continued to elevate his face to the sun. The warmth felt good. He didn't look directly at Grainger but out of the corner of his eye he could see the familiar tufts of short brown hair sticking out from his head at the usual wild angles. *It's like he's never even heard of a comb*, he thought to himself. Not for the first time, he wondered how he could bring it up with the young man. Should he even try? You had to be so careful nowadays. Then he thought about the station's secret Santa that would doubtless be happening next month. Maybe that was an opportunity. He'd have to find out who was organising it this year and arrange to get Grainger in the draw, but he thought the maximum £5.00 ought to cover the cost of a comb. He took a deep breath and reminded himself that such things were not important. Not really.

Somewhere in the distance, beyond the imposing cliffs on which he was standing, he could hear the playful whine of a couple of jet-skis traversing the sheltered waters of Tor Bay. It reminded him that life continued unapologetically all around. Most people remained completely untouched by the tragic events that had taken place on this remote lookout just a few short hours ago. *And that's exactly as it should be*, thought Bobby. It was his responsibility to find out what happened here last night, and to bring the perpetrators to justice. His job made it possible for everyone else to go about their business without fear. And he took that duty very seriously.

"So, what's the current status? Has the scene been fully secured?" Bobby already knew the answer to his question having been briefed by the crime scene manager, but he wanted to check his sergeant was also on top of the basics. This might be a high-profile case first and foremost, but it was also a valuable learning opportunity. And Bobby took his training responsibilities seriously. He hadn't worked with Grainger long, but he saw a lot of himself in the young man. He thought the sergeant could make an excellent detective one day, but also recognised he would need a helping hand on the way. Bobby knew how important that was. He wished he'd had someone to take an interest in his career when he was starting out.

Satisfied with his colleague's response, Bobby moved his questioning on. "Have you ever worked a murder, Grainger?"

"I've had to deal with a few dead bodies, sir. Accidents mainly. Or natural causes. One suicide. But not murder, no." Grainger looked worried, like he'd failed a test. "I am familiar with the protocols though, so nothing to worry about on that score, sir."

"Theory is one thing, Grainger. It's quite another matter in real life. You're going to have to learn on the job. It's not going to be easy. It'll be a steep learning curve, there's no point pretending otherwise." Bobby waited until Grainger met his gaze. "Are you sure you're ready?" He needed to know the young man had understood the seriousness of his words, and that he was up to the task. It was Bobby's experience that if you wanted to know whether a person was telling the truth, you needed only look them in their eyes when they spoke. Someone could lie all they wanted, maybe they even believed some of what they said, but their eyes always gave them away in the end. He guessed that's why the bad guys in films tended to wear sunglasses.

"Yes, sir. You don't need to worry about me. I won't let you down."

"Okay, good. Have we managed to confirm the identity of the deceased?"

"The car is registered to an Irving Hargreaves." Bobby noticed Grainger look away to consult his notebook, although he didn't think his sergeant had read the name from it. "The deceased's wallet was also in his jacket pocket. It contained several credit and debit cards, all of them in the name of a Mr I. A. Hargreaves, so it looks like he's our man." Bobby stood quietly as Grainger paused and looked up from his notebook. *Probably expecting praise*, he thought. He waited for the young man to continue. "Oh, and there was a Torbay Council work pass in the wallet. Issued in the same name and which had the deceased's photo on it, so I think we're clear on the ID front."

"Looks like it *is* Councillor Hargreaves then." Bobby's expression was grave. He was already thinking about how this news would make the investigation more difficult. "The press will be all over this. Not to mention the Chief Constable. They were golf buddies I believe. Anything obviously missing from the wallet?" Bobby was already moving on to potential motives. "Could it be a robbery gone wrong?"

"There was a hundred pounds in twenty-pound notes in the wallet along with the bank cards, so it doesn't look like robbery, sir. I also noticed the victim was wearing a Breitling on his left wrist. The latest Superocean if I'm not mistaken. Very nice. Worth around seven grand. It's only been out a couple of weeks. And that's before you even consider the car. That must be the best part of a hundred grand, and it's just sat there with the keys in the ignition."

"Sat there with a dead body in the front seat," Bobby noted sombrely. "That might have made it somewhat less appealing to a thief, don't you think? But you're right, it does add weight to the argument this wasn't a robbery."

Bobby stared off into the distance. His mind was racing with all the questions that would need to be answered, chief among them how the assailant or assailants got to and from the site. Did they arrive with the councillor or separately? He knew the answer to that question could be key to them identifying the perpetrators.

"Who found the body?" he enquired.

"A couple of youngsters from the technical college in Paignton," replied Grainger immediately. "Boyfriend and girlfriend, or whatever the correct terminology is nowadays."

Bobby noticed that the young officer hadn't consulted his notebook on this occasion.

"They were up here to catch the sunrise, apparently." Grainger paused, as though deciding whether to say anything further. "Although I think one of them had another type of experience in mind, if you catch my drift. Things didn't quite work out as he planned though." He grinned.

"All right, that's enough of that, Grainger. I get the picture. Let's focus on the murder, shall we?" Bobby stifled a smirk. "Where are they now? I'll need to speak to them."

"Just over there, sir." Grainger pointed to the far side of the car park. "In the police car with Officer Perkins."

"Okay, thanks. Have a word with uniform. I want them to conduct a thorough door-to-door to check whether anyone saw anything suspicious last night. Not just suspicious, unusual. Well, anything at all really. Tell them to focus between eleven p.m. and three a.m. That's Faith's best estimate of time of death."

He looked over at the crowd forming by the police tape.

"And push those onlookers further back. This is a crime scene. We're not here to turn on the Christmas lights."

CHAPTER 6

BOBBY REDHILL WALKED AROUND THE front of Officer Perkins' police car and got in the passenger side, closing the door loudly behind him. Officer Perkins was behind the steering wheel, her body turned so she was directly facing the detective. As he slumped heavily into the seat, Bobby automatically turned his head to look at her. He was momentarily startled as, quite unexpectedly, he came face to face with the female officer, their noses only a couple of inches apart. Bobby realised she'd most likely adopted this position just before his arrival, to make it easier for her to address the boy and girl sitting in the back of the car. He managed a brief, self-conscious smile before quickly turning his attention to the young couple behind him.

The boy appeared to have a slim build although his exact proportions were concealed by an oversized black hoodie that hung loosely off his shoulders and a pair of baggy stonewashed jeans that covered his legs like a generously sized blanket. A thin shot of lightly wavy dark red hair protruded from a relatively high hairline before falling just as abruptly over the boy's heavily freckled forehead, coming to rest above a pair of sharp blue eyes. They studied Bobby warily. Not that the detective noticed. He was too busy staring at the boy's head. The sides and most of the back were shaved but the hair along the centre of the skull, from fully front to back and disappearing down into the voluminous folds of the hoodie around his neck, was longer, like the fringe. It looked like a particularly juicy caterpillar was lying along the top of the boy's head.

At first glance, the girl didn't appear an obvious bedfellow with the boy sat next to her. In the way that girls tend to develop quicker than their male counterparts, she looked as though she fitted her skin better, like the butterfly that had escaped the formative chrysalis. Her fine, shoulder-length blond hair was straightened to within an inch of its life and tucked behind a pair of small ears which looked overburdened by shiny metallic additions. Her clothes were smart and appeared expensive. *Not the obvious choice for an early morning ramble on Berry Head*, thought Bobby. In fact, he guessed she'd probably spent some considerable time getting herself ready, notwithstanding the still early hour.

Unlike her companion, the girl looked upset. And scared. She'd clearly been crying. Mascara stains ran down blotchy red cheeks still wet with tears. The sleeves of her heavy winter coat were pulled down low over bare hands that were wrapped tightly around her waist, as though she was trying to keep herself warm. Not that it was cold inside the vehicle. Far from it. With the four of them breathing, condensation had started to fog the inside of the glass. Bobby buzzed down the passenger side window an inch or so. He thought the fresh air might help the young woman feel better. It certainly made the enclosed space more comfortable.

"My name is Detective Chief Inspector Redhill." Grainger had said the kids were students at the technical college which made them somewhere between sixteen and eighteen years old. But, sitting in the back of Officer Perkins' police car, they looked much younger.

"What are your names?" Bobby tried to adopt a relaxed, friendly expression, like that of Officer Perkins, although he wasn't sure how successful he'd been.

"I'm Hunter," responded the boy.

"And I'm Purity," answered the girl.

Whatever happened to normal, sensible names, Bobby wondered? It was as though parents nowadays were in an increasingly desperate race to endow their offspring with ever more unusual names. A race to the bottom, he thought. They were labouring under the misguided impression it would somehow enrich their children's lives.

Or perhaps he was the one who was misguided. Maybe the tech-savvy parents of today were onto something. Had they realised how important it was for their children to stand out in the increasingly influential world of social media? Where nothing was quite what it seemed, and anyone could be whatever they wanted to be. Allegedly.

Not that Bobby really understood such things. But that didn't mean he was blind to the changes. Social media was everywhere. All the young recruits coming into the force were obsessed with it. Always tweeting, liking or swiping something on their mobile phones. It was exhausting just watching it all. Even some of his older colleagues, who Bobby thought ought to know better, appeared glued to their phones most of the time. It wasn't that he was stuck in the past. Not really. He just wanted to do his job. Quietly. He didn't crave recognition. In fact, he believed the less visible he was, the greater impact he was having on the world. Now that's a sentiment he guessed most people today would think completely backward.

"I'm in charge of the investigation," Bobby continued. "I understand you two found the body. Is that right?"

"Yeah," said Hunter although he made no attempt to elaborate so Bobby continued.

"What were you doing here? It's quite an isolated spot and it must have been early?"

"We was up here to see the sunrise." Hunter's eyes glistened as he shot a glance towards Purity but the girl didn't react, preferring instead to stare blankly at her lap.

"*Were* you?" Bobby couldn't stop himself from correcting the young man's grammar, although he had a niggling suspicion the diction wasn't entirely genuine. "What time did you arrive?"

"Must'a been about six thirty." The language was a curious mix of inner-city gangster and educated public schoolboy. It felt exaggerated to Bobby. Hunter looked across to Purity. "That right ain't it, PT?" It took Bobby a moment, but he finally realised PT must be shorthand for Purity. Perhaps it was Hunter's nickname for the girl. Young love.

"'Cos we checked online last night and it said sunrise would be at six forty-three. We wanted to make sure we was up 'ere in good time." Hunter's mastery of the English language continued to impress Bobby.

"Yeah, that's about right," confirmed Purity. It was the first time she'd spoken, other than to confirm her name. "I remember checkin' me phone as we was walking up the hill, 'cos I was worried we was going to miss it." Bobby thought the girl's speech equally as forced as Hunter's.

"*He* was late knockin' for me," she flicked her head towards Hunter, "and then was just messin' about. In no hurry to get here. It was like he weren't really bothered about seeing the sunrise." Purity shot her boyfriend a questioning look. Suddenly it was Hunter's turn to be fascinated with his lap. Bobby wondered whether it might be catching. He stole a quick glance at Officer Perkins to check. She was looking intently at the young couple, a concerned yet compassionate look on her face. She appeared completely at ease, as though used to dealing with teenagers. Bobby wondered whether she had children of her own. Was she thinking about them now? About how she'd feel if it were her child who'd discovered the body? Bobby didn't have children of his own, and there were no nieces or nephews either, but he knew adults were supposed to protect kids from situations like this. He felt the responsibility himself, but guessed parenthood would only make the instinct stronger.

"I remember me phone said six twenty-seven and it weren't much after that we got here and saw the car," Purity concluded. Bobby wondered how long he'd last in a classroom of these youngsters' contemporaries if they all spoke the same way. He was almost glad he didn't have children. Almost.

"So, you walked here, then? You didn't drive or get a lift?" Bobby was keen to move things along.

"Nah, Hunter failed his test again, didn't he?" Purity glared at her boyfriend who refused to meet her eye. Bobby appeared to have hit upon an area of tension in their relationship. Oh well, no one said the path of true love ran smooth.

"Means we still gotta walk or use the bus to get around." Purity continued her rant. "It's proppa annoying, 'specially as we live in Brixham and all the decent pubs and clubs are in Torquay. Most of the guys at college can drive, but they all live in Paignton and don't come down here much. Can't blame 'em." Purity was really in her stride now. Bobby was starting to feel sorry for Hunter who made no attempt to defend himself, preferring instead to continue staring impassively at his lap. Ah, young love.

"Well, maybe Hunter will have passed his test by the time you two are old enough to go out drinking and visiting clubs!" offered Bobby with an encouraging smile. Purity just stared at him, oblivious to the sarcasm.

"Did you have far to walk?"

"Nah, just down the road." Purity again. "Higher Ranscombe Road's where I live. And Hunter's on West-over Close, a bit further down the hill." She nodded almost imperceptibly over Officer Perkins' right shoulder, Bobby guessed in the general direction of home. "He picked me up on the way past. It was supposed to be proppa roman-tic. Hunter loves the sunrise and wanted to share it with me. Told me Berry Head's the best place to experience it and 'cos we'd be the only one's up here at this time of year it would be extra spesh." Bobby assumed she meant 'special' but didn't have the energy or inclination to seek clarification. He couldn't help but feel the interview was losing focus.

"Well, isn't Hunter an old romantic," Bobby conceded. He glanced at the young boy who was looking sheepish. Just as Grainger had implied, Bobby thought his true intentions might not have been quite so honourable. "And then you saw the car?" Bobby prompted.

"Yeah, that's right." Hunter this time. He'd clearly decided now was the moment to reassert himself in the interview. Maybe he didn't want Purity giving away any more of his secrets. Or perhaps he just didn't want his girlfriend analysing his true motives for the pre-sunrise trip to the remote headland. Or how he compared to those other boys from college who'd managed to pass their driving tests.

"When we walked into the car park, we saw it right away," Hunter continued. "Couldn't miss it, could you? Don't see cars like that round here too often."

"Yeah, and Hunter just had to go over and have a closer look, didn't he?" Purity had taken up the story once more, and things didn't look like getting any easier for the young man. "Even opened the bloody door. I wanted to ignore it and go straight to the headland. Should have listened to me, babe. If you had'a done, we wouldn't be stuck 'ere now." *Not Hunter's day*, Bobby thought.

"What did you see when you approached the car?" Bobby enquired. "Why did you open the door?"

"I couldn't see much, to be honest." Hunter suddenly looked defeated. "It had those tinted windows. Then I just tried the door on the off chance. Fancied a look inside, didn't I? I wasn't goin' to do nuffin'." Bobby didn't bother pointing out the boy's inaccurate use of the English language implied the opposite. That he was indeed intending on '*doing something*' with or to the car. "Then I saw that bloke in the driver's seat. Scared the shit out o' me, I can tell you. I said something like '*sorry mate*' and ran back to Purity."

"What happened then?"

"Well, nothing. And that's what was weird. I didn't close the door, see. After I saw the bloke, I mean. He didn't say nuffin' when I opened the door, and then didn't make any attempt to close it afterwards. It was only when I was back over the other side of the car park I thought that was strange. That was why we went back over. Together this time. To take another look. See if anything was wrong."

"Yeah, he didn't want to go on his own." Purity seemed intent on taunting her boyfriend. "If only he'd left it alone,

I wouldn't have had to see that bloke like that. It was *well* gross."

"Did either of you touch anything?" Bobby enquired. "Inside the car, when you went back together to check."

Hunter and Purity exchanged the briefest of glances before answering at the same time. "No." The response was firm. No reason to doubt it. But it was the first time they'd answered a question together. Or so definitely for that matter. If he hadn't been fatigued by the conversation, Bobby might have picked up on that. If he hadn't been so keen to draw things to a close, he might also have taken more notice of the look the couple shared before they answered. It was brief, almost imperceptible, but they hadn't done that before either.

"As soon as we saw he was, you know, dead, we backed away and called the cops straight away." Hunter stared intently at his lap as he spoke. It was the first time he hadn't looked at Bobby when he'd spoken.

"And we missed the sunrise." And just like that, normal service was resumed. "Took those policemen ages to arrive. We were stuck out here all that time with *that body*." Purity shivered slightly as she spoke the last two words, as though trying to emphasise the level of her suffering and discomfort. Bobby wasn't sure whose benefit it was for.

"I can only imagine. It must have been very distressing for you." Bobby hoped he sounded sincere although he was finding Purity's portrayal of herself as the victim increasingly tiresome. "At least you'll have other sunrises to enjoy, all being well. One more thing." He was keen to bring the questioning to a close. "Did you see anyone else this morning? Whether before or after you discovered the body?"

"No, nuffin'," confirmed Hunter.

"It was dead quiet," added Purity, without a hint of humour.

"Well, thank you both. You've been very helpful." The words were spoken without conviction. "You'll need to come into the station in Torquay in the next couple of days to give formal statements. And Hunter, we'll need to take your fingerprints, for elimination purposes. Because you touched the vehicle. But all of that can wait. I'm sure you'll be keen to get yourselves off home now. Or perhaps into college? Lots to learn I suppose," he concluded, more in hope than expectation. "Officer Perkins can give you a lift home if you like." Bobby looked at his colleague who smiled warmly and nodded her consent. "She'll be able to arrange a time for you both to come into the station to give your statements. Your parents can always bring you. Save you getting the bus!"

And with that Bobby got out of the car. He walked away without looking back. Much to his frustration, he wasn't any closer to finding out what had happened here the previous night.

CHAPTER 7

PETER NORTON STOOD ON HIS OWN, to one side of the crowd that had started to form just beyond the police tape that had been hurriedly strung up across the entrance to Berry Head's car park.

To his left, four unnaturally smooth concrete boulders were artfully stacked on top of one another and hand-stencilled with brightly coloured bold letters that announced, '*Berry Head, 400 million years in the making*'. Peter didn't remember the sign from his school visit and wondered now about its purpose. He guessed it was intended to create a sense of mystery and intrigue around the site, but thought it fell wide of the mark and succeeded only in making Berry Head appear to be something it was not. While the military fortifications it housed were old, dating back to the Napoleonic Wars, they were nowhere near the vintage suggested by the sign. And Peter supposed the cliffs themselves weren't any older than the rest of the headland that edged the bay's entire southern flank. So far as he was aware, no other part of the peninsula had received a similar sign. Nevertheless, it did make Peter pause to think about all the things this place must have witnessed over its long history. He realised today's incident was just the latest chapter in an undoubtedly rich and colourful story. Right there and then, the outline for his update piece started to form in his mind.

Stretched out in front of him, the car park was a hive of activity. The near constant stream of people traversing the mottled expanse of grey and white gravel provided some welcome colour against the otherwise sterile backdrop. The unrelenting crunch of coarse aggregate beneath the soles of an army of boots hung heavily in the air, like the fog which often formed over the bay on still, autumn mornings. Among the bustle and commotion, Peter noticed two men stood talking. It was their relative stillness that first drew his attention.

One of the men was older. In his mid-forties, Peter guessed. He was tall and broad-shouldered. The younger man was taller still, but smaller in every other respect. They spoke intently, their heads close together. The older man was doing most of the talking, his companion intermittently checking notes from a pocketbook he held in his hand. They appeared oblivious to everyone else around them. Police, Peter guessed. Behind them, Peter could see a black Mercedes saloon car with what appeared to be a forensics team inspecting something in the driver's seat.

Peter knew the councillor drove a similar car, although he couldn't be sure it was the same one. Nevertheless, he could feel the excitement begin to build once again. Councillor Hargreaves had been a vocal advocate for Oldway Mansion's preservation within a fractured council whose support for the opposing proposals was split almost down the middle. With just four weeks to go before the council voted once and for all to determine the building's fate, Peter had witnessed things starting to get heated at the council meeting last week. Peter knew that if Councillor Hargreaves had in fact died here last night, then that was a massive story that needed to be told. And he intended to be the one to tell it.

The two men finished their conversation and as the older man walked off towards the other side of the car park, his younger companion headed in the direction of the police tape. As he got closer, Peter saw the earnest look he assumed they must teach new recruits at the police academy. Peter estimated him to be in his late twenties and guessed he was a detective constable, possibly a sergeant.

As the crowd started to disperse in response to the young detective's practised combination of verbal instructions and vigorous hand gesturing, Peter moved in the opposite direction. As he approached the police tape, he spoke directly to the detective.

"Peter Norton. I'm with the *Torbay Times*." He extended his hand before continuing. "Are you able to provide any comment on the incident you're investigating here today?"

Grainger didn't make any effort to shake the reporter's hand. "I'm sorry, sir, we won't be making any statement at this time. Detective Chief Inspector Redhill, the senior investigating officer, will issue a formal statement to all media outlets in due course."

"Understood. Thanks, officer…?" Peter raised his voice at the end of the sentence to signal he was enquiring about the man's name and rank.

"Detective Sergeant Grainger, that's G.R.A.I.N.G.E.R."

"Great, got it. And thanks, DS Grainger." Peter finally retracted his hand. "In the meantime, are you able to confirm that a body's been found?"

"That would fall under the category of making a statement, wouldn't it, sir?" Grainger's response was calm. He didn't appear to find the reporter's persistence annoying.

"Then can you provide any comment as to why Councillor Hargreaves' car is in the middle of your crime scene, DS Grainger?" Peter looked closely at the young detective as he asked this question. It was a bit of a punt but, if he was right, he thought the mention of the councillor's name might illicit more of a response. He wasn't disappointed. There was an instant, almost imperceptible flicker of recognition in Grainger's eyes that Peter would have missed if he hadn't been looking for it. His heart spiked. He could sense he was onto something.

"And what might you know about Councillor Hargreaves?" The young sergeant was trying hard to sound disinterested, but Peter could almost hear his brain whirring as he tried to determine the implications of the reporter's question. "What makes you think that is *his* vehicle?" And with those eight words Peter knew he was on the right track.

"I report on all local council matters for the paper and am very familiar with both the councillor and his vehicle." Peter's response was matter-of-fact. He wanted to sound knowledgeable without giving too much away. He sensed an opportunity, if he played it right, to insert himself into the investigation. "I'm writing a piece for tomorrow's edition which relates indirectly to the councillor. I will have to mention this development, one way or another. I can either provide facts or speculation. My editor won't mind either way, but he will expect me to refer to your presence here this morning, close to Councillor Hargreaves' abandoned vehicle." Peter paused before seeking to push home whatever advantage he currently had. "And, given my deadline, I probably won't be able to wait for DCI Redhill's formal statement."

Grainger considered this new information before continuing. "And what's the subject of this piece you're working on? How does it relate to the councillor?"

"It's an update piece on the future of Oldway Mansion. You know, the question of whether it should be sold to Justin King's hotels group and developed into a private members club, or retained in public ownership, restored, and opened back up to the public for everyone to enjoy. You've probably heard about it. Or read some of my previous pieces?" Peter looked hopefully at the detective but was met with a blank expression so he quickly continued.

"No matter." He flicked a wrist disparagingly towards the detective. "There are less than four weeks until the final council vote that will determine the mansion's future once and for all. It's extremely close in terms of which way the vote will go. And it's starting to get fractious. Only last week Councillor Hargreaves got into an argument with Councillor Farmer. I thought they were about to come to blows. I suppose there's a lot at stake but even so, you don't expect it from people in their position, do you?"

Peter could see Grainger processing this information and how it might tie in with the body currently sitting in the Mercedes behind him. "What side of the debate was Councillor Hargreaves on, just out of interest?" he finally asked.

"He was firmly on the side of preservation."

"And what effect would his death have on the vote?" Grainger was trying to sound indifferent, but Peter could tell he was hooked on the story, just like he thought his readers would be. "I mean, theoretically…"

Peter considered the question for a moment, as though this was a connection he hadn't previously made. "Come to think about it, detective, his theoretical death would push things in favour of those who want to develop the site. They took an informal vote at the end of last week's meeting which indicated the preservationists had the majority they required, but only by a single vote. It really is that close. Provided no one changed their mind or voted in a different way to that previously indicated, the vote would be tied – without Councillor Hargreaves, I mean. Seventeen for and seventeen against. In that scenario, the leader of the council would have a second or casting vote." Peter let that information hang in the air for a moment, feeling sure Grainger would bite. He wasn't disappointed.

"Who's the leader?"

"Oh, that would be Councillor Farmer."

"The same Councillor Farmer who argued with Councillor Hargreaves last week?" Peter knew he only had to reel the detective in.

"That's the one. He's the primary sponsor of the development proposals within the council. He's very close to Justin King and during his stint as leader has been a vocal advocate of the developer. He wants the development of Oldway Mansion to be a defining part of his legacy – the cornerstone of his promise to reinvigorate the economic fortunes of this area, I believe he called it." Peter was in his flow now and could see the story developing in front of his eyes. "The death of Councillor Hargreaves would clearly have material implications for the vote which is something my readers have a right to know," Peter finished with a flourish. He felt like a barrister standing in front of the jury as he summarised his case. All he had to do now was wait for the verdict. One, two, three seconds…

"Wait here a moment, Mr Norton, while I go and speak with DCI Redhill."

Grainger walked away from the police tape with mixed feelings. On one hand he was excited about the new information that appeared to provide a clear motive for the death of Councillor Hargreaves. But the knot in his stomach told him his boss wasn't going to appreciate this lead coming from a reporter.

Grainger waited as Bobby walked away from Officer Perkins' police car. He didn't think his boss looked happy, although since DCI Redhill seemed to have a serious, almost pained, expression etched permanently across his face, this lowering of the senior detective's mood wouldn't have been obvious to everyone. But Grainger had worked with Bobby long enough to pick up the DCI's more common tells and was getting quite good at reading the almost imperceptible signs which indicated what was really going on behind the stony outward façade.

At this moment, the DCI's brow was more furrowed than usual, and his hands were pushed right down into the pockets of his knee-length, dark blue trench coat. He was also bent slightly forwards, as though succumbing to the weight of the investigation as it pressed down on his shoulders. Grainger guessed the fists were tightly clenched in those pockets. Not a good sign. He assumed the interview with the two teenagers had failed to produce any tangible leads.

"Anything interesting, sir?" Grainger asked the question more in hope than expectation.

"It doesn't look like they saw anything of note, no. You?"

"It may be nothing, but I've been talking to a reporter." Grainger thought he saw his boss recoil at the admission. He knew Bobby would be concerned about him having spoken to the media, so he continued quickly. "He works for the *Torbay Times*. The man over there." Grainger pointed in the direction of the police tape at the entrance to the car park. Peter was nonchalantly talking into his mobile phone, apparently without a care in the world. "He approached me, sir. I haven't confirmed or denied anything, but he seems to know quite a lot about Councillor Hargreaves. Recognised his car and asked directly for a comment as to why it's in the middle of our crime scene." Grainger proceeded to quickly summarise his conversation with the reporter. "I think you should have a word with him. This Oldway Mansion development could be a legitimate lead. And besides, I guess you'd prefer to get in front of whatever he plans to write in his article for the paper tomorrow."

"Bloody reporters!" Grainger had been expecting the outburst. "They're like vultures feeding on the carcass of other people's misfortune." Bobby paused and looked more closely at the area around the police tape which was now much quieter than when he'd left to speak with Purity and Hunter. "What is he even doing here? I don't see any other members of the press. How did he get here so quickly?" Bobby straightened his tie and ran a hand through his perfectly coiffed dark brown hair before continuing. "Lead the way then, Grainger. Let's see what he's got to say for himself."

Bobby increased his pace as they approached and arrived at the police tape a couple of paces before his sergeant. He ducked underneath without breaking stride, standing up directly in front of the reporter who was still talking into his mobile phone.

"Mr Norton? I'm DCI Redhill." The inspector offered his hand, holding it out while the reporter hastily finished his conversation.

"Pleased to meet you, Chief Inspector." Grainger noticed Peter take a couple of steps back as he offered his own hand in greeting. "And thanks for coming to speak with me." Bobby was taller than the reporter, and broader shouldered. Peter was having to look up at the detective as he spoke, his head tilted backwards at an uncomfortable angle, despite his attempts to create additional space between them. Grainger had witnessed his boss use his physical size to intimidate suspects before. On this occasion, he suspected the invasion of the reporter's personal space was an attempt to assert his authority in the relationship.

"I understand you've been asking questions about a Councillor Hargreaves."

"I was simply asking for an explanation as to why the councillor's car is in the middle of your crime scene. I can see the SOCOs are very interested in something inside the vehicle, so I presume there's a dead body in there and, well, one and one usually do make two. Wouldn't you agree, Chief Inspector?" Peter followed up this summary with a broad smile.

"One and one *do* make two, Mr Norton." Bobby kept his voice neutral. "But in my experience, matters are rarely that straightforward and, more often than not, jumping to obvious conclusions can end up making an investigator look quite foolish."

"I'm not sure I follow." Peter looked confused, although Grainger thought it a little too practised.

"What I mean, is that this is an active crime scene, and we're only at the very beginning of our investigations into what occurred here. As police officers we deal in facts, not conjecture. So, *you* may believe the car over there belongs to a Councillor Hargreaves and you may also speculate that, because there is a dead body inside, which I can neither confirm nor deny, it belongs to the owner of the vehicle. All of that would in my opinion be speculation. Such conclusions have no basis in fact and could easily be wrong in any number of ways."

"So, are you saying that is not the councillor's car over there? And can I quote you in denying that Councillor Hargreaves is dead in the driver's seat?" Grainger thought Peter was enjoying himself. He certainly didn't appear to be intimidated by the inspector.

"I'm not confirming or denying anything, Mr Norton. That is very much my point. Until we've been able to corroborate all the facts, we won't be making any such statements. It would be irresponsible to do so. Victims of crime are people too. Human beings with families who deserve respect." Grainger had heard a version of this speech many times before. "The family has a right to hear from the police in the first instance, not to read about the death of a loved one in the paper or on social media."

"I fully understand that, detective. And, for the record, agree with it absolutely. But you'll appreciate I have a job to do, just like you. I happen to be here, and to have seen what I've seen. I have an obligation to share that information with my readers, who themselves have a right to know what is going on where they live. After that, it's up to them what conclusions they reach. Most of the news is essentially speculation in any event. Well, until it isn't. And the public tend to lose interest by that point, anyhow."

"Yes, I was meaning to ask why you just happen to be here, Mr Norton." Bobby looked at Peter quizzically. "I mean, how did you hear about this incident so quickly? And before you say anything, DS Grainger has checked. You don't live nearby, so don't tell me you saw the police cars from your kitchen window and came to investigate."

"You can't expect me to disclose my sources now surely, Inspector," Peter replied with a dry smile. "Why don't we move on from this impasse? It seems to me that we can be useful to one another."

"Oh yes. And how might that be?"

"Well, I'm sure the highly efficient DS Grainger here has told you all about the story I'm currently working on for tomorrow's printed edition? Concerning the Oldway Mansion development."

"He might have mentioned something to that effect. So?" Bobby's poker face gave nothing away. Even

Grainger couldn't tell whether he was interested in the reporter's pitch.

"I've been covering this story for the last nine months, give or take. Right from the very beginning. I know all the key players and have witnessed several arguments and heated debates on the issue first-hand. To the extent the development turns out to be a legitimate area of investigation in the councillor's theoretical death, then I would be happy to provide any assistance I can. The *Torbay Times* has been at the forefront of the story throughout, and we'd be very keen to retain that position in the event of matters taking an…unexpected twist. Do you follow me so far, Chief Inspector?"

Bobby gave an almost imperceptible nod, so Peter continued.

"Unless I hear from you to the contrary prior to my deadline at six this evening, tomorrow's article will include details of the unexpected and, so far, unexplained death of Councillor Hargreaves on Berry Head last night. It will also explore the potential impact his death might have on next month's council vote. That article will be available online from midnight, but I promise not to publish anything about the events that occurred here last night before then. That should give you plenty of time to confirm your facts and notify whoever you need to. In return, I would be grateful for a heads-up prior to any formal statement being made in advance of my article going live. Just so I'm able to break the story on the *Torbay Times* website first. Prior to any other press outlets, that is."

Bobby appeared to consider the reporter's offer. Or he could have simply been thinking of a suitably diplomatic way of telling him where he could (theoretically) shove it. Grainger wasn't sure which way it was going to go until his boss fished a business card out the pocket of his trench coat and handed it to Peter.

"Why don't you give your business card to DS Grainger, Mr Norton, and I'll let you know if anything we've discussed here turns out to be incorrect. In the meantime, you have my details if you need to contact me."

Bobby was ducking back under the police tape before he'd finished his sentence and was walking back towards the crime scene with his back to the reporter when he added, "I expect we'll speak again soon, Mr Norton."

CHAPTER 8

"Just one moment, sir. I'll check whether Councillor Farmer is available." The young secretary blew on her newly painted pink fingernails while staring at her colleague, Sharon, who was tentatively sipping on a dark green juice she'd allegedly blitzed at home that morning. Sharon was always trying out the latest health fad, although Mandy had never seen her exercising. Mandy smiled. She went to the gym a couple of times a week but didn't really need to. Not like Sharon. She extended her hand in front of her face and nodded agreeably. The colour was great. Bright and vivacious. Just like her. She looked across to the phone on her desk and saw the flashing light reminding her that a call was waiting. Eventually, she leant over and pressed the button that connected her directly with her boss.

"Yes Mandy, what is it?" Councillor Farmer's voice was gruff, as usual. Mandy could hear him just as clearly through the wall behind her as through the headset she always wore when seated at her desk. That's how she knew he reserved his irritated voice just for her. She didn't know why and had long since given up caring. Now she just kept his calls waiting and painted her nails in the bright colours she knew he disapproved of.

"I have Justin King on the line for you. Would you like me to put him through?"

"Yes, of course!"

Mandy looked up and saw Sharon walking towards the kitchen with her green juice. She guessed it was destined for the trash, like so many of her healthy eating ideas. Other than Sharon, the corridor where the secretaries were seated, almost as an afterthought outside the offices of the councillors they worked for, was quiet. Most of the secretaries worked part-time or started later, after dropping children off at school. Mandy liked the peace and quiet of the first and last hours of the day but knew she'd probably go crazy without the constant chatter that reverberated around the confined space during the day. Lockdown had been particularly difficult. Most of the councillors had allowed their secretaries to work remotely, but not Councillor Farmer. He'd been in the office almost every day and had insisted on Mandy's presence.

Finally, she put the call through.

Mandy's voice echoed loudly through the phone's inbuilt speaker, filling the confines of the sparsely decorated office. Councillor Hugh Farmer heard the usual trace of attitude in her voice. Not for the first time he thought about having her moved to work for another councillor. But he dismissed the idea as soon as it formed. He knew he'd miss her. She reminded him of someone he'd known as a young man. Maybe it was the rebellious streak. He'd been in love with her. Still was, truth be told. At the time, he'd thought they'd be together forever, but she'd left him all alone to fend for himself. He knew he'd never got over it. He still felt betrayed. Resentful. And now, all these years later, Mandy had brought those feelings, buried for so long, back to the surface. Stupid really. Still, despite the painful memories, he didn't think he could bear to lose her all over again.

As he waited for Mandy to connect the hotelier and developer, Hugh picked up the receiver, instinctively seeking the greater privacy it offered. He was due to have lunch with Justin King later that day and wondered now about the purpose of the call. He'd just have asked his PA to call Mandy if he simply wanted to rearrange. No, it must be about something else, he concluded.

"Have you heard the news?" Hugh almost didn't recognise the voice on the other end of the phone. It sounded different. Excited maybe. The words were certainly coming more quickly than usual. "It looks like we're going to win!"

"Justin. Is that you? What news? What are we going to win?"

"The development. It's pretty much in the bag."

"What are you talking about? How can we have won? The vote isn't for another four weeks. Are you feeling all right, Justin? You don't sound quite yourself."

"You haven't heard then? I was sure you would have done. He *was* your colleague, after all." Hugh didn't like the way Justin had emphasised the word '*was*'.

"Who *was* my colleague?" Hugh spoke quietly. Like he didn't really want to hear the answer but knew he was expected to ask.

"Irving bloody Hargreaves. Who else?" replied Justin bluntly. "And he's dead!"

"What are you talking about, Justin? If this is a joke, then it's not very funny."

"No joke. His body was found this morning. Up at Berry Head. The police are there now."

"That's terrible!" Hugh's response was instinctive, but then he remembered he'd never really liked Irving Hargreaves. He certainly wouldn't miss the way his colleague constantly tried to undermine him. Never in public, mind, always behind the scenes. Hugh had thought for some time that Irving had one eye on his job as leader of the council. Still, he wouldn't wish him dead. "What happened? Are you sure it's Irving?"

"I have it on good authority." Something about the way Justin said this made Hugh pause. It almost sounded like he knew, for certain. But how could he? Hugh tried hard to suppress the unwelcome thoughts that started to nibble at the edge of his consciousness. Could Justin be involved in Irving's death in some way? Was he even capable? No, the idea was too ridiculous. He'd never had any reason to doubt Justin. And the previous five years had been extremely successful, for them both. Why start questioning him now? But Hugh knew they hadn't faced this level of opposition to their plans before.

He realised with a heavy feeling in the pit of his stomach that he didn't really know anything about Justin King. He was an apparently successful businessman who'd arrived in the bay around five years earlier with money to invest. Hugh had been looking for wealthy backers to support his ambitious plans for the area. It had seemed like divine intervention. And Hugh believed in a higher power. Now he started to question his judgement. Had he exercised caution, done proper due diligence, or had he simply taken Justin at face value? There was a lot riding on the Oldway Mansion development. And Justin had the most to lose. Financially at least. Unsure of what else to say he mumbled, "What was he even doing at Berry Head? He hated going to Brixham."

"No idea, although it must have been something he wanted to keep secret."

"Why do you say that?"

"Because the police believe he was murdered. In the middle of the night. Remote spot to be at that time, don't you think? But typical of Irving to be playing in the shadows."

"Murder? Shadows? What are you talking about, Justin?"

The developer continued without elaborating further. "Of course, his death does present certain opportunities." He was speaking more slowly now, and quietly, in an almost conspiratorial tone. "I don't mean to speak ill of the dead…well, maybe I do… Anyway, Irving's support for those hippie preservationists was getting rather tiresome. He simply refused to see sense, no matter what encouragement I gave him. I always thought that was strange, rather naïve for someone who supposedly had such a successful career in business." Justin was rambling now. Almost talking to himself. "With Irving out of the way, the votes are tied. Assuming no one changes their mind, that is. And without Irving's imposing presence, I'm sure I can win over one or possibly two of the no votes. All being well, there shouldn't be any need to use your casting vote."

"What are you talking about, Justin? Now is not the time to be talking about the development. A colleague has just died."

"On the contrary, Hugh, now is exactly the time. We both have too much riding on the outcome of this development. You just as much as me." Hugh thought the comment slightly threatening. "We can't afford to let this situation derail us. We need to focus and take advantage of the opportunity."

"I wish you wouldn't refer to it as an opportunity," urged Hugh. "It really is most distasteful."

"Maybe so, but that doesn't make it any less true. We need to get on top of this. Think about the bigger picture. About what you want your legacy to be. We've already made such great progress through the development of my other hotels. Job rates are up. Voter satisfaction has never been so high. Just think what Oldway Mansion will do. You'll be held up as the visionary who made it all happen, Hugh. They'll be lining up to appoint you mayor of Torbay after your time on the council comes to an end. If you wanted it, of course."

Hugh was quiet for a moment. He was thinking about the bright red mayoral robes with the thick white fur at the neck and cuffs, and the heavy gold chain. How did Justin know? Hugh had always thought they'd look good on him, but he didn't think he'd ever mentioned it to anyone. "I suppose you're right, Justin. This has always been about so much more than just one individual. We'll have to get the messaging right though." Justin remained silent.

"I'm doing an interview with the *Torbay Times* soon," Hugh continued proudly, the outlines of a plan forming in his mind. "About the development specifically and my vision for the future of the bay more generally. Maybe you should consider doing something similar. An interview with the media-shy Justin King would do wonders for keeping the attention on us and away from the preservationists."

"That's an excellent idea, Hugh." Justin's tone implied he thought it anything but, not that Hugh appeared to notice. He was too busy thinking about what they had to do. "I'll get my PA onto it straight away," continued Justin.

"In the meantime, I'll make some calls." Hugh spoke confidently, once more acting every bit the council's unflappable leader. "If we're going to get in front of this, it'll be important to know exactly what happened. Let's catch up over lunch."

Hugh put the receiver down and slumped heavily in his high-backed leather swivel chair. He couldn't believe this was happening. Not so close to the final vote. The earlier nagging doubts about Justin King started to invade his thoughts once more. He fought them back down. Now was not the time to worry about such things. He realised with a heavy heart that Justin had been right about one thing. He did have too much riding on the development to let it fail. He needed to act decisively.

He leaned forward and pressed the button on the telephone's sleek black console that connected him directly to Mandy. She answered on the fourth or fifth ring. He didn't wait for her to speak. "Get me Chief Constable Parker," he barked. "Urgently."

CHAPTER 9

DCI BOBBY REDHILL SAT IN his office on the second floor of Torquay police station. The door was closed, and the lights were off. The only illumination came from the gaps between the slats in the metal blinds, where they'd been damaged over years of heavy-handed use. His mood was almost as dark as the room. He was troubled by his earlier conversation with the reporter, Peter Norton, and kept playing it over in his mind.

He'd painted a compelling picture that pointed the finger of suspicion in the death of Councillor Irving Hargreaves firmly in the direction of Oldway Mansion and the competing proposals for its future. He'd even suggested the council's own highly respected leader, Councillor Hugh Farmer, as a potential suspect. Bobby sighed heavily. He knew he'd have to investigate but didn't expect it to be easy. Experience told him that politics and (relative) celebrity were seldom happy bedfellows when it came to a police investigation.

Then there was the reporter's presence at the crime scene that morning. It still didn't sit well with him. How had he heard about the incident so quickly? And what were the chances of him having such in-depth, pertinent knowledge about their victim? Bobby was naturally cautious when it came to the media. He was aware of that. He liked to be in control and was suspicious of the media's often sensationalist agenda, fearing its potential to derail an enquiry if not managed carefully. Not that any of that detracted from the task at hand. Bobby knew his biases were a secondary consideration. He'd do whatever was best for the investigation. The truth was all that mattered and he was determined to get justice for the murdered councillor. Even so, he couldn't shake the feeling he was being played somehow.

Just then the phone on his desk started to ring. The sudden noise made Bobby jump and he sat forward abruptly. The small LCD screen indicated it was Chief Constable Parker, the chief constable of Devon and Cornwall Constabulary, calling from his office on the fifth floor. Knowing the Chief Constable and Councillor Hargreaves were friends, Bobby took a deep breath and picked up the phone. "Good morning, sir."

"Redhill, what's this I hear about a murder on Berry Head? I've just had Councillor Farmer on the phone. He tells me it's Irving Hargreaves." The voice was deep, and the words came out slowly, as though each one was being savoured. If forced to put the voice to a person, you'd be forgiven for assuming it belonged to a large, heavily set man. But you'd be left disappointed. The Chief Constable was no more than five foot five inches in his slightly high-heeled shoes. And wiry, like the circular, metal-framed glasses he wore on his impossibly round head.

The questions gave Bobby pause. He hadn't been expecting them. He'd been prepared to break the news of the councillor's death himself. On the drive back from Berry Head he'd even rehearsed what he was going to say. Not for the first time that morning, Bobby felt behind the curve.

"Councillor Farmer? Why was he phoning *you*?" The words came out without him thinking. "I mean, I've only just got back from the crime scene myself. How did he even know about it?"

"I'll take that as confirmation then, shall I?" The Chief Constable's voice remained level, but Bobby suspected it concealed a hint of anger.

"I was about to call you, sir. To let you know."

"I saved you the bother then, didn't I, Inspector? Bloody embarrassing that I didn't know what he was talking about. Especially since Irving and I were friends. So, what do we know?"

Bobby ran through the little he'd been able to put together so far, although he left out his conversation with Peter Norton. Knowing the role of chief constable was as much a political appointment as a policing one, he didn't know how news of the proposed hotel development and its most prominent supporter already being on his radar as potential motive and suspect would be received. He wanted time to work out the lie of the land. His candour proved well placed.

"So, why was Councillor Farmer calling you, sir?"

"He wanted information. He's concerned how Irving's death might impact the plans for Oldway Mansion."

"A strange response to news of a colleague being murdered."

"It might appear crass to you, Inspector, but we don't all have the luxury of forgetting our wider responsibilities in moments of tragedy. For the record, he was devastated about the news, but this development is high up on the political agenda. There's a lot of pressure on him to ensure it succeeds. Councillor Farmer has to stay focused on the bigger picture." Bobby braced himself for what he felt sure was coming next. The real purpose for the call. He didn't have to wait long.

"On that note, are you sure you're ready for this?"

"Ready, sir? I'm not sure I know what you mean."

"Come now, Inspector, don't be coy. I'm referring to your personal situation, as you well know. You only lost your wife last year, and while you might have taken some time off to care for her over the final couple of months, you came back to work straight after the funeral. A case like this can rake up a lot of…unwelcome memories… and we don't need any distractions. This is a high-profile investigation. I don't need to tell you that. There's going to be a lot of scrutiny. The anniversary of Patty's death is in a few weeks. No one's going to think any less of you if you take a backseat on this one. After all, you don't know how it's going to affect you. If you have any concerns at all, better to say now."

Bobby heard the Chief Constable's voice, but the words didn't register. He was thinking about his darling Patricia. Patty to everyone. They'd only met a few short years before. In their late thirties, they'd both assumed the opportunity had passed them by, but it had been love at first sight. For him anyway. She'd never said anything, but he suspected she'd taken a little longer to feel the same way about him.

She was the first woman Bobby had ever met with whom he felt instantly at ease. It had just felt right from the first moment, like it was meant to be. She'd listened without judgement to all the insecurities and fears borne by the scared, lonely little boy who'd found his older brother hanging by his school tie in the basement of the family home. Able at long last to unburden himself, he'd finally come to realise that none of what happened was his fault. He still felt guilty, but nowadays it was simply because he was alive, and his brother wasn't.

Now Patty was gone, Bobby felt cheated all over again. This time it was cancer, not suicide, but the sudden loss led to the same crushing sense of absolute helplessness, of colossal unfairness and utter despair. As Bobby came to terms with the devastating blow, work once again became his primary focus and provided a welcome distraction from the grief. Just like it had before Patricia had come into his life.

Bobby knew he had a weakness for the self-destructive. That was the reason for returning to work so soon after Patty had succumbed to her illness. Growing up he'd rebelled, angry with the world for the pain he felt. As a teenager he'd fallen in with the wrong crowd and had started drinking to forget. It was a dangerous spiral and after leaving school he'd stumbled aimlessly from one dead-end job to the next, never really fitting in. It was only after seeing an advertisement for a police recruitment drive that things had started to change. Urged on by his desperate parents, he had taken the plunge in a last-ditch attempt to finally find his place in the world. It was no exaggeration to say the police force had saved him, before Patty had done so all over again.

Bobby heard Chief Constable Parker's gentle breathing through the receiver and realised he was still waiting for a response. "Thanks for the concern, sir, but I'm fine. Really. The pain never goes away, but Patty knew how important this job was to me. She'd want me to find out the truth about what happened to Councillor Hargreaves. He deserves nothing less. And that's exactly what I intend to do."

Chief Constable Parker was silent for a moment, as though considering his response. When he spoke, his voice gave nothing away. "If you're sure. I'm placing my faith in you, Inspector. Don't let me down."

The line went dead, and Bobby was alone with his thoughts once more. If he'd been in any doubt about the challenges that lay ahead, there was none now: the investigation had just become a lot more difficult.

CHAPTER 10

PETER NORTON WAS DEEP IN THOUGHT. He'd come straight home after leaving Berry Head and had immediately started writing his update piece for the *Torbay Times*. It was now mid-afternoon, and despite having emailed the completed story through to Marcus Payne, his editor, around forty minutes ago, he was still sitting at his dining room table, thinking about Councillor Hargreaves and Oldway Mansion. The more he thought about it, the more compelling the story became. As he reread his work for the twentieth time, he began to believe his own words.

The prospect of there being a more sinister narrative at play, lurking in the details of the seemingly innocent and straightforward story of local council in-fighting he'd been reporting on over the past nine months, appealed to Peter. He felt it justified his decision to move back to the bay and gave meaning to his work over that period. The chance to secure an inside line directly into the investigation also excited him. He thought back to his conversation with DCI Bobby Redhill. Peter could tell the detective had been interested in the information he'd shared and that he hadn't been aware of any potential link to the Oldway Mansion development beforehand. Peter smiled. He thought he'd played his hand well at the crime scene, managing to demonstrate his potential value while not appearing too pushy. He'd also shown he was willing to work with the police rather than against them. DCI Redhill had certainly appeared receptive and grateful. Peter reminded himself to follow up with the detective soon.

He was roused from his musings by a deep rumbling sound coming from his stomach. It was accompanied by a dull ache and Peter realised he hadn't eaten anything today, despite being up since before dawn. His stomach was complaining loudly and demanding attention. Peter stood up and wandered into the kitchen, putting all thoughts of a possible criminal sub-plot to the Oldway Mansion development story completely out of his mind.

As he looked through the kitchen cupboards, he remembered he'd eaten the last can of baked beans for dinner the previous evening. Along with the last piece of bread. A lone bag of quick-cook rice stared back at him. He was reminded of the delicious fridge specials Frieda had been able to cobble together no matter the disparate ingredients to hand. Peter opened the fridge and laughed at the sight of the half-eaten cucumber that sat in depressing isolation on the middle shelf. *Even she'd struggle with that!*

He briefly considered phoning for a takeaway but quickly remembered the promise he'd made his mother to eat more healthily. That was the reason for the cucumber in the fridge. At least he could say he was trying!

He was about to head downstairs to the convenience store when his mobile phone started to ring. He looked at the name on the screen. Marcus.

"Hi, Marcus. Did you get my email? I sent it about an hour ago." Forgetting his hunger completely, Peter didn't bother with niceties. The big-shot reporter, focused solely on the breaking story. The fact he'd answered the call so quickly and was happy to speak with his editor wasn't lost on Peter. *The power of a decent story*!

"Hello, Peter. Yes, I'm fine, thanks for asking." Peter ignored his editor's sarcasm, keen to hear his thoughts on the article.

"I've been through it. It's good work."

Maybe he's not such a bad editor after all.

"This death really adds a fantastic new angle to the whole Oldway Mansion story," Marcus continued excitedly. "It's going to reignite interest, Peter, not just locally but nationally as well. I hope you're ready for that?" Peter smiled but didn't respond. This was the opportunity he'd been waiting for. He was ready, no question.

Marcus filled the silence. "The next couple of weeks are going to be extremely busy, with this death coming on top of the final council vote. And you already have the interviews with Councillor Farmer and Conrad Macpherson." Peter was scheduled to interview the Leader of Torbay

Council and the Chairman of Oldway Mansion Preservation Society in consecutive editions of the paper over the next couple of weeks. The interviews promised to provide in-depth insights into the opposing proposals for Oldway Mansion's future. The *Torbay Times* was the only paper to have secured a sit-down with both men, a coup Marcus was particularly excited about. "Conrad's interview is scheduled for Saturday morning, remember."

"Don't worry, Marcus, I won't forget. I'm looking forward to it."

"Oh, and I received a call from Justin King's personal secretary." Peter noticed the pride in Marcus's voice. "She's offering us an exclusive interview. A rare opportunity to get his thoughts on the development. You know he doesn't usually do much with the press, so it's a real coup for us."

"When did this offer for the interview with King come through?" asked Peter warily.

"Early this afternoon. Why do you ask?"

"Quite a coincidence, don't you think? That we get offered an exclusive interview with Mr King on the very morning Councillor Hargreaves is found dead. We've been trying to get a sit-down with him for months now. He's rebuffed us every time. Quite forcibly, as I recall."

"Coincidences do happen, Peter." Marcus sounded defensive, like the wind had been knocked out of his sails. "Mr King is a very private person who doesn't actively seek the limelight." Peter wondered whether Marcus was quoting straight from Justin King's Wikipedia page. He fought the urge to speak.

"This development is obviously important to him," Marcus continued. "If he's prepared to give us an interview, we should be grateful, not cynically look for ulterior motives. We certainly shouldn't look a gift horse in the mouth. Just think what this could do for our readership numbers." *Here we go*, thought Peter. *It always came down to money in the end*. That was why he could never be an editor. For a real journalist, nothing was more important than the story.

"Everyone in the bay knows him, but no one really *knows* him." Marcus was still talking. "I'm not aware of him giving any other interviews, certainly not locally. People are naturally interested and want to know more about him." Peter decided not to push the point further. You had to pick your battles. "This is a great opportunity, Peter. For you *and* the paper, coming on top of the other splendid work you've been doing these past few months."

Flattery, the quickest way to a reporter's heart.

"I didn't say I wouldn't do the interview. I just think it's interesting timing, is all."

Having secured the final word on the matter, Peter decided to move the conversation on. "What do you know about Councillor Hargreaves then, Marcus? Any theories as to what got him killed?"

Marcus considered the question for a moment. "I never met him personally, although in some ways I wish I had. He had quite the reputation back along. Flash, you know? Expensive cars, beautiful women hanging off both arms and more ex-wives than you could shake a stick at." He laughed loudly. "I guess those last two might have been linked! It's quite a cliché, but I suppose there's just something about that industry."

"Which industry was that?"

"Nightclubs. He owned several in the bay. You're local, Peter. If you ever went clubbing when you were younger, chances are you've been to one of his places."

Peter had an instant flashback to his eighteen-year-old self and a string of Saturday nights during the seemingly endless summer that followed the end of his A-Levels. He could still remember the sense of excitement he'd always felt as he stood in the queue outside the heavily protected entrance to one of those places. You could practically taste the anticipation that hung in the air above the would-be partygoers, like heavily scented cologne, as they eagerly contemplated what lay in store at the end of the line. And the fear. He would never forget the fear shared by all the boys. Would the bouncers even let you in? Girls never had that problem, Peter recalled. Half the time they didn't even have to queue.

Then, after you'd successfully navigated that obstacle, the pay-off came. Pure joy. He remembered the sticky carpets, the awkward, self-conscious dancing and, of course, the crushing sense of disappointment that always accompanied the end of the evening as the girl he'd tried to summon the courage to talk to all night suddenly disappeared home with her gang of giggling friends. Not that he'd be going home anytime soon. There was always an equally long, but infinitely more depressing queue outside the nightclub where he'd stand for hours with his fellow revellers in the cold, and often wet, weather, waiting for a taxi.

A broad smile formed on his face. Great times!

"Although, he had his fingers in a lot of pies..." Peter realised that Marcus was still talking. "Not all of them strictly legal, if the rumours were to be believed. I recall there were some allegations of corruption many years ago. Although, nothing was ever proved and there hasn't been anything recently so far as I'm aware."

Peter was suddenly very interested in his editor's words. "What were the allegations?"

"It was a while ago, but I recall there were some issues with anti-social behaviour linked to the local nightclubs. You know, drug use and petty crime. Nothing we aren't used to hearing about now, but back then it caused more headlines. Several other clubs were either shut down or fined, but Hargreaves' places always seemed to escape blame. His were some of the biggest and most popular establishments at the time. If there was a problem, it just wasn't realistic they weren't also tainted."

"So, what?" Peter asked. "People thought he was greasing some palms?"

"There were inevitably rumours. Some people thought he must have had dirt on certain influential members of the police force and local council. That he was blackmailing them to keep his clubs out of any investigations. As I say, nothing was ever proved at the time and, in any event, it was all such a long time ago that I doubt it had anything to do with his death."

"Interesting all the same. What were you referring to when you said not all his interests were strictly legal?"

"Again, they were only ever rumours, but there was talk at the time about his connections to a criminal gang involved with drugs and prostitution. Ironic really, given his clubs managed to stay clear of any official sanctions."

"Interesting," Peter repeated, almost to himself. "Sounds like he lived quite the life. So how come he's now a local councillor? It doesn't sound like an obvious career move."

"No idea. All I know is he sold up several years ago. He kept a low profile for a year or so before re-emerging on Torbay Council. Still drives around in a nice car but he swapped his big house in Torquay for something more modest in Paignton. Lives alone now. People change, I suppose."

Peter thought about everything he'd just learnt. The description of the flamboyant businessman didn't tally with the unassuming councillor he'd got to know from afar over the past nine months. The story was only growing more intriguing by the hour. Whether it was about local politics, a dispute over planning permission or something else entirely, Peter didn't care. And if Councillor Hargreaves turned out to be villain as well as victim, so much the better. It would only add to the story. Peter couldn't help but laugh out loud. After months in the slow lane, he finally had a story worth reporting on. He felt energised.

He knew there was an opportunity here – for redemption, a return to the big time, he wasn't sure. And in truth, it didn't matter. He was back in the game and that's all that mattered. Wherever it led, he intended to grab his chance with both hands.

CHAPTER 11

THE WARMTH WAS THE FIRST thing that hit DCI Bobby Redhill as he opened the door to the long, thin, windowless room. The second was the noise, albeit only briefly. The excited chatter stopped as soon as he entered, all eyes focused suddenly on him. He was surprised by the number of people crammed inside the relatively compact space. It was clear the Chief Constable was making every resource available to the investigation.

Bobby turned to the white board that had been set up against the narrow back wall, just inside the room's only door, giving himself a moment to compose his thoughts. Someone had already stuck a picture of Councillor Hargreaves, their victim, in the centre. It looked like a typical corporate mugshot that, Bobby guessed, had been printed straight off the council's website. It was accompanied by a couple of pictures taken at the crime scene: one, a wide-angle shot of the car, the other a close-up of the dead body in-situ. Together they formed a powerful reminder of why they were all here, and the little they knew so far.

As he turned to face the crowd, he took in the room for the first time. Within the station it was referred to as 2b. It had always been 2b and presumably always would be, although most of the station's current inhabitants didn't know why. There was no 2a, after all, or 2c for that matter. In fact, none of the other offices within the building were numbered in a similar way. It was on the second floor, which presumably accounted for the 2, but the b was less easily explained.

Those who'd been around long enough knew it was quite simply the room that could be turned into anything you wanted it 'to be'. In the past it had been used for everything from makeshift sleeping quarters to a break-out room for colleagues to discuss cases or make private calls. Most recently it had been a general dumping ground for old case files. Bobby wondered now where they'd all gone and suspected the Chief Constable's influence in getting them moved so quickly.

Bobby had commandeered the space that morning to act as the incident room for the investigation into the murder of Councillor Hargreaves. And, he reflected, they could now be confident they were investigating the councillor's death as Faith Andrews, the pathologist, had formally confirmed the identity of the body at the autopsy that very afternoon. This room would provide a central hub for collating information, formulating hypotheses and identifying and running down leads. Despite being early evening on the day the body had been found, this was the first meeting of the full investigative team and Bobby was about to set out all they currently knew, at the same time identifying the initial focus of the investigation.

Directly in front of him a couple of tables had been pushed together to form a square conference-style arrangement. Bobby noticed Grainger among the officers sat on the chairs that had been arranged around three of its sides. It wasn't lost on Bobby that his sergeant had positioned himself next to an attractive young female officer who'd been seconded to the investigative team from uniform. At the back of the room, Bobby could just about make out a couple of computer terminals. He was impressed. Someone had been busy. It just went to show how important this case was. And how much could be achieved when people worked together. That level of teamwork was exactly what he needed from this group now. He knew it was going to be a difficult and challenging investigation. And a first for many. Murders didn't happen often in Torbay, but he expected the novelty to focus hearts and minds.

Bobby looked at the eager faces and breathed in the scent of stale coffee that hung heavily in the air.

"Councillor Irving Hargreaves..." he began sombrely. "Black male. Sixty-two years of age. Found dead in the driver's seat of his Mercedes early this morning in the car park at Berry Head by a couple of teenagers who were there, so they claim, to see the sunrise. The autopsy took place this afternoon and the forensic pathologist has put time of death between twelve thirty and two this morning. She also confirmed that Councillor Hargreaves was suffocated. So, this *is* murder." He paused and looked around the room, slowly taking in each of the faces in turn. "Looks like some sort of plastic bag was used. There were pressure marks on his neck that pointed to it being done by someone sitting behind him, in the backseat of the vehicle. We haven't found anything matching that description at the scene, so finding the murder weapon is a top priority. It goes without saying that there could be important DNA evidence on it. Was it discarded somewhere on the route down from Berry Head? Let's widen the search area." Bobby paused while he added this information to the white board.

"We've also notified next of kin. A daughter, Kimberley. Late twenties, lives in Torquay in a flat overlooking the harbour. She wasn't particularly upset to hear her dad was dead. I'd go so far as to say she was quite matter-of-fact about it. Almost like she didn't care. Or wasn't surprised. She mentioned something about a disagreement, but then shut down so I didn't press her. She could have been in shock, and I don't want to be accused of insensitivity. But we'll need to speak to her again. Let's look into her before then, find out everything we can, so we're prepared. What was the relationship with her dad like? She's already mentioned a disagreement: can we find out what it was about? Does she inherit under the will? Perhaps there were money worries that her dad's death will resolve. There's no reason to suspect her at this stage, but we all know murder victims tend to know their killers, and often a family member's involved." Bobby let that hang in the air for a moment before continuing. "What do we know about our victim?"

A female detective constable standing in front of one of the computer terminals was first to speak. "He's been a councillor for the past four years, guv. Before that he owned several nightclubs in Torquay. Appears to have been quite successful. There are a ton of pictures from back then on the internet – looks like he knew how to have a good time." She smiled knowingly. "There's much less since his change of career. He currently lives in Paignton, seemingly on his own. He's separated from wife number five. You've already mentioned his daughter. No other children so far as I can tell."

"Okay, thanks, DC Allegri. Keep on it." He looked around the room once again. "I want to know everything there is about Councillor Hargreaves. Connections, family, close friends. His personal and professional life, in other words. And that includes his colleagues on Torbay Council. We should also look into his previous business life. The nightclub scene can be a murky world which, in my experience, can attract the worst society has to offer. Is there a link from that time to his death? We'll also need to interview the current Mrs Hargreaves along with the ex-wives. Same questions that we had for Kimberley apply equally to them. Let's also find out if there were any other women in his life and, if so, whether any of them had boyfriends or husbands who might not have been too happy about it. Did we get anything from the search of his house?"

"Yes, sir." Grainger jumped out of his seat and opened his notebook in one energetic movement. *He's keen*, Bobby thought, *although he's probably just trying to impress the young female officer*. A smattering of sniggers filtered through the room.

"We've boxed up everything from his home office, including his laptop, and we're going through that now." Grainger looked towards a stack of cardboard boxes at the side of the room. Bobby hadn't noticed them before. "Nothing stands out at this stage, although there was a photocopied invoice addressed to Torbay Council on his desk. It was for a substantial sum." He flicked over the page of his notebook. "From a Claude Knight Building Contractors. It's dated nine years ago, so before Hargreaves became a councillor. That may be significant. It's presumably not something he was currently working on. And we also found a newspaper clipping. It looks like it might have been taken from the *Torbay Times*, although we're checking on that. It's an article about the council's summer party. A factual piece, mainly a list of people attending, and details of monies raised for charitable causes. Nothing particularly interesting about that, but the photograph which accompanied the story had been separately blown up." Grainger held up a copy of the image and moved his arms from left to right in a slow semicircle so that everyone, starting with Bobby at the front of the room, could look. "It's of Councillor Farmer and Justin King of the King Hotel Group."

"Thanks, Grainger. That leads us on nicely to one potential lead we already have, courtesy of a reporter at the *Torbay Times* called Peter Norton." Bobby smiled as a groan passed round the room. "I'm still trying to work out what he was doing at the crime scene and why he seemed to know so much about our victim, but what he had to say appears relevant, so we're obliged to follow it up. DS Grainger, why don't you explain?"

Grainger cleared his throat theatrically. "His theory is that the councillor's death had something to do with the upcoming council vote on the future of Oldway Mansion in Paignton. For those of you who don't know, Oldway Mansion is the now abandoned former home of the Singer family which until about ten years ago served as the head offices for Torbay Council. You may already be familiar with this, but apparently there are competing plans to either develop it into a hotel and private members club or preserve it as an historical monument which will remain accessible to the public. If we're to believe our friendly local reporter, Councillor Hargreaves was firmly in favour of preservation which put him at odds with several of his fellow councillors, chief among them Councillor Hugh Farmer, leader of Torbay Council and apparent mastermind behind the development plans. He's closely linked with Justin King of the King Hotel Group that will build and operate the hotel if the development gets the go-ahead. Both presumably have a lot invested in the proposals and would be highly motivated to ensure the vote is passed in their favour. The reporter claims the councillor's death makes it more likely the development will be approved which, if true, points the finger squarely in the direction of Farmer and King."

"But all that's just speculation at this stage." Bobby's voice was measured but the words were delivered with unmistakable force. "There's absolutely nothing to implicate either Farmer or King at this stage. The Oldway Mansion development is one lead and there are several reasons to discount it. Our victim was just one of many councillors to favour preservation, for example. In fact, if we're to believe the reporter, there were seventeen others at last count. So why target Hargreaves and not one of the other seventeen? That fact alone points to another motive. Even if the development does end up warranting greater attention, there are any number of other suspects. It won't just be Farmer and King who have something to lose if the vote goes against them. The development is a political hot potato, and we need to tread very carefully. No one talks to Farmer or King other than me, understood?" The request was accompanied by a wave of nodding heads.

"What's interesting though, sir, is that this Claude Knight fella," Grainger held up the invoice he'd mentioned earlier, "appears to have undertaken building works for both the council and the King Group over the past few years. If we consider Councillor Farmer as the face of the council, then there seems to be a direct link between the three of them."

"Okay, thanks. Why don't you and I pay Claude Knight a visit in the morning? See if he can explain what our victim was doing with one of his invoices. Anything else?"

"Just one thing. We didn't find a mobile phone at Hargreaves' house. As you know, one wasn't found on the victim or in his car, so there's still a question mark over that. Was it taken by whoever killed him, or did he perhaps leave it somewhere else? His office maybe, although people tend to carry them with them, don't they? What with them being mobile and all. Even someone of his generation. I mean you carry yours with you, don't you, sir?" Grainger blushed as he realised what he'd just said. A further smattering of laughter circulated the room.

"Yes, thank you, Grainger. I'm not quite as old as the councillor, but I take your point, I think." Grainger sat down sheepishly while Bobby continued.

"So, the mobile phone is another priority. Where is it? Let's speak to the phone company to see if they can trace it. If the phone's still on, we might get a location. At the very least, we should be able to see where it was last used. I assume we're getting phone records?"

"Yes, boss." The confirmation came from a male officer standing next to DC Allegri. "Should be with us tomorrow or the day after. Mobile and landline. The phone companies are putting a rush on the request."

"Great, thanks, DC Merrali." Bobby paused while he added to a list that was growing on the whiteboard. "So, we currently have one potential motive but are there others?"

The silence that accompanied this question told Bobby it was too early to speculate. "Okay, I'll take that as a work in progress, but we obviously need to identify all potential motives. What about suspects? I appreciate the two are linked, but is there anyone other than those we've already mentioned that we should be looking at?"

"What about the teenagers who found the body, sir?" asked another young male DC leaning casually against the wall. "Are we discounting them, or do we think they might be involved?"

Bobby thought about this for a moment. "Good question, DC Allsop. There's nothing to implicate them at this stage, but they'll be coming in to give formal statements in the next day or so. We can use the time before then to check their story. The key thing is to keep an open mind until we know more. The same goes for all potential leads and suspects. Have we got anything from the door-to-door?"

"Nothing so far, sir, but it's ongoing." It was the female officer sat next to Grainger. "We didn't get a response at a number of houses so will be heading back this evening."

"Thanks, Officer Christenson, good to have you on board." Bobby gave her a warm smile before returning his focus to the wider group. "What about traffic cameras? Has anyone started to look at those?"

"Yes, sir." Grainger again, although Bobby noted he'd stayed seated this time. "The cameras on the road leading into Brixham were out of action last night unfortunately. I've spoken to the council, and they confirmed the camera was hit by an articulated lorry around three weeks ago."

Bobby scrunched his face slightly, as though suddenly in pain. "Considering there's only one road in and out of Brixham, that's either seriously bad luck on our part or extremely convenient for whoever's responsible for the councillor's death. We need to work out which. Are there any possible links between that accident and this investigation? It was several weeks ago which perhaps points to it simply being bad luck, but let's not assume anything. Does anyone involved in that incident or the apparent delay in getting the cameras fixed have links to Councillor Hargreaves? You know the drill."

"Are we assuming the perpetrators arrived and left by car then, guv?" The question came from Dejay Merrali.

"We're not assuming anything at this stage, but Berry Head's an isolated spot, so until we have evidence to the contrary, I think it's safe to assume we're looking for another vehicle. What about other cameras? Did any catch our victim?"

"The camera on Dartmouth Road caught him travelling south at twelve forty-five this morning," confirmed Grainger. "The direct route to Berry Head from his house on Elmsleigh Park would have taken him straight past it."

Bobby thought about this for a moment. "Assuming he adhered to the speed limit and didn't make any other stops along the way, he'd have arrived at Berry Head around one." He looked around the room to see whether anyone disagreed with his conclusion. No one did. "That's right in the middle of our window for time of death, so it's possible he was killed soon after arriving at the car park. The fact he was found sitting in the driver's seat wearing his seatbelt also points to that."

"Could have been an ambush," suggested Klara Allegri.

"That's how it looks," agreed Bobby. "At that hour, Councillor Hargreaves was clearly heading to Berry Head for a reason, not simply for the view or to take a walk. What was that? At this stage I think it's safe to presume he was meeting someone. Was anyone else visible in the Mercedes in the footage from the traffic camera?"

"No, not in the passenger seat at any rate. We have a good view through the windscreen but can't tell whether there was anyone in the back. The side and back windows were tinted which doesn't help. Wouldn't it be strange for him to have passengers in the back though when the front seat was empty? Unless he was moonlighting as a taxi driver, I suppose." Grainger chuckled.

"I agree it sounds strange." Bobby ignored the sergeant's attempt at humour. "But we can't rule anything out at this stage. Why Berry Head? What was special about that spot? Was it his idea to go there? If so, why? Was it a meeting? If so, who with? These are the questions that need to be answered." Bobby paused for a moment, allowing them to hang in the air. "Okay, back to work everyone. DS Grainger will assign your individual tasks and responsibilities. Let's get this wrapped up quickly and efficiently. I don't need to remind you that this is a high-profile investigation. All eyes are on us. We can't afford any mistakes. And remember, the Chief Constable counted the victim as a friend. That means we have his backing when it comes to resources, but there's a price to be paid for every good turn. He won't accept any excuses."

CHAPTER 12

AT JUST AFTER EIGHT THE NEXT MORNING, DCI Bobby Redhill and DS Matthew Grainger were driving to Claude Knight's workplace. They knew builders started work early and were both keen to determine how, if at all, Mr Knight fitted into their investigation. The building invoice that had been found in the home office of their victim, Councillor Hargreaves, was a loose end that needed to be tied. Of potentially more significance were the possible links between Claude Knight, Justin King and Hugh Farmer. It might be nothing more than coincidence, but if proved it could add further weight to the theory linking the councillor's death to his opposition of the Oldway Mansion development proposals. Bobby was eager to show Chief Constable Parker he already had a solid lead, and besides, he'd always been wary of coincidence.

Bobby was concentrating hard as he steered the car down the steep hill into the picture-book village of Marldon on the outskirts of Paignton. Cars were parked nose to tail down his side of the road, forcing him to straddle the white markings that dissected the tarmac. Not that anyone travelling in the opposite direction appeared to notice. They all roared past without reducing their speed or adjusting their steering.

"Bloody idiot!" Bobby's outburst was directed at an oversized BMW, one of the new breed of super-sized four-wheel drive vehicles the animated inspector had only ever seen in places where four-wheel drive was completely unnecessary. The BMW, now just a speck in his rear-view mirror, had only avoided a collision with the unmarked police-issue Vauxhall because of Bobby's quick reactions. He'd managed to quickly steer the vehicle into a conveniently placed driveway between the parked cars as the BMW shot past like a rocket homed on its target.

"Don't they realise there's a primary school at the bottom of the road?" Bobby was shaking his head as he spoke. "And why do people drive those ridiculous things? You never see any passengers in them!"

"It was probably a parent dropping their kids off at the school." Despite being entertained by the outpouring of emotion from his boss, Grainger maintained a professional seriousness as he spoke, keeping his focus firmly on the road ahead. "And I guess it's a status thing. You know, just because you can, rather than because you should."

"Yes, thank you, Grainger. I was posing rhetorical questions but, as ever, your insights into the human condition are greatly appreciated."

"Thank-you, sir. I pride myself on having an acute understanding of my fellow man." Bobby took his eyes off the road momentarily to steal a glance at his passenger. He couldn't work out whether Grainger was being serious. He hoped not, but there was no hint of amusement on the sergeant's face.

After they passed the primary school on their left, the road narrowed suddenly, becoming wide enough for only a single car. Bobby instinctively slowed and was travelling at no more than a gentle crawl when the road bent sharply to the right as it continued its descent towards the centre of Marldon. On the apex of the bend, a partly concealed turning appeared from nowhere. It headed uphill, away from the village. Bobby slowed even further and made the turn cautiously. The manoeuvre was accompanied by an angry blast of a horn from the car behind before its driver accelerated loudly away from the Vauxhall. They were on a country lane now. It looked to have been cut straight through the hillside surrounding the village. Hefty red limestone rock rose threateningly on one side before dropping away sharply on the other. The houses here appeared to cling to the rock-face. They reminded Bobby of the dense, multi-coloured lichen that covered the stone walls he glimpsed intermittently behind the patchwork of vibrant green and yellow hedgerows tightly lining the route. The track was heavily pot-holed and framed both left and right by menacing storm water drains that seemed capable of devouring the Vauxhall's tyres. Bobby maintained a slow and steady speed.

The inspector and his young colleague found what they were looking for around a quarter of a mile further on, just after a shallow bend in the lane. The houses that had loomed large over the Vauxhall suddenly disappeared, replaced by a vast metal chain-link fence about ten feet high. It was strung across a wide opening, maybe two hundred feet in total, that gave way to a large expanse of concrete. Bobby stopped the car in the middle of the lane and leaned forward in his seat to get a better view, his head turned awkwardly to one side as he peered over the steering wheel. A couple of cars and several vans were visible on the other side of the fence, and he could make out two outbuildings, one significantly taller and wider than the other. Both structures had bulky metal roller doors half-opened. The whole area was dominated by a huge cliff face that completely enclosed the space on three sides, as though it had been cut directly from the rock itself.

Bobby saw a narrow gap in the fence and drove through it, parking the Vauxhall next to a brand-new Ford Transit van painted a distinctive dark blue with discreet sign writing on its rear-quarter panel. It advertised '*Claude Knight Building Contractors*' in a large white font and included phone and email contact details in a distinctly smaller size below.

Now he was closer, Bobby could see that all the vehicles in the yard were new. There were several commercial vehicles of varying sizes, all painted the same distinctive blue with the same white markings. One of the cars was a Range Rover. It too was painted the same colour as the vans, but wore a private numberplate, *KN11 GHT*, which Bobby assumed was meant to be read as 'Knight' and was presumably, therefore, Claude Knight's own personal transport.

"Quite the collection of vehicles," said Bobby, clearly impressed. "Business must be good."

With no one else in the yard, Bobby headed towards the first building. The smaller of the two. It was positioned in front of the cliff, parallel to the lane.

"Anyone home?" he called out as he passed underneath the roller door.

There was no response and no sign of anyone inside. It looked as though the building was used as a storage space. Assorted building materials were stacked on the floor while pieces of wood and lengths of metal in a variety of different shapes and sizes were leant haphazardly against the walls. A mezzanine level accessed by a set of metal steps in the right-hand corner ran around three sides. The walls at this level were lined with shelves that appeared to be laden with a multitude of tools, both large and small. A vehicle was parked in the back of the building, underneath the mezzanine. Some sort of hatchback. A dark colour, blue or maybe black. It looked out of place inside the building and, unlike the vehicles parked outside, was old and completely nondescript.

He exited and moved on to the larger building that was built alongside the perimeter fence on the right-hand side of the yard. Entering beneath the open roller door which was at least twice as large as the one in the other building, he called out once more.

"Anyone home?"

An elderly gentleman emerged silently from the shadows. He rubbed his dirty hands on a piece of cloth as he walked.

"Help you?" he asked in a heavy accent. *Devon born and bred*, Bobby thought. The gentleman had a tired, weathered look on his face. Four or five wisps of fine, grey hair sprouted from the top of an otherwise bald head.

"We're looking for Claude Knight," Bobby said. "Is he here?"

"Oh, he's here all right. Up in the office. Looking down on us I shouldn't wonder. Same as always." He gestured in the general direction of the yard.

Bobby turned and noticed a single-storey brick building that had been built on a rocky outcrop about halfway up the cliff, on the left-hand side of the yard, directly across from his current position. He hadn't noticed it before. It appeared to be accessed by a flight of steep-looking steps built into the cliff. The access to the steps was obscured by the Range Rover, which Bobby could now see was parked directly below the office building.

Bobby turned to thank the gentleman, but he'd already disappeared back into the dark recesses of the vast structure.

Bobby and Grainger walked across the yard and started to ascend the steps. It was slow going. The treads rose steeply in varying depths as they zig-zagged their way up the cliff. A thin, metal handrail was the only thing protecting them from the sheer drop down to the concrete below, a drop which only got bigger and more dangerous with every step.

"Not very welcoming, is it, sir?" Grainger's observation reflected Bobby's own thoughts.

When they reached the platform at the top of the steps, they stopped and instinctively turned to check how far they'd climbed. The view took their breath away all over again. From their elevated position there was an unobstructed view across to Dartmoor in the north. Even the church spire, which rose high above the village green below them was a mere speck.

"You can see why the office was built up here," commented Bobby. "There's an almost unobstructed view across the entire yard."

He turned and knocked on the full-length glass-plated door before entering the building. The room he walked into was smaller than he'd expected given the size of the building. Bobby guessed there must be at least one other room within the structure and noticed a door located in the far wall that he guessed provided access.

A chest-high counter ran the entire width of the room, a metre or so in from the door. The hinged access flap was currently lowered, forcing the detectives to remain on the far side. Leaning over the worktop, Bobby observed a cluttered space. A half dozen metal filing cabinets lined the back wall and stacks of boxes and loose papers covered much of what floor remained. There were two desks, both occupied. The first was bigger and positioned more prominently in the centre of the room. It faced the counter and gave a good view of the yard below. Behind it sat a giant of a man. Both tall and fat. A bulky, solid looking stomach forced him to sit further away from the desk than looked comfortable and tested the seams of a herringbone-patterned sweater that didn't quite meet the top of his trousers. He made no attempt to stand and simply stared at the visitors with a look of bored indifference on his face. Bobby noticed a bead of sweat form at the point his mop of unruly brown hair met his bloated face and watched as it rolled down a heavily stubbled cheek before disappearing into the folds of flesh that sat in place of his non-existent neck.

The other desk was in the left-hand corner, squeezed in beside the filing cabinets, facing the wall. It looked like an afterthought. Sitting at it was a small woman with a bun of frizzy red hair perched on top of her head. A pair of old-fashioned horn-rimmed spectacles dangled against her chest, secured by a length of multi-coloured cord that ran around her neck. She didn't look up as they entered.

"Are you Claude Knight?" Bobby addressed his question to the sweaty man mountain. He thought the builder was probably in his mid-forties, but he could have been younger. The ruddy complexion, puffy face and laboured breathing made it difficult to tell.

"That's right." The voice was deep but otherwise indistinct. "How can I help you?" The man's dour expression didn't alter. Bobby wondered whether this was how he welcomed potential customers and, if so, how he'd been so apparently successful.

"Police, Mr Knight. DCI Redhill and this is DS Grainger. Is there somewhere we can talk?"

"We talkin' now, ain't we?"

"Aren't we just." Bobby offered a smile." Do you know a Councillor Irving Hargreaves?"

"Know *of* him."

"He was found dead up on Berry Head yesterday morning."

"So I heard."

"Did you ever carry out any building works for him or meet him in any other capacity?"

Claude shot a glance at the frizzy red bun who continued to stare impassively at her computer screen. "Not as I recall."

"Then can you tell me why Councillor Hargreaves had an invoice in his possession that was issued by your firm to Torbay Council?"

"He was a councillor, wasn't he?"

"Yes, he was."

"We do a lot of building work for the council. It's not that strange that he might have one of our invoices."

"This invoice was from some considerable time ago. Before he became a councillor."

Claude shrugged. "You'd have to ask him…but of course, you can't."

Bobby ignored the comment. He felt like the builder was trying to be provocative and wasn't about to give him the satisfaction of a reaction. "What sort of building work do you do for the council, Mr Knight?"

"All sorts over the years. Been quite successful too. Good work at an honest price, that's the secret."

"I'm sure." The builder wasn't giving much away. "Are you involved with the proposed development of Oldway Mansion?"

"We've submitted a tender. Waiting to hear back."

"And when do you expect that to be?"

Claude looked over to the woman in the corner of the room. "Penelope, do you remember the date we can expect a decision on the Oldway Mansion tender?"

"Four p.m. on the thirtieth of January. Assuming the scheme is approved at council, of course." Penelope didn't hesitate in her response and didn't have to check any records. The information was just there, in her memory, on immediate recall. She spoke in a high-pitched squeal but with a decisiveness that belied her lacklustre physical appearance. At no point did she move her gaze away from the computer screen on her desk or otherwise acknowledge the presence of the two detectives.

Bobby thought about this information for a moment. "The council vote on the development itself is before Christmas, isn't it? Why don't you find out about the tender until a month later?"

"Suppose they don't want to waste time comparing bids if they don't need to."

"But you have to submit them in advance?"

"Has to be done a certain way to make sure everything's above board. There's a strict process to abide by when tendering to public bodies. All set out in law." Claude Knight paused briefly as though considering what he was about to say next. When he spoke, Bobby noticed a smirk form on his lips. "So, you think his death has something to do with Oldway Mansion?"

Bobby ignored the question. "Where were you on Monday evening? From around eight until seven on Tuesday morning."

"Here." Bobby waited for Claude to explain but he just sat there staring vacantly at the detective.

"You were here all night?"

"I sleep here sometimes. Got a sofa in the back room." Claude tilted his head backwards as he spoke, in the direction of the door Bobby had previously noted. "And a small kitchen. It's just easier when I'm working late and don't want to disturb the wife and kids."

"And you didn't leave at any point? To get food maybe."

"Got delivery. Curry probably. That's my favourite. There will be a record on the delivery app. Hang on a second." Claude strained as he leant forward to pick up a mobile phone that was lying on the desk. The sudden movement was accompanied by another bead of sweat making its way slowly down the builder's face. After several taps on the screen, he looked up. "Yeah, delivered at eight oh seven. Chicken bhuna, pilau rice and a garlic naan. From the place on Winner Street in Paignton. Do you know it?" He threw the phone back on the desk in an elaborate display, as though challenging Bobby to accuse him of something.

"Okay, that's all for now. We know where to find you if we have any further questions."

As he closed the glass door behind him, Bobby thought he saw Claude Knight pick up his mobile phone once again. And he thought the builder suddenly looked far more alert than he'd done at any other point during the interview.

CHAPTER 13

BOBBY REDHILL WAS DEEP IN thought as he added to the list on the white board in the incident room on the second floor of Torquay police station. Despite raising more questions than it had answered, the interview that morning hadn't been a complete bust. He now felt certain Claude Knight was a person of interest in the investigation. He thought back to the builder's odd behaviour. He'd certainly been very sure of himself. And quite confrontational at times. Even if he had nothing to do with the death of Councillor Hargreaves, instinct told him that Claude Knight was hiding something, and he intended to find out what it was. In Bobby's experience, people like that always came unstuck in the end. They got over-confident and sloppy and, when that happened, Bobby would be waiting.

"I want to know everything about Claude Knight and his building firm." The instruction was thrown out to the

group that had congregated in room 2b for the daily briefing. "Everything and anything. Don't just look for links to
Councillor Hargreaves or Oldway Mansion. Does he have
a criminal record? What about complaints from customers? The business appears to be doing well, but is that just
show? Anything to suggest his business practices aren't all
above board? You get the picture. Okay, so where are we
with other leads? Who wants to go first?"

Bobby held up the marker pen expectantly. He noticed
DS Grainger sitting down at the table in front of him, in
the same spot as yesterday. He thought his sergeant looked
rather smug. Bobby watched as he leant back in his chair,
puffed out his chest and inhaled a deep, weighty breath.
He looked like he was about to speak, but Klara Allegri
beat him to it. Bobby looked away and quickly forgot all
about Grainger.

"Still no sign of the mobile phone, boss. We've managed to speak to some of Councillor Hargreaves' colleagues though." A sudden change in Bobby's demeaner
made the female DC pause. "Um, yeah, don't worry, no
one's spoken to Hugh Farmer. "Anyway, they all said the
same thing. He was never without his phone. Glued to the
thing apparently. Used it for everything."

"Okay," said Bobby thoughtfully, "so, it's even more
important that we find that phone. Based on what his colleagues have told us, it seems reasonable to assume he had
it with him when he drove to Berry Head, so where is it
now? Do we think the killer took it and, if so, why? Was
that the motive behind the murder? We previously dis-

counted this being a robbery because of all the valuables left on the victim, but maybe it *was* a targeted robbery. Any luck with the trace?"

"Yes, boss. And that's where things get interesting."

"How so?"

"Well, the phone is switched off now. No great surprises there. But its signal last pinged off the mast on the headland near Berry Head at three twenty-two on the night of the murder. That puts the phone somewhere within the general vicinity of our murder scene but, as you say, if it was there then, where is it now? And if the councillor was killed at around one, as we suspect, why was the phone still at the scene at three twenty-two?"

"You mean that if our killer took it then what was he doing for the best part of two and a half hours after the murder? It's a valid question, DC Allegri." Bobby casually spun the pen between the thumb and forefinger of his right hand as he considered this new information. "Perhaps the phone never left Berry Head. It could have simply run out of battery. That would have shut the signal off." He paused and when he spoke again, his voice was laced with a steely determination. "Until we know differently, we assume the phone is still there. And I want it found. Let's redouble our efforts."

"I'll let the search team know, boss."

"What about phone records?"

"They came in this morning. I've not had time to go through them in detail, but one thing jumped out at me.

Our victim received a call on his landline at just before ten on Monday night."

"Do we know who it was from?"

"Not yet, although it was a local number, not a mobile. I've asked the phone company to trace it. We should know later this morning." Klara Allegri bit her lip thoughtfully before adding, "the timing of the call is interesting though."

"How so?"

"It doesn't look like he used his landline much. There have only been a handful of calls over the past few months and most of those were incoming, from what appear to be cold callers." Bobby raised an enquiring eyebrow, so she clarified, "I recognised some of the numbers as being similar to those I tend to ignore when I see them on my mobile."

He nodded slowly. "You think this call could have been our killer arranging the meeting for later that evening?"

"Got to be worth looking into, don't you think?"

"It's possible. Good work Klara. Keep us informed." He looked around the assembled group. "Anything else?"

Grainger shifted in his seat and started to raise his hand, as though he had something to say, but Freddie Allsop spoke before he could.

"A couple of Hargreaves' colleagues confirmed the argument between our victim and Councillor Farmer at the end of the last council meeting on Friday. The meeting had finished about ten minutes before and most had already gone home, but there were still a few people hanging around."

"What happened?"

"They all said it was strange and happened quickly. They were talking one minute but then Councillor Farmer is suddenly in our victim's face, accusing him of going behind his back and trying to undermine his leadership."

"Do they know what he was referring to?"

"They guessed it had something to do with Oldway Mansion. They'd spent most of the evening discussing it, so that sounds reasonable. And Councillor Hargreaves had become something of an unofficial leader among those councillors who opposed the development plans. They all said he was charismatic, and very persuasive in his arguments. That put him directly at odds with Councillor Farmer who's sponsoring the proposals. They all agreed it was out of character though. There was some suggestion that the pressure was starting to get to him. Farmer that is. Apparently, he's invested a lot in the development, and now the vote is getting close, he's started to get twitchy. Especially because there's no guarantee he's going to win. There was some suggestion that he's beginning to take criticism of the development proposals personally."

"And what did they make of our victim?"

"No one had a bad word to say about him, boss. The consensus view was of an exceptionally bright guy who'd added a lot since joining the council. His previous business experience was appreciated, and they all felt he genuinely wanted to improve things. He questioned everything apparently. You know the type. Not prepared to accept the status quo. I guess he might have ruffled a few feathers. It could be relevant. If the council's anything like the police, it's probably suspicious of change."

Bobby smiled. "Bit hard to believe someone would kill him over that though. But I suppose anything's possible. I'll put it on the board, and you can follow up as and when you have time, but it's *not* a priority."

The young DC nodded earnestly.

"Right, who's next?" Bobby was about to put the pen to his lips when he remembered the top was still off. He managed to stop himself just in time. "Come on, don't be shy." He thought he'd styled it out well.

Grainger's hand shot up almost at once and he blurted out, "The CSI's found various prints in the Mercedes. One was a match to someone on our system."

Bobby looked at the young man disapprovingly. "Why didn't you say something sooner, Sergeant? This could be the break we've been waiting for. The rest of it could have waited. Whose prints were they?"

Grainger bowed his head and busied himself with the contents of his notebook. "A Callum Franks, sir."

"The name doesn't ring a bell. Who is he?"

"Career criminal. He's been keeping our colleagues downstairs busy since he was thirteen and he's twenty-seven now. Strictly low-level though, sir. His rap sheet includes arrests for theft and assault, but the majority is for possession and suspicion of dealing."

"Any known links to our victim?"

"Nothing obvious, no. If anything, you'd say they were from two different worlds."

"Well, what are you waiting for? Go and pick him up. It looks like this Callum Franks has got some explaining to do and I for one want to know what he's got to say for himself."

CHAPTER 14

THE INITIAL EXCITEMENT AT HAVING discovered the fingerprints of a known criminal in their victim's car was tempered slightly when Callum Franks couldn't be located. He wasn't at his mum's house, where official records had him residing, although she claimed he rarely stayed there and that she hadn't seen him for weeks. His other known hangouts had similarly come up empty while those of his associates they'd managed to round up all claimed not to know where he was.

That was the reason for DCI Bobby Redhill and DS Matthew Grainger being back in the Vauxhall, driving the short distance to Torquay harbour to see Kimberley Hargreaves. Bobby was keen to maintain momentum and, despite the obvious frustrations at Callum apparently having gone to ground, there were still ample lines of enquiry they could pursue. He knew his mind worked best when it was occupied, so he'd phoned Councillor Hargreaves' daughter and arranged the meeting for later that afternoon. He'd already spoken with her once before, when he'd notified her of her dad's death, but he hadn't wanted to press her on that occasion. Now he needed answers.

"Do you think Callum's done a bunk then, sir?" Grainger asked from the passenger seat. "Because he killed the councillor?"

"It's possible. He certainly has some explaining to do. But we still don't know how Franks and Hargreaves knew each other. It's possible he's a victim himself."

"You think he could be dead as well?"

"I'm not saying that. We shouldn't jump to conclusions is all. There could be any number of explanations for why we haven't been able to pick Franks up yet. But, of course, we shouldn't ignore the fact those people who say they haven't seen him might not be the most reliable witnesses."

"You can say that again." Grainger was quiet for a moment. "What's the story with the daughter then? Do you think she might be involved?"

Bobby looked at his sergeant gravely. "That's what we're about to find out…"

Kimberley Hargreaves lived on the top floor of a three-storey townhouse overlooking Torquay harbour and only a few minutes' walk from the bars and restaurants that lined the waterfront. Bobby could imagine it being a great place for a young woman to live, especially one who had the time and money to properly enjoy it. He wondered again how the councillor's daughter funded her lifestyle. A quick search on social media had showed her out enjoying the local nightlife most evenings, but hadn't indicated any obvious signs of an income.

After being buzzed up, they found the door to Kimberley Hargreaves' flat open when they reached the compact landing at the top of the narrow staircase. The councillor's daughter was in the lounge, sat on a brown leather sofa. It was one of those modern pieces with highly polished chrome legs and a low-level back that Bobby felt certain would be far better to look at than sit in. A glass tumbler containing a clear liquid that only partially covered two large lumps of ice sat on the glass-topped side table next to her.

The sofa faced a large flat screen television fixed to the wall above a traditional fireplace that now housed a modern-looking wood burner. The two large sash windows overlooking the harbour that Bobby had noticed on his previous visit were covered by heavy curtains pulled tightly closed despite it still being light outside. The only illumination came from a couple of brass table lights. Their textured pink glass shades bathed the room in a rich, warm glow.

Kimberley Hargreaves made no attempt to stand as they entered. "Inspector, I hope this isn't going to take long. I'm meeting friends at five."

Bobby bowed almost imperceptibly. "Ms Hargreaves, we appreciate your making time to see us. And we know this is a difficult time. We'll try not to keep you long, but

I'm sure you can understand how important it is that we speak with you."

"Call me Kimberley, please." She picked up the tumbler and took a small sip. "Of course. And I apologise. You're only doing your jobs. Won't you sit down?" She pointed to a couple of matching occasional chairs positioned either side of the sofa. Bobby was pleased to see they had proper supportive backs, although he thought they too looked a little low. He took the one closest to the young woman, knowing he'd be doing all the talking, and perched on the edge of the cushion. "It just feels like he's still here checking up on me," she continued. "Even though I know that sounds stupid."

"Not at all. Why don't you tell us about your relationship with your father? When we spoke yesterday, you mentioned something about a disagreement."

"Did I?" Kimberley suddenly appeared distant. Bobby thought her eyes slightly glazed and he wondered how many drinks she'd had. Right on cue, she picked up her glass and took a sip. "It's no secret. We fell out several years ago." The voice was clear but there was no warmth in it.

"What about?"

"Oh, I don't know. It all seems so unimportant right now. The petty reactions of a spoilt little girl!" She sighed heavily. "He didn't really do anything wrong. It was just who he was. And people don't change, do they? Not really." She looked at Bobby with large, imploring eyes, tears starting to form at the corners.

"Why don't you start from the beginning?" Bobby offered an encouraging smile. "And take your time."

Kimberley took a deep breath and dabbed at her eyes with a crumpled tissue she produced from inside her sleeve before taking another, longer sip from her glass. "In many ways I had the perfect childhood. I was an only child, but I was never lonely. The house was always full of people, and I had everything I ever wanted. Anyone looking from the outside would probably have said it was a loving family. But appearances can be deceptive. It was only when I got older that I learnt the truth." She paused to take another sip. When she didn't look as though she was going to continue, Bobby prompted her firmly.

"And what was the truth, Kimberley?"

"I was an only child because my parents didn't really love one another. Or perhaps I should say, my dad wasn't capable of loving only one woman, and that influence rubbed off on mum. Lots of those people who'd filled the house were their 'special' friends. I was almost invisible to them. They gave me everything I asked for just to keep me quiet. I only realised later that all I ever wanted was to be loved. They divorced when I was sixteen, which was a relief I suppose, but I went off the rails a bit. Having a father who owned the best nightclubs in town was cool for a while. I used to go with my friends most weekends. We'd get the full VIP treatment. It was great. But then you get a bit older and realise it doesn't mean anything. It's all just fake. Smoke and mirrors, you know? It's like going back to the club the next day when it's empty and all the lights are on. You realise it's nothing like you thought the night before. That was my dad. He wasn't what he appeared to be."

"How do you mean?"

"He was charismatic and generous. People were naturally drawn to him. But he could be difficult and self-absorbed. And he always put his own interests first." She attempted another sip before realising her glass was empty. She stood up and went over to an antique wooden sideboard that supported one of the illuminated table lamps. As she pulled open one of its the large wooden doors, Bobby realised it was a well-stocked drinks cabinet. She poured herself another neat vodka but didn't offer her guests anything. "Don't get me wrong, Inspector, I like having a good time as much as anyone. But I never set out to hurt people. Or turn a blind eye when others are doing exactly that."

Kimberley went quiet and Bobby wondered whether he'd pushed her far enough. He decided to try a different topic.

"Do you know a man called Callum Franks?"

"The drug dealer?" Kimberley suddenly appeared more engaged. Bobby thought he saw a flash of anger cross her face. "What's *he* got to do with anything?"

"Just a line of enquiry. I take it you know him then?"

"Most people who go out to the pubs and clubs round here know Callum. Always pushing his filthy pills. I don't know why *you lot* don't do more to stop it." She was quiet for a moment, staring blankly at the fireplace. "Stands to reason, I suppose."

"Why do you say that, Ms Hargreaves?"

"Only that I assume dad was up to his old tricks. He swore he'd changed, but I knew that was too much to hope for."

"What do you mean by that?"

"Oh, nothing. It's just that his views on drugs were the reason we stopped talking. The last straw I suppose you'd call it. I don't agree with them you see, but he never had any problem with people selling them in his clubs. Just part of the landscape, he said. '*People will always find a way to take them whatever my views on the subject.*' I can hear him now. He didn't encourage their use, but he didn't try to stop it either. Turned a blind eye, which was typical of him. If it was good for business, that's all that mattered."

"So, what, you fell out over an ideological difference of opinion?"

"Not exactly, Inspector. One of my best friends died after taking something at a club. Not one of his I should stress. It was around six years ago. She was away in Scotland on a girls' weekend. She'd never taken anything before. I still don't understand why she did it. Just wanted to experiment I suppose. Stupid girl thought she could fly and threw herself off the second-floor mezzanine right onto the dancefloor. They never found out who sold them to her. Who was responsible. I had a family thing that weekend so couldn't make it. If only I'd been there, I might have been able to stop her. She might still be alive."

"That sounds like a tragic accident, Kimberley. You can see that, can't you? It wasn't your fault. There's nothing you could have done."

"Maybe not for Amber. But I was able to take a stand. Dad may not have killed her but by turning a blind eye to the drug use in his clubs, he was just as guilty as the person who sold her those pills that evening."

Despite it being no more than a five-minute drive back to the station, Bobby phoned the incident room as he walked back to the car, keen to hear whether Callum Franks had been located. He soon found out there was no progress on that front, but there had been one interesting development: Justin King's solicitor had been in contact. His client wanted to come into the station tomorrow to give a voluntary statement. They would be there at 9:00 a.m. Now, Bobby hadn't foreseen that. In fact, he really didn't know what to make of it.

CHAPTER 15

THE STATION WAS BUSIER THAN usual the following morning when Bobby Redhill entered at seven thirty. It seemed that word of Justin King's appointment had got around, and everyone wanted to catch a glimpse of the hotelier and developer. Such was the reputation he'd managed to cultivate since arriving in the bay around five years earlier. The big, shiny hotels he'd built and the jobs they'd created were part of that, of course, but mostly, Bobby thought, it was due to his relative anonymity. People were fascinated by him and desperate to find out more. About the real man, not the well-groomed persona they'd been carefully fed through the media. Despite his photograph appearing in the local paper almost weekly, he kept a low profile and never courted attention in his private life. People only knew what Justin King wanted them to, and all of that was focused exclusively on his growing business interests.

The man himself arrived right on time, although with more than just his solicitor in tow. Someone had tipped off the press, a motley assortment of whom were waiting to take his photo and shout questions in loud, earnest voices as he climbed the front steps to the station. Bobby wondered whether Justin King himself might have been the source of the leak. He certainly looked relaxed as he listened to his solicitor confirm they would be making a statement later.

Bobby watched all this unfold from his office on the second floor. He noticed Peter Norton, the reporter he'd met on Berry Head earlier that week, among the assembled group. It reminded him of several phone messages he'd received asking for his call to be returned. Bobby hadn't bothered responding to any of them. He still didn't know how he wanted to deal with the reporter.

The commotion outside died down and Bobby saw Justin King and his solicitor disappearing inside the building. He finished his cup of coffee and straightened his tie. He wasn't sure what game Justin King was playing, but he doubted this little charade would make his job any easier.

"I would like to remind you, Inspector, that my client is here voluntarily, and against my advice I might add, but he felt very strongly that it was his civic duty to come this morning and make a statement." The solicitor sat perfectly straight, his hands clasped together on the table in front of him. He looked young, no older than his early twenties, but he displayed a confidence that bordered on arrogance. It was clearly a proud moment for him. *He'll probably be dining out on this for years to come*, Bobby thought. Not that the detective was impressed. It merely served to support his view that nothing of value would come from this meeting. If Mr King had anything of importance to say, he'd have made sure to bring someone more senior.

"Yes, thank you. I'm aware that you requested this meeting. But we're in the middle of an important investigation and time is of the essence, so please can your client say what he came to and then we can all get on." As soon as the words had left his lips, Bobby chastised himself for being so blunt and letting his frustrations get the better of him. Not for the first time this week, he didn't feel in control of the investigation. He couldn't shake the feeling he was being manipulated. He just couldn't work out to what end.

Justin King looked startled by the strength of the inspector's words although, to his credit, quickly regained his composure. Bobby guessed he was used to being held in rapt attention with people hanging off his every word. *Not today*, he thought to himself.

"Of course, Inspector." Justin smiled but it came across to Bobby as a rather cold, cynical gesture. "And believe me, I don't want to distract you from your important work any longer than necessary. I value the job you and your colleagues do and want you to catch whoever is responsible for this heinous crime as much as the next man. Believe me. That's the reason for my being here really. To try and help. Do my duty, you understand."

"Not really, but please enlighten me." Bobby looked directly at the hotelier as he spoke. Justin's eyes flickered rapidly before they suddenly looked away, down towards the hands he was quietly wringing in his lap.

"Well, it's simple really. Irving was a councillor, and I have a close working relationship with the council. I thought it only natural you'd want to speak with me, so here I am. I have nothing to hide, Inspector, and wanted to come here today to assure you I have absolutely no knowledge of what happened to poor Irving or what he might have got mixed up in."

"Why do you assume he was mixed up in anything, Mr King?"

"Well, it was just a figure of speech, but you don't go to Berry Head in the middle of the night and wind up dead unless you're into something…dodgy." He spoke the last word as though it left a funny taste in his mouth. "Stands to reason."

"But you do think his death was linked to his being a councillor?"

"What…no…I didn't say that…I couldn't possibly know, now could I?"

"But you just said your links to the council made you a suspect."

"Now, hang on a minute, Inspector." The young solicitor's composure had disappeared, and he suddenly appeared agitated. "My client never mentioned anything about being a suspect. He has come here voluntarily to confirm he has no knowledge of whatever Councillor Hargreaves was involved in or how he ended up getting himself killed. He's just a concerned citizen looking to do the right thing."

"And yet, innocent people don't normally come here to volunteer their lack of knowledge about a crime. Not unless they're already on our radar that is." Bobby let his words hang in the air momentarily before continuing. "Is there any particular reason why you think we might be interested in you in connection with this incident?"

"No, none whatsoever. I hardly knew the man. I'd only met him in passing, at council meetings and the like."

"What about the Oldway Mansion development?"

"Oldway Mansion? What about it?"

"Isn't it true Councillor Hargreaves opposed your development plans?"

"Yes, but how could you possibly think that had anything to do with his death?"

"I didn't say I did, but I am interested in whether the possibility had crossed *your* mind."

"No, never."

The solicitor shifted in his seat. "May I remind you, Inspector…"

"Yes, yes, I haven't forgotten. Mr King is here voluntarily. But he was at pains to tell us he wanted to help, so I'm sure he's happy to answer our questions now that he's here."

"Of course, Inspector." Justin King shared a nervous glance with his solicitor.

"Thank-you." Bobby made a point of looking down at the pad in front of him before continuing. "Do you know a local builder called Claude Knight?"

"Claude Knight, you say?" Justin drummed his fingers lightly on the table. "Name doesn't ring a bell. Should it?"

"He's been involved in the development of your hotels, Mr King. He also does work for the council."

"Really? Oh, right, maybe then. Although, all those contracts are awarded by tender. I don't get involved with any of that."

"So, you're confirming you don't know him."

"Well…I didn't say that exactly. We might have met. It's certainly possible, if, as you say, he's been involved in the construction of my hotels."

"My client meets a lot of people, Inspector. He can't be expected to remember all their names. Now, if there's nothing else, we really shouldn't take up any more of your time." The solicitor stood up without waiting for a response, making it abundantly clear the meeting was over.

"What was *that* all about?" Grainger asked as soon as Justin King and his solicitor had left the room.

Bobby considered the question for a few moments. "I'm not sure, although I don't buy all that civic duty nonsense. This has got to be linked with Oldway Mansion some-how. Why else would he come here *and* notify the press in advance? It might be some sort of PR stunt, I suppose.

To spin both him and the development in a positive light ahead of the final council vote."

Grainger ruffled his hair thoughtfully. "It's possible I suppose. Although he must have known we'd want to speak with him, eventually. Maybe he figured he'd rather that happened on his own terms. What with his solicitor being present and the prepared statement, we didn't exactly get anything useful out of him. Other than what he wanted to tell us, of course."

CHAPTER 16

REPORTS OF JUSTIN KING'S VISIT to Torquay police station started to appear online late Thursday. And, as Bobby feared, they didn't paint him or his team in a particularly positive light. Justin King, already the economic saviour of the bay, was now being held out as some sort of moral crusader hell-bent on assisting the incompetent police in uncovering the identity of those responsible for the shocking murder of a serving councillor. Chief Constable Parker had been straight on the phone, understandably concerned by reports his officers weren't making progress with the investigation. He'd made it very clear that if Bobby wasn't up to the task, he'd happily find someone who was.

There was at least one piece of good news as Bobby walked into the station early on Friday morning. Callum Franks had finally been picked up. He'd returned home on Thursday evening and, to everyone's surprise, his mum had phoned the station after her son had gone to bed.

'He's done nothing wrong, so let's get this cleared up. But you didn't hear about his whereabouts from me, all right?'

Sitting in the same interview room on the ground floor of Torquay police station he'd shared with Justin King less than twenty-four hours earlier, Bobby had no intention of dropping Mrs Franks in it with her son. He just hoped her faith in him was justified.

"You're a hard man to find, Callum. Where have you been?"

"I don't have to tell you that, I've not done nuffin'." The manner of Callum's speech reminded Bobby of Hunter and Purity, the sunrise-loving students from the technical college who'd discovered the councillor's body up on Berry Head early on Tuesday morning. He didn't think they'd been in to make their statements and wrote a note on his pad to follow that up with the team.

"You don't have to, but it might be in your best interests. This is a murder enquiry after all."

The young man looked genuinely terrified. "Murder! What you talking about? You crazy if you think I got anyfing to do with no murder."

Bobby smiled. "I've been called worse. And I'm in a bit of a tricky situation here, Callum. You see, we found a set of your fingerprints in our victim's car. The same car where his body was discovered. Now, the crime scene boys tell me they're recent. They weren't left there weeks ago or anything like that. So, how did they get there, Callum?

When were you in Councillor Hargreaves' car, and why?" He paused. "You don't have to talk to me, but if you don't, I'm liable to think the worst, aren't I? You know, put two and two together and conclude you must be guilty of murder. If you don't want that to happen, and if you really are innocent, where's the harm in talking with me?"

"S'pose. What you want to know?"

"Why don't you start with where you've been over the past few days?"

"Exeter. Got some business up there."

"Oh, yes. And what business would that be? I was led to believe you're unemployed."

"Yeah, well, not surprising is it, state of the economy. What hope does someone like me have?"

Bobby smiled and moved on. "So, when did you travel to Exeter?"

"Tuesday afternoon. Been at a mate's until last night. Came home and went straight to bed. Next thing I know, you lot are waking me up and bringing me in here. You know how uncomfortable the beds are in those cells? Didn't get no sleep. I'm proppa knackered."

"It's not a hotel, Callum. Your comfort isn't a priority."

"Maybe it should be. I might be more willing to help."

"Are you aware of a body being found on Berry Head on Tuesday morning?"

"Heard something about it. What's that got to do with me?"

"Were you anywhere near Berry Head on Monday night?"

"Why'd I want to go there?"

"So, where were you?"

"At a mate's place, playing computer games."

"All night? You didn't go out at all?"

"Nah, nothing happening this time of year on a Monday. We was playing computer games all night. You can check."

"And how do you know Councillor Irving Hargreaves?"

"Who says I do?"

"Your fingerprints. And they don't lie."

"Well, I don't know nuffin' about no fingerprints. How'd I even know you ain't trying to stitch me up? I never met that bloke you're talkin' about, and I ain't never been in his car."

"Okay, Callum. We're going to check your alibi. You can go back downstairs to enjoy some more of our great hospitality. I suggest you use the time to think about your situation. I can't help you if you won't help yourself and I have to say, as things stand, it's not looking good."

———

Bobby Redhill went straight back up to his office on the second floor and shut the door behind him. The blinds were closed, and he didn't bother turning on the lights, finding his desk and oversized leather swivel chair through memory alone. He needed some peace and quiet to consider the developments of the past few days. Despite what the press reports would have you believe, he thought they were making good progress and had several potential suspects and a number of interesting leads. The main problem was that no one appeared interested in ruling themselves out. The more people they spoke with, the more potential suspects they had. And he was sure they were missing something. In particular, he was concerned about the picture they were building of their victim, Councillor Irving Hargreaves. It just didn't seem to add up. His colleagues at the council had been universal in their praise, whereas his daughter had painted a very different picture. Who was the real Irving Hargreaves? He didn't know why, but he had a feeling this was the crucial question that needed to be answered if they were going to uncover the truth.

Just then there was a knock at the door and DS Matthew Grainger entered without waiting for a response.

"Bit dark in here, sir. Shall I turn on the lights?" Grainger flicked the switch by the door and the main fluorescent strip light that hung from the ceiling started to flicker.

"What is it, Grainger?"

"The kids who found the body are downstairs giving their statements. Their parents are with them. I think you might want to hear what they have to say."

The statements were being taken in one of the interview rooms directly off the main reception area on the ground floor of the station. It was already quite a squeeze as

Bobby and Grainger entered and they had to awkwardly manoeuvre themselves past two sets of agitated parents to get to DC Klara Allegri who was seated on the far side of the small metal table facing Hunter and Purity.

Bobby sat down next to Klara and gave a friendly smile to the two students. "I understand you have something to tell us that you didn't mention when we spoke on Tuesday. Is that right?"

Hunter was slouched down in his seat. He appeared to be sulking. "We already told your colleagues."

Before Bobby could respond, a fast-moving hand appeared from behind the boy and clipped him smartly round the ear. "That's quite enough attitude from you, young man. You're in enough trouble as it is." Hunter's mum, Bobby guessed. "We're so embarrassed, Inspector. We don't know what's got into him lately." Bobby thought the woman's subtle glance at Purity as she spoke these words betrayed her true feelings as to who was the real villain in this drama.

"That's quite all right. Are you Hunter's mother?"

"Yes, that's right. Maureen Galucsi. And this is my husband, Barry." She paused and Bobby returned his attention to Hunter, but before he could speak, Maureen continued. "As soon as we found out what he'd done we brought him straight here. Heard them talking on the phone. We couldn't believe it. He wasn't brought up like that, I can assure you, Inspector. We phoned Gene and Harold," she nodded to the other couple in the room who bowed slightly, "and got the kids together to confront them."

"Purity's never done anything like this before." It was Harold's turn to defend his child. "She's such a good girl but, you know, easily led." He placed a proud, supportive hand on his daughter's shoulder leaving little doubt who he thought responsible for them all being here, but she just rolled her eyes and continued to stare at the floor.

"Okay, thank you," said Bobby. "If they could tell me in their own words."

Hunter fidgeted and pulled the hood of his sweatshirt over his head. Maureen immediately pulled it back down and gave him a stern look, almost challenging him to argue. "We didn't tell you everything when we spoke before."

"Go on."

"After we found the body of that guy, I phoned someone and told them about it." Bobby thought the boy's voice sounded different today.

"Who did you phone, Hunter?"

"Just a guy I know."

"This guy have a name?"

"Callum. Callum Franks."

Bobby didn't react to the admission. "And how do you know this Callum Franks?"

"He lives in Paignton. I see him around sometimes."

"Why would you phone him after you found the councillor's body?"

"I maybe wasn't quite straight before when I said I didn't recognise the dead guy. His photo's been in the paper, ain't it?"

Another clip round the ear. "Hunter, speak properly. We didn't pay all that money for your education so you could speak like that."

"Mrs Galucsi, please can you let Hunter speak?" Bobby nodded to the young boy, encouraging him to continue.

"I remembered Callum telling me about some beef he had with the dead guy a while ago. I don't know, I suppose I thought he might be interested."

"And what happened then?"

"He said he was only down the road. Told me not to phone the police 'til he got there."

"And what did he do when he arrived?"

"I don't know, had a look inside the car."

"Did he take anything? Please think carefully before you answer. This is very important."

The boy shrugged. "He might have taken the guy's phone."

Bobby let Hunter and Purity off with a strongly worded warning and watched as their parents bundled them out the station and down the steps to the street. He thought they were probably guilty of bad judgement and naïvety rather than anything more sinister, and he didn't want their actions on Berry Head to ruin their futures. Besides, he guessed they were in more than enough trouble with their parents. He couldn't help but smile as Maureen Galucsi gave her son another clip round the ear just before she bundled him across the road and they were lost to sight. He doubted there'd be a repeat of Tuesday morning's sunrise surprise anytime soon.

—••—

Callum Franks had sensibly requested a solicitor ahead of his second interview and she was in place next to her client as Bobby and Grainger entered the room later that afternoon. Before either of them could speak, she leant forward, an officious look on her face.

"Inspector, other than a fingerprint that does not place my client at your crime scene, you have no evidence linking him to this incident and therefore no reason for keeping him detained. I have advised Mr Franks to exercise his right not to incriminate himself and he will therefore be answering no comment to your questions unless you have any new evidence."

Bobby waited patiently for her to finish, ignoring Callum's overly smug look. "How about you listen while we tell you what we now know and then you can decide whether or not Mr Franks is still best advised to keep quiet?"

The solicitor gave a curt nod but otherwise looked completely uninterested. Callum Franks suddenly looked a lot less certain.

"We've checked your alibi, Callum. We know you weren't at Berry Head at the time of our murder, but you haven't been completely honest with us, have you? You did know the victim, Councillor Hargreaves, and you were at Berry Head on Tuesday morning."

Callum grinned. "No comment."

"You received a call on your mobile at six ten on Tuesday morning. From a Hunter Galucsi. Don't bother denying it, we have the records. It lasted fifty-six seconds. Hunter had just found Councillor Hargreaves' body and the first thing he did was call you. Why would he do that, Callum?"

"No comment," but the grin was gone.

"We can come back to that. After receiving that call, you went straight to Berry Head. You didn't tell us this mate you were playing computer games with only lives a few minutes' drive from our crime scene. Probably slipped your mind. Anyway, after arriving at Berry Head you spent a few minutes looking through our victim's car. Starting to ring any bells, Callum? That might have been the point at which you left your fingerprints. Not very clever that, was it? You were then seen taking our victim's mobile phone. Shall I go on?"

Callum gave a desperate look in the direction of his solicitor. She avoided eye contact and just shrugged. *You're on your own here, mate.*

"Fine, but you know I ain't guilty of no murder. You said so yourself. I just took his phone, is all."

"So, how did you know Councillor Hargreaves?"

"Don't know him as no councillor. He used to own a couple of clubs in Torquay, that's where I know him from."

"Go on."

"I used to do a bit of...*business*...in his clubs, you understand?"

Bobby nodded. "I can assure you we're not interested in any of that. Nothing you tell us will be used against you. We just want to know what happened on Tuesday morning."

"His were good places. Always busy with people looking to have a good time and plenty of money to spend. But Hargreaves had a policy. You had to pay if you wanted to operate there and, well, I don't agree with paying no tax."

"I take it Hargreaves took exception to your stance?"

"You could say that. Kicked me out one night and had a couple of his guys give me a going over. Told me I wasn't welcome and if he ever saw me in one of his clubs again, he wouldn't be so understanding."

"That must have been tough to take, losing face like that. So, what, you wanted revenge?"

"Nah, nuffin' like that. What's someone like me going to do against someone like him? I didn't like it, but what could I do? His place, his rules. But it was my gear, and I don't have to share my profits with anyone I don't want to."

"Why go to Berry Head on Tuesday then?"

"Hunter called out o' the blue. He sounded weird, buzzed, you know? I thought he must have taken something but then his girlfriend came on the phone and made a bit more sense. They knew I had beef with the man." Calum suddenly looked embarrassed. "I might have exaggerated that a bit, for effect. Still, when they phoned and told me they'd found his dead body on Berry Head I had to go, didn't I? Keep up the pretence. I have a certain reputation."

"What were you planning on doing when you got there?"

"I didn't exactly have a plan. Never seen a dead body before and don't want to see another anytime soon. It was creepy. I might not have liked the guy, but he didn't deserve that. Still, I had to do something, so I pretended to search the car. I don't know what they thought I was looking for, but they seemed impressed. I didn't go anywhere near the body mind. Anyway, I saw his mobile phone in the cubby at the bottom of the dash. It was partially hidden, but I thought I could probably sell it. You know, make up for some of the lost earnings."

"Where's the phone now?"

"I still got it. The battery was dead when I found it and I don't have a charger for no iPhone, so I just stashed it and headed to Exeter. Forgot all about it to be honest."

"We need that phone, Callum. Where is it?"

"What's in it for me?" Callum's grin was back. He clearly thought he had the upper hand once again.

Bobby leaned back in his chair and smiled. He wasn't sure what to do with Callum Franks, but he had no intention of letting him off with a warning. There was still hope for Hunter and Purity, he doubted the same could be said of Callum. He almost felt sorry for the boy's mother. Her faith had proved misplaced. Still, he knew she'd never give up hope.

CHAPTER 17

PETER NORTON STOOD IN THE middle of the empty car park and looked up at the striking northern elevation of Oldway Mansion. The building's distinctive blueish-grey stone façade was complemented by an abundance of impossibly tall, white columns that stretched heavenwards between the upper two storeys. They had the curious effect of making the building feel both small and contained while at the same time exaggerating its already impressive height and scale. The columns supported a heavily balustraded white roof that gave the appearance of clouds floating. The stone window frames were large and embellished with intricate frescoes while gargoyles and other eye-catching flourishes appeared sparingly across the imposing frontage. It was an undoubtedly grand building, but its grandeur was undeniably faded. The stonework was visibly cracked, now partly covered by quick, temporary repairs, and several of the glass panels in its army of doors and windows were missing, swapped rather incongruously for cheap chipboard replacements.

Peter wasn't given to hyperbole, but he thought it nothing short of a tragedy that a building of such obvious beauty and craftsmanship should have been left to decay like this. Despite covering the Oldway Mansion development story for the *Torbay Times* over the past nine months, he realised that he'd never considered what he'd prefer to happen to the building. In truth, he hoped he wouldn't be in the bay long enough to worry about it either way, but it struck him now as only being a good thing that, whatever the result of the council vote next month, there was at least hope for its future.

A couple of years earlier, the whole structure had been declared structurally unsound and the building unceremoniously closed to the public. The seventeen acres of Italian-themed gardens remained open but, as Peter looked around, he didn't think they seemed to be much of a draw. He wondered whether it might be best if the development proposals were approved after all. At least that would guarantee investment. And, presumably, visitors. A building like this needed to be appreciated, no doubt, but it was obvious to Peter that it needed cash more, and lots of it. Warm words and good intentions alone weren't going to save it.

Peter checked his wristwatch. It was just before three on Friday afternoon. He still had time before he was due to meet the representative of the Oldway Mansion Preservation Society who'd agreed, after Peter had signed numerous liability waivers, to show him around the inside of the building. With the developments on Berry Head earlier in the week, Peter had decided to take up the long-standing offer of a tour, suddenly keen to find out more about the place he believed could hold the key to the suspicious death of Councillor Hargreaves.

Peter walked around the side of the building beneath a battalion of yet more mighty columns and up a set of wide stone steps that brought him out at what might once have been a bowling green or, perhaps, croquet lawn. Unlike the rest of the sizable gardens that were heavily planted, this area was laid entirely to grass and completely flat. It spanned the full length of the building's southern elevation and sat at the bottom of a set of shallow steps which led down from a large stone terrace. Peter guessed the sole set of double doors on this side of the building led from a ballroom or other similarly grand entertaining space. He could imagine the sort of lavish parties that might have been thrown here back in the buildings heyday and could picture weary guests taking a break from the evening's festivities to enjoy the views across Paignton from this elevated spot, before returning inside reinvigorated and hungry for more.

This part of the mansion was protected by temporary metal fencing. It gave the appearance of an active construction site, but on closer examination Peter could see the weeds and brambles that were growing around the base of the fencing panels, as time and nature worked together to reclaim the area. A sign hung loosely from the centre of one of the panels. It was dark blue with white writing that advertised the services of Claude Knight Building Contractors. Peter made a note of the name in his notebook. It wasn't the first time he'd come across it over the past couple of days.

Since submitting his article on Tuesday afternoon, Peter had spent much of his time looking for information about Councillors Irving Hargreaves and Hugh Farmer and their links to Oldway Mansion. He'd managed to corroborate much of what Marcus had told him on the phone about Irving Hargreaves and now felt even more convinced that he didn't recognise the quiet, considered councillor who'd attended every single council meeting over the last nine months. It was like they were two completely different people, and Peter had wondered whether he'd been deliberately deceived. But if so, to what end?

In stark contrast, he'd been surprised to find out very little about Hugh Farmer. Well, anything from before he became a councillor in any event. The internet and the *Torbay Times'* own archives were full of reports about Councillor Hugh Farmer, enigmatic leader of Torbay Council, but there was precisely nothing about him otherwise. It was like he hadn't existed beforehand. Peter thought that strange and had determined to continue his search.

What he had discovered was that Claude Knight Building Contractors had won several tenders for building works issued by the council since Hugh Farmer had become leader and that the building firm had also been involved in constructing the three King hotels that had already been built in the bay during that time. If the current development proposals were approved, Oldway Mansion would be the fourth King hotel in Torbay, all of them built in the last five years, during Councillor Hugh Farmer's tenure as leader of the council. And all of them partnerships between Justin King and Torbay Council or, more accurately, Councillor Hugh Farmer, who'd sponsored each one through the official planning and approvals processes. Peter wondered now whether the link with Claude Knight Building Contractors might be significant.

He'd debated bringing this information to the attention of the police. He was eager for an excuse to speak with DCI Redhill again, hoping for another opportunity to involve himself in the investigation, but he realised he might only have one more chance and needed to make sure whatever he had was both concrete and compelling. He'd tried to contact the inspector on several occasions since they'd spoken at Berry Head on Tuesday morning but had yet to hear back. He wasn't sure whether that meant the inspector was simply busy or just ignoring him. He hoped the former but suspected the latter. He'd seen Redhill looking out of the window of the station yesterday morning when Justin King and his solicitor were giving their press conference. If the inspector was really interested in sharing information, Peter thought that would have been the perfect time to reach out.

"Mr Norton?"

Peter turned abruptly. The melodic voice belonged to a woman standing at the top of the steps he'd only recently climbed. She looked to be in her early forties. Her thick black hair fell below her shoulders with just enough wave to make it interesting and tightly framed a rather plain-looking long, thin face made only slightly more memorable by a pair of tortoiseshell cat-eye reading glasses and full lips painted a bright fuchsia pink.

"I saw another car in the car park and wondered if it might be yours." The voice was confident, with just a hint of a local accent. "I'm Mavis Albright, with the Oldway Mansion Preservation Society." She wore a black and white short-sleeved T-shirt and lightly padded black gillet zipped halfway up over a black pencil skirt that stopped just below the knee. The entirely monochrome colour pallet was broken by a pair of canary yellow high-heeled shoes and matching shoulder bag while both her arms and legs were completely covered with an array of brightly coloured tattoos.

Together the unlikely couple made their way back to the car park and entered the building through an innocuous-looking entrance Peter had noticed earlier. Mavis Albright chatted the entire way.

"The estate was acquired in 1871 by Isaac Merritt Singer who built the original mansion on the site. He invented the domestic sewing machine and founded the Singer Sewing Machine Company." She spoke in an easy, relaxed manner, like they'd been friends for years. "His business had made him extremely wealthy and when he moved down here, he wanted to build something that reflected his status."

"Why did he choose Paignton? It seems like a strange place for someone like that to move to. I assume he didn't have prior links to the area."

"It was for his wife. She'd been advised by her doctors in London that the fresh air would be good for her health. There must have been something in it too, she outlived Isaac by a great many years. She was much younger than him of course, but still, she managed to have another two husbands afterwards. You see, Mr Norton, girl power wasn't invented by the Spice Girls!"

Peter chuckled. "Call me Peter." He was intrigued by Mavis Albright. She wasn't someone who conformed easily to stereotypes.

"It's rumoured she was the model who sat for the creation of the Statue of Liberty," Mavis continued. "Can you imagine? That really is quite something if it's true. And another wonderful feather in Oldway's cap."

Peter looked genuinely surprised. "Wow, that's amazing. Was she still living here then?"

"Sadly not. She moved back to London after Isaac's death. Perhaps in search of husband number two! In all seriousness, I'm not sure she enjoyed Paignton quite as much as he did. Isaac loved it down here and cared for the area deeply. He paid for Paignton Hospital to be built among various other public buildings and was patron of several local charities."

"I was born in Paignton Hospital," Peter said, almost in passing.

"You're local then? You must already know all of this." Mavis suddenly looked embarrassed, her cheeks taking on a similar shade to her lipstick.

"No, not at all. This is all very interesting. I confess to being slightly ignorant when it comes to my place of birth. History has never really been my subject. Please do carry on."

Mavis brightened instantly. "Oh, all right then. If you insist." Her mischievous smile hinted at a playful personality simmering beneath the surface. "It was only after Isaac's death that the mansion we know today came into being. One of his sons, Paris, supervised a significant remodelling. It was rebuilt in the style of the Palace of Versailles while the eastern elevation we've just walked past was inspired by the Place de la Concorde in Paris."

The door needed a bit of encouragement and finally opened with a loud groan. Inside, the building was dark and smelt of mould. A thick layer of dust hung in the air and after no more than half a dozen steps, Peter had walked through several large cobwebs.

Mavis laughed. "The cleaners haven't been in for a while! In all seriousness though, please be careful. There's still a lot of discarded junk from when the council moved out in 2013 and building debris from more recent attempts at maintenance."

Peter moved forward more carefully, his eyes slowly adjusting to the light.

"We can't go into every room I'm afraid," Mavis continued, all business once more. "One of the insurance conditions. But you should be able to get a feel for what an exquisite building this is. It really does have some beautiful features, many of them historically significant. It's such a travesty for it to be locked up like this."

As they walked into the large, double-height hallway, Mavis flicked a light switch and a grand-looking staircase gradually took shape in front of them out of the darkness.

"The staircase is made of marble and the balusters are bronze. Stunning, isn't it?" Peter nodded, not feeling qualified to say anything. They started to ascend before Mavis stopped about halfway up and pointed to the ceiling. "That's an ornate painting based on an original design for the Palace of Versailles by French painter and architect Charles Le Brun." At the top of the stairs, she paused again and pointed at another painting, this one hanging on the wall. "This is a reproduction of Jacques-Louis David's painting, Napoleon Crowning Josephine. The original was purchased by Paris Singer in the late nineteenth century and sold back to the French government in 1946. It hangs in the Palace of Versailles now." There was an obvious sense of pride in her voice. "Can you imagine such a piece hanging in a private residence in Paignton? It's almost incomprehensible." She stood still for a few moments staring at the painting, although her eyes appeared to have glazed, and Peter wondered whether she might be somewhere else. Paris, France perhaps.

From the top of the staircase on the first floor they walked into a long, narrow room covered with paintings on the walls and ceiling. Tall windows lined the walls on both sides, or so Peter thought.

"This gallery is a reproduction of the Hall of Mirrors at Versailles." Mavis spun around slowly, her arms stretched wide for balance and her head tilted back towards the ceiling, a look of childish wonderment on her face, as though she was experiencing the room for the first time. Peter now realised the windows on the inner wall were an illusion created by banks of vast mirrors set in decorative arches that reflected the windows opposite. Peter smiled as he watched Mavis. She moved in quick, tight circles, her unblinking eyes taking everything in while the clicking of her heels echoed loudly around the empty room. "The floor is parquet," she said with a smile before tapping out a little tune with her feet. At the end of the gallery, they walked through impressive full-height double doors that led into the ballroom. Peter saw the doors leading to the terrace that he'd seen from outside, with the security fence and lawn beyond.

Mavis walked purposefully as she continued the tour, pointing as she spoke. "Notice the gilt panelling on the walls and mirrors. Beautiful, isn't it?" At the end of the enormous room, she stopped in front of the fireplace. "This oil painting of Louis de Bourbon dates from 1717. That's over three hundred years old!"

"It's all very impressive, Mavis. Really. As is your knowledge. Do you mind me asking how you got involved with the preservation society? Please don't take this the wrong way, but you're not exactly what I was expecting from my tour guide!"

Mavis smiled. "I'll take that as a compliment. And don't worry, I believe you're interviewing Conrad tomorrow. He's retired and very grey. That should help redress your expectations!" She smiled warmly. "But who says history is only for retired people, or any other group for that matter? Our history has shaped every one of us and we shouldn't be so keen to discard it. I think that's something we'll all regret if we let it happen."

"How so?"

"Buildings like this have had rich and varied lives, Peter. They remind us of important lessons from out past. Lessons which are just as pertinent now. This mansion, for example, was used as a hospital during the First World War and housed RAF cadets during the second. I think you'd agree those are two historical events we shouldn't ever forget. Oldway ceased to be the Singer family home at the end of the Great War when Paris moved to America. For tax reasons. Lots changed after that conflict, of course, and the government needed money to rebuild the country. Not so different from the situation we find ourselves in after the pandemic."

"So, would you call yourself a moral crusader?"

"Not really. I've always had an interest in local history and just felt that I needed to get involved. I work in the library in Paignton and have some spare time to help. And besides, I used to do the tours here before the building was condemned. When I heard what they were planning on doing to the place, I knew I had to take a stand. It's no good complaining if you're not prepared to follow through with actions. If you believe in something strongly enough, you *have* to do whatever it takes."

There was a steely determination to her voice and Peter was left in no doubt that Mavis Albright was a woman of actions as well as words. He decided to press her further. "That's all well and good, and very noble, but how do you plan to fund the restoration works? Even I can see it isn't going to be cheap."

"A combination of sources. Council funds, local donations and Lottery-funded grants."

"Will that be enough, though? I mean, it seems like a massive project."

"It *is* challenging." She paused and looked Peter directly in the eyes. When she spoke, her words were firm. "Just because something's difficult, it doesn't mean we shouldn't try, does it? We owe it to ourselves and future generations."

"I definitely agree this building deserves a chance to be restored to its former glory." Peter was quiet for a moment as he decided how far to push his tour guide. He realised he might not get another opportunity. He was short on time and needed to press Mavis as hard as possible. "Although I'm less certain on how best that can be achieved. Ultimately, that's not my concern, but I am interested in how you think the unexplained death of Councillor Hargreaves might impact the council's vote on the mansion's future."

Mavis appeared surprised by the question. "Councillor Hargreaves? I'm not sure I'd even considered it. Obviously, it's a tragic loss of life and not something you'd expect to happen in a place like Torbay. But, in the context of Oldway Mansion? No, I just hadn't thought about the two together."

"But you were aware of the councillor's support of your cause?"

"Of course. He was one of our most high-profile supporters. And we were very grateful to him. He wasn't scared to stand up for what he believed in, and he helped give us a powerful voice within the council."

"You met him then?"

"Yes, on several occasions. He regularly came to our meetings and helped us plan and strategise."

"What did you think of him?"

Mavis was quiet for a moment, as though choosing her words carefully. "He was a kind and gentle man. Softly spoken but persuasive. And very articulate. When he spoke, people listened. We were lucky to have him on our side and will miss him greatly. His friendship, not just his support."

"But you don't think his death had anything to do with the competing proposals before Torbay Council regarding the future of this place?"

"No, how absurd. This is Torbay! We might all be passionate about this building and have very different visions for its future, but no one's going to commit murder over it."

After saying their goodbyes in the car park, Mavis got into a small, dark green hatchback and drove quickly down the long driveway. Peter watched her go, only turning away as she joined the heavy traffic on the main road and was lost to view. He didn't know what to make of Mavis Albright, but he was sure there was a lot more to her than met the eye.

CHAPTER 18

THE NEXT MORNING PETER WALKED slowly through the chocolate-box village of Cockington towards Conrad Macpherson's thatched cottage. The surrounding roads were narrow, and he'd parked in the main car park, opposite the pub, not wanting to risk the Audi getting pranged. Despite not being far from the busy harbour in Torquay, walking through Cockington felt like taking a step back in time. Peter recalled being told many years ago that parts of this community were mentioned in the Domesday Book. He guessed it made sense the chairman of the Oldway Mansion Preservation Society would live somewhere like this. Everything about the place oozed history.

At the top of a short pathway that dissected a neat lawned garden, Peter knocked twice on a solid wooden door. It was opened almost immediately by a tall, thin gentleman, as though he'd been waiting on the other side.

"Mr Macpherson?" Peter enquired.

"That's me. You must be Peter Norton, from the *Torbay Times*. I've been expecting you." He stood perfectly erect as he offered his hand in welcome. Peter was briefly distracted by the mop of thick, grey hair that was styled into a large quiff, and the disarming smile that displayed an enviable amount of perfectly straight, glaringly white teeth. His host wore a pair of grey woollen trousers, plaid patterned slippers, and a thick, maroon-coloured cardigan over an open-necked checked shirt.

"Well, come in. Don't let all the warm air out." Conrad Macpherson manhandled Peter through the door. He was surprisingly strong for his age.

"I thought we could sit in the kitchen. Not too formal I hope, but I expect you'll want to take notes and will need something to lean on." He turned and leaned in closer to Peter, his voice suddenly quieter. "And this way we'll have ready access to the kettle and the biscuits." He roared with laughter.

"That's fine, Mr Macpherson. Wherever you feel most comfortable."

"Call me Conrad."

The kitchen was at the back of the property. As they entered the cosy space, they were confronted by a sizable picture window above a ceramic white Belfast sink. It overlooked a busy but well-organised back garden that was a sea of colour thanks to all manner of plants and flowers. Peter noticed a small vegetable patch towards the rear, next to a freshly creosoted wooden shed. What little grass there was had been immaculately cut, the contrasting light and dark lines from an old-fashioned cylinder lawn mower perfectly straight and uniform.

"Beautiful garden," Peter observed.

"Another passion of mine. You need plenty to keep you occupied when you retire. The days drag otherwise."

It was only then that Peter turned into the room and noticed someone else already sitting at the round wooden table, a lady in her late fifties or early sixties. She looked familiar and Peter thought he'd seen her somewhere before. Her grey hair was cut short in a functional rather than fashionable style. She was smartly dressed in a tweed suit and white frilly blouse that was just visible at the neck and cuffs of the buttoned jacket. A white pearl necklace matched the pearl studs in her ears, while a pair of sensible, brown shoes on her feet completed the outfit.

"Oh, I'm sorry, I didn't realise there was anyone else here." Peter offered his hand to the seated lady. "I'm Peter Norton, a journalist with the *Torbay Times*. You must be Conrad's wife?"

"Lord, no! How funny you should think such a thing." The lady didn't appear at all put out by Peter's mistake, despite her protestations.

Conrad intervened. "This is Violet Danbury, Peter. She's the society's secretary and general go-to person. Our little group wouldn't function without her. She does everything and knows where all the bodies are buried." He chuckled but Peter noticed Violet didn't join in. She was a picture of professionalism. "My wife's out at one of her women's group meetings," Conrad continued. "She's not interested in historical buildings. Or anything old for that matter. But then, you should see the women's group!" He roared with laughter once again. The sound made Peter break out into a smile of his own. "And she's still married to me. Just!" Another roar. Violet's expression didn't alter and there was nothing in her demeanour to suggest she'd found either joke funny.

"You can call me Violet." She didn't make any effort to stand or shake Peter's hand.

"Pleased to meet you, Violet. Sorry for the confusion. I hadn't realised the interview would be with you both. Not that that will be a problem. The more the merrier. I just thought it was going to be with Conrad, on his own, that's all. In his position as chairman."

"And that's as it should be. I just felt I should be here as well. To make sure you get your facts right. We don't want you printing anything that's not accurate, now do we? I can't abide mistakes." Violet picked up her cup and took a sip of tea before continuing. It was a slow, theatrical gesture and neither Conrad nor Peter dared speak while they waited for her to continue. "I don't expect to be named in your article. Conrad is the figurehead of the organisation, and rightly so. In fact, I would prefer not to be. I don't need recognition. It's enough to know I'm doing my bit behind the scenes." Another sip. "Like I said, I'm here to lend support. And there might be certain information I can provide that Conrad can't. I've quite a long association with Oldway, having lived here all my life. Not like Conrad."

The elderly gentleman chuckled. "Oh, yes, I'm quite the new kid on the block." He winked at Peter before continuing. "I only moved here from Scotland around thirty years ago! No, you're quite right of course, Violet. You'd only tell me off if I got something wrong. Much safer to have you here to correct me as we go along."

Conrad handed Peter a cup of coffee in a hefty mug that matched his own. Peter noticed that Violet was drinking from a delicate bone china cup and saucer. He couldn't see anything similar elsewhere in the kitchen and wondered whether she'd brought it with her.

It was only as he nibbled on a garibaldi biscuit plucked from a well-stocked barrel in the centre of the table that it dawned on Peter where he knew the lady from. "I thought I recognised you from somewhere, Violet, and that your name was familiar, but I couldn't place you. It's just come to me. You're the clerk to Torbay Council, aren't you?"

"That's right, although I'm approaching retirement. Early in the new year. After that I'll be able to devote all my time to the society."

Peter thought he saw Conrad grimace but, when he glanced at his host again, he was all smiles, leaning over the table to fish a bourbon cream from the biscuit barrel.

"And I know who you are of course. You've been at most council meetings this past year, and I've followed all your articles on Oldway in the paper."

After some general chit-chat in which Peter learnt a surprising amount about Conrad and precisely nothing about Violet, and during which Peter's employment history and qualifications had been scrutinised in some depth by the officious old lady, Peter steered the conversation back to Oldway Mansion.

The interview proceeded much as Peter had expected. Conrad's views were firm, just as Mavis Albright's had been.

"Oldway Mansion is an historic landmark and should be cherished as such." Conrad was animated as he spoke. "What we have here is a fantastic opportunity to preserve an important piece of local history and create an attraction the people of Torbay can be proud of. An attraction that would be just as important in drawing visitors to this area as any hotel Mr King and his cronies can build."

Peter pretended to make notes on the pad in front of him. "You don't believe we need more hotels then?"

"I'm not sure that's the right question." Conrad appeared thoughtful. "Tourism is obviously the lifeblood of our community, and we need decent-quality hotels to service that, of course we do. But we already have fantastic hotels. Three of the newest owned by Justin King, I might add. The more relevant question is what all these people who come to visit us are going to do once they're here. They need first-class attractions and things to do, and we have an absolute gem in Oldway Mansion."

It was an interesting argument, and one Peter hadn't considered before, but Conrad soon reverted to an old justification Peter had heard repeated on countless previous occasions.

"When the Singer family sold the estate to the local council back in the nineteen forties, it was at a reduced price on the strict understanding the house and grounds would continue to be freely accessible to the local community." Conrad suddenly looked solemn. "It's completely immoral for the council to try to sell it now and seek to benefit financially by privatising what is, in effect, a public asset."

Peter sensed an opportunity to move the discussion in a more interesting direction. "That's all well and good, but do the finances add up? No doubt your plans are honourable and well-intentioned, and the moral arguments are well rehearsed, but can you really afford to implement them while doing justice to the building?"

Conrad took a bite from a thin pink wafer biscuit. Peter remembered them from childhood but couldn't recall the last time he'd seen one. "It's a valid question, but I genuinely believe that if we manage it properly, the building can be self-sustaining." Conrad finished the biscuit with a second bite. "Our research suggests it could even generate a modest profit, money that could, in turn, be reinvested in the local community."

Peter nodded approvingly and pretended to check his notebook before asking the next question. "How do you think the unexplained death of Councillor Hargreaves will impact your chances of winning the council vote next month?"

Conrad's expression suddenly turned grave, all thought of biscuits apparently on hold. "His death was a massive shock. To all of us." Peter glanced at Violet as she took another sip from her cup. She looked bored by the conversation. "He was a much-valued supporter of our cause, and his loss will be felt by the whole community, not just our little organisation."

"Do you think his death could have had anything to do with Oldway Mansion?"

"I seriously doubt it." A smile briefly formed on Conrad's lips. "This isn't the Wild West you know. And, what would be the point? We have plenty of supporters within the council, all of whom have a voice. I don't think poor Irving's death materially changes the dynamic so far as the vote is concerned. No, Irving's death was a great tragedy, but I suspect its cause will be found to lie somewhere else entirely. There are so many problems within society, even our small and beautiful part of the world is no longer immune." Conrad took a long slurp from his mug. "I understand Mavis showed you around Oldway yesterday." Peter couldn't help but think his host was trying to change the subject. "What did you think?"

"It was fascinating. She's a very knowledgeable lady. I confess to not knowing much about the mansion's history beforehand."

"Yes, it's impressive, isn't it? Even in its current state. Did she tell you about the secret rooms and hidden tunnels?"

"No, what are they?"

Conrad leaned forward slightly. "Oh, it's all very clandestine. Real *Boys' Own* stuff."

"Come now, Conrad." Violet looked annoyed. "Peter doesn't want to hear those old wives' tales. Facts are what he wants."

"Nonsense. Everyone likes a bit of mystery." Conrad leaned back in his chair. "These are the stories we should be telling. They might help to generate interest in our cause. We must do what we can, Violet. Use whatever tools we have available to us."

"Well, I don't agree with that at all." Violet had a look of utter disdain on her face. "You'll end up encouraging all kinds of rogues to snoop around the place. No, we should be maintaining the historical integrity of the building, not trying to turn it into a tacky visitor attraction that appeals to treasure hunters and the like. Not that there's any treasure buried there, you understand," she quickly clarified.

"Careful, Violet. You sound just like Justin King and his stooge Hugh Farmer." Conrad appeared to jump on the opportunity to admonish Violet and did so with obvious relish. He had a mischievous glint in his eye as he spoke. "It's not our place to decide who should and should not be allowed access to the incredible history of this building."

"That's not what I meant, Conrad, and you know it. Go ahead and tell Peter your silly boys' stories if you must."

"Thank you." Conrad took a bite of an orange and white party ring he'd expertly balanced on the top of one of his extended index fingers before continuing gleefully. "Where were we? Ah, yes, the secret rooms and tunnels. Legend has it that Isaac Singer had a secret tunnel built under the original mansion that exited somewhere in the grounds. He used it for clandestine visits to meet his mistress and as a more discreet way for her to enter his private chambers. Then Paris apparently commissioned various rooms during the remodelling that were never included on the official plans. They didn't have the same planning restrictions back then, you understand. Particularly for a family like the Singers. Of course, the only reason for excluding them from the plans would be to keep them secret. There are all sorts of theories as to what he wanted them for."

"That's quite enough, Conrad." Violet appeared flustered. "There's absolutely no proof for any of that. It's sensationalism, pure and simple. Speculation at best. No evidence of any secret rooms or tunnels has ever been found. If they did exist, which they most definitely do not, someone would have found them by now. Please, can we just forget about them and move on!"

Conrad acquiesced with a shrug of his shoulders and another bite of the colourful biscuit. Peter sensed he'd enjoyed having a bit of fun at Violet's expense but knew better than to push her too far.

Peter was about to grab a custard cream from the barrel when Violet suddenly stood up, the legs of her chair screeching across the tiled floor. "Well, I can't sit around here all day. Some of us have things to do." She looked at Peter. "And I expect you'll want to get started on writing up this interview." She ushered him to stand. It was clear that no discussion was being offered. He stood up and was still thanking Conrad for his time and hospitality as Violet escorted him purposefully down the narrow corridor. She herded him outside and closed the front door firmly behind them both without making any kind of farewell to her host.

Peter noticed she hadn't brought the cup and saucer with her.

CHAPTER 19

"IT *IS* SATURDAY, SIR. And it's only one drink. I'm not asking you to marry me."

"All right, very funny, Grainger. Point taken. I accept."

They were sitting opposite one another at the conference table in the incident room. Bobby had just sent the rest of the team home to enjoy what was left of Saturday evening with their families, but Grainger had stayed seated and hadn't appeared in any hurry to leave. Now the inspector realised why. "There's not much we can do here tonight anyway."

Bobby wasn't a big drinker, not anymore. The issues he'd had with alcohol in his past had made that a necessity, and during an investigation he tended to abstain completely in any event, preferring to keep his wits about him. He knew something could break the case wide open at any moment and, when it did, he needed to be able to react quickly and with a clear head. He owed that to the victims and their families. But he decided to make an exception this evening. It had been a long and stressful week and he appreciated the effort Grainger was making.

"Just the one, mind, we have another early start tomorrow." Tech support had promised to have Councillor Hargreaves' phone unlocked by the morning and Bobby was desperate to find out whether it contained anything that could help explain what had happened on Berry Head on Monday night.

Grainger gave a mock salute. "Lansdowne or Fox?"

The Lansdowne Inn and Fox and Firkin to give them their full names, were the two pubs closest to the station and therefore favoured by the people who worked there. Bobby didn't have anything against either establishment, except they often felt like an extension of work, and he didn't feel like engaging in small talk this evening. He especially didn't want to field questions, however well intentioned, about the Councillor Hargreaves murder investigation. Not while it felt like he was yet to make any significant progress.

Bobby rubbed the day's growth of stubble on his chin thoughtfully. "How about the Bull and Bush for a change?" The Bull, as it was known within the station, was a five-minute walk down Belgrave Road, in the direction of the seafront. "I fancy a bit of fresh air and I've heard they often have live music on a Saturday."

They grabbed their coats and exited through the back door. It was cold and they walked quickly, their heads bowed against a strong wind that was blowing up from the bay. Sounds of laughter carried towards them on the breeze and on more than one occasion they were forced to step into the road to avoid unsteady revellers who appeared well into their weekend celebrations.

Bobby looked over at Grainger, wondering whether his young colleague was jealous of the freedom others his age had to make plans and spend their free time as they chose. But he didn't think Grainger had even noticed. By the way his lips were silently moving as he walked, Bobby could tell his colleague was still thinking about the investigation and was quietly working through the evidence. Just like he often found himself doing. In Bobby's opinion, it was that commitment to finding justice for those who couldn't speak for themselves and his empathy for the victim – attributes Bobby himself prized above all others – that marked Grainger out from many other junior detectives.

As they entered the pub, they found a band was playing that evening. The place was busy, but Bobby spotted an empty table in the far corner. He told Grainger to go and secure it while he headed to the bar to order the drinks.

Two women were working although only one was serving. Her colleague, several years younger, appeared to think the band were playing primarily for her own entertainment. She seemed oblivious to the growing crowd on the other side of the bar, somehow managing to ignore the increasingly loud shouting and animated arm-waving of ever more frustrated customers clamouring for her attention.

When it was eventually Bobby's turn, he was not surprised to see the older woman approach him.

"Sorry 'bout the delay, love."

"No problems. Having a few staff issues?"

"Don't get me started." She raised a thick black eyebrow that was so precise in its construction that Bobby assumed it must be drawn on. "Boss's daughter." It was clear she didn't think any further explanation was necessary. She simply gave Bobby a knowing look. He got the hint and ordered an IPA for himself and a lager for Grainger.

After he'd paid, he carried the drinks over to his colleague and immediately understood why the table had not been taken by anyone else. Grainger was perched low, on an uncomfortable-looking stool, his bum positioned lower than his knees which were level with the tabletop. Not that Grainger seemed to mind. He appeared completely unaware of how ridiculous he looked. Bobby didn't feel as though he could say anything since it had been his idea to send Grainger to this table in the first place. In for a penny he thought, as he prepared to sit down on a similarly inappropriate stool on the other side of the small round table. He lowered himself slowly, hoping that no one was watching.

"What do you think will happen to Callum then, sir?"

"His case has been handed over to the CPS. I've made my recommendation, but it will be up to them to decide whether he's charged with anything."

"He's messed us about though, hasn't he? Obstructed the investigation."

"It's out of our hands now. We need to focus on things we can control. Like the phone. Hopefully there's something on it. We need a break."

"We have quite a few leads though, sir."

"Yes, lots of interesting theories, but nothing concrete. We've yet to find the silver bullet that makes sense of everything. That's what we need to discover. Every case has one. I just hope we find it on the mobile. The Chief Constable's already talking about reassigning the case."

"He can't do that, can he, sir?"

"He can do whatever he wants. All I can do is try to get to the bottom of it all as quickly as possible, while it's still my investigation."

"So, what's your current feeling? Who do you think did it?"

"I really have no idea, Grainger. The more people we speak with and the deeper into the investigation we get, the more questions I have. It doesn't feel like anyone is telling the whole truth though. I just don't know which bits are real. Or what they're trying to hide."

"You still think there's more to our victim than meets the eye?"

Bobby nodded and took a sip of his beer. "At the very least, we need to understand who Councillor Hargreaves really was. We currently have two very different descriptions from the people who should have known him best. Why is that and which version is correct? That's why I want you to speak with anyone who was involved with Hargreaves in the nightclub scene, to see what their views are."

"And whether he was still involved in that world despite selling his clubs?"

"Exactly. There could be something from back then that's relevant to our investigation."

"I have appointments to see a couple of people on Monday."

Bobby was suddenly aware of movement around him and realised the music had stopped. Several people were getting up to leave. Just then he heard a female voice addressing him.

"DCI Redhill. I thought that was you."

Bobby turned his head towards the voice. From his position close to the ground, he was confronted at first by a pair of tight stonewashed denim jeans, two shapely legs and a couple of bright red high-heeled shoes. As he raised his glance, he immediately recognised the face smiling down on him. It was the same one he'd been charmed by on a couple of previous occasions already this week.

"Faith." He felt his cheeks redden as he considered how silly he must look perched on the low stool next to Grainger. "What are you doing here?"

"A friend of mine is in the band. He's been trying to get me to come and see him perform for a while. What about you?"

"Oh, we just popped in for a quick drink after work. It's been a long week. You can probably imagine."

"Yes, of course. How's the investigation going?"

"Slowly, but we're making progress." The words were spoken without much conviction. "You remember DS Matthew Grainger?"

Faith glanced at Grainger and smiled but quickly returned her focus to Bobby. She was wearing her blond hair down this evening. It was perfectly straight and fell just below her shoulders, a couple of inches longer than Bobby had imagined when he'd seen the pathologist at the autopsy earlier in the week and her hair had been neatly tied back. Her lips were a bright shade of red that matched her shoes. Bobby noticed her eyelids shimmering as they caught the light, echoing the effect of the sequins on her black halter neck top.

With Bobby sitting so low and Faith towering above him in her heels, conversation was difficult. Bobby, who hadn't stood up when Faith first arrived, now found himself in a quandary. Did he stand or stay seated? He realised he didn't know whether she intended to stay and chat or was just saying a quick hello as she passed by. He didn't want to appear presumptuous so ended up doing neither, instead adopting a weird hovering stance, his bum off the stool but his legs still bent.

"What did you think of the band?" Faith asked.

Bobby realised he hadn't paid much attention to the music. "Great," was all he managed before seeing the disappointment on Faith's face. "We only arrived ten minutes ago, but they seemed to be going down well. What does your friend play?"

"Lead guitar. He also sings. Such a cliché, I know. He's even got the long blond hair. But he's so talented and such a sweet guy."

"I dislike him already," replied Bobby, not entirely joking.

"So, do you come here often? I thought you guys all went to the Lansdowne after work. That's where Jake had his retirement drinks, wasn't it?"

Once again Bobby felt his face flush with embarrassment as he recalled mistaking Faith for Jake Twyford, the now retired forensic pathologist, when they'd first met on Berry Head on Tuesday morning. "That *is* one of our favourite haunts. But it's good to try something new every now and again. And we thought they might have music on tonight."

"Well, I won't keep you. I just wanted to say hi. It was nice to see you, Bobby. You too, DS Grainger."

And with that Faith turned and walked confidently back towards the stage. Bobby sank back onto the stool, his legs suddenly burning from the effort of holding the half squat. He followed her progress until she pushed between a large group standing at the bar and disappeared into the crowd.

"Nice of her to come and say hi," said Grainger before taking a gulp of his lager. "She clearly likes you, sir."

"What are you talking about, Grainger?

"She couldn't stop looking at you. And she barely even acknowledged my existence."

"I'm sure she was just being polite. She's still relatively new round here remember, and it *is* the first time we've worked together."

"If that's what you want to tell yourself, sir. I'd be over there now if it were me."

Bobby took a long sip of his drink. He didn't want Grainger to see the smile on his face. After putting his glass back down on the table, he changed the subject.

"What's going on in that department with you? Anyone special in your life, or are you still young, free and single?" As the words left his mouth, Bobby cringed. He hoped he didn't sound too much like an embarrassing father trying hard to be hip. Not that the young man appeared to mind.

"There is someone, sir. I met her at a party a few weeks ago. She's a solicitor with a firm in Exeter. A real high-flyer."

"Sounds like quite the catch. What's she doing with you!" Bobby laughed but stopped abruptly when he saw Grainger's expression darken. He hoped he hadn't offended his colleague. No one seemed to have a sense of humour anymore.

"The thing is, I haven't spoken to her yet. Not on her own. Not like *that,* anyway."

Bobby laughed again but through relief this time. Perhaps he and Grainger were even more alike than he'd realised. "Aren't we quite the pair? So much for your earlier bravado. But seriously, you really should follow your own advice and tell her how you feel. You don't want to end up like me. Married to the job."

As they finished their drinks and got up to leave, Bobby found himself looking round the pub for any sign of Faith. He caught a glimpse of her as he approached the front door. She was talking closely to a young man with long, blond hair and impossibly tight trousers. The friend, Bobby presumed. He felt a knot of anxiety forming in the pit of his stomach and found himself pausing in the doorway. Embarrassed by his behaviour, he took a final quick look before walking outside, just as Faith leaned forward and flung her arms around her male companion.

CHAPTER 20

PETER WOKE EARLY ON SUNDAY morning after a fitful night's
sleep, the frustrations of the past week finally having
caught up with him. Only five days earlier he'd felt excited
about the future, for the first time since before his return
to Torbay. The circumstances surrounding Councillor
Hargreaves' death and its potential links to the Oldway
Mansion development story had energised him in a way
he hadn't imagined possible outside the big investigative
pieces he'd become known for in London. It wasn't just
the national interest and the effect that could have on his
career, although he'd be lying if he denied that was a factor,
he realised he needed the buzz that came with chasing an
important story to give his life meaning. With the glamour
of local celebrity, suggestions of government conspiracy
and the intrigue of an historic building with a mysterious
past, he certainly thought this one qualified. Added to

that, he'd been confident of securing an inside scoop by developing a collaborative relationship with DCI Redhill, the SIO on the case. But after a week of unanswered calls and nothing to show from his own investigations, he was as far away from breaking the story as he'd ever been.

He'd spent Saturday evening writing up the notes from his interview with Conrad Macpherson but had soon tired of the mundane task, his thoughts quickly returning to theories of collusion and conspiracy. He'd been surprised that neither Conrad nor Mavis Albright had levelled any accusations of foul play in the councillor's sudden and unexplained death. In fact, both had dismissed the notion out of hand, while Violet Danbury had just appeared bored with the conversation. The more Peter thought about it, the stranger that seemed. Justin King's impromptu press conference on Thursday had made it clear their opponents had no intention of resting on their laurels. It didn't make sense for the preservation society to do otherwise. Even if they genuinely believed there was no link, he'd have expected them to stoke the fires and use the opportunity to garner support for their cause. After all, the sympathy vote could be a powerful one, and Peter knew endorsement of the opposing proposals within council was extremely close. A vote here or there could make all the difference.

He'd briefly questioned whether his personal situation might be clouding his judgement, that perhaps he was reading too much into things because he wanted there to be more to it. But he quickly dismissed the idea. He was convinced the death of Councillor Hargreaves had something to do with the contested future of the stately home. And he didn't think the members of the Oldway Mansion Preservation Society were being completely honest with him.

In the absence of other leads, Peter had spent time continuing his research. The preservation society had existed in one form or another for many years but appeared to have taken on more prominence after the council relocated to new premises in 2013, leaving the mansion empty and, to all intents and purposes, forgotten. In the years since, official investment and maintenance had almost completely dried up and the building had started to deteriorate, evidenced most ominously by its closure to the public on safety grounds a few years earlier. Its members now almost single-handedly maintained the mansion's extensive grounds and had plans to open a tea-room to generate much-needed funds.

From what Peter could gather, membership was made up of a disparate collection of locals: retired professionals, bored housewives, history buffs, the green-fingered, business owners (likely, Peter guessed, with vested interests) and those who just needed a cause to champion. Peter had wondered which category Mavis Albright fell into. There was no doubt she was a history buff, but some of the ideas attributed to her in the detailed minutes of the group's recent meetings that Peter had found online hinted at someone who also needed a cause. One of her suggestions had been for direct, positive action in the event the council vote went against them. For those of the group's members who weren't familiar with the terminology, which appeared from the subsequent debate to be most of them, it was described as occupation of the building and martyrdom until the group's aims were achieved. However long it took.

Mavis continued to surprise. A quick online search had provided some context. In her youth she'd been a fervent campaigner and habitual protester for all manner of social interest groups. And direct, positive action had very much been part of her armoury. There were pictures of her living in the branches of an old oak tree scheduled to be cut down to make way for a new motorway, and reports of her living in a tunnel for several weeks underneath the proposed site of a controversial new nuclear power station. Peter had been impressed by her commitment although noted her efforts had ultimately all been in vain.

The group appeared well supported and were clearly organised, a fact Peter attributed, at least in part, to their chairman's '*decorated military background*' and the skills of their secretary, '*clerk to Torbay Council for the past 30 years*'. All in all, interesting but nothing to explain why they'd seek to downplay any potential link between the death of Councillor Hargreaves and the future of Oldway Mansion.

Peter had gone to bed disheartened, but not before vowing to get up early to go surfing. It had been weeks since he'd made it out on the water, and he needed to clear his head and get his muscles working.

For Peter, there was no better place than out on his surfboard, in the middle of a seemingly never-ending expanse of water, the headland rising in front of him like a beacon. Just him, his board and absolute silence. No matter how busy it was on the water, or how jumbled his thoughts, he always managed to find a level of calm and a clarity of thought he'd never been able to replicate on land.

He smiled at the prospect.

After putting on his swimming shorts, he dressed in a pair of baggy tracksuit trousers and a T-shirt beneath a shapeless sweater. He'd learnt many years ago that the key to a successful surfing trip was loose-fitting clothing that could be easily taken on and off at the side of the coast road as you changed in and out of your wetsuit. And a large towel to cover what little modesty you had left to protect.

With his bag packed and his thermos brimming with steaming hot coffee, Peter put on a Gore-Tex jacket, loaded the Audi and secured his surfboard to the roof. He was on the road before eight feeling smug. He'd always thought there was something incredibly virtuous about being up and out before the crowds, on any day, but even more so on a Sunday.

The roads were quiet, and on a whim, Peter decided to head to one of his favourite spots in North Devon. It was a ninety-mile drive that would take around two hours although Peter knew it would be well worth the effort. It wasn't a trip he made often given the typically fierce tourist traffic, particularly in the prime summer months. But today, Peter had the whole day ahead of him, the locals were still in their beds, and the holiday traffic was non-existent.

As he left the residential streets behind, he pressed down hard on the accelerator. The Audi's engine responded immediately, and he felt the vehicle reverberate excitedly beneath him. As the turbos spooled up and did their thing, Peter was forced back into his seat with gratifying force. He laughed out loud and pressed down harder with his right foot.

Around thirty miles into the journey, Peter took the second exit, straight ahead on a wide, empty two-lane roundabout a little too quickly. It was only the car's clever electronic safety systems snapping the rear back in line behind the front wheels that stopped him making an unscheduled tour of the local hedgerows. Suitably chastised, he slowed down and relaxed into the journey, reminding himself he was in no rush and that the excitement was supposed to arrive at the end of the drive. He turned on the car's stereo and Frieda's homemade CD picked up from where it had left off earlier in the week.

Peter was singing along with Taylor Swift as she lamented the end of yet another doomed relationship when he arrived in Croyde at just after ten. There were only a handful of cars parked in the road and he didn't see anyone as he changed into his wetsuit. Walking down the narrow passage to the beach he shared a wordless moment with a shivering but smiling surfer travelling in the other direction. Peter stopped momentarily as the vast expanse of Croyde's beautiful beach opened out in front of him. Other than a few bodies bobbing rhythmically on the tide, there was no one around. Peter closed his eyes and breathed in deeply before attaching the leash to his right ankle and running purposefully down to the water, jumping onto his board when it reached his waist. He paddled his arms hard to get out beyond the waves before sitting up and taking in the view from his new position.

The vast stone cliffs on his left and striking green hills further off to his right, that together formed the delightful Croyde Bay, felt so familiar and he immediately relaxed, for the first time in weeks. In front of him the golden sandy beach enclosed by rolling yellow sand dunes called to him and he caught the next wave, working his arms hard for a few seconds before jumping effortlessly to his feet in one fluid, practised movement. As he approached the shore, he jumped headfirst into the wave, gasping as he was briefly submerged in the freezing cold water. It took his breath away, but he emerged feeling invigorated and grabbed his board to do it all over again.

Over the next ninety minutes, Peter alternated between brief periods of explosive effort and longer interludes of calm, sitting quietly, bobbing with the tide and not really thinking of anything. Just enjoying the silence. As he walked back up the beach his arms burned and his whole body ached, but he felt happy and content. After changing into dry clothes, having narrowly avoided the attentions of a young beagle who wanted to play with his towel, he poured himself a cup of coffee from his flask and sat in the Audi with the engine running, the heated seat on full and the heater blasting him with hot air.

The journey home was mercifully uneventful, and Peter used the time to call his parents, making the most of the car's Bluetooth function to connect his phone. He hadn't spoken to them in over a week and knew that if he didn't call today, he'd be in trouble with his mum. Not something he'd recommend to anyone. His dad was less concerned about hearing regularly from his only son, but if Peter didn't call his mum every week, she got upset and that *was* something his dad cared about.

It didn't sit well with Peter that the task currently felt like a chore. It hadn't always been that way but he'd noticed a definite strain in the relationship with his parents since he'd left London. His mum had adored Frieda and Peter knew she couldn't understand his decision to move on. He guessed it might have been different had there been another woman but, as it was, she just saw the prospect of grandchildren slipping further away. While he hadn't said so directly, Peter knew his dad agreed with Frieda and thought he'd needlessly discarded a promising career and that he was wasting his talents and education working for the *Torbay Times*. Families... Peter sighed. Rather than addressing any of these issues head-on, each side skirted around the edges, leaving what they really felt unsaid.

As luck would have it, Peter called at just the right time. His mum was heading out the door to meet a friend for lunch while his dad was at the golf club, so the conversation was mercifully short, and Peter hung up satisfied his duty had been done for another week.

He arrived back in Paignton just before two and parked in the spot outside his flat he'd vacated earlier that morning. After unstrapping the surfboard and carrying it to his front door, he left it propped against the wall outside while he went back to the car to grab his bag. When he returned, he unlocked the door, threw his bag inside and proceeded to haul his board up the stairs, kicking the door closed with his foot as he passed through. As darkness descended he immediately regretted the instinctive action. He stumbled up the stairs and used the torch function on his phone to locate the lock on the door to his flat.

With his surfboard safely inside, he went back down to collect his bag, making sure to leave his front door open to throw some light into the stairwell. Not for the first time, he reminded himself to get a new bulb. As he grabbed the bag's handles, he noticed an envelope on the floor. His bag had come to rest on top of it when he'd thrown it through the doorway earlier. He bent down and picked it up before carrying both items up the stairs to his flat. After dropping the bag on the floor next to the surfboard he closed the door and absently ripped open the envelope. It contained a single sheet of A4 paper folded into three equal segments. There were eighteen words in total, arranged over three lines across the middle of the page.

'Hugh Farmer is not what he seems'
'Look into his past'
'The Oldway Mansion development cannot go ahead'

CHAPTER 21

AT JUST AFTER EIGHT THIRTY on Sunday morning, Bobby Redhill was back in the incident room sat at the conference table opposite Matthew Grainger. The rest of the team were yet to arrive.

"Well, that's a first!"

Bobby leaned back in the uncomfortable plastic chair, a look of total disbelief on his face. In front of him on the table was Councillor Hargreaves' mobile phone. The tech guys had been as good as their word and, having unlocked it overnight, had identified the voice recorder as the last app to be used before the battery died. A quick check had revealed a recording of two hours and twenty-three minutes starting at twelve fifty-nine the previous Tuesday morning.

Grainger blew the air out of his puffed-up cheeks. "Have we just listened to someone being murdered?"

"I think we have, yes."

"Creepy. Although it doesn't tell us much...does it?"

Bobby leaned forward and pressed play on the recording. He wanted to listen to it again, this time prepared for what was to come. Immediately a slight background hum played through the phone's inbuilt speaker. "That's the engine of the Mercedes," Bobby announced confidently. "He must have started the recording before arriving at the car park." A light thud was followed by the unmistakable sound of tyres on gravel. "That must be him putting the phone down in the central console, where Callum found it." A pause. "He's in the car park now. You can hear the gravel crunching." They continued to listen as silence descended. "It sounds like he turns the engine off and just sits quietly for a moment. Maybe he's waiting for someone. Yes, is that someone getting into the vehicle? There, listen." Bobby pointed at the phone as vague sounds of gusting wind could be heard alongside what appeared to be the whisper of distant waves crashing. "But notice how no one speaks. Does that suggest he knew the identity of the person he was meeting?"

"Could be," Grainger agreed. "But we think the assailant sat in the backseat, don't we? We can't tell from the recording which door is being opened. It could be Irving getting out the vehicle."

Bobby shook his head. "I don't think so. He was found in the driver's seat, remember, with his belt still on. And listen to that."

"What?"

"Exactly. There's a slight noise and then nothing. Just silence. That must have been the door closing again. I think someone got into the car. And from what we already know, it's likely that was into the backseat, behind the driver." They listened to the silence for a few more seconds. "There," Bobby suddenly exclaimed. "That sounds like a scuffle of some sort."

"Yes," agreed Grainger. "You can hear heavy breathing. Like someone trying to catch their breath. That must be Hargreaves." They listened to the increasingly desperate noises until silence descended once more. Both Bobby and Grainger automatically bowed their heads, all too aware of what that meant. Bobby was the first to speak.

"You can hear the wind again. That must be the assailant getting out the car." Then two more periods of silence interspersed with the now familiar sounds of wind and sea. "That could be the assailant opening doors and checking inside the car. But what were they looking for? And did they find it, whatever it was?"

The question was rhetorical and, unusually, Grainger didn't respond.

"We'll have to get someone to listen to the full recording," Bobby continued, "but I'd bet it's just static after the first nine minutes as the recording gradually runs down the battery. See, you can hear another car driving away here. That's the sound of the engine…and the faint crunch of tyres on gravel. And then silence. Nine minutes in. That's 1:08 a.m." He paused the recording. "The whole thing was over in less than ten minutes."

Grainger was quiet for a moment. "But does it tell us anything we didn't already know?"

"Maybe not, although it does corroborate certain facts. Time of death for one. And then there's the recording itself. Why would he record the encounter?"

"It points to a meeting, doesn't it, sir?"

"I agree. But what sort of meeting requires a recording?"

"And a secret one at that."

"How do you mean?"

"Well, we can hear the assailant searching the car afterwards. At least that's what we think they're doing. They didn't find the phone though, did they, so it must have been hidden. That could have been what they were looking for."

Bobby nodded deliberately. "We know Callum found it in the small cubby at the bottom of the centre console. It's not much bigger than a mobile phone, and shallow, you probably wouldn't notice it unless you knew to look. Callum told us he only found it because he was trying so hard not to look at the body!"

"Are we looking at some sort of shakedown?" Grainger asked.

"Could be. But if that's the case, who was doing the shaking and who was being shook?"

———•———

As mid-afternoon turned quickly into night and darkness descended abruptly outside, the gaps in the broken blinds threw shards of light onto the ceiling of Bobby's office from the streetlights that lined the road outside the front of the station. They roused the inspector from his thoughts, and he checked his watch. Another day was coming to an end with yet more questions and no meaningful answers. He was considering sending the team home for the night when he received a call from the incident room. *'We've got something you'll want to see, boss.'*

"These were sent by Veronica King?" Bobby was standing at the conference table staring down at Councillor Hargreaves' mobile phone. Freddie Allsop, Dejay Merrali and Anna Christenson were sat down in front of him. Grainger and Klara Allegri stood at his shoulders, one on either side. A wire protruded from the bottom of the phone and connected to a flat screen television mounted on a tall stand in front of them. The television replicated the images on the phone's screen.

"Yes, sir." Freddie Allsop, sat directly in front of the phone, was manipulating the images on the screen. "No doubt about it. The messages were sent on an encrypted messaging service. Mrs King has tagged her account with a picture. See?" He tapped on the screen and the messages were replaced by Veronica King's smiling face."

Bobby had never met the hotelier but recognised her instantly. *Like everyone else in the bay*, he thought. The picture appeared to have been heavily edited. Or professionally shot. Maybe both. Bobby wondered whether she'd undergone a bit of professional alteration herself. He guessed Veronica King was in her late forties or early fifties, but she looked much younger in the picture. Bobby was no expert, but he'd expect her to have at least one or two wrinkles. Maybe a grey hair or two. And he thought her teeth looked a little too straight and white to be entirely natural.

"So, Veronica and our victim knew each other, is that what we're saying?"

"Maybe more than that, boss." The photo disappeared and was replaced by a stream of texts. "The messages suggest a closer relationship, like they were having an affair." Freddie slowly scrolled through an extensive archive of historical communications. "They start around six weeks ago, innocent enough at first, but quickly become quite suggestive. And Mrs King sent a couple of photos that appear to support the theory of an intimate relationship." He paused briefly on a thumbnail picture of Mrs King resplendent in nothing but dark blue lingerie. The photo had been taken in front of a mirror and showed Mrs King in a provocative pose. A phone was visible in front of her stomach, near an area of light distortion from a camera's flash.

"Anything to suggest this might be linked to the councillor's death?" Bobby asked, now very interested.

"It's possible. The frequency of messages changes about two weeks ago. Mrs King is still messaging relatively frequently, but Councillor Hargreaves stops responding, and then, the Friday before his death, she sends a slew of quite abusive texts. There's no further communication between them after that. Not on this app anyway. We're still going through phone records."

Bobby read the most recent batch of messages. Mrs King was clearly angry and upset. In the last message, sent around 10:00 p.m. on the Friday before his death, she appeared to accuse the councillor of dishonesty.

"So, what do we think?" Bobby asked. "Is this a crime of passion? What about Justin King? Did he know about the relationship between his wife and Councillor Hargreaves? Is that why he came to see us last week? Was he trying to get in front of this, to point our investigation in another direction? He must have realised we'd find out about it. Was he trying to protect his wife? Maybe he thinks she had something to do with his murder."

CHAPTER 22

BOBBY REDHILL AND MATTHEW GRAINGER were parked on the road outside the Kings' imposing residence in the exclusive Ilsham Marine Drive development of Torquay well before eight on Monday morning. They hadn't phoned ahead and didn't announce their presence now. Instead, they sat and waited, neither of them speaking. Bobby was thinking about the case, rehearsing different scenarios in his mind of how Veronica King might react when they confronted her. He couldn't be certain about his colleague, but he doubted the investigation was at the forefront of his thoughts at that moment. He looked across just as Grainger bit down hungrily on the bacon sarnie he'd picked up at a roadside café he'd insisted they stop at on the way. Bobby cracked the Vauxhall's driver side window to let in some fresh air. The smell was making his stomach rumble.

Ilsham Marine Drive curved around the edge of a rocky outcrop of cliffs overlooking Thatcher Rock, a small island situated around three hundred meters off the coast. The arc of the road followed the contours of the cliffs, rising from Meadfoot beach on one side and taking in Hope's Nose and Hope's Cove on its way round to Wellswood, an upmarket primarily residential area of Torquay. The road was one of the most expensive addresses in the bay and therefore one of the most prestigious postcodes.

At exactly eight fifteen the pair of imposing double-height wooden gates in the high boundary wall that surrounded the King estate started to open inwards and a dark grey Range Rover edged slowly onto the road before accelerating quickly past the Vauxhall, without giving it a second glance. Bobby watched in the passenger side mirror as it disappeared and waited a couple of minutes before pulling forward onto the wide pavement in front of the now closed gates.

Bobby pressed a button on the intercom located at the top of a metal pole fixed in the ground. A cheery sounding woman's voice answered and, after Bobby had identified himself, the gates started to open without any further words being spoken.

The property was set back from the road in the middle of a generously sized plot. The driveway wound around the edge of a heavily sloped front garden that led up to a house built in an elevated position where the ground began to flatten out. Initially the drive passed along the inside of the front wall before taking a sharp left and proceeding to track a thick laurel hedge which, Bobby guessed, marked the boundary with the next-door property. Bobby's view of the house briefly disappeared as he passed through the gates, but it gradually reappeared as he made his way up the drive, its secrets unveiling themselves piece by piece, teasing him just enough that he wanted to see more, like the work of a seasoned burlesque dancer. Up close, it was even bigger than it had appeared from the road. And even more modern. Its entire frontage was made of glass while an infinity pool spanned its full length and appeared to flow out of the structure itself. In the reflection of the early morning sun, it looked as though the house was floating in the same bright blue waters of the bay that its prominent position, high on the cliff edge, gave it an unobstructed view of.

Bobby followed the drive round to the back of the house and parked in front of a triple garage, on an expanse of block paving so vast it looked as though it could accommodate a small army of vehicles. The front door was at the back of the property, along with the garage, a tennis court and an Olympic-sized outdoor swimming pool.

The door was located up a shallow set of steps. Like the front of the house, it was nothing more than a large pane of glass. It afforded views into the depths of the property and out the other side, to the shimmering waters of the bay. Bobby was about to press the doorbell when a glamorous woman appeared and opened the door. She was dressed casually in grey tracksuit bottoms and a matching hooded jumper, although both items looked expensive. The material appeared soft, and its silvery colour reflected the light from outside as she walked, as though she was the living embodiment of the house around her. She wore a massive diamond ring on her wedding finger and an equally large diamond necklace around her neck. Mrs King, Bobby guessed. She smiled but there was no warmth in it. In fact, she looked decidedly anxious.

"I can guess why you're here." Veronica King spoke without introducing herself. "I assume you waited for Justin to leave. Thank you for that courtesy. You'd better come in."

They followed her through an enormous double-height hallway into the front of the house, passing a set of functional metal stairs leading to the first floor. They appeared to be suspended in mid-air without any visible supports. The whole ground floor was just one enormous open space dominated by the oversized floor-to-ceiling windows that overlooked the infinity pool. A few colourful paintings, which Bobby thought might qualify as 'modern art' hung on the walls, and several heavy-looking statues had been positioned artfully on waist-high plinths that dotted the space, but the real focal point here was unmistakably the view.

Veronica led them to the kitchen in the front left-hand quadrant of the ground floor, next to the lounge, although they were really one and the same room given the lack of a dividing wall. Without asking, she started making coffees at a professional-looking machine. Bobby walked over to the window and looked out. A couple of sailing boats bobbed lazily on the water, their progress constrained by the stillness of the morning. Bobby followed the surprisingly graceful flight of a seagull as it glided effortlessly in the distance. Further out, the bright blue of the sea merged seamlessly at the horizon with the equally vivid blue of the sky.

"What a fantastic space, Mrs King. And that view. You'd surely never get bored of it."

"You didn't come here to discuss architecture, Inspector. Or the view. Shall we get on with it?" There was no malice in the voice, just a hint of resignation. She placed two cups of black coffee on a marble-topped central island and pointed to a couple of high stools, inviting the detectives to sit while she leaned against the counter from the other side.

"Of course." Bobby offered a friendly smile. "What can you tell us about Councillor Irving Hargreaves?"

"I presume you've seen our…communications?" She looked down at her hands. "Did he keep the photographs?"

"There were a few pictures on his mobile, yes, but they're of no interest to us, Mrs King."

Veronica gave an almost imperceptible nod of thanks. "It really is very embarrassing. I assure you I don't make a habit of this sort of thing. You must believe that. And I need you to understand that I love my husband very much. It's complicated, but we haven't had a close… physical relationship…for some time now. I've never done anything like this before, but Irving was very persistent. At first at least. And he could be very charming. I was flattered I suppose, and I was attracted to him. Although I suppose I was probably just trying to make Justin jealous." She paused and played unconsciously with her wedding ring. "Everything was fine for a while. Exciting. But recently he'd become distant and cold. I'm ashamed to say I became a little…temperamental."

"We've seen the texts you sent him the Friday before last."

"Not my finest moment. I'd had a few drinks and he wasn't answering my calls. Well, you've seen that I was…upset."

"What did you mean when you accused him of using you?"

Veronica inhaled deeply. "I'd started to get the feeling he wasn't really interested in me. Not like *that*, anyway. That perhaps he had another agenda."

"That must have hurt?"

"You could say that. Although it's not the first time I've experienced rejection in that department and my husband's still very much alive, so if you think Irving's behaviour sent me into such a rage that I killed him, you're way off, Inspector."

"Okay, so if not romantic, what do you think his motives were in pursuing an intimate relationship with you?"

"Apart from the sex you mean?"

Bobby blushed at the woman's candour.

"I apologise. That was crude. And unnecessary." Veronica was quiet for a moment. "I want to be honest with you, Inspector. I can assure you I had nothing to do with Irving's death. But there are certain…delicate matters…that I'd prefer remain private."

"I can't make any promises. I do need to know everything. Not just to rule you out of our investigation, but to build a picture of our victim and his movements in the weeks before his death. But what I can say is that if anything you tell me has no bearing on the investigation, I will do my best to keep it out of the formal reports."

"Thank you, Inspector, I can't ask for more than that." She took a deep breath. "I have no proof that any of this is at all relevant, you understand, but a woman's instinct can be a powerful thing."

"And what did your instinct tell you about Councillor Hargreaves?"

"Irving always wanted to talk about my past. At first, I thought it was sweet. That it proved he was interested in me. But then I began to doubt his motives. Particularly when he started backing away. I hadn't told him what he wanted to know you see. Anyway, I began to realise it wasn't so much *me* he was interested in as *us*. My husband and I."

"In what way?"

"In the way he was only really interested in one period in my past. Or perhaps I should say, one specific event."

"And what was that?"

Veronica took another deep breath, exhaling slowly. "Before we moved to Torbay, Justin and I lived in Leith in Edinburgh. We ran a nightclub there." Veronica was quiet for a moment, as though transported back in time.

A sad-looking smile formed on her face. "It was successful. *We* were successful. Life was good. We held an important place in the community. People looked up to us. Justin and I were happy. But after *that* night, everything changed."

"What happened, Mrs King?"

"It was a Friday. We were busy. Fridays were always popular with the young professional crowd. Everyone was having a great time. There were no issues. Nothing to suggest anything was wrong. If we'd have known, we'd have done something."

Veronica dabbed at her eyes with the corner of her sleeve. Bobby gave her a moment to compose herself.

"It all happened so quickly. Justin and I were in the office on the top floor. We didn't see the incident, but the eyewitness accounts all said the same thing. A young woman climbed onto the railings on the second-floor mezzanine and fell onto the dancefloor below. Well, jumped I suppose. No one had time to react. There was nothing anyone could have done. It was just a tragic accident. We only found out later she'd taken something and must have jumped thinking she could fly." Veronica's face darkened slightly. "Stupid girl." The words were barely audible and there was no venom in her voice, only sadness.

"I'm very sorry, Mrs King. That must have been a difficult time."

Veronica stared directly at Bobby but appeared not to see him. "There was nothing left for us there after that. We had a zero-tolerance policy on drugs, always had, but people just assumed she'd brought the drugs from our club.

From us! Once you're tarnished with that brush, there's nothing you can do to change people's opinions. We had to leave. Make a fresh start somewhere new. Funny that we chose Torbay. It's a long way away, that was the point, obviously, but also very similar in many respects. I suppose that's what drew us here. We like being part of a community. And I'm not sure I could live away from the sea."

"Did you tell your husband about your suspicions?"

"Yes, I had to. It threatened the business. Everything we've worked so hard to build up these past five years."

"Was that why he came to the station last week? Your husband, I mean. He must have realised we'd find out about it."

Veronica suddenly looked panicked. "I didn't tell him *everything!* He didn't know about the…*physical*…relationship." She quickly regained her composure. "I just said that Irving was snooping around. Asking questions about our past. About *that* incident. He knew we were friends. He didn't question it. Besides, he's not that creative. No, that was business, pure and simple. The final council vote is next month. We just wanted to get ourselves in front of the media, in case the news of Irving's death gave the preservationists a bit of a boost. All a bit unsavoury I know, but necessary nonetheless. Optics are everything in this game, Inspector. Even if it did make poor Justin look like a bit of a wally!" She laughed but there was no joy in it. "I'm genuinely sorry he used you to do it, though. I know your time is incredibly precious. Especially now. If it's any consolation, he hated doing it. The media thing, I mean. He really is quite shy and prefers to stay out of the limelight. We both do. For obvious reasons."

Bobby wasn't about to excuse the behaviour but decided not to make an issue of it. He realised he might need the leverage with Justin King at some point. "The Oldway Mansion development is important to you then?"

"Of course. We've invested a lot of time and money into it. But it's not just important for us, it's vital for the economic future of the whole area."

"Where were you and your husband last Monday evening? Say from eight until eight the following morning."

"We were out for dinner. At Hugh Farmer's house. To discuss the development. We arrived at his around seven thirty and got back home just after eleven."

"And then?"

"And then we went to bed. We both got up around six thirty the next morning, as usual."

"Forgive my directness, Mrs King." Bobby paused while he considered how best to ask his next question. "You mentioned before that you and your husband are no longer… intimate. Does that mean you sleep in separate rooms?"

"Well, yes, but I don't see what that's got to do…"

"Simply put, it means that neither of you have an alibi for our time of death."

CHAPTER 23

PETER NORTON PRESSED SAVE ON the interview with Conrad Macpherson. It was late Monday morning and Marcus was expecting it by lunchtime. It had taken longer to write than anticipated, mainly because his attention had been elsewhere, focused on the note he'd found on his doormat the previous afternoon. Peter looked over at the single sheet of white paper lying face down on the other side of the dining table. It was a standard A4 size, neither thick nor thin, just normal office quality. The sort that could be bought from any number of retailers. There was absolutely nothing remarkable about it, and yet it had unsettled him. He leaned forward and picked it up carefully as though it might explode, turning it slowly in both hands and tilting it towards the light as he checked every inch for clues. Not that he expected to find any. He'd done the same thing a hundred times already but was still no closer to understanding who'd sent it or why.

Eighteen words, each one constructed from individual letters cut out of a combination of what appeared to be newspapers and magazines. The letters were of different sizes and styles and covered the full spectrum of the rainbow in their colours. Some were capitals and some lower case. There didn't appear to be any reason for the distinction.

He put the letter down and picked up the envelope, examining it in the same way. Like the paper, there was nothing distinctive about it. His name, 'P.Norton', had been hand-written in large, generic block lettering with a thick black marker pen. There was no address and no postmark, confirming the sender had delivered it personally. Not for the first time, Peter wondered whether any local cameras had picked up the unexpected delivery.

He looked again at the letter. It was almost cartoonish in its construction, like a parody of what such a note should be. As though a child had written it, or someone who watched too many mysteries on television, and yet, somehow, it was even more threatening as a result.

Two questions kept spinning around his mind. Why had it been sent to him? And, because it had, did it mean he was now in danger? It seemed unlikely, but why else would someone go to such extreme lengths to conceal their identity?

Peter's thoughts turned to the Oldway Mansion Preservation Society and, not for the first time, he wondered whether the timing of the letter was significant. After all, it had arrived the day after his meeting with Conrad Macpherson. But he dismissed the idea of the retired military man sending it. It didn't seem like his style. Besides, what would be the point of sending such a mysterious note? Next, the intriguing image of Mavis Albright appeared in his mind. She'd already surprised him on a couple of occasions. Could he add this mysterious communication to that list? He guessed it probably qualified as direct, positive action but, again, if she'd sent it, what was the purpose? Then Peter remembered his interview with Hugh Farmer scheduled for later in the week. It was possible that could explain the timing. The series of interviews with Conrad and Hugh had been heavily previewed in the *Torbay Times*. Did someone want him to confront Farmer? But, if that was the case, it didn't slim down the list of suspects. Or provide any insights as to their motives.

As these thoughts raced around his increasingly weary mind, Peter realised that four of the words stood out more than any of the others. They were the only ones to be constructed entirely in bright colours and to feature no lower-case letters.

'Hugh Farmer Oldway Mansion'

He hadn't noticed it before and wondered now whether the distinction was intentional. He thought it could easily have been done sub-consciously by the sender. After all, those four words appeared to form the crux of the message. And just like that, the fog cleared. He finally understood what the note meant. Peter leaned back heavily in his chair and exhaled a weighty breath. Whoever had sent it was trying to point him towards some unidentified link between Hugh Farmer and Oldway Mansion.

Peter thought about the argument between Councillors Farmer and Hargreaves at the end of the last council meeting and the familiar, intoxicating tingle of excitement once again coursed through his body. He realised the link had to have something to do with the death of Councillor Hargreaves. What else could it be? Someone was trying to tell him the respected leader of Torbay Council had something to do with the death of his fellow councillor!

———•———

Later that afternoon, Peter entered Torquay police station with a noticeable spring in his step. The anonymous note and its envelope were stored safely in his rucksack.

He'd decided the note offered his best opportunity to get DCI Redhill's attention and finally secure himself a ringside seat to the Councillor Hargreaves murder investigation. Provided he could convince the inspector of his theories. That's why he'd come in person rather than simply phone. Redhill had dodged his calls too many times already and he didn't want to give him that option again. He was determined not to end up empty-handed this time.

To Peter's surprise, DCI Redhill appeared at the front desk within five minutes of his arrival. "Mr Norton, good to see you again. Please follow me." Bobby led Peter into an empty interview room just off the main reception. It was a small space, with just enough room for a single metal table and four metal chairs, two on either side. Despite the sparse decoration, Peter thought the room claustrophobic. The ceiling was low and there was no natural light, just a single bright fluorescent tube that made the skin on his face prickle like the mid-afternoon summer sun.

"What can I do for you?" Bobby pointed to one of the chairs on the far side of the table and took a seat in the one opposite. "The desk sergeant said you have information concerning the Councillor Hargreaves murder investigation."

"Potentially, yes. It's all a bit strange really. I'm not sure what to make of it to be honest."

"Well, you're here now. Spit it out and let me be the judge." Bobby's expression didn't change. If he was interested in what Peter had to say, he wasn't giving anything away.

Peter placed his rucksack on the chair next to him and carefully pulled the envelope out of the front pocket with both hands. "I received this yesterday. There's no postmark but it is addressed to me." He handed the envelope to the inspector. "Read the note inside."

Peter watched as Bobby turned the envelope over in his hands a couple of times before proceeding to take out the piece of paper it contained. He read it slowly and then checked whether there was anything else in the envelope. "When exactly did you receive this?"

"I found it yesterday afternoon, but I don't know when it was put through the door. It must have been after the postman had been on Saturday morning though. I recall checking the post around midday, as I was heading out. It wasn't there then, I'm sure of that."

"And what do you think it means?"

"It's a clue, isn't it? In the Hargreaves murder."

Bobby looked unconvinced. "How do you figure?"

"I told you about the argument Hargreaves had with Councillor Farmer at the end of the last council meeting. And Farmer's motive. What did *he* say about the argument by the way?"

"We haven't spoken to Councillor Farmer yet."

"Sorry, what did you just say?" Peter couldn't believe what he'd just heard. "What have you been doing this past week?"

"We have several active lines of enquiry, Mr Norton. None of which I'm at liberty to share with you. But rest assured, we are working through all leads thoroughly." He paused briefly. "Why do you think it was sent to you of all people?"

"I work for the *Torbay Times*, as you know. I've been covering the Oldway Mansion development and am now reporting on the murder investigation. Who better to send it to if you want to expose a murderer?"

"Why not go to the police?"

Peter thought about this for a moment. "Perhaps they don't trust you to investigate *all* leads."

"Very funny." Bobby turned the letter over in his hands and appeared to consider his next question carefully. "Okay, I can see why someone might send the note to you, but if they want to expose Councillor Farmer in some criminal enterprise, as you claim, why send you something so ambiguous? Why not just provide the evidence?"

"I'm interviewing Councillor Farmer later this week. For the paper. It's been well advertised. Perhaps they want me to confront him."

"That sounds like a sure-fire way to get you and that paper of yours sued. Are you sure this isn't just someone trying to get *you* into trouble?" Peter didn't offer a response so Bobby continued. "Chances are it's just a prank. Whether directed at you or Councillor Farmer, I think it highly likely it's just intended to cause trouble. But we'll investigate nevertheless. After all, it could be the real killer trying to muddy the waters. It does happen you know."

Bobby stood and looked at the paper in his hand. "I'll keep this for the time being. And I'd be grateful if you'd let me know straight away if you receive any more of these notes. Now, if that's all?"

Peter wasn't ready for the conversation to end. He hadn't achieved his main objective. "There was something else, actually." The words tumbled out of his mouth almost before he'd formed them.

"Yes?" The inspector sat back down although Peter didn't think he looked happy about it.

"I was over at Oldway Mansion on Friday, for a tour with the preservation society. It might be nothing, but I saw a sign advertising a Claude Knight Building Contractors on some temporary fencing. It struck me as potentially relevant, and I thought I should mention it."

Peter was sure he saw a glimmer of recognition accompany his mention of the building firm, but the inspector's expression was blank again when he spoke. "Relevant how?"

"It's not the first time I've come across that company in the context of my reporting on Oldway Mansion. They've done a lot of building work for the council since Councillor Farmer became leader, and it has recently come to my attention that they also have strong links to Justin King. It could just be coincidence, but…"

"We have several active leads, Mr Norton, as I said before. But thank you for the information." The inspector stood abruptly and walked over to the door without another word. The conversation was over.

———

Bobby was in the incident room when the call came through. A Peter Norton was in reception. He had information related to the investigation and would only talk to DCI Redhill. Bobby was sceptical and wondered whether it was just a ploy to get information not already released to the public. He'd not returned any of the reporter's calls. Perhaps this was just a new tactic to get his attention.

He checked his watch. According to DC Allegri, Grainger had only just popped down to the canteen for a late lunch having been to interview some of Hargreaves' contemporaries in the Torquay nightclub scene. Bobby was keen to hear what he'd learnt but guessed he had time to see what the reporter wanted first. Besides, he realised it could be important. Following the interview with Veronica King that morning, he knew he couldn't afford to ignore any potential leads.

When Peter handed over the envelope, Bobby didn't know what to expect although he still suspected some sort of ruse. As he opened the letter, the contents of the note hit him like a train. He had to read the words several times, slowly digesting them as his brain kicked into damage limitation mode. He knew it was most likely harmless, a childish prank, but the timing was suspicious. Hugh Farmer was well known locally, but the murder of Councillor Hargreaves had garnered national attention. With his links to Oldway Mansion, it was possible Farmer had been mentioned in those reports. Bobby knew he'd have to check. But first he needed to placate the reporter. The last thing he needed was Peter Norton running around undertaking his own investigation.

He tried to clear his head and was careful to look uninterested in the note. He needed to sound believable, even though he had doubts. He cursed himself for letting slip that he'd yet to speak with Farmer, but thought he'd dealt with that mistake well.

Bobby was anxious to get back upstairs and wanted to bring the meeting to a close as quickly as possible. But the reporter was persistent. The mention of Claude Knight was unexpected and caught him off guard again. Bobby had to grudgingly admit, the reporter had done his homework. And his instincts for this type of investigative work were impressive. It was clear Peter Norton was not some-one who could simply be ignored. Bobby knew he could cause trouble if left to continue poking around unchecked. And he now felt sure that he would. Bobby realised he'd have to keep a closer eye on the reporter from here on in.

CHAPTER 24

BOBBY WALKED UP THE STAIRS to the second floor deep in thought, but quickly forgot his concerns as he entered the incident room. There was a noticeable energy that hadn't been there when he'd left less than twenty minutes earlier.

Grainger bounded over as soon as he walked in. "Looks like we might have finally caught a break, sir."

"What's happened?" Bobby responded eagerly, desperate for some good news.

"Well, I was having lunch just now in the canteen with Jack Brady, from uniform. We play football together sometimes. He's a wicked striker. Scored this goal once…"

"Thank-you, Grainger. And this is relevant, how…?"

"Oh, yes, sorry, sir. He was telling me about a call-out he got last night. A drunk and disorderly at the Church House Inn." Grainger paused. He had Bobby's attention and it appeared obvious to the inspector he intended to enjoy his moment in the spotlight.

"Okay, Grainger, I'll bite." Bobby raised an inquisitive eyebrow. "As in the public house in Marldon? The one located just down the hill from Claude Knight's building yard?"

"That's the one, sir. And it was Claude Knight who'd had a few too many to drink."

"Interesting. Is he downstairs now, in the cells?"

"Unfortunately not. He wasn't arrested." Seeing the confusion on Bobby's face, Grainger continued. "He's a regular there apparently and they didn't press charges. I got the impression he's too good of a customer."

"Pity. I would have liked another word with him. On our patch this time and after him having spent a night in the cells. So, what's the story?"

"He'd been in the pub drinking since they opened at six that evening. We got the call just after ten, so he'd obviously had a fair amount. It sounds as though the staff just wanted some help to get him out at closing time. He'd started to get aggressive, going on about having a lock-in after hours. He's a big guy, as you know, and they didn't fancy their chances of getting him out if he decided he didn't want to leave. They didn't want any trouble, so, they called us."

"But, as you said earlier, that wasn't unusual." Bobby was trying to work out how any of this was relevant to the investigation. He wished Grainger would just get to the point. "Weren't there any locals in the pub who could help? Why call the police if you aren't going to press charges?"

"Jack did say there were a few locals about when he arrived, but none of them wanted to get involved apparently. He also mentioned it's not the first time they've been called out to deal with Mr Knight. It sounds as though they view us as there own private bouncer service where Claude Knight is concerned!"

"Okay. But how does the news that Claude Knight is an aggressive drunk help us with our investigation?"

"I'm coming to that, sir." Grainger looked down at his notebook despite not having referred to it up to that point. Bobby wondered whether it was for dramatic effect. "It's not the fact he was drunk, but what he was saying that's interesting."

"Go on."

"Apparently, he was talking a lot about Oldway Mansion. To anyone who'd listen. And plenty who wouldn't. It seems that he became quite a nuisance. A couple in the restaurant left early because of him and another group celebrating a birthday complained about him repeatedly coming over and disturbing them."

Bobby was starting to get impatient. "What was he saying?"

"That the development was definitely going ahead. In fact, he said he was celebrating. It's going to make his fortune apparently."

"We're sure that's what he was saying?"

"Jack's certain. Said he made a note of it afterwards."

"Interesting." Bobby thought about this information and how it fitted in with what they already knew.

"That's not what he told us last week, is it? He said the winning tender for the development work would only be announced next year, well after the council vote to decide whether the development proposals are approved. And that vote doesn't take place for another couple of weeks in any event. There's no way he could be so confident…"

"Unless he had some inside information." Grainger finished Bobby's sentence excitedly.

"You need to speak to those barmaids, Grainger. And anyone else who was in the pub last night. We need to confirm what Claude Knight was saying, and then we'll need to have another word with him."

Bobby stood still for a moment. The investigation seemed to finally be gaining momentum. He knew now was the time to double down on their efforts. He clapped his hands together loudly to quieten the room. "Okay, listen up everyone. We're starting to make some real progress here. We're close to uncovering the truth, I can sense it. But we need to keep pushing." He looked around the room at the tired faces and knew they wouldn't be able to keep the pressure up indefinitely. "Grainger and I went to see Veronica King this morning. She confirmed the affair, and we still can't rule out a crime of passion, but I want to focus on an incident that happened at a club the Kings owned in Leith, Scotland, around six years ago, before they moved to the bay. A young woman died after taking an illegal substance. It can't be a coincidence that Kimberley Hargreaves' friend died after taking drugs at a club somewhere in Scotland around the same time. That friend's death appears to have caused a falling out between father and daughter and now, just before his own death, our victim was allegedly using Veronica King to try to find out more about what happened that night at the Kings' nightclub. The two events must be one and the same, but I want it confirmed." He waited as pens wrote frantically on notepads. "What else do we have?"

Klara Allegri was the first to speak. "The phone company have finally come back to us with the details of that call Hargreaves received on his landline last Monday evening. Interestingly, it came from a payphone in Paignton, near to the train station. Who uses a payphone anymore? Unless you want to keep your identity secret."

Bobby nodded thoughtfully. "It sounds likely that it was our assailant arranging the meeting."

"I've checked and there's no CCTV down there, but uniform are going to ask around. It's a long shot, but someone might have seen something."

"Okay, good work. Grainger, did you get anything interesting from the current nightclub owners in Torquay? Any reason to think Hargreaves was still involved in that world?"

"Not really, sir. They all confirmed he left the industry well and truly behind when he sold his clubs. Several expressed surprise by that decision though. They hadn't seen it coming. Said it all happened very quickly. I got the impression they were disappointed more than anything. I think they looked up to him to be honest, like some sort of father figure."

"So, we can drop that line of enquiry as a priority?"

"Looks like it, yes."

"Anything else?"

"Only that they all described Hargreaves as ruthless. He had a nasty streak apparently. Again, they didn't sound bitter. If anything, I think they admired him more because of it. But it does suggest he was the type of man who could make enemies."

"It adds weight to the theory he rubbed someone up the wrong way. That revenge could have been the motive behind his murder." Bobby added this new information to the whiteboard. "All right, back to work, everyone." Bobby was about to head towards the door when Grainger stopped him.

"I forgot to ask. What did the reporter want?"

The inspector looked blankly at his sergeant. "Reporter?"

"Yeah, Peter Norton. You were downstairs with him when I got back from lunch, weren't you?"

"Oh, nothing important," Bobby replied vaguely as he continued to walk towards the door. "But I do need to speak with Councillor Farmer. Right away."

CHAPTER 25

PETER WALKED DOWN THE STEPS outside the police station in a bit of a daze. The conversation with DCI Redhill hadn't gone the way he'd expected. And he was still no closer to an inside scoop.

He couldn't decide whether the inspector had taken the contents of the note seriously. Peter thought he'd been dismissive and hadn't asked many questions. And then there was the admission he'd not even spoken with Hugh Farmer yet. Peter still couldn't believe it. As he walked back to his car, he couldn't shake the feeling he was missing something. That perhaps he'd been fobbed off somehow.

As he walked, Peter thought about it some more and began to wonder whether that was just how the inspector was. Cautious. Distrusting even. That he didn't like to give anything away. Particularly in connection with an active investigation. And certainly not to a civilian or, worse, a reporter! That certainly made more sense. Peter remembered that Redhill had behaved in a similar way on the first occasion they'd met, at Berry Head, on the morning of Councillor Hargreaves' death. He'd been aloof then and hadn't said much. But he had listened to what Peter had to say. And he'd kept his word. There was no reason to doubt him now.

By the time he reached the Audi, Peter felt a lot happier. He might not be any closer to his exclusive, but he had at least done the right thing by notifying the police of the note and his theory as to what it meant and why it had been sent to him. It was up to them what, if anything, they did with that information.

As he got into the car, he dropped his rucksack on the passenger seat and unzipped the main compartment. He pulled out his laptop and switched it on, turning on the mobile data function on his phone while he waited for it to load. This turned his mobile into a Wi-Fi hotspot and enabled him to log on to the internet from anywhere he had a signal.

He opened the internet browser and typed *'Robert [Bobby] Redhill, Police'* into the search box. Most of the results were reports of crimes where the DCI had been the senior investigating officer, although there was also a link to an article about a Patricia Redhill who'd died of breast cancer aged 42. She'd been a surgeon at Torbay Hospital. Her husband was named as Robert Redhill, 44, a police officer from Torquay. Peter read the article with interest. Next he found a LinkedIn entry for the inspector. It didn't look as though it was maintained and included little infor-mation, although Peter was able to learn that Redhill had originally served with the Greater Manchester Constab-ulary before moving to Devon in 2001. Peter checked the Devon and Cornwall Constabulary's own website, but it didn't include biographies of its personnel. Peter thought that made sense.

Peter wasn't sure what he'd been looking for, but the simple act of looking and not finding anything reassured him. He turned off the laptop, put it back in his rucksack and was about to start the engine and head home when he had another thought. He was near the offices of Torbay Council and, since he wanted to get hold of some informa-tion ahead of his interview with Hugh Farmer, decided he might as well kill two birds with one stone and head down there now.

He got out of the Audi and walked along East Street before taking a left at Palm Road which took him across to Union Street, from where it was a straight shot down to the council offices. He walked through the automatic double doors and approached the young man sitting behind the reception desk. Peter wondered whether he was on work experience. He didn't look older than sixteen or seventeen. And he appeared to be wearing his dad's suit. Although wearing might have been too strong a term. It was far too big for him. He looked like he was drowning in it.

The partly submerged child appeared to hold his breath as he slumped down in his chair, as though hopeful Peter might not see him. Although, in truth he was difficult to miss. He was gangly with straggly pieces of hair shooting out at odd angles from various clumps on his face. Peter guessed it was intended to make him look older but thought it succeeded only in having the opposite effect. Still, it did help to hide some of the blotches of angry red acne that pitted his skin. He looked absolutely terrified as Peter leaned over the desk and asked for his assistance.

After several false starts, including an initial denial that anyone by the name of Violet Danbury worked for the council, or that there was even such a role as clerk, the boy managed to find her details and phoned through to inform her she had a visitor.

Mrs Danbury appeared less than a minute later. She was dressed similarly to the way she'd been on Saturday. "Hello, Peter. I didn't expect to see you again so soon. At the council meeting on Friday, perhaps, but not before. How's the piece for the paper coming along? Do you need my help with something?"

"Hi, Violet. I hope you don't mind me popping by. I know you're probably very busy." Violet ignored the compliment, so Peter continued. "It's coming along well, thank you. It'll be in this week's edition. I really hope you approve." Still nothing. "I wanted your help with a related matter actually."

Violet looked at Peter warily. "Oh yes, what's that?"

"As I think you're aware, the interview with Conrad is the first in a series. You know, to address both sides of the debate."

"That makes sense," Violet agreed grudgingly. "Everyone has the right to be heard and to put their views across. What's that got to do with me?"

"I have an interview scheduled with Councillor Farmer on Wednesday. To get the pro-development perspective."

Violet nodded. "Councillor Farmer is very passionate about the development. Along with his friend, Mr King. I'm sure he'll put his case across very eloquently indeed."

"I've been doing some research, in preparation for the interview." Peter noticed Violet looking around the reception, perhaps for an escape route. Remembering she'd told him on Saturday how much of a stickler she was for accuracy, he added, "to make sure I have my facts straight and ask the right questions." Peter smiled hopefully.

"Go on," she said without much commitment.

"I've noticed Councillor Farmer appears to have a very close relationship with Mr King. You just mentioned it yourself, in fact. And I can see from the public records that a lot of the council's development projects since Mr Farmer became leader have centred around Justin King and his King Hotel Group, in one way or another..." Peter paused to allow Violet a chance to respond to the subtle accusation.

"They are close, that's true. And Mr King has been very supportive of the council since he moved here." It was clear that Violet wasn't going to say anything further, so Peter continued.

"I was hoping you could let me have copies of any council records related to those developments. You know, minutes, approvals and objections, that sort of thing. Anything in the public domain. I noticed, for example, that all three of the new King hotels have been built on land originally owned by the council. Public land in other words. And each of them valuable sites in their own right. One had been refused development over many generations, another was a cliff-top location with unobstructed sea views close to an established guillemot nesting site, and the third was a prime town centre location. I'd be interested to see whether any objections were raised and, if so, how they were addressed. A quick search of the Land Registry showed me that each of those sites I just mentioned are now owned outright by the King Hotel Group. There's no mention of Torbay Council retaining any interest in the land."

Violet looked at Peter quizzically but didn't respond, so Peter continued. "Each of those three developments pre-date my working for the *Torbay Times*. And I couldn't find anything online."

"Well, you wouldn't. Find it online, I mean. We're only just getting round to digitising our records." Peter looked at Violet inquisitively, waiting for her to continue, but she just stared back blankly. She clearly had no intention of making this easy.

"And the hard copy records?"

A pained expression suddenly formed on Violet's face. "Oh, I can't let you have those. Out of the question."

"But they're all part of the public record. There shouldn't be any privacy or confidentiality issues."

"No, quite right. They are part of the public record, technically at least. My reticence stems more from a practical issue."

"Which is?"

"We had a fire at our storage facility recently. We're still going through everything, but I don't hold much hope that anything survived."

The news was a blow but Peter knew there was no point taking out his frustrations on the clerk. These things happened. It wasn't her fault. Now that he thought about it, he recalled something about a fire being mentioned at a recent council meeting. And there'd been a short article in the paper. He hadn't paid either much attention at the time.

He was quiet for a moment, desperately trying to think of what else he could request to avoid this being a completely wasted trip. "What about the conflicts of interest register? I presume Hugh Farmer declared the nature of his relationship with Justin King before any of these arrangements were discussed and concluded?"

"Yes, of course. But the register does nothing more than record the existence of any personal interest a councillor might have in connection with the business to be discussed by the council. It doesn't go into any more detail than that. Councillor Farmer is a close friend of Justin King and, so far as I recall, that fact is recorded on the register as a permanent conflict of interest. That means he doesn't have to declare the same interest every time something new comes before council involving Mr King or his hotels group. It's good practice to have two lists, one for permanent conflicts and one that's project-specific. Just as well, really. Mr King's name is mentioned so often at meetings, it sometimes feels as though he's a member of the council himself!"

Having said his goodbyes, Peter walked back to his car slowly, preoccupied with his thoughts. *A conflict of interest…* Maybe there was something more to that. He thought again about the argument between Farmer and Hargreaves after the last council meeting. He was sure the councillor's death was linked to his opposition of the Oldway Mansion development proposals. He knew that he couldn't give up, no matter the obstacles. He'd just need to find another way to get the proof he needed.

CHAPTER 26

BOBBY WALKED INTO HIS OFFICE and closed the door behind him. The blinds were drawn, as usual, but the small anglepoise desk lamp next to his computer was on so the room wasn't completely dark. He walked around the desk and sat down in the high-backed leather swivel chair. He fidgeted noisily but couldn't get comfortable. Eventually, he leaned back and closed his eyes. He needed to think.

After several minutes he leaned forward purposefully and picked up the receiver of the telephone on his desk. He dialled a number he knew by heart and, putting the phone to his ear, briefly heard the familiar ringing as the connection was made. Almost immediately the call went to voicemail, as he'd expected it would. There was no personalised message, just four simple words: *'Please leave a message'*. He did so. One that was equally short and to the point. Then he replaced the receiver and leaned back in his chair. All he could do now was wait.

Just then there was a knock on the door and Grainger entered before Bobby could respond. "Dark in here again, sir." He flipped the light switch and the office's main fluorescent strip light immediately flickered into life. "We've had some information back on the accident that took out the traffic camera on the Brixham Road."

"Oh, yes, what's that?"

"As we know, the damage was caused by an articulated lorry colliding with the camera. It turns out the lorry was delivering a load of aggregate to the sewage treatment works in Churston. Foundations for a new storage unit they're building there. The local water board, which owns the site, ordered the aggregate from the suppliers, a Zambucchi Aggregates, directly. It was the supplier's lorry that had the accident. No red flags so far. What's interesting is that Claude Knight's firm is involved in the construction of the new building. They were engaged in connection with the groundworks."

"Okay, that's something else we need to speak to Mr Knight about. But why hasn't the camera been fixed? That accident was weeks ago."

"That's less clear at this stage. Although traffic cameras like that one are the responsibility of the local council."

Bobby nodded and was about to speak when Grainger continued. "There's something else, sir. We found details of an appointment on Hargreaves' phone. With Claude Knight. It was a couple of weeks ago now, at Hargreaves' house. Claude said he didn't know him, didn't he? I wonder why he didn't mention it?"

At that moment Bobby's mobile phone started to ring. He looked down at the number on the screen and then back to Grainger. "I need to take this. It's personal. Do you mind?" Bobby nodded towards the door and, for once, Grainger appeared to pick up on his meaning without further clarification. He slipped out the office without comment, closing the door quietly behind him.

"Thanks for phoning me back."

"It sounded important. Although I thought I'd have heard from you before now, in connection with Irving. But probably not on this number."

"I've been trying to keep you out of it, although you should expect an official visit soon."

"Okay. So, what's up?"

"It might be nothing, but I've just had a reporter from the *Torbay Times* come to see me. He had a letter with him that he claims to have received over the weekend. Well, not so much a letter, more a note. One where the words are constructed from letters cut out of magazines and newspapers."

"How odd. What's it got to do with me?"

"It was encouraging this reporter to look into your background."

"I see. What did you tell him?"

Bobby was surprised by the calmness in Hugh Farmer's voice. "I think I managed to put him off. For the time being at least. But I can't be certain he's going to drop it completely. He already thinks it might have something to do with Irving's murder and he's got the bit between his teeth. There's every possibility he might start poking around into your past, which is the last thing we need."

"I doubt he'll find anything if he does."

"Maybe not, but I'd prefer he didn't try in the first place."

"Who do you think sent it? Should I be worried?"

"I don't have any reason to be concerned. I haven't heard anything. You?"

"Nothing. It's probably just some crackpot."

"Let's hope so. The reporter mentioned he was interviewing you soon. Is that right?"

"What's his name?"

"Peter Norton."

"I'm doing a piece with the *Torbay Times* later in the week. I think it might be with this Norton fellow. I'm quite looking forward to it as it happens. It'll give me a fantastic platform to sell the wider economic benefits of the development."

"Well, be careful. He's no fool. He used to work for one of the big boys in London. Had quite a reputation as an investigative reporter, so don't underestimate him."

"I think I can handle it, Bobby."

"Just stay vigilant. We can't be certain he won't receive any more of those notes, or what they might say if he does. I've told him to let me know if that happens, but there's no guarantee he will. In the meantime, I'll reach out to a few contacts and see if you've been mentioned. You should keep your head down while we work out what's going on."

"Bit difficult in my position. Besides, this is a crucial moment for the Oldway Mansion development. I need to stay visible if we're going to be successful in getting it through the council vote. There's only a couple of weeks to go now."

"If you're sure. But remember, this murder is getting national coverage. You could be compromised."

"I don't think so, it's been too long, but it's a risk I'm going to have to take. Besides, I'm heading down to Plymouth tonight to watch the football. How much trouble can I get into down there?"

"I didn't take you for an Argyle fan, Hugh. I didn't think you'd be able to take sides like that. Not in your position."

"I'm not, and I can't. It's just business. Some friend of Justin King's has invited us to his box. I've not been before, but Justin assures me it'll be fun. But how much fun can Plymouth and Scunthorpe in the second round of the FA Cup really be?"

Bobby laughed. "I hear you, it's not quite Manchester City, is it?"

"Those days are long gone. For both of us."

"Yeah, typical isn't it? They only start winning when we move away and give up our season tickets."

"A lot has changed since then."

"You can say that again." Bobby was about to hang up when a question popped into his head. Always the detective, he never intentionally left any information off the table. "Who's the guy you're going to the football with? The one with the box?"

"Some local builder. A chap called Knight. Claude Knight, I think his name is."

CHAPTER 27

"WHAT AM I EVEN DOING HERE?" I've got a business to run. This is harassment. Wait 'til my solicitor is finished with you. You'll be lucky to get a job sweeping the floors at my yard!"

Claude Knight was red-faced as he stomped heavily down the corridor on the ground floor of Torquay police station sandwiched tightly between two police officers. Given his size, he towered over his guards who resembled a pair of scrawny, emaciated wings loosely attached to the side of an angry, overweight bird that had long since forgotten how to fly. Sweat ran down Claude's face and he brushed a chubby hand through his greasy, thin hair, forcing it to stand up in the middle of his head, like some sort of elaborate plumage.

After depositing their quarry in an interview room, the officers left Knight pacing alone in the confined space, his head bobbing up and down as his feet shuffled back and forth, like a chicken scratching the ground for food. His ramblings became muted as they closed the door behind them, although they were still able to make out the occasional shouted threat as they walked away down the corridor.

Bobby Redhill and Matthew Grainger watched Claude being brought into the station on a monitor, from the relative safety of the desk sergeant's office. They quickly decided to leave him for a while, hopeful that he might calm down, and headed off to the canteen in search of coffee.

They entered the interview room about twenty minutes later and sat down on one side of the metal table, across from Claude who was slumped quietly on a chair, apparently resigned to his fate. Or perhaps just worn out. His head was down, facing the table, and his shoulders were hunched forward. Bits of white spittle had dried at the corners of his mouth.

Bobby placed some papers on the desk and leaned forward. "Mr Knight, thank you for coming in to speak with us today."

"Didn't realise I had a choice."

"You always have a choice, but we'd obviously prefer you to speak with us voluntarily. We don't want to have to arrest you." Bobby chuckled, but it was clear from his expression that the words were meant as a warning rather than a joke.

"Do I need a solicitor?"

"Only you can answer that. Is there any reason why you think you might? Like I said, you're not under arrest. We just want to ask you a few questions concerning matters that have come to our attention in connection with the death of Councillor Irving Hargreaves."

"That's why!" Fresh bubbles of spittle began to form at the sides of Claude's mouth. "You keep going on about a murder. I don't know nothing about that. I didn't murder anyone. Why would I? Doesn't make any sense. You ain't gonna pin that on me. I hardly knew Councillor Hargreaves. What possible reason could I have for wanting him dead?"

Claude looked first at Bobby and then Grainger, back and forth one after the other, his head moving in quick, exaggerated movements like a spectator at a tennis match. He looked defiant and his complexion was starting to turn red once more. Bobby knew they wouldn't get anywhere if Claude continued to get agitated.

"Calm down, Mr Knight. No one is accusing you of anything. Not yet anyway. But you understand we have a job to do. For the moment, our investigation has led us in your direction. We need to ask you some questions and the sooner you answer them, the sooner we can all move on. Provided you had nothing to do with the unfortunate incident on Berry Head last week, you've nothing to worry about and you'll soon be able to get back to that yard of yours."

"Fine, go on then. Ask your questions and get this over and done with. I assume someone will give me a lift afterwards. I've no other way of getting back."

"Don't worry, we won't leave you stranded." Bobby gave a reassuring smile. "You mentioned just now that you hardly knew Councillor Hargreaves. That's not exactly what you said last week, is it?" Bobby checked some notes in front of him. "You told us then that you *'knew of him'*. That implies a passing recognition, he was a public figure after all, not that you'd met him. But we now have evidence that you went to his house recently. Is that true?"

Claude looked down at the table again, his anger now completely gone. "He made an appointment for a consultation. Said he was looking to build an extension and wanted a quote. That's what I spend most of my time doing now, the customer-facing side of the business. I swear I didn't know it was Councillor Hargreaves at the time. Not 'til I got there. I recognised him straight away though. Like you said, he's well known."

"Why didn't you tell us about this before?"

"I didn't think it was relevant. I was only there a couple of minutes."

"What happened?"

"Nothing. It was a waste of time. It quickly became clear there was no extension."

"What do you mean?"

"After I arrived, he took me into his office and started asking about some works I'd done years before for the council. He waved an invoice in my face and asked about various other contracts I've won over the years. There was no mention of an extension and I've checked since. There's no planning application and he's not spoken to any other builders. I told him what I thought of him wasting folks' time and left sharpish."

"What do you think he wanted to know?"

"No idea. The guy was crazy. I didn't know whether my life was in danger!" Bobby looked at the sizable frame of the man sat across from him and doubted he intimidated easily.

"You weren't remotely curious?"

"I don't have time to be curious."

"And you never heard from him again?"

"Never."

"Okay, Mr Knight. What do you know about the sewage treatment works in Churston?"

"What sort of question is that? I know what it is. And where. Who doesn't round here? There was a massive uproar when the council approved it being built there. All those poor folks in their expensive houses suddenly with a sewage plant at the end of their gardens. Your heart goes out to them, doesn't it? Although something didn't smell right about that decision. No pun intended."

"Okay, we're less concerned with conspiracy theories and more about your familiarity with the site."

"I don't have any."

"But your company *is* currently engaged in pre-paring the groundworks for a new storage unit they're building there?"

"Yes, so? That doesn't mean I'm familiar with the site, does it?"

"But you *have* been there?"

"To do the initial scope of works. That was months ago though."

"And I presume you know who Zambucchi Aggregates are?"

"Of course. We use them all the time. They're the main suppliers of cement and ready-mix concrete in the bay. Not much competition nowadays, mind."

"So, you have a close relationship with them?"

"I'd like to think so. We have a close relationship with several suppliers. It's the only way to operate successfully."

"What do you know about a collision between a Zambucchi Aggregates articulated lorry and a traffic camera outside the sewage works around four weeks back?"

"Might have heard something about it. It's a close-knit community. The guys talk to one another, you know how it is."

Bobby realised they weren't going to make any progress on the point so decided to change tack. "We heard you had a spot of trouble at the Church House Inn on Sunday night."

"What about it?" Claude suddenly sounded defensive. "I had a few too many drinks and got escorted out by a couple of your colleagues. No big deal. Not the first time it's happened and probably won't be the last."

"Why drink so much that night?"

"Why not? I get drunk a lot."

"And do you always shout about your business dealings when you do?"

Claude looked at the inspector curiously. "Possibly. What am I supposed to have said?"

"Several witnesses heard you bragging about the Oldway Mansion development. You were very confident about it being approved by Torbay Council. How could you possibly be so sure when the decision, a democratic vote among councillors I might add, isn't for another two weeks?"

Claude stared at the table and didn't offer an explanation.

"And I understand you've already secured the contract for the development works. Congratulations! I hear it's going to make you rich! I suppose that's cause for a celebration. Just one thing. I'm curious how you could know that when you've already told us the tenders won't be looked at until after the council vote." He paused and stared at Claude. The builder sat impassively, as though without a care in the world. "And didn't your assistant confirm that the successful tender won't be announced until the end of January next year? That's more than a month after the council vote and, by my count, still the best part of two months away."

Claude shrugged his shoulders. "What can I say? I'm a naturally positive person. And I talk a load of rubbish when I've had too much to drink. Ask anyone and they'll tell you the same thing. My friends normally just ignore me. I'm surprised anyone even bothered to mention it."

"So, for the record, you aren't denying what you said, simply the truth behind it. Is that correct?"

"Listen!" Claude banged the metal table loudly with his meaty fists and his beady eyes flickered with rage. "I don't know what I was saying on Sunday night. Or why." He sighed heavily and his shoulders dropped. As quickly as his anger had appeared, it was gone again. "The truth is I don't remember much of the evening. I only know the police escorted me out because someone mentioned it to me in the village the next day. If people told you that's what I was saying, I've no reason to doubt them. But I can assure you I have absolutely no way of knowing the outcome of the council's vote on the development, or the competitive tender process in the event the development is approved. How could I?"

Bobby shrugged. "You could have inside knowledge. I hear you're friendly with Justin King. Didn't you take both him and Hugh Farmer to the football in Plymouth last night?"

"That's no secret. Like I said before, this business is all about relationships. I entertain people at Argyle all the time. I have a box down there. And they weren't the only people I invited. There were ten of us in total, and a thoroughly enjoyable evening we had too." Claude suddenly looked defiant. "I don't appreciate what you're implying about my business practices. I'm not saying another word without my solicitor being present."

CHAPTER 28

THE HOUSE WAS A LARGE, detached property built in the Georgian style that was popular in this part of Torquay, off a tree-lined street built into the cliffs high above the town. It had a long driveway accessed between a pair of tall stone pillars, but there were no gates, a fact Peter thought strange. All the other houses on the road had them and, at this moment, they were all closed, presumably to deter unwanted visitors. They leant an air of exclusivity and a sense of mystery that was missing from Hugh Farmer's house. Peter wondered whether that was intentional. Hugh Farmer, man of the people.

As he turned off the road, he noticed a pair of ornamental stone eagles, one on top of each pillar. With heavily textured wings folded back dramatically behind powerful-looking bodies, it appeared as though the magnificent birds were swooping to catch their unsuspecting prey in sharp talons that extended down low in front of them. Given his suspicions about Hugh Farmer, Peter wondered whether that image might not be more prophetic. Danger. Enter at your own risk.

The only car on the drive was a small, cherry red hatchback. It was tucked in neatly by the side of the house, almost apologetically, as though the owner was trying hard to conceal it. Peter parked in front of a double garage, a separate structure which appeared to be a more recent addition, located to the left of the main building. The door was shut and he couldn't see inside.

He got out of the Audi and looked around. The three-storey house was characterful and imposing, with delightful proportions and a pleasing symmetry. Painted a pale cream colour, its white windows were flanked by matching shutters on the ground and first floors while two small dormer windows that looked like a pair of eyes protruded out from the slate roof, above the stone copings that capped the top of the house.

Several palm trees were dotted around the front garden which was otherwise laid to lawn. They left Peter in no doubt he was in a traditional, upper-class area of Torquay. Palm trees had been an exotic feature of the bay's public gardens and seafronts since Victorian times, providing some justification for its claims of being the English Riviera, but were far less often found in private residences.

Peter rang the doorbell and waited. When the door opened, an elderly woman greeted him with a half-smile that looked more like a grimace. She had thin, grey hair pinned up around the sides and back of her head with heavy metal slides and wore wire-rimmed glasses high up on the bridge of her nose, directly in front of sharp-looking eyes. Underneath a woollen cardigan with only the top pearl-effect button fastened, she wore a beige-coloured blouse. An ankle-length pleated skirt in a rich burgundy colour hovered above comfortable, black patent shoes.

Peter introduced himself and was informed that Councillor Farmer was waiting for him. The words were delivered in a clipped, accusatory tone, like Peter was late for the appointment. He automatically checked his watch, noting with relief that he was right on time.

He followed the woman down a long, narrow corridor to the back of the house. She walked quickly and Peter had to concentrate to keep up. Neither spoke. She knocked on a heavy wooden door and entered without waiting for a response. Hugh Farmer was sitting behind a mahogany desk that was covered in papers. He stood as Peter entered the room and extended a smooth, manicured hand in welcome. "Mr Norton. Please come in." Peter walked across the room and shook the councillor's hand. It was warm and dry. The grip was firm, but not overly so. Well-practised, Peter thought. As you'd expect from a politician.

"Make yourself at home." Farmer pointed to a chair in front of the desk. "Can we get you anything? Mrs Aiken will be only too happy to oblige." Peter looked at the woman who'd answered the door, the housekeeper presumably, whose expression suggested anything but happiness. He asked for a coffee, not wanting to disappoint. Black, no sugar.

Mrs Aiken disappeared through a different door to the one they'd used to enter. Peter hadn't noticed it before. There was no frame and the door itself was covered with the same heavily patterned wallpaper as the walls that surrounded it. A secret door. Peter had seen something like it once before, at an old country hotel he'd stayed in with Frieda.

"What a wonderful home you have here, Councillor Farmer."

"Call me Hugh, please. And may I call you Peter?" Peter nodded his agreement as the councillor continued. "I've seen you so many times at council meetings and the like, I already feel like we're old friends. I can't believe we haven't met before."

Peter smiled and took his seat. The councillor was certainly charming, and he appeared very relaxed. Could this really be someone who'd only recently been involved in the death of a colleague? Peter admitted it seemed unlikely. He watched as Farmer sat down in his chair and rested his elbows on the wide wooden arms, bringing his fingers together thoughtfully in front of his face in the shape of a pyramid. He suddenly looked serious. "This house was once owned by Benjamin Disraeli, the former British Prime Minister. That's what appealed to me, I suppose. I respect the history and wanted to safeguard it for future generations. Legacy, that's what's most important to me, Peter. Disraeli achieved so much during his time in office, if I can only achieve a fraction of what he did. I just want to do my bit. To try to make things better. For everyone."

Peter wondered if he'd stumbled into an election husting by mistake. "That's very commendable," he mumbled, although he doubted Hugh needed much in the way of encouragement.

"It's a peaceful place to live and work," the councillor continued. "You didn't mind coming here to do the interview, I trust. It's so much more comfortable than the council offices. Between you and me, they aren't what they used to be. Not since we moved out of Oldway Mansion. Does that surprise you, Peter?" He stared at the reporter who managed a non-committal shrug of his shoulders. "It shouldn't. I support preservation as much as those guys in the preservation society. We just disagree on the best way to achieve that objective. The upkeep of the mansion was too much for the council, Peter. What does that tell you? The only way to maintain its historical integrity is for it to pay its own way. And that means passing it over to the private sector. A hotel operator with deep pockets, now that's exactly what's required." The smile which accompanied these words appeared well-practised but not particularly sincere. "But we're getting ahead of ourselves."

At that moment, Mrs Aiken appeared in the room again, this time holding a silver tray laden with two individual cafetières, two mugs and two small plates of biscuits. She unloaded her offerings on the desk, one set in front of Hugh, the other in front of Peter.

"Mrs Aiken, what would I do without you?" Hugh smiled again, this time aiming a disconcerting wink in the direction of the housekeeper. "I'd be completely lost, that's what!"

Mrs Aiken displayed no reaction and quickly disappeared back through the secret door.

"I met the clerk of the council recently," Peter said, more as a means of keeping the conversation flowing than anything else. "I must have seen her a hundred times at council meetings, but I'd never spoken to her before."

"Oh yes, Mrs Danbury. Violet. What a marvel she is. Another in the Mrs Aiken mould. All too rare nowadays, unfortunately. I'm not sure what we'll do at the council when she goes. She's been there forever. Long before any of us councillors. Or any other members of staff for that matter. She keeps us on our toes, I can tell you. Rules us with a rod of iron!" Hugh chuckled.

"Is that right? She certainly struck me as a very…professional lady."

"That's the word, Peter. She can come across as a bit of a stickler, but she means well. And she's always put her job first. She'd have made a good councillor in that way." Hugh's overused smile was beginning to make him look slightly manic.

"She's retiring then?" Peter asked, although he already knew the answer.

"Yes, early next year. It comes to us all I suppose, although it really will be quite a shock. We all rely on her absolutely. Me especially. But we must look at the positives

and keep moving forwards. We still have so much important work to do. And there are certain…opportunities…
which arise with her retirement."

"Oh, yes," responded Peter, suddenly interested.
"Such as?"

"You heard about the fire which destroyed a lot of our
records, I suppose? Of course you did, we discussed it in
council." Peter nodded slowly and hoped there wouldn't
be a test! "Violet's given the council thirty years of dedicated service. That's quite something, particularly in this
day and age. The world has advanced greatly in that time,
but Violet has stayed delightfully consistent throughout. In
many ways there's something comforting about that. She
has strict procedures and protocols that haven't changed
in all that time. And she doesn't trust computers. A gen-
erational thing I suppose. *'You know where you are with paper,'*
that's what she always says." Hugh took a sip of coffee.
"Violet's departure, sad as it undoubtedly is, will allow us
to speed up the process of change and put new safeguards
in place to ensure nothing like the disastrous loss of our
historic records can ever happen again. The digitisation
of whatever survived the fire has already begun in earnest
and moving forwards everything will be recorded electronically. No longer will everything go through just one
person. Poor Violet's inadvertently become the gatekeeper
for everything that's gone on within the council over the
past thirty years. Even more so since the fire. It really is
too much responsibility for one person. I feel sorry for her,
I really do. But she doesn't complain. She's a proper stal-

wart." Hugh leaned forward slightly and spoke in a quieter, almost conspiratorial voice. "Although I think she probably enjoys it. You know, being needed. Since her husband left, I often wonder whether the council is the only real family she has."

It was suddenly clear to Peter that Hugh liked to gossip. That surprised him. Peter picked up a biscuit and took a bite, hoping Hugh would fill the silence. Chocolate digestives. A more grown-up choice than Conrad's eclectic selection. Peter wondered what a person's biscuit choices said about them.

"Although that might not be a bad thing," Hugh continued, still sitting forward, still speaking softly. "I'm not one for rumours, you understand, but since we're on the subject…" He paused, appearing to choose his next words carefully. "It was before my time, and I'm only repeating what I've been told, but her husband wasn't a nice man. A drunk and a womaniser!" Hugh's face contorted like he was chewing on a lemon. "Made poor Violet's life a misery by all accounts. But she put up with it. As you'd expect from someone of her generation. Stiff upper lip and all that. Anyway, one day he just disappeared. Walked out and hasn't been heard of since. She's better off without him of course, but that sort of thing has got to have an impact, hasn't it? It's almost inevitable she threw herself into her work."

Peter wasn't concerned with the direction the interview was taking. He'd learnt many years ago to follow the chain of thought of the person you're interviewing, however far off topic it went. You never knew where it might lead and, besides, Peter wasn't in any rush. If anything, this background was helping to explain Violet Danbury's slightly odd behaviour at Conrad's house last week. It was for those reasons he decided to keep the next question centred on the clerk. "I met Mrs Danbury when I interviewed Conrad Macpherson. He's the chairman of the Oldway Mansion Preservation Society. I'm sure you know she's the secretary of that organisation."

"Yes, they're lucky to have her."

"I'm sure. But doesn't that create any difficulties in your relationship? What with you being on opposite sides of the debate?"

"Not at all." Hugh leaned back in his chair, all business once more. His voice louder, more authoritative, as it had been when they'd first been introduced. "Differences of opinion are what life's all about. Debate and discussion, that's what's important. Violet knows that as well as the next man…or woman. And she can hold her own, believe you me. No, the council is broadly split down the middle on the Oldway Mansion proposals. Living with differences of opinion is just part of the job. Debate is encouraged within council and all views are welcome. It's certainly not a dictatorship where only my opinions count, I can assure you of that."

"And were you simply having a lively debate with Councillor Hargreaves after the last council meeting?"

Hugh's shoulders slumped forward slightly. "Aaah, you heard about that did you?" Not my finest moment,

Peter. I told you that I encourage discussion and debate, I didn't say that I'm always able to control my emotions. And Irving, may he rest in peace, was just the same. But he wasn't against landing the odd low blow, either. He was used to winning at all costs, I suppose. I'm sorry to say I let him wind me up. But we sorted out our differences before we left that night. Parted on good terms."

"Do you think Councillor Hargreaves' death will have an impact on the debate?"

"I don't see how. They've lost a very articulate advocate for their cause, but I can assure you, he wasn't the only one within council."

"His death does potentially tilt the balance in favour of the development though, doesn't it? That's if the informal vote taken at the end of the last council meeting is any indication."

"I wouldn't set much store by those informal votes, Peter. When you've been doing this as long as me, you know better than that."

"You don't think the vote should be postponed then, until a replacement for Councillor Hargreaves can be elected?"

Peter thought he saw a flash of anger cross the councillor's face. "Not at all. Oldway Mansion can't wait. This issue is too important, and the cost of waiting is just too high. I fear the mansion won't survive any further delay."

It was clear to Peter he'd hit a nerve. He was concerned now that Farmer might not be so open for the rest of the interview. And so it proved. Hugh was more guarded in his responses although he appeared to relax again after an effusive explanation of the development scheme's many social and economic benefits, which lasted a full twenty minutes. After deftly outlining a cost-benefit analysis of the proposed development which underlined the fiscal disadvantages to residents of the mansion being preserved solely as a tourist attraction, he excused himself for a few moments.

Peter took the opportunity to stretch his legs. He walked along a wall of bookcases laden with books of all shapes and sizes, casually fingering the spines of history books, leadership manuals and autobiographies of politicians and famous businessmen. Next, he wandered over to the mantelpiece behind Hugh's desk, to look more closely at the pictures displayed proudly in shiny silver frames. Hugh appeared in all of them, flashing the same manic smile Peter had witnessed first-hand on several occasions over the past hour. Peter recognised Justin King, the Mayor and several other local dignitaries.

As he turned back into the room, Peter saw the piece of paper Hugh had used earlier, during his explanation of the cost-benefit analysis. Leaning forward to take a closer look, his eye caught on another silver picture frame he hadn't noticed before. It was positioned to the far side of the bulky computer monitor, out of sight of anyone sitting in the chair on the other side of the desk. It was of a young woman. That intrigued Peter. He'd not come across any mention of Hugh's relationship status in the research he'd undertaken prior to the interview, and there'd been no suggestion of any children. Peter wondered now whether this woman might be the someone special in the councillor's life. He bent forward to take a closer look. She was a very attractive young woman. Not more than a girl really. He felt his stomach tighten and his breath caught. She looked very familiar. He thought for a moment and then took out his phone and opened the email his friend, Steve Earl, had sent him the previous week. On the morning of Councillor Hargreaves death.

The familiar likeness of George Best, the famous Northern Irish footballer appeared on the screen next to the notorious Manchester crime boss Steve had told him about. And next to Harry Bannister was, without question, the young woman staring back at him now, from the photo on Hugh Farmer's desk. Peter couldn't believe what he was seeing.

The young woman in both photos appeared identical: same confident pose, same clothes, same hairstyle and the same mischievous glint in her eyes. Peter looked more closely and thought he could make out the outline of Harry Bannister's shoulder at the edge of the photo on Hugh's desk. Yes, he was certain that the photo had been cut down from the one Steve had sent him. But why did Hugh Farmer have a picture of this girl on his desk? How did he know her and what links did he have to Manchester?

Just then Hugh's distant voice reverberated through the walls. Peter realised his host was nearby, in one of the downstairs rooms, probably talking with Mrs Aiken. He quickly took a photo of this new picture with his phone and was back round the other side of the room pretending to admire a monstrous painting of bold shapes and bright colours that Peter doubted even a child could be proud of, when Hugh appeared.

"I was just admiring some of your pieces, Hugh. Fascinating."

"Oh, thank you. I wouldn't say I'm a collector, but I know what I like."

Peter looked directly at the councillor. "I couldn't help but notice the picture on your desk."

The same flash of anger that Peter had seen earlier passed across Hugh's face but, as before, it was gone as quickly as it had appeared.

"I hope you haven't been snooping in my absence?"

"No, not at all. I haven't offended you, have I? I couldn't help but notice, that's all. She's a very striking young woman. I just wondered who she was, but it's none of my business. Please, forget I mentioned it."

"I'm sorry, Peter. I shouldn't have reacted like that. Forgive me. I just prefer to keep my personal life private. I'm sure you can understand. You're right, though, she is very beautiful." He paused, appearing deep in thought. "She's just someone I was close to a long time ago. A different world really." Hugh suddenly looked up, his eyes clear and focused once again. "Shall we continue?"

He sat back down behind his desk and gestured for Peter to resume his own seat. Peter caught him steel a glance at the picture of the young woman before he picked up seamlessly from where he'd left off with his eulogy about the most efficient ways to stimulate the tourist economy in the bay.

But Peter wasn't listening anymore. He was thinking about the mysterious young woman and trying to come up with some rational explanation for why her picture might be on Hugh's desk.

CHAPTER 29

PETER WOKE FROM ANOTHER RESTLESS night during which he'd dreamt more than usual, the image of the mysterious young woman invading his thoughts on an almost continuous reel while he slept. Each time it was the same scene that played out. He was back in Hugh Farmer's office. Mrs Aiken, the housekeeper was there, holding her laden tray. Only now, Mrs Aiken had become the younger lady. After serving the coffee and biscuits, she walked towards the secret door, as she'd done in real life. But now, after opening it, she turned towards Peter and beckoned to him before disappearing through the door which closed firmly behind her. When Peter tried to follow, he realised there was no handle, and he was unable to do so. He turned round to see Hugh sat behind his desk, pointing, and laughing at him.

Peter tore off the duvet and jumped out of bed. There was no point just lying there replaying the dream over and over. That wasn't going to achieve anything. He needed to do something proactive. He needed a plan.

After a long, hot shower, Peter went to the kitchen and made coffee. As he sat at the dining room table waiting for his laptop to load, he considered everything he knew so far. Hugh Farmer and Irving Hargreaves had been on opposing sides of the debate surrounding the future of Oldway Mansion. A debate that Peter had witnessed becoming increasingly fractious as the date for the final council vote drew closer. In fact, he'd seen both men having a heated argument, presumed to be about the mansion, at the end of the last council meeting, just four weeks before the crucial vote. Then, three days later, Irving Hargreaves had been murdered on Berry Head. Less than a week after that, Peter had received an anonymous note cautioning him against Hugh and encouraging him to *'look into his past'*. That same note appeared to link whatever was in Hugh's background with the Oldway Mansion development. For his part, Peter had brought the note to the attention of the police, but they had played down its relevance, suggesting it was likely just a hoax. Then Peter had discovered a picture of a young woman in Hugh's private home office. It was a photo he knew had been taken at some point in the 1980s in Manchester, in a bar frequented by a notorious local gang and in the original of which she was standing next to the gang's ruthless leader, Harry Bannister.

With his laptop loaded, Peter typed *'Harry Bannister, Burford Boys'* into the internet search engine. He read the articles that appeared with interest. Details of the gang's unofficial 'office' in the bar of the Shire, the building that Peter's friend, Steve Earl, was now renovating into a themed hotel, were mentioned as was their acquaintance with several of Manchester's more famous personalities, George Best included. The story behind Harry's moniker, *'The Torch'*, was laid bare in far more detail than Steve had gone into. One article provided a vivid description of numerous buildings that had been burned down during that time and a couple of still-smoking bodies that had been found on two separate patches of wasteland in different parts of the city, all attributed to the handiwork of Harry Bannister. One of the bodies was named as local man, Albert Henshaw, who was reported to have had an argument with Harry in a Manchester club the night before his body was found. The other belonged to a woman who'd tragically never been identified.

Peter was surprised to learn that, despite his alleged crimes, Harry had never been charged with a single offence, let alone prosecuted. The author of a different article speculated on the network of spies and culture of fear that had protected the Burford Boys and referenced unconfirmed reports of senior police officers and politicians being paid to keep the gang safe.

Peter then came across an article outlining the case that finally led to Harry's imprisonment on fraud charges. He read it quickly, with a hunger he hadn't experienced in more than a year and, to his surprise, what he read seemed remarkably familiar. By the early 1980s, the seemingly untouchable Burford Boys had branched out into financial crime. They acquired an option to purchase Lancaster Arcade, a derelict Victorian shopping arcade near Victoria train station in central Manchester and proceeded to secure significant grants from the city council based on promises to reinvigorate the area with a new mixed-use commercial and residential complex. Those promises perhaps inevitably proved hollow and went unfulfilled while the Burford Boys disappeared with two million pounds' worth of the council's money.

Peter read the article a second time and the embers of a theory started to glow in his mind. If Harry was in prison by the mid-1980s, the photo of Harry with George Best and the mysterious woman had to have been taken at some point before then, likely the early eighties based on George Best's appearance in the picture. He thought about the anonymous note he'd received – *'look into his past'* – and opened the picture Steve had sent, focusing his attention this time on the third man, the one standing on the edge of the frame. Peter still thought he looked startled, like he didn't know the photo was being taken. But, as he looked again now, Peter realised there was something strangely familiar about him. Was it the way he was standing, or perhaps his face? Peter zoomed in closer and noticed two moles on the man's left cheek. He'd seen someone else recently with similar markings. Hugh Farmer.

Could the third man be Councillor Hugh Farmer? Was it possible?

He did a quick calculation and thought the ages of both men just about worked. They could be the same person. He then remembered the story about the fraud that had finally caused Harry Bannister's downfall. A fraud involving council funds and an historic building. He had to admit there were similarities with the Oldway Mansion development proposals.

Peter wondered if it was more than just a coincidence. If Hugh Farmer had known Harry Bannister in Manchester back in the early 1980s, could he have been involved in the Lancaster Arcade development fraud?

He leant back in his chair and closed his eyes. The contents of the article that had mentioned police corruption tumbled heavily around his mind. He recalled the search he'd done on DCI Bobby Redhill a few days ago. Hadn't that reported the inspector working in Manchester prior to Devon?

Was that just another coincidence or could DCI Redhill be involved, somehow? Was he protecting Hugh Farmer just like the police had allegedly protected Harry Bannister all those years before?

And, if he was right about all of that, it wasn't a massive leap to think that Hugh Farmer could be responsible for the murder of Irving Hargreaves. If Hargreaves had found out about a fraud involving Oldway Mansion, a fraud masterminded by the respected leader of Torbay Council, that would surely be motive for murder. Hugh Farmer had far too much to lose for that truth to ever come out.

Peter recalled struggling to find any information online about Hugh Farmer prior to his becoming a councillor and he wondered now whether that might be significant. Could he be trying to cover his tracks by distancing himself from his past?

All the pieces seemed to fit, although he couldn't explain who'd sent him the anonymous note, or why. No matter, it was a minor point, and he didn't have time to figure it all out. Not at this stage. The council vote was in two weeks. After that, it could be too late. Peter knew he had to do something, and quickly. But he couldn't risk taking his theory to the police, he didn't know who he could trust. A large grin accompanied the realisation that he didn't need their help. He was an investigative reporter after all, and a good one at that. Or at least, he had been. In that moment Peter knew he was going to follow the story wherever it took him. And whatever the consequences. This was his chance to prove to himself, and everyone else who'd doubted him, that he wasn't finished yet.

He realised that to prove his theory he would need to establish that Hugh Farmer was the third man in the photo, and there was only one way he could think of to do that. He had to find the mystery young woman, or someone else from back then, who could verify the identity of the startled young man and confirm his links to Harry Bannister, the Burford Boys and the Lancaster Arcade fraud.

He picked up his mobile phone and called his friend, Steve Earl, in Manchester. Steve answered on the second ring.

"Mate, is that offer of a weekend in Manchester still on the table?

"Sure, what's up?"

"I need your help. You're probably going to think I've finally gone crazy, but this is what I need you to do…"

CHAPTER 30

Bobby Redhill stood at the front of the incident room just before eight on Friday morning ready to begin the daily briefing. The familiar aroma of strong coffee hung heavily in the windowless room. Today it was laced with the slightly sweet smell of stale sweat. Behind him, the white board was almost full, covered with names and faces that only two short weeks ago would have been alien to every member of the team but were now intimately familiar. Together they mapped out a detailed timeline of the key events in the case so far.

"Right then." A hush immediately descended over the room as Bobby started to speak. "We're approaching the end of the second week of the investigation. You've all done great work and gathered a ton of information." He looked proudly at each member of the team in turn. "We have several active leads and I want to use the time this morning to take a step back and recap everything we know so far. Afterwards, we can agree the areas we should be focusing on over the next few days. It goes without saying that weekend plans should be cancelled." There were a few groans, but no one appeared particularly surprised.

"Councillor Hargreaves," Bobby pointed to the photo in the centre of the board, "his body was found in the public car park at Berry Head around six thirty last Tuesday morning by a couple of teenagers who were there hoping to see the sunrise. We now know their involvement extended beyond merely finding the body. Before notifying the police, they phoned Callum Franks, local small-time drug dealer, who by chance was at a mate's house nearby. He came immediately to the car park where he searched our victim's car and stole his mobile phone. We've ruled out all three for the murder, although the CPS have decided to charge Callum with perverting the course of justice." This news was accompanied by universal nods of approval. "That mobile phone has proved to be a key piece of evidence, not least because Hargreaves unwittingly recorded his own murder. That recording gives us an accurate time of death and corroborates earlier conclusions reached from the autopsy and the traffic camera on the Dartmouth Road. Hargreaves was killed almost immediately upon his arrival by an assailant we believe was lying in wait for him. That suggests pre-meditation."

Bobby paused. No one disagreed with anything he'd said so far, so he continued his summary.

"We still don't know the purpose of the meeting although Hargreaves did receive a phone call at ten on the evening of his death. From a payphone near the train station in Paignton. We believe that was the assailant arranging the meeting for later that night. Again, everything points to this being pre-meditated." He paused. "So, we have a meeting in an isolated location in the early hours of the morning. That narrative suggests this could be about something illegal. But why would Hargreaves record it? Was he trying to protect himself? Perhaps he was intending to blackmail someone?" Bobby paced in front of the white board as he considered the next point. "This remains a key question and to answer it we need to know our victim better. Currently we have conflicting descriptions. One of a tough, no-nonsense businessman who splashed the cash, chased after women and fell out with his daughter over a casual attitude to drug use in his clubs. The other of a quiet, caring councillor who stood up for the rights of the common man. Who was Irving Hargreaves and what was his real motivation? Did he care about saving Oldway Mansion or was he playing another angle and, if so, what was it?" Bobby waited while the team finished taking notes. "Okay, suspects. Who else have we managed to rule out?"

"His colleagues on the council for a start," replied Dejay Merrali. "Well, other than Hugh Farmer, but you've spoken with him, haven't you, boss?" Bobby nodded thoughtfully but didn't answer directly.

"He was well respected," continued the young constable. "People admired his work ethic and valued his input.

He was one of the newer councillors, but most appeared to look up to him. He was always asking questions, wanting to know how things worked and whether there was a better way of doing them. I think he made his colleagues look good, to be honest. Although not everyone appreciated his approach. He had a few run-ins, mainly with the clerk. She's been in the role for thirty years and isn't used to being questioned. I've spoken with her and can confirm she's quite prickly."

"But there's nothing to implicate any of them?"

"No boss. Two of them, Councillors Danford and Newman, were a bit reticent to confirm their whereabouts at first, but they soon caved when I threatened to speak with their other halves. Turns out they were able to alibi each other." He raised an eyebrow and gave a knowing look. "I've verified it with the hotel they were staying in. There's also Councillor Freegard. He spent the early part of the evening with his wife at the members' spa of the new King Hotel in Torquay. He's not a suspect, but Mr and Mrs Freegard only became members recently, around the time he was reported to have changed his stance on Oldway Mansion from preservation to pro-development. It might just be a coincidence, but we couldn't find any evidence that either of them pay for their memberships."

"Interesting," said Bobby. "That might suggest some greasing of wheels. Give whatever you've uncovered to the local government ombudsmen, let them deal with it. Who else?"

"The four ex-wives," offered Klara Allegri. "None of them had spoken to the deceased in years and were very happy about that too. Three of them are remarried now and they all have alibis, boss, so no reason to think they had anything to do with it."

"Okay," said Bobby. "What about the current Mrs Hargreaves?"

"There was no love lost there. I don't think she'll be losing any sleep over his death, put it that way." Bobby looked at the female constable inquisitively. "They were in the process of getting divorced and it was getting very acrimonious," she explained. "I spoke to Hargreaves' solicitor who confirmed she was playing hard ball and trying to get every last penny she could."

"Is she a suspect? She'd inherit under his will I assume, as next of kin."

"She has a solid alibi, and Hargreaves had already changed his will. The solicitor thought his death would make it difficult for her to get anything."

"Who benefits now?"

"Everything goes to his daughter, Kimberley."

Bobby paused to look at the picture of Kimberley Hargreaves on the whiteboard. She didn't look like a killer, but he'd been around long enough to know appearances could be deceptive. And money could make people do surprising things. "What do we know about Kimberley Hargreaves?"

"On social media she calls herself an influencer," confirmed Freddie Allsop, "but in her case I think that just means she doesn't work."

"How does she afford to live in that flat overlooking the harbour?"

"Her dad's been paying her two thousand pounds a month for the last six years, ever since he sold his nightclubs."

"Anyone else think that's strange?" asked Bobby as he added this new information to the board. "Kimberley told us she hasn't really had a relationship with her father over the last six years, and yet he's been paying her a substantial sum every month throughout that period. Why would he do that?"

"Didn't she say they fell out over his views on drug use in his clubs?" asked Anna Christensen. "Could it have been guilt money perhaps? His way of trying to make amends."

Bobby thought about this for a moment. "It's certainly possible. Have we managed to confirm that Kimberley's friend died at the King's nightclub in Leith?"

"Yes, sir," said Grainger. "We've had it confirmed by the police in Scotland, but it looks like Hargreaves had already made the connection. We found several files on his phone. Links to newspaper articles and even a copy of the autopsy report."

Bobby was quiet for a moment as he considered this information. "Why was he so interested in that unfortunate incident? Everything seems to link back to it. It caused a falling out with his daughter who he's since been making significant monthly payments to. He also sold his night-clubs shortly afterwards before recreating himself as some sort of Good Samaritan, and we know he started a relationship with Veronica King recently, apparently with the sole intention of finding out more about what happened back then. What was he up to? We need to find out, and quickly." Bobby paused and consulted the whiteboard again. "That brings us to Claude Knight. Our victim had an invoice from Claude's building firm which links indirectly to Oldway Mansion as it concerns works they carried out on the new council offices before the council moved their operations over to Torquay. He'd also cut a photo of Hugh Farmer and Justin King out of the paper and had it blown up. Have we confirmed when it was taken?"

Klara raised her hand. "We traced it back to a picture printed in the *Torbay Times*. Three years ago, in August." She checked her notebook. "The sixteenth. It was taken at the council's annual summer drinks. There's nothing special about it and, so far as I can tell, Hugh Farmer and Justin King are both regular attendees."

Bobby nodded thoughtfully. "We'll focus on the invoice for now. It provides a clear link to Claude Knight, and there's something off about him. I'm convinced he's trying to hide something. What do we know so far?"

"He's owned the building firm for the past nineteen years," confirmed Freddie. "He joined the business right after leaving school at sixteen and worked as a labourer for a couple of years. Claude left school with a few GCSEs but clearly wasn't an academic so that all seems to track. What's more surprising is the fact that two years later he bought the owner out, becoming boss in the process. He changed the name soon afterwards. I've done some checking and the business was in financial trouble so that perhaps explains the timing, but there's no evidence of Claude's family having money, so it's not clear how he managed to afford it."

"Interesting," agreed Bobby. "Let's see what else we can find out about that transaction. It's quite a jump from labourer to boss, particularly at that age. What else?"

"He doesn't have a criminal record," confirmed Dejay, "but he was interviewed at Paignton police station back when he was still a minor."

"What about?"

"Allegations of bribery while he was a pupil at the community college in Paignton. All pretty unsophisticated. He supposedly threatened to tell the parents of some of his fellow students about them stealing sweets from the local shop, unless they paid him to keep quiet. One of the teachers found out and notified the police. Claude was interviewed but no one pressed charges. I think the parents were keen to brush it all under the carpet. None of their children came out looking good after all."

"Great work. We're starting to build a picture of Claude Knight. Go over everything again, in case there's anything we've missed. What about CCTV and the door-to-door?"

"Nothing of interest from the door-to-door," confirmed Anna, "and nothing on any of the private CCTV and doorbell camera footage either."

"I might have something, boss."

Bobby looked at Klara who was flipping through the pages of her notebook, a look of concentration on her face. "I took a call on the incident line about half an hour ago. From a local resident in Brixham." The page flipping stopped. "Yes, here it is. A Michael Choudary. He lives on Marina Drive and recalls seeing a car heading down the lane towards the car park at just after twelve thirty last Tuesday morning."

"Why has he only just come forward? Marina Drive was part of the door-to-door, wasn't it?"

"He was heading off to Heathrow at the time. Had an early flight to Germany. For work. He's only just got back and found the card we posted through his door asking for information."

"He hadn't heard about the murder before, from a wife or neighbour maybe?"

"He lives alone apparently. Said he keeps himself to himself."

"That sounds about right, sir," agreed Anna. "I recall the name. We put a card through his letterbox when we didn't get any response, but I know that none of his neighbours told us he was away."

"Okay. And he's certain on the timing, is he?"

"Yes, boss. He said he left home at exactly twelve thirty. The lane heading down to the car park is no more than a minute's drive from his house."

Bobby thought about this information. "That's too early to be our victim, but it could have been our assailant. We know from the recording that they were already in place when Hargreaves arrived. Was he able to give a description of the vehicle?"

"Not really. By his own admission, he's not much of a car guy. He did think it was a hatchback though. Possibly an older model. And he thought it was a dark colour."

"Go and get a statement. See what else he can remember. And press him for details." Bobby started to add this new information to the whiteboard. "It's not much, but it's the best lead we have. Afterwards, compare the description against the footage from the traffic cameras that were working that night. You never know, we might get a match. Our luck's got to change soon."

CHAPTER 31

A COLD WIND WHIPPED ALONG the concourse as Peter stepped off the train at Manchester Piccadilly station at eleven thirty on Saturday morning. He instinctively zipped up the collar of his jacket and nuzzled his face into the soft fleece lining. All around, people moved quickly, some hurrying to get connections, others headed to the exits. Peter stood still for a moment and watched the commotion unfold around him. It seemed appropriate somehow. The truth was, he didn't know what to expect from this trip, or whether he'd even find what he was looking for. In fact, he knew it was a long shot. Over thirty-five years had passed since that photo of George Best and Harry Bannister had been taken. There might not be anyone left from back then, and even if there was, there were no guarantees they'd be willing to talk to him. But he also knew he had to try. He was done spinning his wheels in Devon. It was time to take back control. Peter Norton, calmly seeking the truth amidst the chaos. He smiled at the idea of himself as some sort of dignified hero but, as he took a deep breath and strode confidently down the platform, he couldn't shake the feeling this was a make-or-break moment.

The taxi dropped him at the kerb outside Deansgate Locks. The bars that lined this trendy section of canal were already busy with people making an early start to their weekends and the gentle hum of conversation and laughter filled the air. Steve lived in a loft-style apartment in a converted warehouse a couple of minutes' walk away. Despite never having been there before, Peter found it easily enough. Steve was waiting and buzzed Peter up. "Do you want the grand tour, or shall we just get straight down to business?" Steve waved a piece of paper in his hand.

Peter gave his friend a bear hug. "I'm loving the commitment, mate. It's great to see you." He pointed to the now slightly crumpled piece of paper, "the results of the homework I gave you, I presume?"

Steve smiled. "After you called the other day I got in touch with a chap we used during the restoration of the hotel. He was like a consultant. He helped to ensure the décor was authentic and the photos we hung on the walls were all genuine, things like that. Anyway, he's lived in Ancoats all his life and knew Harry Bannister and the Burford Boys back when they ran the city." Steve held the piece of paper in the air triumphantly. "He's given me the names of five places where he thought we might be able to find some of the guys from back then."

"Great, but if he was around at the time, couldn't he just have given you some names directly, set up some meetings?"

"I did ask, but he refused. Even made me promise to keep his name out of it. Said he didn't want to get involved, that he'd kept out of trouble with the Burford Boys all his life and wasn't about to get on the wrong side of them now."

"I thought you said the Burford Boys disappeared after Harry Bannister went to prison in the eighties?"

"I did. And *they* did. But these things are all relative, right? The Burford Boys still hold a lot of sway in Ancoats, particularly among those who knew them in their heyday. Some people have long memories. I know you've read the stories of what they got up to, mate. Harry especially. Fear is a powerful weapon. I don't blame him for being careful. He wished us luck, but doubted anyone would talk to us."

Peter felt his stomach knot. Perhaps this was a fool's errand after all.

"I also asked him about that photo," Steve continued, apparently oblivious to the disappointed look on Peter's face. "The one with George Best and Harry Bannister. He doesn't recognise the girl but thought the third guy looked familiar. He couldn't remember a name but did say something about him being involved with the incident that led to Harry going to prison."

Peter made his friend repeat that, and a wide grin formed on his face as he considered the potential implications. If the third man had been involved in the Lancaster

Arcade fraud, and he turned out to be Hugh Farmer, his theory could be right after all.

They set out from the apartment and headed north towards Ancoats on foot. Steve said it would take around thirty minutes.

"So, you really think this Hugh Farmer fella could be involved with the death of one of his colleagues?" Steve asked.

"It's only a theory, but the pieces fit. I just need some proof, something to tie it all together."

"I'll admit it sounds crazy, but I've known you long enough, mate. When you get like this, you're usually onto something." Steve laughed. "And there was I thinking you were exaggerating when you said the story you've been working on for the past few months was exciting! Shows what I know."

Their first stop was a pub called the Greyhound which, according to Steve's source, had been a regular haunt of the Burford Boys back in the day. They found it easily enough, in the middle of a row of terraced houses about a mile from the Shire, but as soon as they stepped inside, they knew it wouldn't be much help to them. It had recently been renovated and was now a gastropub serving exotic lagers at seven pounds a pint and truffle burgers for fifteen. Sides extra. Besides, everyone in the place was under thirty. Peter's stomach knotted again. He wondered whether it was an omen. Either way, he didn't think it boded well for the rest of the places on the list. It certainly raised a question mark over the extent to which Steve's source still had his finger on the pulse of what was going on locally. He checked his watch. It was early afternoon and they had plenty of time so he ordered a round of drinks. No food. He hadn't seen Steve in over a year and if this was destined to be a fruitless search, he could at least make sure they had a proper catch-up.

The next couple of places on the list also proved a bust. One had been turned into a wine bar and the other specialised in gin. It claimed to sell over two hundred different types and, from the number of bottles that lined the wall behind the vast bar, Peter could well believe it. They had a drink in both establishments though, taking a recommendation from the barman in the gin bar rather than wade through the menu that was thicker than the average copy of the *Torbay Times*.

After finishing their gin and tonics, they moved on to the fourth venue on their list, a pub called the Lord Nelson. It was a mile or so from the Greyhound but a little closer to the Shire. As they approached, it immediately looked more promising. The brickwork was worn and the building itself appeared tired, as though it hadn't seen a lick of paint in more than half a century. It looked small, being no wider than the terraced houses that flanked it on either side. To the left of the front door, a large, square window faced the street. It was split into four smaller sections of glass by thin lengths of wood that crossed both vertically and horizontally. Each pane had a thick raised circle of glass at its centre. The design, which made it difficult to see through, was one Peter had seen in numerous pubs throughout the country. Not that he'd have been able to see anything in any event, the glass being covered with a thick layer of black grime.

The two friends hesitated on the pavement outside. It was quiet and there was no one around. Neither spoke but they were both thinking the same thing. It didn't look welcoming, not like the gin bar they'd just left.

Peter thought back to the station concourse earlier that day. *This* was why he was here. *This* was his destiny. He chuckled at the drama he was able to conjure in his mind, seemingly at will, took a deep breath and strode forward confidently.

The door opened directly into the minimalist confines of a single-roomed bar. It was like walking into a stranger's lounge uninvited, only more intimidating. As soon as the door opened, everyone inside stopped what they were doing and stared at the new arrivals. And the place was busy. They lowered the average age by around thirty years though. A good sign.

They made their way to a compact bar built against the back wall. The tables and chairs they passed on the way were all different sizes and styles, like the place had been furnished at an auction. All eyes followed their progress through the deadly quiet room.

The barman was probably in his sixties. He was tall and thin with a few isolated strands of unnaturally black hair combed over the top of his otherwise bald head. A stained tea towel was stuffed into the top of an equally dirty apron tied tightly around his thin waist with a frayed piece of string. Peter thought both items might once have been white. Maybe they'd been brought around the time the windows had last been washed. Perhaps they'd been used to wash them!

When they arrived at the bar, Peter nodded at the barman and ordered a couple of pints. *Nothing to see here, just two guys looking for refreshment.* It was almost as though he'd uttered some magic words and the other customers immediately returned to their conversations. Peter took a sip of his pint and tried to engage the barman in conversation. He asked about the pub and the local area but didn't get more than a monosyllabic grunt in response.

Steve tried next. He was the local lad, after all, so figured he might fare better. He explained how he'd overseen the development of the Shire and how fascinated he'd been by all the photos from back when the Burford Boys had used it as their unofficial headquarters. But there was still no reaction. The barman just stared absently into the middle distance as he polished a wine glass with the dirty tea towel.

Peter was looking around the room while Steve tried to engage their host. He couldn't be certain, but he thought that for a brief second or two the noise level in the bar had decreased a fraction when Steve mentioned the Burford Boys. Convinced he was just being paranoid, he quickly put the idea to one side and opened the photo of Harry,

George Best and the mystery man and woman, on his phone. He showed it to the barman and told him they were trying to find the young woman. Did he know who she was, or anyone who might? He zoomed in closer on the young woman's face and showed the barman again. Still no reaction. The barman continued to stare at something just below the ceiling, his eyes never flickering and not once looking at the phone. Again, Peter thought the noise levels had briefly decreased at the mention of the young woman. It was as though everyone in the bar was listening in on their conversation.

After a couple of further unsuccessful attempts at getting the barman to talk, Peter decided they should cut their losses and try the last place on the list. He had a suspicion that everyone in the bar probably knew who Harry Bannister and the Burford Boys were, but it was clear they weren't going to admit it. Perhaps Steve's source had been right. People were too scared to talk.

Before they left, Peter dropped one of his business cards on the bar, asking the barman to call if he should remember anything. He guessed everyone in the room had heard the request so didn't bother to canvass further. Silence once again accompanied their walk through the confined space. As they approached the door, Peter momentarily turned back into the room. All eyes were on him, except for the barman's, who was facing the other way. Peter noticed his business card was no longer on the bar, and he could have sworn he saw the barman putting something into the pocket of his apron.

CHAPTER 32

They approached O'Rourke's Snooker Club, the final venue on the list Steve's source had put together, with mixed emotions. They both agreed the Lord Nelson had been a promising lead, but the reluctance of anyone inside to speak with them served as a stark reminder of the difficulties they faced. Still, the several drinks they'd both consumed so far during their quest helped temper their frustrations.

The snooker club was located on a dismal-looking road, above a furniture store surrounded on both sides by boarded up units. The entrance was located round the back of the building, accessed from a car park that was almost empty. Luckily, the place was open. They climbed a dimly lit staircase to the upper floor where they entered a cavernous room which held around twenty tables, most of them in use. Low-level music played from overhead speakers and, refreshingly, no one paid them any attention.

They walked over to a bar that ran the length of one of the walls. There was a lone barman. He was younger than his compatriot in the Lord Nelson, probably somewhere in his forties.

"Snooker or pool?" he asked in a heavy Mancunian accent. He was a short, stocky gentleman, with powerful-looking arms bursting out the short sleeves of a heavily patterned Hawaiian shirt. A full handlebar moustache framed his mouth and complemented the thick, dark hair on his head.

"Neither. Not just now, at least." Peter leaned against the bar. "We're after some information, actually."

"Is that right? Suppose you buy a drink before we get to that?"

Peter ordered pints and waited as his new friend poured them. "So, what do you want to know?" he asked as he placed the drinks on the bar.

"We're trying to find anyone who was around in Manchester in the nineteen seventies and early eighties and knew Harry Bannister and the Burford Boys. Have you heard of them?"

"Oh, yeah, I've heard of them all right. Known them most of my life. This place has been in my family for years. I used to come here to help when I was younger." He made quotation marks in the air with his fingers as he said 'help' and added a tired-looking smile. "My dad was in charge then, God rest his soul. The Burford Boys were in a couple times a week in those days. Often gave me a few quid, for sweets or whatever. I thought they were great. Always had a big crowd with them. There was a real energy in the place whenever they were around. You could feel it." He smiled at the memory. "Excitement, I suppose you'd call it. Of course, I didn't realise back then that they never paid for anything while they were here. I could never understand why we didn't have any money when this place was always so busy. Only found out later, when I was older. Some of those guys still come in, from time to time. Still don't pay. My dad wouldn't want them to, that's what they tell me." He scoffed. "They live in the past, those guys… Still trying to trade on past glories. At least they don't come in very often now."

"Are they likely to be in today?"

"Not today, no. Manchester City are playing at home. They never miss a match, that lot. Even now."

The news was a blow, but Peter hadn't expected it to be easy. This was by far the most promising lead they'd had all day, he wasn't about to just give up and walk away. "I was hoping to speak with them. Do you know where I might be able to find them later, after the game?"

"You could try the Fox and Anchor in New Islington. It's a pub for City supporters. They usually go there after the game. Same as a lot of fans." The barman paused and looked at Peter with inquisitive eyes. "What do you want with them, anyway? They aren't the sort of people you just strike up a conversation with, if you know what I mean."

"I've heard the stories. But that was all a long time ago."

"If you say so." The barman picked up a cloth from underneath the bar and tossed it casually from one hand to the other. His face wore a serious expression, as though thinking carefully about what to say next. "I can see you're not from around here, so I'll give you some advice. These aren't people you want to mess with. Even now. They might be older, but don't let that fool you. They still have plenty of influence, particularly in this part of town."

"I appreciate that. And thank you. But it's very important that I speak with them. We don't want to cause any trouble. We're just trying to locate someone, and we have reason to believe they might have hung out with the Burford Boys back along." Peter took out his phone and opened the picture he'd shown at the Lord Nelson. "This lady."

The barman looked at the photograph carefully. "You police or something?"

"No, nothing like that. It's a personal matter."

"All the same, my advice would be to forget about this woman and walk away. While you still can. The Burford Boys don't like people asking questions about them, and they certainly don't appreciate people snooping into their past. Especially strangers."

Peter thanked the barman for his help, and his advice, but proceeded to ask what time City's football match finished. He also handed the barman a business card, in case he thought of anything else, or spoke to anyone who might be willing to talk to him. The handlebar moustache assured Peter that neither of those things was likely to happen, but did confirm the football match would finish at around seven thirty.

Peter looked at his watch and saw that it was only just after five. They had plenty of time. He figured they might as well play a couple games of pool while they waited. They paid for an hour on a pool table in the back corner and ordered another round of drinks. By the time their hour was up, they were both quite unsteady on their feet and, as they stumbled past the bar and down the stairs, they didn't notice the two guys who followed them.

It was dark outside and there were no lights on the pathway that ran along the rear of the furniture store. Only the waist-high metal railing that separated the path from the car park beyond guided their route back towards the main road. About halfway along the length of the building, Peter stopped suddenly. If you had asked him later, he wouldn't have been able to explain why. Maybe it was a primitive instinct, some call to survival, because when he turned round he saw two silhouettes looming up threateningly behind him. They were big, like the barman, but taller and wider. And there were no colourful shirts on display here. They wore serious, dark clothes, that matched the expressions on their faces. Peter immediately had a bad feeling.

"We don't want any trouble." He held up both hands in a gesture intended to calm the situation.

Steve had continued walking and was a few paces further along the path when the two strangers reached his friend. The first man pushed past Peter without breaking stride, forcing him to stagger backwards. He hit the brick wall of the furniture store hard, the impact knocking the wind out of his lungs and he automatically leant forward as he struggled to replace the missing air, just as the second man pushed him back violently by his shoulders, pinning him against the wall.

The second man's face was only inches from Peter's. The pungent aroma of cologne filled his nostrils and burnt his already dry throat. "Why are you asking questions about the Burford Boys?" The voice was surprisingly high-pitched.

Peter was still struggling to breathe and couldn't have spoken even if he'd known what to say. Fortunately, the guy didn't wait for an answer. "You don't know what you're getting involved with here, Mr Norton."

Hearing the stranger say his name sent shivers down Peter's spine. He suddenly realised how foolish it had been to leave his contact information behind after asking questions about Harry Bannister and the Burford Boys. His head was swimming. He wasn't sure whether from the lack of oxygen or the effects of the alcohol. Probably both, he concluded with a growing sense of dread. He thought he felt some movement around his waist but guessed his mind could just be playing tricks on him. His legs were numb after all, and his assailant's face was so close to his own that he couldn't move his head. He didn't know where the first guy was and had no idea how Steve was fairing.

"You need to back off. Now. Go home and mind your own business, or there will be consequences. We know your name. We have your phone number…and now we know where you live."

The man released the pressure on Peter's shoulders slightly, just enough to allow him to move his head. Looking down he saw a wallet discarded on the floor. The man sneered and his eyes flicked momentarily to whatever he was holding in his free hand. Peter's eyes focused slowly. The object was white and appeared shiny. It looked tiny in the guy's enormous, meaty fist. A driver's licence. *His* driver's licence. The realisation hit Peter like a powerful blow to the stomach and he sucked in a deep breath.

"If you know what's good for you, you'll drop this. You're way out of your league. Leave the past where it is. Poking your nose into other people's business isn't going to do anyone any good. Especially you. We can be very persuasive when we need to be. And next time, we won't be so nice."

Without warning, the man released the pressure on Peter's shoulders. Peter instinctively took a step forward, away from the wall, to steady himself, but before his foot could touch the floor, he felt a sudden, shattering impact on the left side of his face and his standing foot briefly left the ground. He landed heavily on the concrete floor a metre or so further back, his shoulders once more resting against the wall of the furniture store.

CHAPTER 33

PETER WOKE THE NEXT MORNING FEELING SORE. His back hurt from being forced up against the wall of the furniture store, his lip was painful from where he'd been punched and he had a throbbing headache unquestionably, he conceded, his own fault for having drunk too much. He winced as he swung his legs over the side of the bed, standing up carefully before walking with slow, considered steps to the bathroom. He stared at his reflection in the mirrored doors of the vanity unit above the sink. His face didn't look as bad as he'd been expecting. His left eye was partially closed and the skin around it was starting to turn an elaborate blend of bright yellows, dark blues and faded blacks, but the cut on his still swollen lip had already started to heal.

Not for the first time since last night, Peter chastised himself for having let his guard down. In some ways he knew it was understandable. He'd not seen Steve in ages and had been enjoying catching up. Even so, it had been stupid to have had so much to drink. He shook his head in embarrassment, or frustration, he wasn't sure which. Probably both, he admitted. He knew better than that. At least, he should have done. He certainly used to. Maybe he just wasn't up to chasing down the big stories anymore!

Standing in the shower Peter could almost feel the aches and pains leave his body as the hot water washed over him. By the time he walked into the kitchen, he felt like a new man. Steve was sitting at the breakfast bar eating a piece of toast. He looked at his friend cautiously. "How are you feeling?"

Peter grabbed a cup from the cupboard and poured himself a coffee from a pot on the counter. "Not too bad, surprisingly. The shower helped. It's probably my ego that's most badly damaged."

"It could have been a lot worse. I think we got off lightly."

"Speak for yourself!" Peter took a sip of his drink and grimaced theatrically as the edge of the cup touched the cut on his lip.

Steve shrugged. "If it's any consolation, I've got a stinking hangover."

After getting home last night they'd ordered delivery pizza and had sat up until the early hours discussing every detail of what had happened. Peter had been relieved to hear the first guy hadn't laid a finger on Steve, simply standing over his friend in a threatening manner to prevent him from getting involved. Peter had taken that as a positive sign. It suggested the Burford Boys were only interested in him. Not exactly great news but a relief in the circumstances, considering Steve had to continue living in the city. Peter felt bad enough already, he didn't want to cause his friend any further trouble.

They'd both agreed that it must have been someone from the snooker club who'd instigated the attack on them, with the Hawaiian-shirted barman the most likely suspect. He'd warned them off after all, and given them every opportunity to walk away, but they hadn't listened. In fact, Peter had made it very clear they still intended to try and contact the Burford Boys later that night at the Fox and Anchor. Perhaps that had forced the barman's hand and left him with no choice but to act.

"So, are you going to drop this now, mate?" Steve took a sip of coffee. "Last night you said you planned to sleep on it, but you can't seriously be considering still trying to speak with those guys, not after what happened? They clearly don't want to talk to you."

Peter knew his friend was right, but the events of the previous day had convinced him he was onto something, and he wasn't ready to give up at the first sign of trouble. The stakes had been raised, but they'd been high already. If anything, the Burford Boys' reaction to his asking questions had only made him more determined. "There must be another way of finding out who that woman is. Or the identity of the third man. We don't have to speak with the Burford Boys directly. After all, we never set out with the intention of doing that. Someone, somewhere in this city must know."

Steve didn't look convinced. "You could always go to the police." He stood to pour himself another coffee. "What about that inspector you showed the anonymous note to? You haven't told him about the photo you saw on Hugh's desk and how it links to the one up here at the Shire, have you? He might be willing to help. They have access to all sorts of information we don't. And they might have more luck getting information from the public, if it comes to that."

Peter was quiet for a moment. He still didn't trust DCI Redhill, although he didn't want to get into that with his friend right now. Just then his mobile chimed to signify the receipt of a text message. Peter took the phone out of his pocket and looked at the screen. It was from a number he didn't recognise. He opened the message and read it through a couple of times. When he finally spoke, his voice was full of intensity. "Listen to this, mate. It's from an unknown number. *I knew the girl you've been asking about. Do you want to meet?*'"

Steve looked at his friend sceptically. "I don't know. After everything we've learnt about the Burford Boys, what are the chances of someone popping up out of the blue and offering to speak with you?"

"We won't know unless we respond, will we?"

"It could be a trap."

Peter thought about this for a moment. "I don't think so. What would be the point? Those guys had their say last night. And they already know my name and where I live. It makes no sense for them to try to lure me into a trap now."

"I suppose you're right. But you should set the meeting place. Make sure it's somewhere you can control."

"You've watched too many spy films," Peter replied, laughing. He paused. "But it can't do any harm. You're the local round here. Where do you suggest?"

"What about the bar in the Shire? That would be quite poetic, don't you think? Since that's where the photo was taken."

"Like the story coming full circle?"

"If you say so." Steve smiled at his friend's theatrics. "But seriously, it's the perfect place. I know the manager and can get us a private table. Besides, the bar has only just reopened to guests of the hotel. There'll be no chance of those goons turning up without us knowing about it first."

———

Peter was in place at a circular table in one corner of the Shire's comfortable bar twenty minutes before the scheduled meeting. Three other tables were occupied by people enjoying lunch while a young couple shared a bottle of wine at a high bench positioned against the wall opposite. Steve sat alone at the bar nursing a lager shandy.

Peter saw her as soon as she walked in. She was petite, with fashionably cropped, short grey hair. She paused briefly in the doorway and looked slowly around the room before walking straight over to his table. "I haven't been here in donkey's years." She spoke quietly, the deep lines that shadowed her expressive brown eyes dancing with the delivery of each word. "It's been closed for a long time of course, but even before that I'd stopped coming. They've done a good job. It looks like it did back in its pomp. Only nicer."

Peter recognised her from the Lord Nelson. She'd been sat at a table close to the bar. "Why don't you sit down?" he asked. "Can I get you a drink?"

The woman shook her head. "I won't be here long." Peter waited while she placed her handbag on her lap and busied herself with something inside. "I'm Peter," he said gently when she finally looked up.

She started to fidget once more. "I'd rather not tell you my name, if you don't mind. The Burford Boys are still revered in these parts. It wouldn't do me any good if they were ever to find out I've spoken to you." She looked at Peter's face, as though seeing it for the first time. "But I guess you already know that?"

"I guess so." He carefully touched his swollen left eye. "That's fine with me. I don't want to get anyone into trouble."

"Visiting that pub yesterday afternoon wasn't very clever, if you don't mind me saying. It was full of friends and acquaintances of Harry and his cronies."

"That was kind of the point."

"Still, no one was ever going to talk to you." Her eyes flicked around the room constantly. "Not there, anyway. We all heard what you were asking Lenny." The barman, Peter presumed.

"Is Lenny responsible for this?" Peter pointed to his face.

"He let them know you were in the bar asking questions. Of-course he did. It would have looked suspicious if he hadn't. Plenty of others had probably already reported back within minutes of you arriving. But, no, you've only got yourself to blame for that."

"That's fair, I suppose. But he kept my business card? I presume that's how you got my number."

For the first time since she'd arrived, the woman appeared to relax. Her eyes settled momentarily on Peter. "I've known Lenny for longer than I care to remember. He's one of the good guys. Doesn't have much time for Harry or the Burford Boys, same as me, but he knows how to play the game. What he has to do to keep safe. I saw him put that card of yours in his pocket and asked him for it after closing, when everyone else had gone home." The woman suddenly looked earnest. "I couldn't speak to you yesterday. You understand that, don't you? But I heard you asking about a girl, and it got me interested. When Lenny confirmed the photo was of Emily, I knew I had to contact you."

Peter gave a surprised laugh. "I didn't think he'd even looked at it. Who's Emily?"

"Emily Jones. Do you still have the photo? I'd love to see it."

Peter opened the photo on his phone, the close-up taken in Hugh Farmer's office.

"That's her all right. Oh, Emily. Poor Emily."

"Who *is* she?"

"A lovely girl, that's who. At least, she was. So young and so full of energy. Beautiful too. But you can see that for yourself. Everyone loved her. It was her greatest gift, but also her biggest curse as things turned out."

Peter's heart sank. He guessed from the way the woman was talking that he wasn't going to get the chance to meet the mystery young girl, after all. "How did you know her?"

"We worked together. Only for a couple of months, but I'll never forget her. We were both hostesses. You know, serving drinks and keeping the punters happy. Most places round here had them back then, especially on Friday and Saturday nights. You don't see so much of it now, but it was a good job, and you could earn decent money with the tips and all. I hadn't done much at school and there weren't the opportunities for women back then like there are now. Emily was in the same boat as the rest of us girls, I guess. Not that she ever spoke about her family. I got the impression she'd fallen out with them, maybe run away from home. I never asked. Not my business."

She paused, apparently lost in her memories. Peter gave her a moment. He could see the pain in the woman's eyes. She took a crumpled tissue out of her handbag and dabbed at them gently. "I liked her. I was a bit older and could see she needed a guiding hand, so I took her under my wing. She was very trusting and with looks like hers got a lot of attention. But she never saw the risks. Not her fault, I suppose. She was young, and she was having the time of her life. She'd even met a young man who she was very serious about. She was happy, I suppose. But then she caught the attention of Harry Bannister and everything changed."

"What happened?"

"Harry was drawn to Emily immediately. She was beautiful, of course, but also young and innocent. Just the type he was attracted to. But, no, that wasn't it. The fact that every man in the room dreamt of being with her, that's what did for Emily. Harry had to have her, didn't he? Like some sort of trophy. It was just the way he was." The tears were running freely down her cheeks now and she made no attempt to stop them. "Not that Emily was interested. Like I said, she already had a young man, and they were very much in love. But you don't say no to Harry." The woman was quiet for a moment. "She didn't realise how things worked round here. I tried to warn her, but she wouldn't listen. She just thought I was worrying unnecessarily. Stupid girl." The woman shook her head in a slow, sad way. "She was too trusting. A fat lot of good that did her."

"What do you mean?"

"She disappeared. I have my suspicions, although nothing I can prove. All I know for sure is that one day she was there and the next she was gone. And afterwards, no one was allowed to even mention her name."

"What do you think happened?"

"Harry, that's what. She must have done something to upset him. He got rid of her, I'm sure of that."

"Got rid of her? How do you mean?"

"Some burnt remains were found a few days later, on waste ground in Salford. They've never been identified, but I know they were Emily's. Poor girl."

Peter remembered reading an article about Harry Bannister that mentioned two sets of still smouldering human remains, one of the victims, a woman, never having been named. "That's awful. I'm so sorry."

"It was a long time ago. But Harry did get a comeuppance of sorts. A few weeks later he was arrested for some fraud or other. He ended up going to prison. No one round here could believe it. He'd always been untouchable. No one was stupid enough to give evidence against him of course. But the police had proof, apparently. They didn't need anyone to testify. He served ten years and by the time he got out the Burford Boys were no longer top dog round here. Don't get me wrong, they're still powerful and still have influence, as you found out last night, but it was never the same as before. Thank God."

"What happened to Emily's boyfriend?"

"Oh, he left Manchester. Very soon afterwards as I recall. Never heard of him again. Not that I could blame him. The memories round here must have been too strong."

"What was his name?"

"Ben. Ben James. A lovely lad he was. Shy I guess you'd call him. The opposite of Emily really, but he was also ambitious and clever. They made a lovey couple. He worked for Harry. Well, I suppose everyone round here did in one way or another." She paused and looked at Peter's phone on the table. The screen had gone dark from where it had been left. "Can you tell me where you got it from? The photo, I mean. I haven't seen her face in over thirty years. I never imagined I would again. I thought all photos of her had been destroyed. Harry's orders."

"It's from here actually. Up on the wall." Peter pointed to a row of frames on the other side of the room. The woman stood up and walked over, as though in some sort of a trance. Peter followed a few paces behind. As she looked at the original picture hanging on the wall, her whole body began to shake. "My goodness, she was only eighteen when this photograph was taken. I remember the evening so well. Almost like it was yesterday. It's not every day you get to meet George Best though, is it? That was the night she first met Harry. And there's Ben, as well."

Peter did a double take. "Sorry, that's Ben?" He pointed to the third man in the picture. The one with the startled face who looked like he didn't belong. "Well, that's another mystery solved. But why are they standing so far apart? They look like they don't know one another."

"Well, they didn't back then. Not so far as everyone else was concerned at any rate. Their relationship was a secret. I was one of the only people who knew."

CHAPTER 34

PETER NORTON STARED THROUGH THE windscreen of his bright red Audi. The engine was switched off and it was quiet inside the car, reflecting the peaceful suburban scene outside. He was parked about two hundred metres from the entrance to Hugh Farmer's house and had a perfect view of his driveway. It was early, around seven, but he'd already been sat there for a couple of hours. That's how he knew Hugh was still inside.

After leaving the Shire on Sunday afternoon Peter had returned to Steve's apartment armed with two new names and a renewed determination to uncover the truth. He'd spent the next few hours online, trying to find out anything he could about Emily Jones and Ben James. He'd been about to give up when he stumbled across Ben James's name in an old newspaper article covering the fraud trial of Harry Bannister. It was only a brief mention, no more than a couple of lines, but it clearly referred to Ben as the face of the grant applications. He'd been the one who'd sat in front of the council bureaucrats and convinced them to part with hundreds of thousands of pounds in development grants.

As the early morning light lazily pushed back the night, the first dog walkers of the day began to appear. They remained only vague images on the periphery of Peter's consciousness as he thought back to the article he'd read yesterday. It had gone on to report that Ben James was entirely blameless, as much a victim in the whole sorry affair as the hapless council. *Blameless. Victim.* Those words tumbled around Peter's head like washing on a spin cycle. Then he remembered the former hostess saying that Ben had worked for Harry. If that was true, and he had no reason to doubt her, then how realistic was it to believe that Ben had no idea what Harry and the Burford Boys had really been up to? Peter thought Ben must have known the Lancaster Arcade development was a scam.

In fact, he was certain that Hugh Farmer was using his experiences as Ben James in Manchester all those years ago to try and defraud Torbay Council in connection with the Oldway Mansion development. And that he was ulti-mately responsible for the murder of Irving Hargreaves who, Peter guessed, must somehow have uncovered details of the nefarious scheme. These ideas had dominated his thoughts on the train journey back to Devon yesterday evening and had prevented him from sleeping last night. He'd finally got out of bed and, still restless, had gone for a drive to try to clear his mind. The roads had been empty and after driving around aimlessly for an hour or so, he'd found himself parked here outside Hugh's house.

While admittedly circumstantial, Peter thought the evidence he'd already managed to piece together was persuasive. Even so, he knew it wasn't enough to take to the police, or even Marcus for that matter. His editor would never authorise the publication of such damning accusations without first having hard evidence to back them up. No, he needed more, and he thought he knew how to get it.

The Audi's starter button pulsed in front of him. It felt like the car was challenging him. *I'm ready, are you?* Peter leaned forward and thumbed the control purposefully. He might only have a name, but that was more than he'd had last week. He pulled the Audi away from the kerb and headed straight for Hugh Farmer's drive.

The house was quiet and there were no lights on in any of the windows. The old hatchback he'd seen in the driveway last week was also missing. Peter guessed it must have belonged to Mrs Aiken, the housekeeper, and that she was yet to arrive this morning. He walked up to the door and rang the bell. Somewhere high up in one of the trees, a lone bird chirped a doleful song. Peter waited but when no one answered he rang the doorbell again, this time holding the buzzer down longer. Eventually he could hear muffled shouts through the heavy wooden door. It sounded like *'I'm coming'* but Peter couldn't be sure, so he rang the bell for a third time. The door opened almost immediately. Hugh Farmer stood there wearing stripy pyjamas and he didn't look happy. Or particularly awake. His hair stuck up at odd angles on one side of a puffy face lined with creases, as though he'd been lying on something with a similar texture.

"What are *you* doing here?" It wasn't a polite enquiry. "Do you know what time it is?"

"We need to talk," Peter responded calmly.

"We need to do no such thing." Peter thought he saw the councillor sneer. "We're not friends. You need to make an appointment like everyone else. And I don't fancy your chances of getting one anytime soon. Not after this little stunt." He looked down at his pyjamas and then back into the house, as though suddenly confused as to why he was standing there. "Where's Mrs Aiken when you need her?"

"We really do need to talk. Are you going to invite me in, or shall we do this on the doorstep?"

"Do what? I don't know what you're talking about. Have you gone quite mad? I should never have invited you here for that interview…"

"Councillor Farmer!" Peter's voice was loud in the silence of the early morning. "I need to talk to you about something very important."

Hugh peered out the front door cautiously, as though concerned Peter's raised voice might have drawn a crowd. "You'd better come in." He stepped back into the hallway and waited for Peter to enter before closing the door slowly behind him. "What's this all about?"

"Your past."

"My past? What are you talking about?"

"I'm talking about who you really are. About Ben James and Emily Jones." Peter saw a momentary flash of recognition on the councillor's face, overlaid with a flicker of fear. But, when he spoke, Hugh's voice was friendly, and calm. "Now, Peter, I don't know what you're talking about. Why don't you explain yourself? You really aren't making any sense I'm afraid." He flashed the familiar smile Peter had seen on several occasions last week as the polished façade of the seasoned politician returned. "I'm not sure whether that's because you got me out of bed and I'm still half asleep, or because you're talking nonsense." Another smile. "Now, who are Ben James and Emily…what did you say her name was?" Jones, was it?"

"Emily Jones, that's right. She's the young woman whose picture you have on your desk."

"Picture?"

Peter felt surprisingly calm. He knew the truth was going to come out. He was in control here, not Hugh Farmer. "Come now, Councillor, let's not play that game. You know very well what picture. You told me she was a friend from your past. Well, I recognised that photo and I saw the original this weekend up in Manchester."

"Manchester? What's Manchester got to do with anything? I don't think I've ever even visited…"

"I think you've done more than visit, Hugh! I think you used to live there. Or should I call you Ben?"

"Ben? Who is this Ben character?" Peter saw a flicker of concern in the councillor's eyes.

"Ben James. He was Emily Jones's boyfriend. They both lived in Manchester in the early nineteen eighties. Ben worked for Harry Bannister, leader of the Burford Boys, the local gang that ran the city at that time. Emily was a young woman who worked as a hostess at various bars across Manchester, including the Shire in Ancoats. She caught Harry's eye but wasn't interested because she'd already found the love of her life. Ben James. Or, should I say, *you*?"

Peter paused and studied the councillor's face before continuing. The smile was gone, and Farmer's eyes had glazed over slightly, as though he was remembering something, or someone. "She disappeared at a very young age, no older than eighteen or nineteen, soon after being introduced to Harry. Presumed dead. Murdered at the hands of the notorious gang leader if the rumours are to be believed. Ben, meanwhile, was the chief negotiator for a massive development scam that Harry had masterminded, and for which he ended up going to prison. Ben disappeared from Manchester soon afterwards, never to be heard of again. I've not been able to find out anything about him since." He paused for effect. "I also haven't been able to find out anything about *you* prior to your joining Torbay Council. A strange coincidence, don't you think?"

Hugh had regained his composure and stood impassively as the charges were read out to him. "I really have no idea what you're talking about. You obviously have quite an imagination, I'll give you that. It's a fascinating story, no doubt, but just a story nonetheless. I have no idea who any of these people are. The identity of the woman in the picture on my desk is of absolutely no concern of yours. And as to why there's only limited information about me on the internet, that's simply a reflection of how I choose to live my life. Not everyone has a desire to share their every waking moment on social media. Some of us still value our privacy. A concept your generation finds hard to understand, I know. I accept that as a councillor I am in the public eye, so tolerate an element of publicity, but only when it comes to my public role. Now, if you don't mind, I would like you to leave. You've forced yourself into my home at this ungodly hour and thrown around all manner of malicious and completely unfounded accusations. I've listened out of courtesy, but enough is enough! If you don't leave now, I will be forced to call the police and have you arrested for trespass…and intimidation." Hugh stepped forward and opened the front door. "And if you dare print any of this rubbish in that paper of yours, I'll sue both you and it."

Peter could see he wasn't going to get anything more out of Hugh Farmer. Not today anyway. Although he had him rattled. He was right, he knew it. He walked past the councillor slowly, but Hugh Farmer continued to look straight ahead, avoiding all eye contact with his accuser. As soon as Peter stepped outside, he heard the door slam shut loudly behind him.

CHAPTER 35

HUGH LOOKED OUT OF THE large window in the hallway and watched as the Audi drove away. The brake lights flashed brightly as it navigated the shallow right-hand curve in the driveway before it was lost to sight behind the thick, green hedge. He stood silently for a few moments as he decided what to do. He wasn't a man prone to overreaction, but the reporter had him worried.

He walked into his office, closing the door silently behind him, and picked up the photo of the young woman from his desk. He missed Emily every day, but that part of his life was over now. He *was* Hugh Farmer, not the boy he used to be. He'd made a success of his life, just like he'd promised Emily he would. He wasn't about to allow a small-time reporter ruin everything he'd worked so hard to achieve. He deserved the success he was getting. He'd certainly made enough sacrifices.

He ran his hands along the underside of the desk and clicked a small metal lever that unlocked a hidden drawer concealed above the kneehole. It housed an old-fashioned clamshell mobile phone. He picked it up and opened the contacts directory. It contained only a single number. He dialled and waited. A male voice answered on the fourth ring. It was quiet and carried an unmistakable hint of concern. "Is everything all right?"

"I'm fine, but we do have a problem."

"What's happened?"

"I just had that reporter at my house. You know, Peter Norton, from the *Torbay Times*. Uninvited, I might add. He knows, Bobby. What are we going to do?"

"What do you mean he knows?"

"Exactly that. He knows who I am, everything. He was asking about Ben James and Harry Bannister. He even knew about Emily. He's been up in Manchester apparently. Has quite the shiner, so I guess his questions weren't well received by our friends up there. It hasn't put him off, mind, not if his display this morning is any indication. Quite the opposite in fact."

"Tell me exactly what he said."

Hugh told Bobby everything that had happened that morning, starting with his being woken up by the reporter. And then he got angry with the inspector. "Why didn't you know what he was up to? We could have got in front of this if only you'd done your job properly. How could you not know he was going up to Manchester? This could ruin everything."

"Calm down, Hugh. It doesn't sound like he has anything concrete. He was just fishing, trying to scare you."

"He did a pretty good job, I can tell you. I didn't expect to hear those names again."

"I'll take care of it. Just carry on as normal. And don't talk about this to anyone else." Bobby's words were clipped, like he was annoyed. Hugh was about to say something, to defend himself, when he realised the inspector had hung up. He stood there quietly for a few moments, the phone still in his hand, and thought about how quickly life can change. Less than an hour ago he'd been on top of the world. Unstoppable. Now he was about to be exposed and everything he'd worked so hard for over countless years was in danger of coming crashing down. And yet, he realised that in many ways nothing had changed. The threat of Harry Bannister and the Burford Boys had hung over him like a dark cloud for most of his life. He wondered if it would ever end.

CHAPTER 36

PETER KNEW HE WAS IN TROUBLE as soon as he answered the phone. He'd been expecting the call, of course he had, he just hadn't anticipated it coming so quickly.

"What were you thinking, Peter?" Marcus's voice was angry. It brought Peter back from the thoughts that had been whirling around inside his head.

"Were you thinking at all, more to the point?" Marcus generally didn't raise his voice. It only really happened when someone, or something, was threatening him or his career. And Peter guessed a call from the chief constable of Devon and Cornwall Constabulary would probably fall into both categories.

"The Leader of Torbay Council! Why did it have to be *him* of all people?"

Peter decided not to interrupt. Better to let him get everything off his chest.

"He's got friends in very high places. The Chief Constable! They don't come much higher than that." Marcus was no longer shouting, in fact Peter thought he might be about to burst into tears. "He wasn't happy, Peter, let me tell you. And I have to say, I don't blame him. He made it very clear he holds me directly responsible for your actions. *Me*! I didn't know what you were up to. And I'd have stopped you if I had. Nevertheless, this is my problem now, and I have no intention of losing my job because of your mistakes. Do you understand?"

Peter thought now might be a good time to say something. "In my defence, Marcus..."

"Defence! What are you talking about? There is no defence, Peter." Marcus sighed heavily. "If it was just this thing with Hugh Farmer, I might have been able to help you. But Justin King called earlier to cancel the interview with us. Because of *your* actions. You know what a coup that was going to be. The powers that be aren't happy. I'm sorry, but there was nothing I could do."

The conversation had quickly taken an unexpected turn, and Peter was struggling to keep up. "What are you saying, Marcus?"

"You're being suspended, Peter, with immediate effect, pending a formal investigation into your behaviour."

Peter sat at his dining table in a daze. The small flat suddenly felt hot and he realised his forehead was covered with beads of sweat. He couldn't believe what had just happened. *'Suspended…Immediate effect…Investigation.'* The words rattled around his head like marbles in a bag.

He knew confronting Hugh had been impulsive. And he'd fully expected the Leader of Torbay Council to come out swinging. But he hadn't expected him to use the police to do his dirty work for him. Or to weaponise Justin King. He had to grudgingly admit that had been clever. With Peter sidelined, Hugh Farmer was free to operate with impunity. He'd won! The thought hit Peter like an unsighted punch to the solar plexus. He was convinced Hugh Farmer was Ben James. Now more than ever. But, as things stood, he was unable to prove it. And Hugh knew that. He'd been rattled though. When Peter had first mentioned those names – Ben James…Emily Jones…Harry Bannister – the respected leader of Torbay Council had recognised them. Peter was certain of that. And they had scared him.

Peter was onto something, and he wasn't the sort of person to give up easily. Besides, he no longer had anything to lose. Marcus had strongly advised him to drop *'his crusade'*, but Peter knew he was never going to do that. Even if it cost him his job. The truth was more important, and he was sure he knew what that was. Now he just needed to prove it.

CHAPTER 37

PETER PICKED UP A COPY of the *Torbay Times* from the pile on a low shelf in the corner of the convenience store below his flat on Wednesday morning. He stopped in his tracks as he scanned the headline on the front page.

'*Leader of Council takes a step back*'

He read it again, open-mouthed, before skimming the article that accompanied the headline. There was no mistake, Councillor Farmer had taken a leave of absence. With immediate effect. Unspecified personal issues were cited and no time frame was given for his return.

Peter threw some coins on the counter and raced back upstairs. He'd not anticipated this development and needed time to consider what it meant. He slumped down heavily on the sofa and read the article several times. The council vote to decide the future of Oldway Mansion was next week and Peter wondered how Farmer's unexpected move impacted that. The article provided an explanation. The vote was set to go ahead as planned, with Hugh appointing a proxy to vote on his behalf.

So, Hugh had managed to get himself out of the firing line with no apparent impact on his plans for Oldway Mansion. It felt like a fatal blow. Time was running out and with Hugh now in hiding, Peter had no idea how he was going to expose the truth about the Leader of Torbay Council.

He reluctantly made the decision to phone DCI Redhill. He still didn't trust the inspector but realised he was out of options. Peter needed his help although he didn't want to go to the police station. That was Redhill's turf, where he was in control.

DCI Redhill didn't appear surprised to hear the reporter's voice. "Mr Norton. What can I do for you?"

"We need to talk. It's important. But not over the phone."

"You know where I am. You've been to see me before. Feel free to drop in whenever convenient."

"Not the station. Somewhere neutral."

"You make it sound like we're about to have a duel." The inspector chuckled before suddenly thinking better of it. "We're not, are we?"

"This is serious, inspector!" Peter's tone was more heated than he'd intended, but the flippancy of the inspector's response had angered him. He could feel his cheeks starting to redden and he took a moment to compose himself before continuing. "Can you meet me on Torquay seafront in thirty minutes?"

"I'll be there," Bobby replied firmly.

———•••———

Peter was leaning against the Audi and staring out to sea when Bobby arrived. It was busy, despite being the middle of the afternoon, and cars were parked all along the road that fronted the beach. The detective didn't bother trying to find a space, opting instead to simply pull up next to the Audi and switch on his hazard lights. Horns blared loudly as he walked towards Peter.

"What's this all about, Mr Norton?"

"I want to talk about Hugh Farmer." He took a deep breath. "I want to know where he is and why he's suddenly disappeared."

"And what's that got to do with you? Or me, for that matter?" The inspector's face was deadpan, his response giving nothing away.

"I think it has more to do with you than you've been letting on. And it impacts me because I almost got beaten up trying to find out who Hugh Farmer really is."

"What do you mean? He is who he is!" Bobby looked closely at the bruise around Peter's eye. "Do you want to report a crime, because we really should do that back at the station."

Peter was frustrated by the inspector's attempts to stall him, so he decided to just lay out his theory and see how Redhill reacted. "Is Hugh trying to defraud the council through this Oldway Mansion development? Like he did thirty-five odd years ago in Manchester. When he was Ben James. With the Lancaster Arcade. Did Councillor Hargreaves find out what he was up to? Is that why he's dead? Are you covering up Hugh's involvement in his murder?"

Bobby stood quietly for a moment and watched as the seagulls circled in large groups above the gently lapping waves that took on a smooth almost creamy appearance where they hit the shore. When he spoke, the inspector's question took Peter by surprise. "What are you doing here, Mr Norton?"

"I'm here because of Hugh Farmer…"

"No, not here specifically. What are you doing in Devon? I've done my research. You had a great job in London with a respected paper. You were a proper high-flyer breaking important stories. No offence, but now you're working for the *Torbay Times*." He paused. "Maybe not even there anymore. What happened?"

"I'm not sure that's got anything to do with this."

"I'm not the enemy here, Peter." Bobby's voice was soft. Against his better judgement, Peter believed him. He sighed heavily.

"My editor refused to publish an exposé I'd been working on for several months. About corruption in the police force." Peter looked at the inspector, daring him to say something. When he didn't, Peter continued. "Two men died in custody. They were both young and healthy. There was no plausible explanation for their deaths. It reeked of a cover-up, but no one was talking. A few weeks later, I received an anonymous tip-off and followed the lead until

I uncovered the truth. The story was explosive. One of my best. But my editor buried it. Said it wasn't in the public interest." Peter was angry now. "The police had got to him. Or more likely his bosses. We had a frank exchange of views which ended with me deciding I couldn't work there anymore."

"Is that why you don't trust me?" Bobby spoke with a hint of disbelief in his voice. "Because I'm a policeman and, what, you think we're all corrupt?"

"It's not as simple as that. But I know you're not telling me the whole truth."

"Have you ever considered that I might be trying to protect you?"

"Are you saying my life's in danger…are you threatening me, Inspector?"

"Not threatening, no. Just telling you straight. This is much bigger than that paper of yours, and there's a lot more at stake than your reporter's pride. I can't say any more than that, but you need to back off, now. Let me get on with my job."

And with that Bobby walked back to his vehicle and drove away without a backward glance.

Peter watched him go, none the wiser as to what was going on, but more intrigued than ever. The inspector's reaction had been telling. He was getting closer to the truth. He just had to keep going.

CHAPTER 38

HUGH FARMER STOOD AT THE window in the compact kitchen of the small cottage and looked out at the wild, open moorland that reached to the horizon. He turned towards Bobby Redhill, clearly frustrated. "Is being stuck out here in the middle of nowhere really necessary?"

"It's just a precaution, hopefully it won't be for long, but we can't afford to take any risks."

"The vote on Oldway Mansion is next week. I should be canvassing my colleagues for their support."

"I know it's not ideal, but we've been through this. The murder of Irving Hargreaves has received national attention and now that reporter has been up to Manchester asking questions. We need to make sure you haven't been compromised."

Hugh looked around the room sullenly. "I don't see why I have to stay *here* though. Couldn't you have found somewhere a bit more…comfortable?"

"It's all I could organise on short notice. And it's perfect. Quiet and secluded."

Hugh appeared to be sulking. He stomped over to the farmhouse-style table and dragged one of the wooden chairs along the flagstone floor before sitting down heavily. "Just make sure I'm not here long."

Bobby sat down on the other side of the table, opposite the councillor. "There is something else we need to discuss."

Hugh looked up, suddenly interested. "Oh, yes. What's that?"

"Peter Norton."

Hugh scoffed. "He's the reason I'm stuck here. What do I want to talk about *him* for?"

"We can't underestimate him, Hugh. He's managed to put a lot together already. If we continue to ignore him, he's going to cause more problems, I'm certain of that."

"I thought he got suspended?"

"He did, but he contacted me yesterday asking to meet up. He's not about to back down. If anything, he's more determined than ever. He's throwing some wild theories about. We need to shut him down before he does some real damage. You know better than anyone how mud sticks."

Hugh was quiet for a moment. When he spoke, his voice was calm. "What do you propose?"

Bobby took a deep breath. "I have an idea. You're probably not going to like it, but I think it's the only way to get him off our backs, and to keep you protected…"

CHAPTER 39

THURSDAY MORNING AND PETER was once again parked on the road outside Hugh Farmer's house. It was early, like last time, although on this occasion he'd only arrived about ten minutes earlier. After confirming that no one was home, he'd hastily retreated to the warmth of the Audi to wait. It didn't take long. Five minutes later, the cherry red hatchback he'd seen parked in Hugh's driveway on his first visit, came into view in his rear-view mirror. It was moving slowly, down the centre of the road, it's headlights on full despite the growing brightness of the day.

He ducked down low in his seat, not wanting to be seen. Mrs Aiken was behind the wheel. She concentrated hard on the road in front of her as she passed and paid him no attention. After watching her turn cautiously off the road, Peter waited a couple of minutes before following her into Hugh's driveway. As he walked towards the front door, he noticed the hatchback parked close to the side of the house, just as it had been on his first visit.

Peter rang the doorbell, a short, sharp blast, and Mrs Aiken answered almost immediately. She was putting on an old-fashioned light blue housecoat. *Must be cleaning day*, Peter thought.

Peter gave a warm, friendly smile. "Good morning, Mrs Aiken. Do you remember me?" He didn't give the house-keeper an opportunity to respond. "Peter Norton, with the *Torbay Times*. I was here last week to interview Councillor Farmer. I'm sorry for coming round so early, but I only realised last night that I left my hand-held voice recorder in Hugh's office. After the interview." Another smile. "I called last night but there was no answer. Is Hugh in? I really do need to pick it up."

Mrs Aiken looked flustered. "I'm sorry, sir, but Mr Farmer is away. I'm not sure when he'll be back."

"Oh dear." Peter tried his best to look distressed. "I'm in serious trouble with my boss if I don't get it back. Is there any chance I could just pop in and check? I think I know where I left it."

"I don't know. Mr Farmer doesn't like anyone going into his office when he isn't there."

"I'll be quick, I promise." Peter leaned forward and lowered his voice in a conspiratorial tone. "And he doesn't need to know. I won't tell him if you won't." He stopped himself from winking. He'd seen how creepy it was when Hugh had done it last week.

Peter could tell from the look in her eyes and the way she tilted her head slightly to one side that Mrs Aiken felt sorry for him. She wanted to help. He was just a fellow worker trying to keep on the right side of his boss. They were in the same boat. People like them had to stick together. And perhaps the opportunity to do something against Hugh's wishes appealed to her. Maybe she'd been dreaming about it for a long time. Besides, Farmer would never find out. Where was the harm?

"Okay, but you need to be quick." She took a step back into the hallway and let Peter enter. At that moment, the phone started to ring. Mrs Aiken immediately looked torn.

"Don't mind me," Peter said jovially. "You carry on. Go and answer the phone. It might be important. I can find my own way."

The housekeeper didn't look convinced, but after a second or two considering her options, she nodded and scurried off into the back of the house. Peter checked his watch. He guessed he had three or maybe four minutes. Five at the most. It all depended how long Steve Earl, his friend from Manchester, could keep her talking. Peter was optimistic. He knew Steve could be extremely charming when he wanted to be.

Peter had phoned his friend last night with the outlines of a plan. He needed evidence to prove that Hugh was Ben James, and he couldn't think of a better place to look than Hugh's office. But, despite Hugh going AWOL, he knew gaining access to his home wouldn't be easy. He'd asked Steve to phone Farmer's house phone this morning, five minutes after his signal, and to distract the housekeeper, who he'd been sure would still be working despite her boss not being in residence, for as long as possible. He'd sent Steve a text outside, just before he'd started the Audi and followed Mrs Aiken into the drive.

Peter hurried along the corridor and entered the office through the same door as the previous week. Everything looked the same as it had done then. Somewhere on the other side of the secret door, he could hear Mrs Aiken talking. He couldn't be certain, but he thought he heard her laugh. A promising sign.

He got to work quickly, making his way straight for the desk. He immediately noticed the photo of Emily Jones was missing and wondered whether Hugh had got rid of anything that linked him with his past. But, on reflection, he thought it more likely he'd just taken it with him when he'd gone into hiding.

There were three drawers on either side of the desk, two the same size on top of one much larger at the bottom. There was nothing of interest in the first three drawers, just a load of old notebooks and assorted bits of stationery, so he moved to the ones on the other side. They appeared to contain more of the same, until Peter got to the large drawer at the bottom of the stack. He pulled it open to reveal a silver tray containing several bottles of whisky and a couple of stubby, thickly cut, crystal glasses. They had dense, heavy bases and long, thin triangular shards cut into the outside of the glass, starting at the bottom and shooting up towards the rim. Two of the bottles were almost empty. It looked as though Hugh liked a drink.

As he closed the drawer, he knocked the leather swivel chair that was pushed in tightly beneath the desk. It collided noisily with the central panel above the kneehole. Peter instinctively looked towards it and noticed that the panel appeared to be protruding further than the wood on either side. He pulled the chair out of the way and knelt down for a closer look. It was definitely out of line. He positioned his fingers either side of the raised panel, clamping it tightly, and pulled. To his surprise it moved. He realised it must be a drawer. Or a secret compartment. His heart started to race and he pulled harder.

Fully opened, it revealed a surprisingly large space. Not that it contained much, just a few pieces of what appeared to be blank paper. Disappointed, he was about to push the drawer closed when he stopped himself. It might have been the change of light as he altered his position above the desk, but he suddenly noticed the outline of various shapes on the underside of the top piece of paper. They seemed familiar. He picked it up and stood motionless. He couldn't believe what he was looking at. There were three pages in total. He picked up each one and laid them on the desk, reading them in turn.

They were just like the anonymous note he'd received. The words were arranged on the same innocuous, A4-sized white paper and had been composed using similar letters cut from a mixture of newspapers and magazines. Read together, they carried a message just like the one Peter had received, only these had clearly been sent to Hugh Farmer.

The first one said:

'I know your secret. Stop the Oldway Mansion development now.'

The second one read:

'I know who you are. If you want the truth to remain our secret you will pull out of the Oldway Mansion development.'

The third one was simpler. More final:

'Time is running out.'

CHAPTER 40

AFTER LEAVING HUGH FARMER AT the secluded cottage on Dartmoor, Bobby returned to the police station and went straight to the incident room on the second floor. He had a murder to solve and between them Hugh and Peter Norton were becoming distractions. To make matters worse, the Chief Constable was still on his back, threatening to bring in someone else to run the investigation if Bobby didn't make progress soon.

Grainger called over as soon as he walked through the door. He seemed excited.

"Where have you been, sir?"

"Just following up on a lead. Why, what's up?"

"Do you remember the description of that car we were given by Michael Choudary?"

Bobby nodded. "He saw it driving down to Berry Head car park on the night of the murder."

"That's right."

"It was generic though wasn't it? Dark-coloured hatchback. An older model."

"Yes, not much to go on, but we checked back through the traffic camera footage from that night and got an interesting match."

Grainger paused and consulted his notebook. *Inflating his part again*, thought Bobby. "And?"

"And a twenty-some-year-old dark blue Fiesta was caught going past the camera near Roselands, heading towards Brixham, just after nine on the night of the murder. We don't have it going back the other way."

"Who did it belong to?" Bobby asked the question sharply, frustrated by the time it was taking his colleague to get to what he presumed would be the good bit.

Grainger smiled. "Claude Knight."

Bobby thought back to the first time he'd met the builder and remembered the incongruous-looking hatchback parked under the mezzanine in the storage shed. He could feel the excitement growing in his stomach.

"There's more." Grainger appeared to be enjoying himself. "We've been looking into the invoice we found in our victim's home office. The one from Claude's firm that relates to renovation works undertaken at the new council offices back in 2013."

"I remember."

"Well, it turns out that one of the other contractors who tendered for the work filed a complaint."

"What about?

"They claimed the selection process wasn't conducted fairly. Apparently, they'd lost a few other council tenders to Claude's firm over the years and so, to prove that something fishy was going on, purposefully submitted a very low price. They were confident no one else would beat them because it would basically have cost *them* money to do the work at the price they'd quoted. When they didn't win, yet again, and the contract went to Claude, they were naturally suspicious."

"So…what, they thought Claude was being given inside information on the other bids? What happened?"

"Ultimately nothing. They withdrew their complaint, which is also strange, don't you think?"

Bobby nodded thoughtfully. "Particularly after going to all the trouble of setting their trap. How did you find out about this?"

"A couple of the councillors we interviewed remembered it. It was only mentioned in passing. We probably wouldn't have thought anything about it if Claude and that invoice weren't already on our radar."

"Okay, good work. Did any of these councillors admit to concerns that Claude Knight might be getting preferential treatment in the council's tenders?"

"No. And when the complaint was withdrawn, the council didn't investigate further. They did say there haven't been any complaints since though, so it could have just been a case of sour grapes."

"Have you managed to get hold of a copy of the complaint?"

"Unfortunately not. We asked to see their records, but it turns out the council suffered a fire a few weeks ago at their storage facility. All their historic records were destroyed."

"A fire? Interesting timing. Do we think that's suspicious?"

"It's possible. The fire started a week before they were due to digitise their old paper records."

Bobby looked at his sergeant thoughtfully, but he couldn't hide his excitement. This was the break he'd been waiting for. "See if you can track down the company that made the complaint. I want to know why they withdrew it. And get a warrant to search Claude's office. That man has got some explaining to do, and this time I want it done formally, under caution."

CHAPTER 41

PETER LOOKED AROUND THE TINY, windowless room and fidgeted anxiously. Just like the table in front of him, his metal chair was bolted securely to the floor. It was hard with sharp edges that stuck painfully into his back every time he moved. He hadn't been able to get comfortable since being dumped in the cold, clinical space around twenty minutes earlier.

Two uniformed police officers had picked him up at his flat around forty-five minutes ago and bundled him into the back of a marked police car. They hadn't said much on the drive to Torquay police station and he still didn't know what he was doing here, but he hadn't been arrested, he was certain of that. He stood up and started to pace around the room. It was now well after six on Friday evening and he wondered how long he was going to be stuck here for. He walked over to the door and tried the handle. It was locked. He doubted that was a good sign. In fact, he was beginning to think he'd been forgotten about when DCI Bobby Redhill walked purposefully through the door.

"Mr Norton." He was reading something and didn't look at Peter as he spoke. "Please take a seat."

"What's this all about, Inspector? The officers who picked me up wouldn't tell me anything."

"Just a few questions, shouldn't take long."

Peter looked at the inspector for any further clues but when none were forthcoming he waited quietly. He was back on Redhill's turf and didn't want to push his luck. Bobby continued to read from the piece of paper he'd brought in with him. When he'd finished he smiled at Peter. "Why don't you tell me what you were doing at Hugh Farmer's house yesterday morning."

"Who says I was there?"

"We've received a complaint from a Mrs Aiken, the housekeeper. She alleges you tricked your way into his home office before proceeding to rifle through his belongings."

"That's ridiculous. She let me in. And she has absolutely no reason to accuse me of rifling through anything."

"So, you admit you were there then?"

Peter laughed at himself for having fallen into the inspector's trap. "Okay, I was there. It's no secret." He held his hands up in front of his chest in an act of surrender. "I was looking for my digital recorder. I must have dropped it when I interviewed Hugh last week."

"I know that's what you told Mrs Aiken. But she's certain she's tidied Hugh's office on more than one occasion since the interview without finding anything. She's suspicious of your real motives, and I have to say, so am I. She also claims to have received a strange phone call just after you arrived. You wouldn't know anything about that, would you?"

"I don't know what you're talking about, Inspector. I went there to retrieve my recorder. I didn't want to get in any more trouble with the paper. Those things are expensive, you know."

"You were alone in the office for a full five minutes. What were you doing all that time?"

Peter shrugged his shoulders. "Not much. I found the recorder quickly enough but thought I should wait to say thank you to Mrs Aiken before I left. She went to answer the phone, like you said, and was gone longer than I expected."

"Mr Norton." Bobby was getting frustrated by the reporter's evasiveness. "We both know you didn't go there to get your recorder. For one thing, the interview with Councillor Farmer has already been printed. If your recording of the interview was missing, you'd have been in contact with Farmer before now." He leaned back in his chair. Bobby looked more comfortable on the hard metal object than Peter felt. Probably used to them, Peter guessed. When he spoke again, Bobby's voice was softer and his words more considered. "Didn't we just have a conversation about this, Peter? Can I call you that?" The reporter shrugged. "I asked you to back off and let me get on with my job. And what do you do? Less than twenty-four hours later."

Peter looked at Bobby defiantly. "Don't ask me to back off again, Inspector. You know I can't do that. I'm a reporter, it's who I am."

Bobby sighed. "I realise that now. But what do you think is going to happen if Hugh Farmer presses charges? Things could get very difficult for you. Particularly after that altercation with him earlier in the week. What are the chances of getting your job back then?" Bobby didn't expect an answer. He let the question hang in the air for a moment before leaning forward in his seat. "There is another option."

Peter looked warily at the inspector, unsure whether this was another trap. "Go on."

"I can't have you conducting your own separate investigation. You understand why, don't you, Peter? It takes my attention away from what really matters. So, my offer is one of cooperation. Something to benefit us both."

"Okay." The word dripped with suspicion as it slowly left Peter's lips.

"If you agree to drop your…interest…in Councillor Farmer, I promise to tell you the truth. You won't be able to print any of it, but it will put your mind at rest, I can assure you of that. And, as an additional incentive, I'll bring you into the Hargreaves murder investigation. As it happens, we're close to making an arrest. You could have the exclusive." Peter's mind was spinning and he didn't speak. "It'll be a great story, Peter. It should be enough to get you reinstated at the paper. I'll make it clear to your bosses that this offer is open only to you."

"I'm not sure what to say. Can I think about it?"

Bobby stood up suddenly. "Don't take too long. I'll be back in ten minutes for your answer." And with that he walked out the room and closed the door firmly behind him. It shut with a solid-sounding clunk and, once again, Peter found himself alone.

CHAPTER 42

PETER WAS PACING WHEN BOBBY walked back into the room. Twenty minutes had passed rather than the promised ten.

The inspector took a couple of short steps into the confined space but made no effort to sit down. "Now, about this offer. I haven't got all day."

Despite his best efforts, Peter hadn't been able to work out the DCI's motives for offering this olive branch. He still didn't trust him, but he remembered his editor's words from a couple of weeks back, just after the offer of an interview with Justin King had fallen in the paper's lap: '*we certainly shouldn't look a gift horse in the mouth*'. He realised he had nothing to lose by accepting, and potentially a lot to gain. An exclusive on the Hargreaves investigation was exactly what he'd been striving for. A real coup. That sort of opportunity could do wonders for his career. And it was sure to get him back in Marcus's good books. Peter was surprised by how strong a motivation that was.

"You've got a deal, Inspector." Peter had been standing, but now he sat down. He expected the inspector to do the same but watched instead as he walked back to the door and pulled at the handle. When it opened, Hugh Farmer was standing in the doorway.

"What's *he* doing here?"

Bobby responded as the councillor entered the room and sat at the table, on the opposite side to Peter. "You wanted the truth, Peter, who better to give it to you than *him*?" Bobby took the seat next to Hugh and leaned forward. He chewed on his bottom lip as though deciding what he wanted to say. "Hugh wants to tell you the truth. Not that he has any obligation to do so. He feels like you deserve it though, after all your…*efforts*. But everything he's about to tell you has to remain a secret. That's not open for discussion." He glanced at Hugh who was sitting impassively, just listening to the inspector's words. "You can't print a word of it, or tell another living soul. I cannot stress the importance of that enough. Now, do we have a deal?"

"I don't think I have a choice, do I?"

Bobby nodded and glanced at Hugh. The councillor took a deep breath and looked Peter straight in the eye. "You were right about Ben James. That was the name given to me when I was born, but I've been Hugh Farmer for so long now that it's Ben James who feels a stranger to me." He paused. "I was born in Manchester, not that I knew much about my family. I was abandoned at a young age, you see. I grew up in care. That's probably why I was so determined to make something of my life. But my ambition made me a target. Well, that and my naïvety. Those were two qualities Harry Bannister and his friends fed on. They lied to me. Used me to front their fraud."

"The Lancaster Arcade?"

"Exactly. I'd done well at school and had never been in trouble with the police. Not something everyone who'd come through the system could say. And I've always been good at relating to people. I've never been scared to stand up in front of a crowd and sell an idea. Not if it's something I truly believe in. I guess that's why I've done so well in public service. They took advantage of that though. I was just a kid."

"You didn't know it was a scam?"

"Of course not! Not at the beginning, anyway. I genuinely thought we were going to develop a run-down part of Manchester. That's what the council thought as well. They were excited by the vision I set out. But Harry never had any intention of building anything. He didn't give a damn about improving people's lives. He just cared about money and maintaining the status quo."

"But he ended up going to prison."

"He might have got away with it, probably would have, if it hadn't been for Emily."

"Emily Jones?"

"Yes." Hugh went quiet, lost in his thoughts. Peter gave him a moment with his memories. "We fell in love. I couldn't believe my luck. She was a couple of years younger than me, but we had similar backgrounds and connected straight away. We had such plans. I was going to be a successful businessman and together we'd have five or six children. A happy, stable family. The opposite of what we'd both experienced growing up." Tears started to run down both cheeks. Hugh rubbed at them with his sleeve and looked embarrassed. "I'm sorry. I've not spoken about any of this before."

Peter offered a reassuring smile. "So, what happened?"

"Harry Bannister, that's what. He decided he wanted Emily the first time he saw her."

"He didn't know you were together?"

"No one did. It was our secret. Something that only we knew. It gave us both a power we'd never had before. It sounds silly now, but it didn't at the time."

"So, did Harry find out?"

"I'll never know for certain what happened that night. I suspect only Harry really knows. Maybe one or two of his close friends. There was never any evidence to prove it, but I know he killed her. Human remains turned up a few days later. Burnt! I know they were Emily. He just dumped her on some wasteland, like a piece of rubbish." The tears were running freely now and Hugh made no attempt to wipe them away. "It was a Saturday night. We were in the Shire. Harry was there, as usual, along with the rest of the Burford Boys. Things were going well with the Lancaster Arcade and Harry was in a mood to celebrate. I saw him proposition Emily but she just laughed and walked away, as usual. This had been going on for a couple of weeks. I suppose that was enough for Harry. I saw his demeanour change straight away and he stormed out. A few minutes later I realised Emily was missing. I asked around. Some of the girls had seen her leaving with a couple of Harry's guys. That was the last time anyone saw her." He was quiet for a moment. "God knows what he did to her. I mean, why else would he burn her body? I just pray she didn't suffer too much."

"I really am very sorry, Hugh." Peter thought the councillor looked broken. "But how did you end up living in Torbay under a different name?"

"I was so angry. I knew what Harry had done, but I couldn't prove it. If I wanted to get revenge for Emily, I knew I had to be smart. By that stage, I was already having doubts about the Lancaster Arcade project. We were getting all these grants, but there hadn't been any progress on the actual development. It probably took me longer than it should have, but I got there in the end. I guess what happened to Emily helped to clarify things. I could finally see what Harry was really like. He didn't care about anyone else. We were all expendable. After Emily, I had no doubts he'd leave me as the scapegoat for the fraud."

"What did you do?" Peter was wide-eyed, hooked on every word.

"I took a leaf out of Harry's book. Only I acted first. I sacrificed him to save myself."

"You went to the police?"

Hugh nodded. "I had the records of the money coming in and where it had gone. This was all new to Harry, remember. The Burford Boys had been strictly old school prior to that. Extortion, protection, the occasional bank robbery. I'm not trying to belittle those crimes, far from it, but they were relatively simple. People-focused. And people can be intimidated and controlled. That's how they'd managed to get away with their crimes for so long. But investment fraud was an entirely different beast. And they didn't understand it. Not that they'd ever admit that. Too proud. But, that was why they needed me. And I used that to my advantage. There's one big difference between fraud and the crimes they were used to: the paper records. They couldn't be argued with. And no one had to testify to secure a conviction. I agreed a deal with the police to provide them with enough evidence to send Harry to prison in return for a new life."

"Witness protection?" Peter asked.

Hugh nodded. "Although I hung around for the trial. Even went to court a couple of days. I didn't want to run the risk of Harry and the Burford Boys getting suspicious and coming to look for me afterwards. I sat in the gallery with the other guys and listened to my name being mentioned as part of the fraud. Then, a few weeks after the conviction, I just left. They probably didn't even notice to be honest. They had bigger things to worry about. Harry's imprisonment had emboldened their rivals and the Burford Boys were busy trying to keep hold of what they had."

"I was his last witness protection officer." Bobby picked up the story. "Until around seven years ago, there was no national system. The service was operated by local police forces. It wasn't strictly necessary, but when Ben, sorry, I mean Hugh, relocated down here, he was joined by an officer from the Greater Manchester Police. The powers that be thought it would be helpful given the potential reach of the Burford Boys if they ever found out about his involvement in Harry's conviction. That officer retired in 2001 and I was his replacement. There hadn't been any rumblings about Ben James for over fifteen years by then, but Harry was out of prison and the top brass still wanted someone with local knowledge on the ground down here."

Peter appeared stunned by the revelations. "It's not often I'm left speechless." He suddenly appeared wide-eyed as he thought about the potential consequences of his recent actions. "I haven't caused any issues, have I? By going to Manchester and asking questions, I mean? With the Burford Boys. They aren't looking for you, are they?"

"No, nothing like that." Hugh's eyes were clear now and the colour had returned to his cheeks. "Ben James is still in the clear, so far as I'm aware. Although Bobby has me holed up in a safe house twiddling my thumbs." Hugh glared at the detective.

"With you stirring things up in Manchester, I had no choice. We couldn't take any risks while we determined whether there was any threat to his life."

Peter suddenly remembered the anonymous notes he'd found in the secret compartment of Hugh's desk. He couldn't work out how they fitted in, although he didn't want to admit having found them. He didn't want to give Redhill any excuse to go back on their deal. "What about that anonymous note I received?" he asked. "Are you sure that wasn't sent by the Burford Boys?"

Hugh chuckled. "I don't think so. It's a bit too subtle for them. I received a couple of similar notes myself, actually." Peter tried to look surprised. "I didn't take them too seriously. In my position I'm used to receiving all manner of threats through the post."

"I still think it's just some joker, trying to cause trouble." Bobby's face suggested he thought it anything but funny. "But we aren't taking any risks. Hugh will stay in the safe house until after the council vote next week."

CHAPTER 43

AFTER ARRANGING AN OFFICER TO take Hugh Farmer back to the cottage on Dartmoor, Bobby led Peter upstairs to his office. It was more comfortable than the interview room, and his back was starting to ache from sitting on the hard metal chair for too long. The door to the incident room was open as they walked past and before Bobby realised what was happening, the reporter was standing in front of the white board completely immersed in the details of the investigation.

"You can't be in here, Peter."

Peter looked around the room. "There's no one around. And you promised to bring me inside."

"I meant after we've made an arrest."

"Oh, yes, I remember. Who's the suspect?"

"You know I can't tell you that. Not yet. We're still waiting on a couple of warrants."

Peter shrugged. "I'm here now. Where's the harm? Besides, you either trust me or you don't."

Bobby sighed. "Okay, but we need to be quick."

Peter looked back at the board. "So, where does Violet fit in to your investigation?"

"Who's Violet?"

"Violet Danbury. She's the clerk of Torbay Council. And secretary of the Oldway Mansion Preservation Society."

"Nowhere, so far as I'm aware. Why do you ask?"

"You've got a picture of her on the board."

"Picture? What picture?"

"This one." Peter pointed at the photo of Hugh Farmer and Justin King that had been found in Irving Hargreaves' home office.

"That's Hugh with Justin King. Both of whom you know. It was taken at the council's summer party a few years ago. We found it in Irving's office."

"Yes, but that's Violet in the background." Peter took a step to one side and inspected a headshot of a large, angry-looking man. The name Claude Knight was written underneath it. "And if I'm not mistaken, that's Claude Knight she's talking to."

Bobby stepped forward. "Let me look at that." He inspected the photo carefully. "That's Violet Danbury with Claude Knight?" His voice was quiet, like he was talking to himself. "I don't think we'd noticed that before. We'd all been focusing on the two main subjects, Hugh and Justin King."

"Maybe they weren't what was interesting about the photo. You said you found it in Hargreaves' office?"

"Yes, along with that." Bobby pointed to the invoice that had been found alongside the photo, the one from Claude's building firm for renovation works at the new council offices in Torquay.

Peter looked at it excitedly. "So, I was right about Claude Knight's involvement? His name kept popping up, in relation to the council and Justin King. I thought it had to be important. Is *he* your suspect?"

"He's a person of interest, yes." Bobby looked at Peter carefully, a serious expression on his face. "An old model hatchback was spotted at Berry Head on the night of the murder, not long before Hargreaves was killed. Claude Knight owns an old-style Fiesta that was caught on a traffic camera headed towards Brixham that night. He's got some explaining to do."

Bobby ushered Peter out of the incident room and down the corridor to his office. He was relieved it was Friday night and the station was quiet. He didn't think anyone had seen the reporter looking at the white board. He knew the Chief Constable would have a fit if he ever found out.

They sat down either side of his desk. Bobby was deep in thought. He didn't know much about Violet Danbury and wondered whether that was a gap in the investigation. He remembered DC Merrali mentioning he'd spoken with her. She'd been interviewed alongside all of Hargreaves' work colleagues at the council. Bobby recalled the young DC had called her prickly. "You've met Violet Danbury. What is she like?"

Peter thought for a moment. "A bit odd, but harmless enough."

"Odd? Why do you say that?"

"Maybe that's not the right word. She was there when I interviewed Conrad Macpherson. He's the chairman of the preservation society. I hadn't expected anyone else to be present, but she made it very clear the interview would not be taking place without her being there. And she route-marched me out of the house when she wanted to leave. It was clear she didn't want me speaking to Conrad on his own." Peter considered this for a moment. "I did think *that* was odd."

"Did she have much to say for herself?"

"Not really, no. She said she was there in case Conrad needed assistance. That she knew more about the mansion than he did because she's lived here all her life. That was a strange comment, in retrospect. Having heard him talk, it's clear he's very knowledgeable on the subject. Perhaps more than her. He had some fascinating stories… Apparently, there are tunnels hidden under the mansion that aren't on any of the plans. They were used by the original owner to sneak his mistress into the house." Peter smirked. "Violet dismissed them out of hand. Said they were rumours with no substance, but Conrad seemed convinced. I got the impression he tolerates her because of everything else she does for the organisation."

"Such as?"

"Administrative stuff, I guess. Their website praises her thirty years' service as clerk of the council. They do seem very well organised for a group of local volunteers. I'd bet she's responsible for much of that. Conrad's a military man, which probably helps, but I reckon they generally do whatever Violet tells them to. I certainly did!" Peter laughed. "Hugh said much the same thing. She rules the councillors with a rod of iron, apparently. Although he thought she was probably just lonely. Her husband left her many years ago. Disappeared suddenly and hasn't been heard from since. Sounds like the council and Oldway Mansion are the only things she has to keep her occupied now. He was concerned about how she'll cope next year."

"How come?"

"She's retiring. The end of an era, Hugh called it. Still, after the fire that destroyed all their historical records, I guess it's long overdue."

At that moment, there was a knock on the door followed quickly by Grainger crashing into the room. Bobby hadn't realised his sergeant was still at work. The young detective stopped in his tracks when he saw the reporter. "Oh, sorry, sir. I didn't know you had company."

"It's all right, Grainger. What is it?"

"There's been an incident." He paused and glanced at Peter warily. Bobby nodded, indicating he should speak freely in front of the reporter.

"A body's been found. In Marldon. At Claude Knight's yard. From the initial description, it sounds like it might *be* Claude. And a fire has been reported at the same location. We need to get up there."

CHAPTER 44

BOBBY GUIDED THE VAUXHALL DOWN the hill towards the village of Marldon carefully, despite the urgency of the mission. In the backseat Peter was tutting intermittently and checking his watch every ten seconds or so. Bobby could see his exaggerated movements in the rear-view mirror. Grainger sat in the passenger seat looking bemused. He hadn't spoken since they'd left the station. Bobby regretted agreeing to the reporter travelling with them, but he knew he'd just have come anyway. This way he could at least keep an eye on him.

Bobby slowed even more as they approached the primary school and was forced to stop the Vauxhall completely soon afterwards as they came up behind a dense crowd blocking the road. The flashing lights from the emergency response vehicles lit up the faces of the assembled throng as they strained to get a glimpse of whatever was going on. The illuminated faces provided a strangely macabre backdrop to proceedings before Bobby, Grainger and Peter had got near the actual crime scene.

The trio got out of the car and pushed themselves through the sea of people. Bobby was surprised to see that several onlookers – if their comfortable and, in some cases, inappropriately suggestive attire was any indication – had vacated their beds to join the friendly mob.

As he struggled through the crowd, Bobby heard fanciful reports of at least two different crimes that were rumoured to have taken place that evening. Someone told him excitedly that there was an active hostage situation involving the Roberts family, Mr Roberts having apparently just found out about his wife's infidelity with the mechanic at the local garage. *What took him so long?* appeared to be the consensus view. Certainly, the majority were rooting for the scorned husband who was reported to have barricaded himself in the kitchen of the family home. Another villager passed on the rumour that a raid had taken place on a secret cannabis farm that had been discovered in the basement of the abandoned home formerly owned by the Jenkins family. The illegal activity had apparently only come to light after the high-powered heating lamps used to grow the plants had set the building on fire.

Bobby was pleased to reach the police cordon and ducked under it enthusiastically. Progress was easier from this point and, after rounding a shallow bend in the lane, the three men were confronted by a warm yellow glow emanating from Claude's yard. As they got closer, Bobby stopped and shielded his eyes against the glare of the powerful spotlights that had been set up to illuminate the area. It was like walking from night to day. The imposing cliffs that enclosed the yard on three sides magnified the light while appearing to hold it close, caressing it like a mother might her child. His eyes took a moment to adjust, but the familiar space soon revealed itself to him.

The gates to the yard had been pushed wide open and two fire engines were parked just inside. Firefighters buzzed all around, as hoses sprayed water on the still smouldering remains of Claude's cliff-top office. Bobby looked around and saw Faith Andrews, the forensic pathologist, at the foot of the stone steps. She was struggling with a large plastic sheet which she appeared to be attempting to use to cover the body that lay at her feet. Bobby winced as he saw the torrent of water flooding down the steps. Whatever evidence there might have been was probably halfway down the lane by now.

Bobby made his way towards her. It was a cold night, but he unbuttoned the top half of his overcoat as he walked.

"What do you have for us this time, Faith?"

"Hey, Bobby," she said breezily. "I didn't think I'd be seeing you again so soon."

She appeared to be wearing a large, padded jacket underneath her forensic coveralls and Bobby could see a glimpse of a stripy beanie hat under the integrated hood. The hat was pulled down tightly around her face, but she still looked cold.

"Can you give me a hand with this?" She nodded at the plastic sheet. "We've taken photos of the body, but I want to cover it up to protect whatever evidence might be left. There's a lot of water around." She tilted her head in the direction of the fire engines, as though Bobby might have missed them. "He's completely soaked. I doubt we'll get much from him, but we have to try."

Bobby leaned over the body and looked at the contorted expression still visible on the heavily cut face. It was definitely Claude Knight. "If you've got photos, you might as well move him. As you say, the longer he stays here, the less chance we have of collecting any evidence."

"Okay, great. Thanks Bobby." She signalled to a couple of her colleagues to move the body. "Shall we say tomorrow afternoon for the autopsy?"

Bobby nodded. "Any initial thoughts on cause of death?"

"The injuries are consistent with a fall down those steps."

"Anything to suggest foul play?"

Faith looked up towards the office. "There's only a flimsy handrail. It wouldn't have been much help if he tripped. And he'd been drinking. Heavily would be my guess. The smell of alcohol is unmistakable, even with all the smoke and water."

"So, accident then?"

"Maybe. The first responders said the place was pitch dark when they arrived. If he'd been drinking, it would presumably have been relatively easy to slip and fall. I'll know more tomorrow." Just then Faith noticed Peter for the first time. She couldn't immediately place him although she recognised his face. She offered a casual smile by way of acknowledgement.

"Do you really think it could just be an accident, sir?" Grainger's question caught Bobby by surprise.

"It's possible. We know he used to sleep here sometimes. He told us it was when he was busy, but I guess the same logic applied to when he'd been drinking. Probably more so. He could have fallen, but the timing is suspicious. Just before we were about to arrest him. And what about the fire? If he fell on his way up, how did it start?" Bobby was quiet for a moment while he thought things through. "We know he used to drink at the Church House Inn. Get yourself down there now, Grainger, see if anyone's still around. If not, I want you there first thing in the morning. We need to know if Claude was there tonight. And if he was, I want to know who he was with, what he was saying and what time he left. And if he left alone."

CHAPTER 45

"And this was a man you say?"

"Yes, definitely. Well, I suppose it *could* have been a woman."

It was Saturday morning and Bobby had joined Grainger at the Church House Inn. They were sat at a chunky wooden table framed by a bay window overlooking the green that formed the centrepiece of Marldon's pretty village. They were talking to Brenda, one of the members of staff who'd worked behind the bar last night. She also happened to be one of the women Grainger had spoken with the previous week, after she'd phoned the police for assistance getting a drunk and aggressive Claude Knight out of the pub at closing time.

Brenda suddenly looked worried. "It *was* Friday night. It's always busy on Friday night. And, I only saw them briefly, whoever they were. It's not like I was keeping tabs or anything."

She'd already confirmed that Claude had been in pretty much all night, arriving at five, along with the rest of the after-work crew, and not leaving until ten thirty. Nothing out of the ordinary there, apparently. He came in every Friday night, regular as clockwork. And he normally stayed until around the same time. You could set your watch by it. A lot of the regulars had similar routines. It was because of that predictability that Brenda had remembered Claude talking to someone she hadn't recognised.

"It was about nine, something like that. I remember we'd started to receive orders for cognacs and other nightcaps from customers in the restaurant. Anyway, this stranger comes in and sits down at the table in the corner." Brenda pointed to a square table next to a door leading to the ladies toilets. "Claude had been sitting there alone, keeping himself to himself, and then all of a sudden he had someone with him. They had their back to the bar and were wearing a floppy hat, with the sides folded down over their face, so I didn't get a good look."

Bobby looked frustrated. "Is there anything helpful you *can* tell us?"

Brenda suddenly looked pleased with herself. "They handed something to Claude. An envelope. White. The sort you get bills in. I remember thinking about my gas bill. I'd only received it that morning."

Bobby looked at Brenda. "And? Did you see what was inside?"

"No, sorry. Claude got up shortly afterwards and went to the toilet. Left the stranger at the table on their own. The next time I looked, they'd gone and Claude was standing at the bar chatting with some of the other locals. He'd been in a strange mood before, but afterwards, he was a different person."

"How so?"

"He was happy. He even brought me a drink, and he *never* did that. I remember thinking he must have won the lottery or something…"

Bobby cut in. "Let's take a step back for a moment. You said this person was wearing a large floppy hat. Wasn't that suspicious?"

Brenda smiled. "And a long coat. A waxed one. Went down almost to the ground as I recall."

"That sounds like an unusual outfit," Bobby prompted. "Distinctive, even. Are you sure you don't remember anything more about what this person looked like?"

Brenda suddenly looked offended. "This is a village pub, you know. People wear all sorts. Especially in winter. We don't tend to judge. I just didn't pay it much attention. And, like I said, it was busy."

"Bobby tried one final time. "So, you couldn't really see this person's face, or even if it was a man or a woman. If you had to come down on one side…"

"If I had to say one way or another, I'd say a man…or possibly a woman. No, a man. Definitely."

CHAPTER 46

PETER SAT ON HIS SOFA half watching a home improvement programme on the television. It was after 11:00 a.m. but he was still in his pyjamas. He'd finally arrived home from Claude Knight's yard around 2:00 a.m. after grabbing a lift with one of Bobby Redhill's colleagues, but despite feeling absolutely shattered, hadn't been able to sleep.

Last night had been a complete whirlwind and he was still trying to process everything that had happened. From the shock of getting picked up by the police, to the surprise offer of collaboration from DCI Redhill, through Hugh Farmer's bombshell revelations and ending with the death of the main suspect in the Irving Hargreaves murder investigation. Peter wasn't sure where Claude Knight's death left his arrangement with the inspector, but he sensed his big scoop slipping agonisingly out of his grasp, and with it any chance of getting his job at the *Torbay Times* back.

During the frustratingly slow drive to the crime scene, the inspector had warned him in no uncertain terms to stay out of the way, so he'd hung back in one corner of the cold, wet quarry minding his own business while people rushed about all around. He'd found that hard, but it had given him time to think. And his thoughts had kept returning to the invoice the police had found in Irving Hargreaves' office. There was something about it that kept niggling at Peter's brain, he just hadn't been able to put his finger on what it was.

As he sat there now, it came to him. The council's records had all been destroyed in the fire at the storage facility. So, how did Hargreaves have a copy of it? Surely it should have been destroyed along with all the other records. Redhill had told him it related to works undertaken almost ten years ago, well before he'd become a councillor, so why did Hargreaves have a copy of *that* invoice in particular? Peter knew it had to be important. The invoice linked back to the council's decision to move their offices out of Oldway Mansion and over to Torquay. Peter thought that had to be significant. And then there was the photo that had been found alongside the invoice. It focused on Hugh Farmer and Justin King, the two main players behind the Oldway Mansion development proposals, but Claude Knight was also visible in the background. Peter didn't believe that was a coincidence. He knew the builder had links to both the council and Justin King and he'd seen the sign advertising Claude's building firm on the security fencing at Oldway Mansion prior to his tour with Mavis Albright.

The more he thought about it, the more determined he became that Hugh Farmer was the common link between the invoice and the photo. He'd been leader of Torbay Council for the past ten years and was in charge at the time the council moved offices. Peter didn't know for sure, but he suspected that decision had also been taken under Farmer's leadership. It had left Oldway Mansion empty, which had in turn presented the opportunity for the development proposals that were about to be voted on by the council. Proposals that Hugh himself had put together alongside his friend, Justin King.

Peter thought about everything he'd learnt since his recent trip to Manchester. There were definite similarities between the proposals Hugh had put forward for Oldway Mansion and those he'd overseen years earlier in connection with the Lancaster Arcade, back when he'd been Ben James. Peter realised that Hugh Farmer had the knowledge, experience and power required to pull off something similar now.

But what about the story Hugh had told him yesterday in the interview room? It was compelling and Peter knew he had no reason to doubt it. But it also struck Peter that Hugh being in witness protection almost gave him automatic immunity from consideration for the current murders. At the very least, he thought it might be enough to blinker the DCI's investigation.

He then recalled the inspector mentioning an old model hatchback being spotted near Berry Head just before Irving Hargreaves had been murdered. Mrs Aiken, Hugh's housekeeper, drove an old Nissan Micra. That certainly fitted the description. Peter wondered whether Hugh could have borrowed it on the night of the murder. He certainly thought it was possible.

Peter continued to mull things over. If there was some sort of scam involving the Oldway Mansion development, he wondered whether it could be linked to the tender process for the building contract. That would tie back to Claude Knight and might explain why he'd just been killed. If Hugh was trying to fiddle the costs involved in converting the former stately home and its grounds into the flagship of the King Hotel Group, he'd need a cooperative building contractor. But a partner would also represent a loose end. Particularly when a reporter with nothing to lose was snooping around and asking questions.

If he was right, Peter realised it was also possible that this wasn't the first time the pair had worked together. The invoice for the renovation of the new council offices in 2013 flashed back into his mind. Perhaps that was why Irving had a copy of it. If he'd stumbled across some evidence that proved a conspiracy, or he had suspicions and had gone in search of evidence, that could have been enough to get him killed.

Peter recalled his conversation with the clerk at the council offices a couple of weeks back. He'd asked her about conflicts of interest, but at the time he'd been focused on Hugh and Justin. What if the relevant conflict was between Hugh and Claude Knight? He realised he needed to establish whether Hugh had ever disclosed any links with the builder. And there was only one person who could answer that question: Violet Danbury. She'd worked at Torbay Council for thirty years. If anyone knew what was going on, it would be her.

He stood up and rummaged through the sideboard that stood against the wall in the lounge. It had come with the property and he recalled seeing a telephone directory in there when he'd moved in. He finally found it underneath a stack of old magazines and quickly opened it to the relevant section. There was a single entry for a Mrs V.E. Danbury with an address in Laura Grove, in Paignton. That had to be the one.

He sat back down on the sofa and typed the number into his phone. After pressing the button to connect the call, he listened to the rings. Three, four, five... No one answered. Maybe she wasn't in. He was considering hanging up and trying again later, when the ringing stopped and, after a short pause, an electronic voice spoke. Her answering machine. Peter hadn't planned on leaving a message, but now he'd got this far, he didn't see the harm. He waited for the beep.

"Mrs Danbury. It's Peter Norton, the reporter with the *Torbay Times*. We've met a few times recently. I'm sure you remember. I hope you don't mind me calling, but I need to speak with you. It's quite urgent. And delicate, actually. It's about the council's tender process for building contracts…

I think it's why Claude Knight was killed last night – you've probably heard the news. And Councillor Hargreaves a few weeks ago. The murderer has to be someone high up in the council. It's probably better if we speak in person. Would you mind if I just came to see you? Say around four this afternoon. I hope that's okay. I look forward to seeing you then."

He disconnected the call and smiled. It felt good to be doing something positive again. He hated standing on the sidelines twiddling his thumbs, and he was sure Violet Danbury would be able to provide him with the answers he needed.

CHAPTER 47

BOBBY PULLED THE VAUXHALL INTO a space in an isolated part of Torbay Hospital's car park, near the entrance to the mortuary. He was running late for Claude Knight's autopsy and hurried into the building and down the sterile corridor. He was breathing heavily as he pushed through the double swing doors into the morgue. "Sorry I'm late."

"Great timing, I've just finished and was writing up some notes." Faith, dressed in scrubs, was standing at the back of the room with her back to the door. As she turned, she gave the inspector a concerned look.

Bobby's cheeks reddened. "So, Claude Knight," he said quickly. "What did you find?"

Faith turned to the body lying on the gurney in the centre of the room. Apart from the head, it was completely covered by a white sheet. "The headline conclusion is that this was not an accident."

Bobby wasn't surprised by the news. "Go on."

"There was a significant amount of alcohol in his system, as I thought at the scene. Clearly liked his malt whisky, but I don't think he was fussy. Quite the celebration he was having."

"Enough to make him unsteady on his feet?"

"Oh, yes, certainly. For a normal person at least. I'm not sure you or I would have been able to stand after consuming that much alcohol, let alone walk up that steep hill to his yard. Or climb those steps to his office, for that matter. But Claude wasn't a normal person. Not when it came to alcohol, anyway. He had extensive scarring of the liver, the tell-tale signs of a serious and dedicated drinker. It's likely he'd have been able to function pretty well. Actually, he might have functioned better *because* he'd been drinking!"

"Okay. That aligns with the witness reports from the pub. He was in good spirits, no pun intended. Definitely drunk, but not staggering about. We know from our earlier enquiries that it wasn't unusual for him to drink to excess. He could become boisterous and, because of his size, intimidating, but never unsteady on his feet. And he always walked back up the hill to his yard. When he wasn't being escorted by the police, that is. So, what are we saying? Was he a functioning alcoholic?"

Faith thought about this. "Quite possibly, yes. I obviously never met him, so couldn't comment on his ability to function in the real world, but I would certainly be inclined to agree he was an alcoholic."

"This could have been an accident, then? He could have simply fallen down those steps."

"We can't rule it out as a contributory factor. People who've consumed that much alcohol are always going to be less capable. Even someone with Claude's tolerance. My reason for believing this was *not* an accident is the large amount of sleeping tablets in his system."

"Sleeping tablets?" The revelation had taken Bobby by surprise. "Why on earth would he have taken sleeping tablets before heading out for a night at the pub? When did he take them?"

"I can't be precise, but at least an hour before he died. Maybe two, but no more than three. Most of the tablets had been absorbed into his system, but there were still trace amounts in his stomach."

"So, he took them at some point during the evening, while he was still in the pub. That makes even less sense, doesn't it?"

"I agree taking sleeping tablets in the middle of a night out would typically be considered unusual behaviour, but I try not to judge what people get up to."

"How much is a large amount?"

"Enough to seriously impair his ability to walk and talk. Especially on top of the alcohol. Even for someone with his tolerance for substances."

"Not the amount he might have taken by accident then?"

Faith laughed. "I'm not even sure how you'd go about taking a sleeping tablet by accident, but, no, I don't think he'd have taken that amount accidentally."

"Any idea how he took them?"

"They were dissolved in liquid. One of his alcoholic drinks would be my guess."

Bobby recalled Brenda mentioning Claude going to the toilet while the stranger was still sitting at the small table in the corner of the Church House Inn. Could the tablets have been dropped into his drink then? It was possible, he decided. And the timings worked. "What about time of death?"

"I can be pretty precise about T.O.D." Faith smiled. "And not just from a medical perspective. He was found by a neighbour just after eleven and was apparently already dead at that point. That's likely given the nature of his injuries, although we can't rely on that report because the neighbour didn't check for a pulse. The ambulance arrived at eleven fourteen and he was pronounced dead at eleven fifteen. He hadn't been dead long at that point. No more than an hour. Say T.O.D. somewhere between ten and eleven fifteen."

Bobby considered this for a moment. "That's helpful. We know he was alive at ten thirty when he left the pub. We have any number of witnesses to that effect. And it would have taken him around five minutes to walk back to the yard. Maybe a bit longer given the amount he'd drunk. No more than ten, though. So, he'd have been back at his yard at around ten forty. It might have taken him a couple of minutes to climb those steps, of course, but either way he must have died very soon after arriving back at the yard.

Probably somewhere between ten forty and eleven when the neighbour came to investigate the fire."

"Sounds about right," agreed Faith.

"So, a twenty-minute window to, what, ambush him, push him down the steps, set fire to the office and then disappear before the neighbour arrived on the scene. He was adamant there wasn't anyone else in the lane, and he stayed with the body until the ambulance arrived." Bobby appeared to be talking to himself, so Faith remained quiet. "I meant to ask," he continued. "Did you find an envelope on the body? Apparently, he was handed one in the pub, but we didn't find it at the scene."

"Nothing like that, no. Some keys and a wallet, that's all."

"Okay, thanks." Bobby paused. "For all your help over the past couple of weeks. It's really appreciated." He offered a slightly sappy smile.

"No problem." Faith beamed warmly in return. "You'll have my report by the morning."

As Bobby walked back to his car, his mind was spinning, but only one thought was clearly in focus. That he wouldn't mind another body turning up if it meant being able to see Faith again soon. He forced himself to push the ridiculous notion away. He knew he had to focus. There were now two victims, two families who needed justice. That was the only thing that mattered. And that was where he needed to concentrate his energies, not Faith. There would be plenty of time for that later.

Back in the Vauxhall, Bobby considered the little he currently knew, starting with the fact that Claude had almost certainly been murdered. He thought it impossible to believe his death was unconnected to the murder of Irving Hargreaves. Claude had been his prime suspect in the councillor's death and Bobby knew that both victims had crossed paths recently. The presence of Claude's hatchback on the traffic camera also suggested the builder had lied about his whereabouts on the night Irving died. And then there was Oldway Mansion. Both men had links to the historic building, albeit on opposing sides, with Irving a fervent supporter of preservation and Claude desperate to win the development work. He wasn't sure how the stately home fitted into things, but he couldn't shake the feeling it was at the centre of both investigations.

CHAPTER 48

PETER PULLED TO THE KERB in Laura Grove and looked up towards Violet Danbury's bungalow. It was a pleasant-looking property, clean and tidy with a freshness that hinted at a recent coat of paint. There were no lights on in any of the windows overlooking the well-tended front garden, though, and the house looked deserted. Peter wondered whether she might still be out.

He got out of the Audi and walked up the drive. He could see now that each of the windows was covered on the inside by lace curtains. They were bright white and appeared to shimmer as the late afternoon light reflected off the gleaming panes.

At the top of the drive stood a single garage, but the door was closed so Peter couldn't tell whether there was a car inside. Halfway along the side of the bungalow a wooden storm porch protected a white front door made of

UPVC. It gleamed as though only recently cleaned. Peter knocked and waited. There was a small panel of patterned glass at the top of the door and he peered through. It was dark on the other side, but then he saw a light appear. It was only faint, as though someone had opened a door at the back of the house, and was followed moments later by the unmistakable sound of a lock turning.

When the door opened, Violet Danbury stood there wearing an apron over a dark skirt and an equally dark cardigan. She was wiping her hands on a tea towel. "Hello, Peter. I got your voicemail. I've been expecting you. Come in."

"Thanks, Mrs Danbury."

"I told you before, call me Violet."

"Thanks, Violet. I hope you didn't mind me phoning earlier, and now…just coming round like this?"

"Not at all. It's nice to see you. Although, I really don't know how I can possibly help."

She showed him into the lounge. It was a long, narrow room that ran the full width of the house and had large, picture windows that dominated each end. The one at the front had views out across the bay while the other over-looked a large patio area and a sizable back garden beyond.

"Would you like a cup of tea?"

"That would be great, thanks, Violet."

"I was just in the kitchen when you arrived. Doing some baking. Give me a minute to sort myself out and I'll be back."

"That's fine. There's no rush, really. Please, take your time."

Violet disappeared leaving Peter alone. After a few moments he could hear cups clinking in another room. He wandered over to the front window and pulled the net curtain to one side to take in the view.

When Violet returned, Peter was looking out over the back garden. She carried a large heavily laden tray. He rushed over to help her, taking the tray and setting it down on a low table positioned between a two-seater sofa and a matching chair. It contained a teapot hidden beneath an old-fashioned cosy, two cups on saucers and a side plate covered with what appeared to be freshly baked biscuits. The cups and saucer were adorned with images of brightly coloured flowers. The side plate appeared to be from the same set, and Peter had no doubts that beneath its knitted jumper, the teapot would be sporting the same design.

"This is a lovely house, Violet. The views out the front are stunning. I bet you don't watch the television much. And what a lovely garden." He was back at the rear window. "Must be great for entertaining. Especially with that patio. What a fantastic space. I'd love something like that. With a barbecue and a few friends, I'd be in my element."

Violet looked down her nose, slightly. "I don't really go in for barbecues. Although my husband used to like them. That was the only time he'd cook. And he loved to enter-tain. It was his idea to build the patio. I thought it frivolous. And far too big. But he disagreed. And he got his way, of course. But then he left before it was finished, so he never got to enjoy it. Still, I've had a lot of pleasure out of it over the years. More than I expected to. I like to just sit there, in the peace and quiet. He said I'd grow to love it. I guess he was right about that, at least."

Violet went quiet and appeared to be thinking about something. Some distant memory perhaps. About her husband, Peter guessed.

"I'm sorry, Violet, I didn't mean to upset you."

"That's quite all right. It was a long time ago now. Water under the bridge."

"Have you really not heard from him since he left all those years ago?" Peter regretted the question as soon as he'd asked it. Violet would wonder where he'd got the information from. He didn't want her to think he'd been gossiping behind her back. Fortunately, she didn't seem to notice and answered straight away, almost without thinking.

"No, I haven't. Not a word. But I'd rather not talk about *that* man. Life is for the now, don't you agree?"

Violet picked up the teapot and poured the steaming, dark liquid into the two cups. They already contained milk and there was no offer of sugar. She handed one to Peter. It tinkled in its saucer as she released her grip. Peter instinctively held it in two hands, fearful of spilling anything on the thick carpet, and ended up balancing the saucer on his knees.

"Let's talk about something more interesting," Violet continued. "Like why you've come to see me. It's all very mysterious, I must say. And exciting. I don't get many visitors." She suddenly looked sad. "I don't have any family to speak of. Not since Malcolm left. We never had any children you see. It's just me now." Violet paused and took a sip of tea. "You mentioned in your message something about the deaths of Councillor Hargreaves and someone called Claude Knight. I was aware of poor Irving, of course, from being on the council together. But I only heard about the other man today. On the wireless. I like to listen to the local station. He was a builder or something, wasn't he? I must say, the name didn't ring a bell, although now I think about it, I do remember seeing his vans around the area on occasion. But you think his death has something to do with Irving's, and that there might be a link with Torbay Council? I must admit, it all sounds too improbable. Like something off the television. I really don't know how I can possibly help you."

"I probably didn't explain myself very well on the phone. I was quite excited. And tired. I haven't slept much over the past couple of weeks. But, yes, I do believe the deaths of the two men are linked to the council. Specifically, the tender process that the council operates for building contracts."

Violet picked up the side plate and held it towards Peter. "Would you like a biscuit? I baked them myself when you said you might be popping round. I remember you mentioning at Conrad's how much you liked a biscuit."

"Thank you, Violet. That's very thoughtful of you. I don't mind if I do." Peter took a bite. "Chocolate chip cookies, my favourite."

Violet put the plate down without taking one herself. "Sorry, Peter, I interrupted you. What were you saying?"

Peter smiled. "No problem. I was talking about the council's tender process for large building contracts. Like the development of the King hotels and the renovation of the council's current offices. Or the development of Oldway Mansion. I was wondering…are there any records which show how those tenders were run? Or the basis on which the winning tenders were chosen?"

"Well, the tender for the Oldway Mansion development has yet to be considered. It's subject to the council first approving the development at the vote next week, and that's by no means a certainty."

"I understand that. I was just using Oldway Mansion as an example. What about those projects that have already been approved and tenders awarded? Say over the last ten years." Peter knew he'd asked her about these records before, but he didn't think there was any harm in doing so again. "Do you have records for those?"

"Records?" Violet looked surprised by the question. "Probably not, no. Like I told you before, we had that unfortunate fire at our storage facility a few weeks back. Most of our records were destroyed. It was such a shame. I've been saying for years that we should be making digital copies of everything but, you know bureaucracies!" She sighed loudly.

"But even without the records, *you* must know how those tenders are run. Who oversees them? It must be someone high up in the council."

"Another biscuit?" Violet picked up the side plate again and held it towards Peter who was too preoccupied to respond. "Just help yourself." She put the plate down and moved it closer to him before looking at the uneaten biscuits with exaggerated head movements and big, hopeful eyes when he didn't make an immediate move to choose one. "I can't eat them all."

Peter didn't think he could refuse. Hadn't she said she didn't get many visitors? And she had gone to the effort of baking. His favourites too. "Thanks, I don't mind if I do. So, about the council tender process?"

Violet took another sip of tea. "All of our tenders are run in accordance with the law. There's no way around that. There are strict guidelines, and we comply with them absolutely. Our procedures are robust. We don't do anything improper, I can assure you of that."

"And I wasn't accusing anyone, Violet. I just need some information."

"I'm just not sure I can help you."

"How about the winning tenders? How are they chosen?"

"In accordance with the rules and pursuant to the criteria set out in the tender document. It really is quite straightforward."

Peter was starting to get frustrated. He felt as though Violet was being deliberately vague in her answers. "I understand that, but who makes the decision? Who decides which bid adheres to the rules and best fits the criteria?"

"That would be the leader of the council. Responsibility ultimately falls on him. For *all* council matters."

It was the admission Peter had been waiting for. He breathed a heavy sigh of relief. "What about the relationship between Hugh Farmer and Claude Knight?"

"What do you mean?" The question appeared to have taken Violet by surprise, although she soon regained her composure. "I'm not aware there *was* a relationship. Like I said before, I didn't even recall knowing who Claude Knight is, or was, I should say, before I heard about it on the wireless this morning." She looked at Peter curiously. "What are you saying, Peter? Are you accusing Councillor Farmer of some sort of involvement in that man's death? And the death of Councillor Hargreaves? I simply can't believe it."

"It's the only thing that makes any sense. Hugh has a connection to both men and the common link is Oldway Mansion. I'm sure their deaths have something to do with the building contracts that the council awards."

Violet picked up her cup carefully, expertly gripping the delicate handle between her thumb and forefinger. "Who have you shared these theories with, Peter?"

"No one. Not at this stage. I was hoping to get some evidence first. I thought you might be able to help me, because you've worked at the council for so long. I guess I thought if anyone would know what's been going on, it would be you."

"I appreciate the vote of confidence, and I'm sorry I haven't been any more help. But I just can't believe anything you've said. And I certainly can't provide any evidence. I just don't think there is any. I've worked with Hugh for fifteen years. I can't believe he'd do what you claim. He's such a gentleman. And as you say, I'd have noticed if he was up to something." Violet paused and gave Peter a warm smile. "Don't worry, I won't mention anything you've said to anyone else. And I'd advise you to keep it to yourself as well. Talk like that could get you into serious trouble. Hugh's a very influential man. He has friends in very high places."

Peter looked at Violet blankly. "You have no idea."

"What was that?"

"Nothing." Peter was starting to feel despondent. And tired. The energy he'd felt earlier was quickly disappearing. "Perhaps you're right, Violet."

"Why don't you have another biscuit? And another cup of tea?"

Peter leaned back in his chair. The tiredness was washing over him now in waves. The room was warm and the chair comfortable. "Sure, why not." He found himself responding without even thinking. "That would be lovely."

Peter stayed for another ten minutes while he finished his second cup of tea and managed a couple more biscuits. Violet was surprisingly good company, and it made a welcome change to think about something other than Hugh Farmer for a while. By the time he got outside, he was looking forward to getting home. He felt certain he'd sleep well tonight. He yawned as he got into the car and was still yawning as he pulled the Audi away from the kerb. His mind felt dulled, like he was operating on autopilot.

It had gone dark while he'd been inside Violet's house and all the cars on the road now had their lights on. It was the end of the day and traffic was heavy. He pulled up behind a queue of cars, all waiting for a gap in the traffic to allow them to merge onto Marldon Road, the long, steep hill that joined the village of Marldon at the top with Paignton town centre at the bottom.

The cars edged forward slowly as one by one they joined the faster flowing traffic of the larger road. And then, finally, it was Peter's turn. He was going to be turning left, towards Paignton and home. As he waited at the junction, the cars on Marldon Road travelled past in a constant, steady stream. Their headlights were bright and the light seared into his brain, hitting an area deep behind his eyes.

He really wanted to get home. He could feel the tiredness start to envelop him.

He buzzed down the driver's side window to let in some air. It helped him focus and, when he spotted a gap in the headlights he took his chance, pulling out quickly into the stream of traffic. He checked his rear-view mirror as soon as he'd completed the manoeuvre and saw there was already a car right behind him, its headlights illuminating the inside of the Audi as though parked in its backseat. The bright light reflected off the rear-view mirror straight into his eyes.

Marldon Road was busy in both directions and an endless stream of headlights headed towards him on the other side of the road. Like those of the car behind, they appeared brighter than usual. Too bright. It was as though all the cars around him were driving with their main beams on. It felt like an endless assault on his brain. Even the brake lights of the cars in front glowed a blazing red that seemed far brighter than usual. He narrowed his eyes, trying to shut out some of the glare. It seemed to help.

And then, gradually, the dazzlingly bright lights disappeared. Peter was suddenly floating home on a wave of warm red brake lights that flowed serenely from the line of cars in front of him.

The sound of a blaring horn brought him back to the present with a jolt and a bright white light suddenly filled his vision. He realised with a shock that he must have closed his eyes and veered onto the wrong side of the road. He was driving directly towards a car travelling in the opposite direction. It was moving quickly and didn't appear to be slowing down. Its lights were flashing frantically and the driver was blaring his horn, as though under some mistaken illusion he could prevent the seemingly inevitable impact with bright light and loud noise alone. Peter quickly yanked at the steering wheel, pulling the Audi violently to the left, just as the approaching car flew past, narrowly missing his front wing.

Peter breathed a heavy sigh. He shook his head and slapped his cheeks a few times to try and wake himself up. His side window was still open and cold air was streaming in, but he suddenly felt hot. He touched his forehead. It was wet with sweat.

He shook his head again and turned the radio on to try to force himself to stay awake. He was only five minutes from home. He just needed to concentrate. Once he was there, he could lie down and sleep. But he felt so tired. He yawned again. Several times. They were coming so frequently now, he hardly even noticed. And then he was back floating, on the same wave of comforting red brake lights…

He heard a loud bang and a sickening crunch of metal before everything went dark.

CHAPTER 49

EARLY ON MONDAY MORNING, Bobby was back at Claude Knight's yard. He stood at the top of the stone steps and looked across to Dartmoor in the distance. The view from this elevated vantage point never seemed to disappoint, no matter how often he stood here. There was always something new to see, some detail in the landscape he hadn't noticed before. This morning it was snow visible on some of the higher peaks of the moor.

His thoughts turned to Hugh Farmer. He knew the Leader of Torbay Council would likely be pacing nervously in the isolated cottage somewhere among the vast expanse of open moorland, the frustrations of his enforced absence from the world having only increased in the past few days. The council vote to decide Oldway Mansion's fate was now only a matter of days away and Hugh felt very strongly that he should be an active, and visible, part of it all. So far, Bobby had managed to convince him to stay put, but he wasn't sure how much longer the councillor would continue to do as he asked.

It was another headache he could do without. He was back to square one with the Hargreaves investigation and, since Claude Knight had been his prime suspect for that murder, he was currently at a loss to explain who might have been responsible for killing either man. The only thing he was certain about was that the two crimes were linked. But he needed a breakthrough, and he needed one quickly. The Chief Constable had started to talk more openly about bringing in a fresh pair of eyes.

He had at least managed to solve one mystery. Following news of Claude's death being broadcast around the bay by local media outlets, Penelope, Claude's redhaired assistant, had come forward with information that explained his being caught by the traffic camera driving towards Brixham on the night Irving Hargreaves had been killed. And which gave the builder an alibi for the councillor's murder.

Claude had been on his way to the Manor House Inn, an out-of-the-way pub in Churston village. Penelope had been with him. She admitted they used to go to the Manor regularly, because it was quiet and no one there knew them. Claude often used the old Fiesta on those trips apparently, to avoid unwanted attention. He thought the Range Rover too flashy and knew he would likely be over the limit by the time he was headed home. That was also the reason he'd used the back roads on the return journey. That at least explained why he hadn't been caught again on the traffic camera going in the opposite direction. Penelope confessed to often spending the night with her boss in the back room of the office. And she confirmed they'd gone back there that night too.

Bobby was having difficulties picturing the gruff builder with the petite and, clearly much older, secretary. Fortunately, his attention was drawn away from the unwelcome image by a noise behind him. It was Grainger. "We're ready for you, sir."

Bobby followed his sergeant into the remains of Claude's office.

They'd discovered a safe in a heavily burnt cupboard in one corner of the building's back room, although discovered was perhaps too strong a word. They'd have found it anyway, of course, but Penelope had already mentioned it. And that was the reason for Bobby being present this morning.

Penelope had told him an interesting story. When Claude returned from his meeting with Irving Hargreaves, the one arranged by the councillor under the pretence of wanting a quote for a non-existent extension, he'd apparently been in a very strange mood. *'He was rattled. I'd never seen him like that before'*, she'd said. *'He ordered me to start going through all our old records. Cleaning house he called it. But he made me run everything by him before I threw anything away. After all that fuss, he was only interested in one piece of paper. An old invoice. From years back. His mood changed immediately he saw it. And he put it straight in the safe.'*

That had led Bobby to ask the obvious question. Why would Claude put an old invoice in the safe when all other records were kept in filing cabinets or left on the floor? And another thing. The fire inspectors had confirmed an accelerant was used. A spot underneath Claude's desk had been identified as the point of origin. So, second obvious question: why go to the trouble of setting fire to Claude's office, if not to destroy something. A piece of evidence perhaps? Some loose end Claude's death alone could not resolve. Which got Bobby thinking again about that invoice.

The remains of the cupboard had been cleared and the safe, a large old-fashioned affair, was the only object left in the charred room. Bobby handed the key to Grainger. "Do you want to do the honours?"

The keyhole was covered by an oversized piece of metal and positioned next to a big, ornate brass handle that looked a bit like an angel, it's two wings radiating off a central stalk. Bobby wondered whether that was a good sign. Some sort of omen. He certainly hoped so, and found himself offering up a prayer to a God he no longer believed in.

Grainger knelt in front of the safe, turned the key in the lock and grabbed hold of the angel wings firmly. With the lock released, the handle turned to the left with a reassuring clunk and the door swung open easily. It revealed a space that was both large but at the same time smaller than the outside dimensions suggested, such was the thickness of the safe's metal body. Grainger turned on the torch function on his phone and shone the light into the darkness. Bobby could see a shelf separating the space into two equal-sized areas before Grainger leaned forward and blocked his view completely.

"There's not much in here, sir. Just some cash and a few papers."

He proceeded to take the items out one by one before passing them behind him to his boss. He didn't seem particularly interested in anything he'd found. If anything, he looked disappointed. "I was sure we'd find something in here."

Bobby didn't respond. He was looking at the last piece of paper Grainger had handed to him. It was an invoice, the only one among the papers he was now holding. *The* invoice Penelope had told him about. It was a single sheet of paper. Bobby read it carefully, focusing on each word in turn. He was surprised to see that it hadn't been issued by Claude's firm. Was that significant? He read it again, more slowly this time, and something in his brain clicked. A completely unexpected connection suddenly came together. He stared at the paper for another long moment. It couldn't be, could it? And yet, it would explain everything.

Keeping hold of the invoice, he handed the remaining contents of the safe back to Grainger and hurried outside.

Grainger called after him. "What do you want me to do with this lot, sir?"

Bobby didn't slow his pace. "Bag it up, Grainger. And then meet me at the station. We have work to do."

Bobby almost ran down the stone steps. He'd finally found the silver bullet. That crucial piece of evidence that helped to explain everything that had happened over the past few weeks, including why Irving Hargreaves and Claude Knight had been killed. He needed to get back to the station to check a couple of details, but he was certain they'd only confirm what he already knew.

CHAPTER 50

BOBBY REDHILL SAT IN HIS office on the second floor of Torquay police station. The blinds were drawn and the only light came from the lamp on his desk. A copy of the *Torbay Times* was spread out in front of him.

The headline on the front page read '*Local Reporter Killed in Car Accident*'. The related story explained how Peter Norton, 34, a much-respected reporter with the paper, had died at around 5:45 p.m. on Saturday evening after his car left the road and hit a wall. Marldon Road in Paignton was closed for several hours as emergency services responded and tried to free Mr Norton from the wreckage. Despite their efforts, he was pronounced dead at the scene. No other vehicles were involved and the incident was being treated by police as a tragic accident.

A secondary story at the bottom of the page declared '*Oldway Mansion Development Plans Shelved*'. The article explained that following the bad publicity that had accompanied the death of Councillor Hargreaves, and in the wake of the mysterious absence of Hugh Farmer, millionaire developer Justin King had decided to pull out of the development.

Bobby turned the page, where the story continued. It suggested that the alternative proposals put forward by the Oldway Mansion Preservation Society, to renovate the fine old building and preserve it as an historical monument for future generations, would now be successful. There was even a quote from Conrad Macpherson, Chairman of the preservation society, expressing his delight at '*common sense finally having prevailed in this matter*'.

On page four, Bobby skimmed two further stories. The first one concerned the death of Councillor Irving Hargreaves and made it clear the police were no further forward in uncovering a motive or identifying the killer.

The second related to the death of Claude Knight and confirmed it to be another tragic accident. The paper reported that Mr Knight, 37, a local builder, had fallen to his death late on Friday night. It speculated that alcohol might have been a contributory factor and, quoting a source familiar with the investigation, confirmed that Mr Knight had accidentally knocked over a kerosene heater causing a fire in his office before tripping over and falling down the stone steps that led to the builder's yard below in his haste to escape the flames.

Bobby sighed and leaned back in his leather chair. He'd played his hand, now all he could do was wait.

CHAPTER 51

THE HAMMER CAME DOWN HARD on the long, metal crowbar. Once, twice, three times. The sound echoed around the empty corridor. It seemed to get louder with each hit. Grainger took a step back and covered his ears.

He was standing approximately two floors' distance below the main ballroom of Oldway Mansion, in one of the many corridors that made up the building's vast basement complex. By the looks of the cobwebs hanging from the ceiling and the thick layer of dust that covered every surface, no one had been down here in a great many years. A stale aroma pointed to fresh air having been similarly absent during that time.

He'd initially taken DCI Redhill's instructions to take the lead on this part of the investigation as a vote of confidence. Now he wasn't so sure. He pictured his boss sitting in his centrally heated office back at the station and sighed. *He should be here instead of me. After all, he likes sitting in the dark!*

The crowbar finally split the wood panelling on the third strike, offering encouragement to the workman delivering the barrage of blows that followed. Grainger's head started to throb.

With the assistance of a second workman, the panelling was levered away from the wall before a third colleague joined in to help carry the solid, heavy structure out of the way. The three men strained under the effort.

With the panel gone, Grainger could see a door. It was small, no more than three quarters the height of the corridor in which it stood, and particularly narrow.

The first workman tried the handle, but nothing happened. He tried again, this time both pulling and pushing. Still the door didn't move. He grabbed a torch from his toolbox and examined the gap between the door and frame on all three sides before getting down on his knees and resting his face against the floor while he checked the gap there. When he stood up, his cheek was black, covered in a thick layer of grime. Neither of his colleagues seemed to notice. They just looked on quietly as he picked up a screwdriver, one with a long, thick, metal shaft. He walked back to the door and proceeded to poke the gap between door and frame, in the area next to the handle.

"There's a lock going into the frame," he said to no one in particular. "But no keyhole."

He looked more closely at the door. "There might have been one here once. It could have been filled in. What do you want to do?"

The question was directed at Grainger. He took a sip of water from his bottle as he considered his options. He could feel all three of the workmen staring at him, waiting for his decision. He was in charge, but he didn't know how far his authority extended. Could he instruct the workmen to damage the door? Oldway Mansion was a listed building after all. He briefly considered phoning DCI Redhill, but quickly thought better of it. If this was a test, he didn't want to fall at the first hurdle.

"Can you break it down?" he asked.

The first workman shrugged his shoulders. "Could do."

"Even if you unblock the keyhole, we don't have a key so that's not going to help much, is it?" Grainger looked hopefully at each of the workmen in turn.

"If you say so." The first workman was clearly the senior of the three. His colleagues were yet to speak, and they just stared blankly at the sergeant now.

Grainger finally reached a decision. "No, it needs to come down." He pulled his shoulders back as he spoke. Confident.

"If you're sure, guv. Your decision. We just do as we're told."

Helpful, Grainger thought. *Really supportive. A proper team effort.*

He was about to second-guess his decision when several heavy blows rained down on the doorframe. *No turning back now!*

The frame splintered more readily than the panel before it had done. The foreman worked the crowbar methodically until he was able to remove a small oblong piece of wood, exposing the lock in the frame. After some further effort, he removed the last remaining splinters and pulled the door open with the lock still sticking out of its housing.

Grainger was relieved to see the door was still in one piece. He stepped forward and peered into the gap. It was dark inside. In fact, he couldn't see a thing. He grabbed his flashlight and switched it on. The powerful beam revealed a tunnel running off into the distance.

He tentatively put one foot over the threshold and, after taking a final deep breath, stepped forward. The tunnel was much smaller than the corridor he'd just left. He had to stoop to make sure his head didn't hit the ceiling. He could sense the walls closing in on either side of him as he slowly moved forward. The sensation only got more acute the further he walked. He began to feel claustrophobic and started to take deeper breaths. The air tasted stale in his mouth.

After four or five minutes, he was starting to feel quite disoriented. It felt as though he'd been walking in a straight line, and relatively flat, but he couldn't be sure. He wondered where he was, relative to the mansion and its grounds. He stopped and shone the torch, first against the walls and then against the roof. He hoped they were strong enough to support the weight of the soil around him. He didn't much fancy getting trapped down here. He instinctively took his phone out of his pocket and checked the screen. No signal. If the tunnel collapsed, he'd be stuck down here alone, with no way of contacting the outside world. He thought about the workmen he'd left in the basement behind him. He assumed they were still there but realised with a jolt that he hadn't told them to wait.

He flashed the torch back hopefully in the direction he'd just come. The darkness instantly evaporated in the sudden onslaught of light, but quickly crept back at the edges of the beam. The darkness was everywhere. Grainger prayed the battery in his torch would last, and he wished he'd put in a fresh set as he'd briefly considered doing that morning.

He took a deep breath and pushed on. He wasn't about to give up. He started to hum but stopped almost immediately when he heard a noise. It had been faint, but there had definitely been a sound of some sort coming from further along the tunnel. He listened hard and even held his breath for a few seconds. The silence encompassed him. It was so heavy he could feel it. And then he heard the noise again. It was a scratching sound. He flashed the beam of the torch up and down and side to side until it caught on a pair of tiny, yellow eyes close to the ground. They stared at him for a second or two before disappearing into the darkness. Rats! Now he really wanted to get out of this tunnel. He hated rats. His mind flicked back to the earlier image of DCI Redhill in his office and he cursed his boss under his breath.

After a few more steps into the darkness, close to where he'd seen the piercing yellow eyes, he found what he was looking for. He got close enough to confirm he was correct but didn't touch anything. That would be someone else's job. Thank God.

He pulled out his mobile phone and was about to make a call when he remembered he had no signal. He would have to wait until he got out of the tunnel. He turned around carefully and headed back the way he'd come, his pace now quicker, and he soon saw the light from the doorway and the voices of the workmen chatting in the basement corridor. He felt an immediate sense of relief and sped up just a little bit more.

As he stepped back over the threshold, he peered around the open door and saw the workmen lined up against the wall. Two standing and one sitting. They looked relaxed. Not remotely concerned about the policeman in the tunnel. They were drinking something out of hard, plastic cups. Grainger could see steam rising. Tea, or coffee, he guessed. He wondered where they'd got that from. And why they hadn't offered him a cup earlier.

"Find what you were after, guv?" asked the foreman casually.

"More than we could have hoped," Grainger replied cryptically.

He turned and walked away. Once outside, Grainger pulled his phone out of his pocket and, seeing that he finally had a signal, swiped at the screen until the number he wanted appeared. He dialled and waited for the call to be connected. He heard the familiar ring, but it was gone almost as quickly as it started. The call had obviously been expected.

"Sir, we've found them." Grainger's voice was composed and hid the excitement he felt inside.

On the other end of the line, Bobby smiled. He didn't speak. He didn't need to. They would have to run some further tests, just to be certain, but he knew they finally had the evidence they needed to close both murder investigations down. The last piece of the puzzle had just fallen into place.

CHAPTER 52

Bobby Redhill was driving. Carefully as usual. Grainger sat to his left, in the passenger seat of the Vauxhall. Neither spoke.

Bobby glanced in his rear-view mirror at the marked police car behind. There were two officers inside, both staring straight ahead, neither speaking. They wore serious expressions and looked as though they carried the weight of the world on their shoulders. Blue lights flashed from the light bar on the vehicle's roof and from lights hidden in its front bumper but, like Bobby, the officers weren't in any great hurry and no siren accompanied their sedate progress. The police car appeared content to follow the Vauxhall's slow, deliberate movements as though the two vehicles were joined by an invisible tow rope.

When they reached their destination, Bobby pulled into the kerb while the police car stopped in the middle of the road, its lights still flashing. Bobby took a deep breath and got out. Grainger followed his lead. They walked up a short drive towards a single garage with a small, black hatchback parked inside. It was old but its immaculate paintwork gleamed as though only recently polished. When they reached the front door, sheltered under a porch halfway along the side of the house, Bobby knocked before taking a step back and waiting for it to be answered.

Less than a minute later, shadows appeared through the glass panel at the top of the door which was opened by Violet Danbury. "Can I help you?"

Bobby and Grainger introduced themselves and showed their warrant cards before asking to be let in. The lady inspected the two gentlemen and their credentials carefully before catching a glimpse of the police car with its flashing lights abandoned in the road at the bottom of her drive. She suddenly looked troubled and stood still for a moment, apparently deep in thought. Eventually she stepped back into the house and walked slowly down the hallway. "Take your shoes off and close the door behind you."

They followed her into a comfortable lounge that ran the width of the house. She was perched on the edge of a narrow armchair with a high back.

"Mrs Danbury." Bobby spoke slowly. "We have some news about your husband."

Violet looked at the inspector but didn't speak. She didn't offer either of her visitors a seat.

"We've found Malcolm, Mrs Danbury." Bobby paused to let the news sink in. Violet looked startled but also, the inspector thought, relieved. As though a weight had been lifted from her shoulders.

"I'm sure that news comes as a surprise to you, although I also know it's not a complete shock."

"I don't know what you're talking about, Inspector. When you say *'found'*, what do you mean?" She looked at Bobby with piercing eyes. "And he's not my husband. Legally maybe, but not in any way that really counts. You can't divorce someone who is classified as missing. At least not until sufficient time has passed and they can be declared legally dead."

Bobby smiled. "I'm glad you mentioned that. Over seven years, isn't it? Your husband has been missing for far longer than that and yet you've never made any attempt to have him declared dead. Until recently that is." He paused for dramatic effect. "You filed the papers with the court a few weeks back. As soon as they're approved, you'll be entitled to claim his life insurance, won't you?"

Violet briefly looked sucker-punched before quickly regaining her composure. "I don't know what that's got to do with anything. That's a private financial matter."

"I disagree. I think it's very relevant."

"You still haven't told me about Malcolm. Where is he?"

"Your husband's remains were found in a tunnel beneath Oldway Mansion. He's been there for almost twenty years. But you already knew that, didn't you?"

Violet Danbury was starting to look flustered. "I don't know what you're talking about. Are you saying Malcolm's been dead all these years?"

"That's exactly what I'm saying. And I also believe you knew he was there because that's where you put his body after you killed him."

Violet spluttered. "That's preposterous. What an allegation. How could you…"

"We know Claude Knight was working here twenty years ago building a new patio for your husband. Around the same time as Malcolm disappeared. Claude was a labourer for the firm back then, but less than a month later he owned the business. He paid ten thousand pounds in cash to buy it. Not that he had access to that type of money and no bank lent it to him. We now know you remortgaged this property soon after your husband went missing. For an additional ten thousand pounds. You withdrew the whole amount in cash."

Violet stared at the inspector but didn't interrupt him.

"I don't know what happened with your husband, whether you meant to kill him or if it was just an accident, but I think Claude witnessed it, or somehow worked things out, and that he blackmailed you into paying him the money he used to buy the building firm. And I think he's been blackmailing you ever since." Bobby paused, but still Violet didn't speak. She appeared to be in a trance. It was as though she was hearing the story for the first time.

"Irving Hargreaves had an old invoice in his home office. It related to the renovation works Claude Knight's building firm carried out on the council's current offices in Torquay. Just before they moved out of Oldway Mansion in 2013. We know that another firm who tendered for the contract complained about irregularities in the tender process. They'd submitted a deliberately low bid which they knew no other contractor could beat, because they couldn't do the work profitably for that price themselves. When they didn't win and the work went to Claude Knight, they made accusations about Claude having had access to their bid. Is this sounding familiar?"

Violet didn't react.

"They withdrew their complaint before it was investigated, so the truth never came out. We've spoken to the owner of that firm and he confirmed that Claude Knight threatened him. Forced him to withdraw his accusations. That was fortunate, wasn't it, Mrs Danbury? What would an investigation have uncovered, do you think? You've run that council for the past thirty years. Nothing happens there without your knowledge. If confidential tenders were being shared, there's no way that could have happened without you knowing about it."

Violet suddenly looked defeated, but still she didn't speak.

"And then the council's storage facility suffered a devastating fire and all of its historical records were destroyed. Records that might have proven the accusations in that complaint from 2013. Again, more good luck for you." He paused. "I hear you're due to retire in the new year. Well-deserved after such a long and dedicated period of service. And just in time to enjoy your husband's life insurance. You'd want to tidy up any loose ends before then, of course. Make sure there are no records that could link you with Claude Knight. But you didn't reckon on Councillor Hargreaves, did you? He wasn't like the other councillors. He didn't simply do as he was told. He asked questions and challenged decisions. I guess you didn't realise that he'd already managed to get hold of that invoice from 2013. But he was the reason for setting fire to the storage facility, wasn't he? He was poking around into things that didn't concern him and you had to act quickly. It was a crude solution, but effective nonetheless."

Violet's shoulders slumped forward and she appeared to shrink right there in front of Bobby's eyes.

"But, it didn't stop Irving asking questions, did it? In fact, I suspect it just convinced him even more that something was going on. Made him even more determined to uncover the truth. Is that why you lured him to Berry Head that night? He wasn't about to drop his suspicions, was he? He wasn't going to let you retire quietly, so you had to do something."

Violet suddenly looked defiant. "He was so self-righteous. He acted like he was some sort of saint. But he didn't fool me. I'd heard the rumours about him from back when he owned his clubs in Torquay. I assumed he was just working an angle. Looking for an opportunity to make some money. Like that mercenary, Claude. I couldn't let that happen. I wasn't going to be a victim. Not again."

"What happened?" Bobby's voice was soft and encouraging.

"Irving was always asking questions. He'd noticed that Claude's firm had won a lot of council tenders, but it was Claude's links to Justin King that he was most interested in. He was obsessed with the Kings. Claude had won the tenders to build the other three King hotels and Irving thought that was suspicious. He kept asking for information about the links between Hugh, Justin and Claude and how the developments had been approved. Just like that reporter."

"Peter Norton?"

"Yes, he started asking the same questions Irving had. I knew it was only a matter of time before he worked it out." Violet's eyes misted over. "A nice boy. I liked him. But I knew he wouldn't let it go, not until he had all the answers. Just like Irving. It was a nightmare. I just wanted it all to stop."

"Why did Claude have to die?"

"He'd been blackmailing me for years. Ever since Malcolm… He never asked for money. Not after the initial ten thousand I gave him to buy the business. It was always information. About tenders, councillors, it didn't matter. If he thought he could use it to his advantage then he wanted it. I hated doing it, but what choice did I have? He had me exactly where he wanted me. He'd seen what had happened with Malcolm. I thought that once I retired, I'd be free. But then Claude contacted me out of the blue last week. He told me he knew where Malcolm's body was buried, that he'd found the proof, and then he made some comment about Irving's murder. I think he'd guessed I was responsible for that. Said he wanted money to keep quiet.

That's when I knew it was never going to end. I was never going to be free of him."

"Is that what you handed him in the envelope on Friday night. At the Church House Inn?" Violet nodded. "We didn't find it anywhere. I assume you took it back off him, after you pushed him down the steps?"

Violet sat in silence for a moment. She looked defeated. "My whole life has been controlled by men. First Malcolm and then Claude. I just wanted something for myself. To retire in peace. Is that too much to ask? I'd never even considered claiming the life assurance before, but then I thought why not? It isn't a lot of money, but I saw it as payment for all those years of suffering. I'd earned it. I filled out the forms and contacted the insurance company. It was going to be something just for me. For my retirement. I wasn't about to let anyone get their hands on it." Particularly Claude and certainly not Irving Hargreaves.

"And the fire at Claude's yard? Was that intended to destroy the invoice he'd found? The evidence that proved where you'd hidden Malcolm's body?"

"I didn't have much time. There were houses next door to the yard. I thought someone might have heard him fall."

"What happened to Malcolm?"

Violet scrunched up her face. "He was a horrid man. Spent most of his time gambling or drinking. Often both. And he loved to pick a fight, especially when he was drunk. I suppose that one day I'd just had enough. I remember I'd burnt a mark in one of his shirts. He was standing right there, where you are now. He was so angry. He was shouting and I knew he was going to strike me. I just lashed out. Got in first. Caught him on the side of the head. Only I was still holding the iron. He went down hard. Hit his head against the fireplace." She nodded to the heavy stone surround in front of the grate. "I knew he was dead straight away. I remember feeling relieved. I could have gone to the police, claimed self-defence. But I didn't. I just wanted him out of my life." Violet stared at the empty fireplace, a contorted smile forming on her face, as though reliving the events of that day. "I was a bit of a history buff and had read about the tunnels under Oldway Mansion. Only I knew they were more than just folklore. I'd worked at the council for about ten years by then and had spent most of my lunch breaks and several evenings and weekends exploring. I had complete access and nothing much to come home for. It's such a magical building." Her eyes glistened at the memory. "When Malcolm had his...accident...I knew exactly where to put him. I was sure no one would ever find him there."

"But you used Claude's boss to seal the tunnel entrance. And paid the invoice with council funds."

Violet shrugged. "Money was tight and I didn't want to waste any more of it on *him*. We lived on my wages and Malcolm often spent more than I earned. Mr Lancaster, he owned the building firm, was one of Malcolm's friends. That's why we used him to build the patio. He wasn't as bad as Malcolm, favoured gambling over drinking, but he wasn't much of a businessman. That's how Claude was able to buy the business off him so cheaply. I didn't think for one second he'd keep hold of that invoice."

"And then Claude found it all these years later?"

"What are the chances? As soon as he saw it he worked everything out. He was clever like that. The date and the description of the work carried out was all he needed. Just when I was about to get away from him."

"He didn't know where Malcolm was buried before?"

Violet shook her head. "I didn't realise at the time, but he'd seen me lash out and Malcolm fall and hit his head. I thought everyone had already gone home, but Claude was still hanging around. He's always had a sixth sense for an opportunity, that man. When Malcolm wasn't there the next day, he got suspicious and started asking questions. I brushed them off at first, but then people started to gossip about Malcolm walking out on me. That's when Claude saw his chance. I should have denied it. Let him go to the police if that's what he wanted to do, although I doubt he would have. It was stupid, but by paying him that money I effectively told him I was guilty. I gave him the rope to hang me with. He's blackmailed me ever since. I wish I'd done things differently, but once you start down a path…"

Bobby shook his head in disbelief. It had pretty much gone down just as he'd thought, but hearing Violet Danbury admit it now, it all seemed so incredibly sad. "How did you manage to get Malcolm's body into that tunnel?"

Violet chuckled but it sounded hollow in the circumstances. "I surprised myself there. I suppose shock, or necessity, can make you do extraordinary things. I waited until later that night and loaded him in the back of the car. This place isn't overlooked, so that was easy. And I had a key for Oldway Mansion. It was deserted late at night and they didn't bother with security back then. It was hard work, but I managed to drag him down to the basement. I thought I'd been so clever. No one else knew the tunnels were there and with the building being used as council offices, I knew no one would ever find them. I was in the perfect position to make sure that never happened, after all. But then the council took the decision to move and then there was talk about developing the building. I knew I couldn't let that happen, that they might discover the tunnels and Malcolm's remains. That's when I joined the preservation society. I thought that if we could defeat the development proposals, I could ensure the tunnels remained hidden. Killing Irving was unfortunate. He'd become a liability, but he was also our most prominent supporter. After he died, it became more likely Hugh would win the vote. I'm not sure what I'd have done then. Move the remains, I suppose."

Violet went quiet, her confession over. All three of them remained still for a moment as they considered everything that had just been said. Eventually, Violet stood up and quietly walked out to the police car sandwiched between the two detectives. She suddenly looked old, and frail, but she held her head high as a small crowd of neighbours, no doubt seduced into leaving their homes by the flashing blue lights, looked on, unsure what to make of the curious scene unfolding in front of them.

CHAPTER 53

Bobby Redhill stood on the pavement and pressed the buzzer to the top floor apartment. Several days had passed since Violet Danbury's arrest and the inspector was tying up a few loose ends.

"Kimberley, it's DCI Redhill. Can I come up?"

Kimberley Hargreaves seemed pleased to hear Bobby's voice and buzzed him straight up. She was waiting at the door as he reached the third-floor landing. She rushed forward and enveloped him in a big hug.

"Thank you."

The gesture took Bobby by surprise and he stood there awkwardly as the young woman hung off his neck. Sensing his unease, she stepped back. "I'm sorry. It's just that after Amber, it's a relief to have closure. To know who was…responsible."

Bobby smiled. "That's why I came, actually."

Kimberley looked at the inspector quizzically.

"I thought you'd want to know."

"Know what?"

"It became clear during our investigation that your dad was working hard in the weeks before he died to try to find out the truth about what happened to Amber. To prove who was responsible. So far as we know, he didn't get any answers, I'm not sure we ever will, but he was trying."

"What are you saying?"

"I think he wanted to change. For you. He was even committed to saving Oldway Mansion for the benefit of the local community. Does that sound like the dad you thought you knew?"

Kimberley laughed and choked back tears. Bobby had no evidence of anything he'd just said, but it was the only explanation that made sense to him. And he knew Kimberley was the type of person who needed answers. He guessed they'd never know for sure what Hargreaves had been up to in the weeks and months before his death: whether, as Bobby had just said, he'd been working hard to prove to his daughter that he'd changed or if, as Violet suspected, he was running an elaborate scam with a view to extorting money from her, just like Claude Knight had been doing for so many years. Bobby had never met Irving, but everything he'd learnt over the past few weeks pointed to a man who'd changed. Or at the very least was trying hard to. Besides, Bobby thought Kimberley needed this explanation. Too many people had been hurt. It was time to start the healing.

CHAPTER 54

PETER SAT UP IN BED, his mouth hanging wide open like an old-fashioned ventriloquist's dummy. "She drugged me!"

Bobby laughed. "Sleeping tablets crushed up in the biscuits. If I'd known that's all it would take, I'd have done it myself weeks ago!"

They were in a quiet ward on the third floor of Torbay Hospital. Bobby had come to visit Peter who was now off the critical list and recovering well from his recent accident. Peter was only just getting up to speed with everything that had happened since then. He'd been particularly surprised to hear about Violet's arrest but had then recalled the photo he'd seen on the white board in the incident room at the station. The one from the council's summer party that the police had found in Irving Hargreaves' home office, with Violet and Claude talking in the background. He remembered with a sinking feeling how she'd denied knowing the builder that afternoon at her house, not long before he'd had his accident. It was a tough lesson, but he realised he'd been so focused on Hugh Farmer's guilt that he'd missed that discrepancy. Still, it was a mistake that could easily have had far more serious consequences so, despite everything, he felt lucky.

"I see reports of my death have been greatly exaggerated?" Peter smiled as he picked up a copy of the previous week's *Torbay Times* which had been lying on the table by the side of his bed. Care to explain my miraculous recovery, Inspector?"

Bobby shuffled uncomfortably in his seat. "Yes, well… it was you who put me onto Violet in the first place. Did you know that? Not immediately, but something you said at the station, on the night Claude Knight was murdered, stuck with me. About the tunnels under Oldway Mansion. And Violet's husband having suddenly left her. He just disappeared, you said. I didn't realise the significance at the time, but when the evidence started to come together, those words came back to me and helped explain everything. By that point, I'd heard about your accident. We were all very concerned. You were in a serious condition, but the doctors were optimistic. Once I was confident you were going to pull through, I realised there was an opportunity to use your accident to help us get the evidence we needed, but without tipping Violet off to the fact we were onto her."

Peter looked confused so Bobby continued.

"Once the doctors told us you'd been drugged, we retraced your steps. People had seen that distinctive red car of yours parked outside Violet Danbury's house, so I guessed that's where you'd been. Probably continuing your own investigation." He tutted light-heartedly. "I don't know what you said to her, but you had her worried. You know she thought you were onto her?"

"She did?" Peter sounded surprised. "I still thought it was Hugh!"

Bobby looked disappointed but didn't dwell on the admission further. "I spoke with your parents and they reluctantly agreed to my plan. Your editor, Marcus, was only too keen to help. It was crucial Violet believed not only that you were dead and that your suspicions, whatever they were, had died with you, but also that the Oldway Mansion development had been defeated."

"I saw that article in the paper as well. Are you saying that's not true either?"

"It wasn't when the article was written, although Justin King has since pulled out. Reckons recent events have made the scheme too challenging. Although he could have simply been trying to get his excuses in first." Peter looked at the inspector curiously. "The council voted overwhelmingly in favour of preservation at the end of last week. It's possible he was given a heads-up beforehand."

Peter nodded thoughtfully. "You were concerned Violet might try to move her husband's remains and get rid of the evidence once and for all?"

"I thought there was a risk, yes. And we needed time to find the tunnels. Conrad Macpherson was helpful there. He didn't know where they were exactly, but he was familiar with the stories and was able to point us in the right general direction. We used some high-tech sonar equipment to do the rest."

Peter was quiet for a moment. "So, it was Violet who sent those anonymous notes to Hugh and me?"

"Yes, she was trying to put pressure on Hugh to scrap the development. When her initial attempts failed, she turned to you. She'd read all about your career as an investigative reporter and obviously thought you might have more luck. She didn't know exactly what Hugh was hiding but had always been suspicious. He never spoke about his past and the background checks they'd conducted when he joined the council had thrown-up a few anomalies."

Bobby suddenly noticed Peter smiling at something over his shoulder. He turned and was surprised to see Faith Andrews, the forensic pathologist, standing there. "Faith, what are *you* doing here?"

Faith smiled at the inspector before walking straight over to the bed and giving Peter an affectionate kiss on his cheek. "You look so much better." She picked up his hand and held it softly in her own.

"I feel it. The doctors said I should be able to go home tomorrow."

Bobby stood up and awkwardly rubbed his hands together. "I didn't know you two knew one another?"

Faith smiled. "We met at the Claude Knight crime scene. I took pity on him and offered him a lift home. We got talking in the car and realised we had a lot in common. We met up for a coffee the next day and had plans to see one another again, but then Peter had his accident. Later that same day!"

"I suppose we have you to thank, Bobby." Peter grinned. "I'm not sure we'd have ever met if you hadn't brought me into the police station that night."

"Yes, well…you're welcome." Bobby coughed. "I suppose I should be going. You've probably got a lot to talk about." He hesitated. "I forgot to mention, I spoke to your editor, Peter. They're expecting you back at the paper next week. They want you to write a detailed piece on both murders. Congratulations."

Peter fidgeted in the bed, as though trying to get comfortable. "What I still don't understand, is how Violet thought she'd get away with it. I mean, hiding her husband's body in a public building like that, it's just so brazen."

"I suppose she just hoped no one would find it."

Peter shook his head and laughed out loud. "Imagine gambling your whole life and future happiness on something as fragile as hope!"

"Well, you know what they say." Bobby glanced at Faith before turning purposefully towards the door. "It's the hope that kills."

AUTHOR'S NOTE

This book includes references to real-life people and places and certain historical facts. Oldway Mansion does exist, for example. It was once owned by the Singer family before being sold to Torbay Council at the end of the Second World War. All true. And George Best was a famous footballer who will be familiar to many people, not only football fans, particularly those of a certain generation.

Harry Bannister and the Burford Boys, by contrast, along with all the other characters in the book, are figments of my imagination, as is the story itself, which is a work of fiction. Any similarity or resemblance to actual people, places or events is unintentional, while all errors or mistakes, whether in history, geography, science, medicine, procedure or any other matter, are entirely my own and a result of my exuberance and imagination.

I hope you enjoyed the story.

ABOUT THE AUTHOR

At the start of 2020 I was working in London as a corporate lawyer. In many ways it was a fantastic job, and I'm grateful for the opportunity to have practised law, although it had been many years since I'd felt fulfilled at work. Maybe twenty years of anything will do that to you. But what to do instead? It was a question I'd been struggling with for a while, and at that point I still didn't have an answer.

Fast forward a few months into the new decade and a global pandemic had unexpectedly presented a once in a lifetime opportunity to embrace the unknown and try a new challenge. Within four months of the UK's first lock-down, my employer had accepted my request for voluntary redundancy, and I was finally free from the daily grind. Not that I had a plan. That took a little longer. After all, what does someone who's been indoctrinated into office life do when there's no longer an office to go to?

The idea to write a book formed gradually over time, first as a bit of a joke (yeah, of course, write a book!) before crystallising into something more realistic. A few years earlier I'd completed an executive MBA and had enjoyed writing the essays (not something I recall saying the first time I went to university). That got me thinking. If you break them down, essays are essentially condensed stories, why not attempt a novel? The pandemic had presented a unique opportunity, so if not now, when?

With the decision finally made, the hard work really began. How do you go about writing a book in any case? Where do you even start? If you're anything like me then you read for many reasons: to learn, to feel inspired and, often, simply to be entertained. I've read any number of novels for entertainment, but I've never really bothered to consider how they were pieced together. It turns out these things don't just happen by chance. A lot of work goes into it.

It's something I've read many times before, but I think it's worth repeating. Writing a book is hard and anyone who attempts it requires a tremendous amount of support. I was fortunate to have more than my share. Thanks to everyone who encouraged me along the way or read the early drafts and managed to remain positive. I won't name you all here, you know who you are, but please know your support was, and continues to be, greatly appreciated. Thanks also to the select band of professionals I worked with who helped polish my manuscript into what you see today.

I won't lie, at times it was a daunting project. I frequently felt out of my depth, like I didn't know what I was doing – I didn't – but I always came through those moments of doubt. And best of all, I now have something to show for all the effort.

If you're reading these words then I hope it's not too optimistic to assume you've persevered through my novel from beginning to end. If that's the case, thank you. If you're lucky enough to live in the South West of England then maybe it will remind you of the beauty all around and inspire you to get out and reacquaint yourself with the area. If you've never visited, then I hope it might encourage you to do so. Devon and, more specifically, Torbay is a picturesque part of the world with many wonderful places to explore. Perhaps you might even be inspired by my own journey and challenge yourself to try something new? If so, good luck. After all, what's the worst that can happen? Not convinced? I'll let you into a secret. Compared with the alternative, doing is easy. It's the hope that kills…

Johnathan

Printed in Great Britain
by Amazon

28175050R00249